D1510804

Sophie's Lies

a novel

JuliAnne Sisung

ISBN-13: 979-8612814580

This is a work of fiction. Characters and incidences are the product of the author's imagination and are used fictitiously.

Published February 2020 by JuliAnne Sisung

Books by JuliAnne Sisung

Sophie's Lies
a novel

The Hersey Series
Elephant in the Room
a family saga

Angels in the Corner
a family saga

Light in the Forest
a family saga

Place in the Circle
a family saga

The Idlewild Series
Leaving Nirvana
an account of love and oppression
race, gender, honor

The Whipping Post
a story of oppression, enlightenment and
redemption of those who tied and were tied
with ropes seen and unseen

Ask for the Moon
a tale of love, growth and acceptance
as Idlewild comes of age

Acknowledgements

Sophie's Lies was born after hearing many accounts of women surviving under the harsh hands and voices of their partners. When their stories are told on the nightly news in the form of brutality, friends and families invariably shake their heads in confusion and disbelief – because they didn't know. The truth is in the back closet tucked under the photograph albums, collecting dust. It isn't spoken. I hope my words bring a little understanding to the falsehoods those strong women tell and the choices they make. Their lies are wishes in disguise.

Thanks to my beta reader and brother, Mark Jessup, for giving sound advice. I appreciate his talent as a writer, as well. His poem *Magic Bob* is a bridge to Sophie's heart and land, as well as a summary of a gardener's prudent mind. Waste not, want not. Cherish the earth.

And to my editor who works tirelessly to improve my work – sometimes without any help from me – thank you, Larry.

One – Meet John Wayne, 2018

The screech of the metal gate traveled down a half-mile driveway through a thick copse and was almost buried by the distinctive growl of a Harley. Its deep rumble intensified as if being sucked by the winding path that kept her safe and sealed away from the rest of the world.

She left her chair on the concrete porch to go inside, and the screen door slammed behind her hard enough to perk Fannie's long ears but not enough to make her rise. The hound cocked her head, listened to the engine's roar, and watched for her mistress to return while she kept an eye on the end of the path, waiting for the intruder to burst through the trees and into sight. The elevated porch provided a good vantage point for the dog. She could keep an eye on the driveway as well as the animals in their pens without having to move unless some stranger came into the yard. They never had – right up to this moment.

Fannie groaned and stood as the old woman pushed through the door with her shotgun and pumped a shell into the breach as the motorcycle came into view. He didn't stop even as she raised the gun and pointed it at his chest, but he slowed to a crawl and inched his way toward her, his feet on the ground, his eyes fastened on the round open end of the barrel. He shut off the machine, dropped his feet to the ground, and listened for the snick of the safety catch.

"Can't you read? Says private property. No trespassing."

A sharp breeze stirred the thick hair streaming around her shoulders and down her back like a silver shawl, and her green eyes snapped with anger and mistrust. She looked like a grandma you'd love once you got to know, but wilder, like she'd sprung fresh from the forest around her.

"Saw all the signs. Thought they were for everybody else. Not me."

He leaned back against the black leather seat and crossed his arms, not ready to leave or ask permission to stay.

"I learned how to use this thing a long time ago."

She wiggled her shotgun to make sure he understood what thing she was talking about and then steadied it to point at his chest again.

"Bet you did. Nice place you got here." He let his eyes wander the grounds surrounding her home.

A lean-to housed an ancient tractor, an almost-ancient automobile he thought would qualify as a first-rate antique, an old lawn tractor and several scattered pieces of garden equipment. Only the car looked like it had moved in a long while. Dust, loose straw, leaf debris and bird poop covered the rest in undisturbed layers.

So, she still drives, he thought, *but that's about all.*

Goats lined the wires of their enclosure, bleating like they wanted something from him or wanted him gone. Chickens and guinea hens scratched at the ground in front of a weathered shed and a couple of peacocks came out of a tree at the end of what had once been a garden. He hadn't seen a peacock fan its tail before and forgot about the gun pointed toward him in his fascination with the bird as it squawked and strutted.

"Don't know why he doesn't fall over backwards," he said to the woman.

"He's had that tail for a while. Got kinda used to it."

A fat calico rubbed against his boot. He leaned to scratch at her ears as she climbed his leg and planted herself on his leather chaps.

"Nails in, cat. Leather doesn't heal."

She poked the gun his way, reminding him she held all the cards, along with the gun, and he was trespassing.

"What do you want?"

"I was out driving around and talking to people. Old man down the road told me about your place, and I thought I'd check it out." He grinned and watched the weight of the shotgun drag at the barrel which now pointed directly at his bike. "I'd really rather you didn't shoot Miss Lily. I heal, but she doesn't."

"Lily?" Her head spun looking for another snooper.

"My Harley. She's a girl."

Sophie frowned and inched backwards, dropping onto the chair that bumped into the back of her legs. She didn't like growing old, didn't like being hampered by the weakness of age. But the alternative sucked, too, and she wasn't ready to leave her home and her animals. They needed her, and she'd paid a high price for her land. She owned it and every square inch of dirt on these hundred twenty acres.

Propping the shotgun on her legs, she aimed it vaguely at the man and kept her trigger finger steady and ready.

"Still don't know what you're doing here. I don't like people coming onto my property. You need to start talking or get walking."

The cat climbed higher and tried to make a nest out of his stomach, while others who had fled from the noise of his bike crept low to the grass toward him like they were stalking prey. He didn't count them all but figured there had to be at least twenty slithering their way through the grass, a crazy high number to be sure.

He wanted to get off the bike and walk around the property, saunter down the overgrown but still visible paths veering off into the trees surrounding the house. He pictured the many garden plots in full bloom as they must have been

3

years ago, and he wanted to dig his hands into their soil. He needed a slice of heaven like this appeared to be, a place secreted away from people, a sanctuary.

The man he'd talked to down the road said these folks might be ready to sell, but it didn't look that way by the slant of her shotgun. And what the hell – he didn't have the money anyway, but he couldn't help checking it out.

"Mister?"

The gun raised and a sliver of fear crawled up her spine as he showed no inclination to leave and no discomfort about encroaching and staying.

"Do you mind if I look around?"

"I do. Get."

She heaved from the chair and stepped toward the edge of the porch. Fannie, the long-legged coon hound, stood and bumped against her, a low, half-hearted growl sliding from deep in her chest.

"But I might like to make an offer on your property."

She pointed the gun to the sky and pulled the trigger. The blast trembled in the air long afterwards, scattering birds and causing her own critters to run for cover. Only Fannie stayed still, and Sophie pumped another shell into the chamber.

The man raised his hands in submission and gave a tentative, slanted grin, took another long look around and scratched his head, fingers rippling through dust colored, blond hair.

"I get it. I'm going. Name's John. John Wayne."

She snorted and the gun jolted, wanting to bark again.

"It is not. Liar. Who do you think you're kidding? I'm not a stupid, old woman."

His pale eyes narrowed, and he lowered his head, bobbed it back and forth sideways as if he didn't want to face her mockery.

"Of course, you aren't. But the name really is John Wayne. My mother loved him. I'm going."

He thumbed his bike to life and duck walked it across the grass to the driveway, feet on either side to keep it from falling over. He'd never get it up again if it went to the ground. And he knew it.

Peacocks screamed a discordant displeasure with Miss Lily's melody. Goats bleated, chickens cackled, and guineas flapped their wings and tried to fly. Sophie wanted to frown at their noise but couldn't, and a smile crossed her lips and lit her eyes.

She listened to the life around her and the sound of John Wayne traveling down the long path; it couldn't claim to be a driveway. No one else kept it up, now, and the tractor wouldn't start so she could do it herself.

She knew when he turned onto the road by the revving thunder of the Harley and took a long-held breath of relief, wiping at the sweat that had collected under her breasts. She didn't wear a bra most days anymore, and they rested against her stomach, overheating her whole body. Damned things.

Sophie couldn't help the look of satisfaction stealing over her face. It wasn't like he fell off the bike when she pulled the trigger, but the look in his eyes and the set of his shoulders said it all. Clearly, he didn't know she wouldn't shoot him – or maybe nick his Harley.

Well, she'd never hurt it, not intentionally. The machine was positively beautiful.

She let the shotgun hang from her hand, a heavy burden, as she maneuvered slowly down the three concrete steps to the ground and moved toward the chicken coop and goat pen. She wasn't about to leave it behind in case the stranger changed his mind and decided he didn't want to leave. But she didn't think he'd return, and he hadn't seemed totally malicious. After all, he let Cali climb his leg and sit on him. Not all men would do that.

But the *other one* had liked cats, too, had let them crawl all over him, had more than twenty in the house at one time. Liking cats doesn't mean a damned thing.

Goats bleated and guineas shouted *Chi-chi-chi* at her, all wanting to talk about the noisy stranger.

"Little late now, don't you think," she said. "He's gone, and you didn't even let me know he was coming. I'd have baked a cake," she said with a sardonic laugh. "And then you could eat it because I can't. I'm getting fat."

Sophie filled the bucket with feed for the chickens and talked to them while she scattered it, enjoying the comfortable sound of their soft clucking. The smaller guineas darted around the slower hens, making noise much larger than their size.

"Settle down, you loud mouths." But a smile warmed her face because she loved her birds. They were for laying eggs and for the pure joy of listening to their chicken songs. They weren't for eating, unless something horrible happened to them. Then she'd wring their necks to keep them from pain and pop them in the pot. She wouldn't be wasteful, but it had taken years for her to get to where she could do that.

"I'm coming," she yelled over to the goats who were stomping the ground impatiently. "Petunia, Billy, Gladiola! The rest of you, too. Behave."

She squinted into the sunlight, deepening the lines on her brown face and wondered what would happen to her babies if she dropped dead at this moment. How long would she lay in the middle of her chicks before someone else ignored the *No Trespassing* signs and drove down her driveway again? How long before someone came to pick her up off the ground if she died? How many days before someone came to feed her critters?

She cussed at herself and flung the empty scoop bucket into the feed barrel, closed the lid and wrapped her arms around a half bale of hay to feed to the goats. There was a time, not so long ago, it seems, she could carry the whole bale. But she had muscles yesterday. Not so many today.

She tossed it over the wire fence, milked her ladies and went back for the second half, thinking about the stranger – John Wayne. She didn't care he had invaded her privacy. In fact, he gave her something to think about. Every once in a while, she'd like to talk to someone besides her animals.

"Come on, Fannie. Let's take a walk."

Two – Meet Carl, 1960

After work, Sophie and her girlfriends stopped at Henry's Bar for a couple of drinks and to check out the men playing darts, shooting pool, or sitting on barstools telling each other lies. In their small town, strangers were rare, so they knew everyone in the shabby neighborhood bar, even if only by name or face. Henry's provided a safe place to meet and have a drink and some fun on a Friday night.

Familiarity comforted and unfettered them.

As Sophie looked around, her eyes stopped at a man who gave the word handsome a different meaning, even in baggy jeans and a plaid shirt that had known a lot of better days. Although she and her friends had seen him in Henry's a few times, he was essentially a stranger.

An out of towner.

But unlike the other men and for a long while, he ignored the women and carried on an animated conversation with a friend, acting like the ladies weren't there. That alone made him desirable to a few of them who watched through secretive, half-lowered lids.

Somewhere between dancing and telling stories with her friends, Sophie decided something was special about the man. Something more self-assured than the others, like he didn't give a damn what anyone thought or said, like he knew things they couldn't possibly know. His insolent attitude bordered on arrogance until he ducked his head and grinned, and that look made up for the rest. Perhaps the guise was calculated, practiced.

She didn't know how she could tell so much about a man from the lengthy distance between them, but it became firmly planted in her mind. Could have been the drinks. Could have been him. She looked his way periodically, and he looked back to catch her eye a few times. When Dee dared her to walk right up, give him a hug and plant a kiss on his cheek, she told her to forget it.

"I don't hug," she said. "And you know that."

"Go on. You know you want to. It's written all over your face," Dee told her.

Dee was right. She did want to, and, after several glasses of cheap wine, Sophie decided she liked his eyes. They were magnets that drew her toward him.

He watched her walk across the room and admired her shape, hourglass and perky. She had dimples, a dazzling smile and a glint in her eyes that said she was game for a whole lot of almost anything. She didn't hug him like they'd dared her to do, but she did plant one on his cheek.

"Sophie Saxon, just what are you doing?" He wrapped an arm around her back to draw her closer, but she held her ground so she could see his eyes.

"Don't believe I know your name. How do you know mine?"

"Guess your reputation precedes you. Carl. My name is Carl."

"Well, Mister Carl, I just came up here to order a drink, and you got in the way," she said in a tease.

"You're lying, Sophie. I don't like lies."

His hand pulled at her waist, maintaining contact like he wasn't about to let her go, and he smiled. But the creases at the corners of his eyes said he might have meant the harsh words, and she stepped back with wide eyes of her own.

"Let her go, man. You're scaring her," his friend Freddie said, shaking his head at Carl. "Ignore him, Sophie."

Carl threw his head back in a laugh that drew attention and she proceeded to order the drink she'd lied about. And it *had* been a lie, though she'd only meant it as a funny fib. But he'd turned a cute comment into a calculated falsehood, or maybe she'd imagined irritation that hadn't been there.

Sophie returned to her friends, feeling the prickle of his eyes on her and wishing she had the guts to turn around and stare back. Check his expression.

They didn't talk again that night, but she couldn't stop thinking about him.

He came by her apartment the next day with an invitation for dinner – at his place.

"I'm grilling steaks," Carl said with a grin, "and one has your name on it."

Light brown hair curled around his ears and the back of his neck like he needed a haircut. Most guys wore it long now, some all the way down their backs, but she liked his. He wore a light scruff on his cheeks that couldn't be called a beard, and cat hair clung to his dark shirt. *Had he never heard of a lint brush?* But Sophie still liked his eyes and his quirky grin, so she nodded.

"I guess that would be fine. What time? Want me to bring anything?"

He handed her a piece of paper with an address in the next town over.

"I like A-1 on my steak," she said as he sauntered away, shoulders hunched in a slouch she found both familiar and exotic. Much later, she'd translate the distinctive stance as his way of coping with a disappointing world he couldn't change, couldn't make work acceptably.

They ate half-pound T-bones in his living room, their plates teetering on wobbly, metal TV trays, their arms waving in the air to scatter cats trying to climb on laps and shoulders to snag a piece of meat from a too-lazy fork. Sophie had never seen so many felines before and, though she liked them,

11

figured she'd hack up a hairball in the morning, for sure. But the giant bottle of A-1 Steak Sauce standing next to her plate caused a smile to tilt her lips and made up for having to fight for her food.

Carl talked about his work, about how he could improve conditions on the job if the bosses would only listen to him. But they wouldn't. They weren't smart enough to recognize his suggestions would save time and money for the company. He shook his head, forehead lined with annoyance.

Sophie didn't say much about her job because it didn't require much of an explanation. When she told him about the diner, he didn't appear interested. And she figured he was right. What she did wasn't nearly as interesting as what he did, but she enjoyed waitressing, liked the people and the socializing.

After dinner, he let her wash the dishes while he got beers from the fridge, leaned against the counter, and talked about people they both knew. He knew everyone, and he knew everything about them.

Carl showed her a workshop where his newest project awaited final development, a robot with multi-programmable processors. Arms moved and lights blinked where his eyes would be. It looked cute but creepy, and an odd chill traveled down her spine.

"Does he have a name, and what's he going to do when you're all done? Your laundry? Dishes? If so, better make it a female," she said with a giggle.

They'd been drinking beer from quart bottles, and she thought her comment funny, but he stepped back, affronted, and covered the shiny metal contraption with a grimy sheet.

"Course not. I'm gonna program him to shoot intruders. Nosy trespassers."

"Excuse me?" Her eyes widened. His said he wasn't kidding. "You mean, if I come back to see you, I might get a bullet in my head from the tin man? Or the mailman? Or your brother? I don't mean they'll shoot me, but he'll shoot them. The robot." She squirmed. "You know what I mean." "He'll recognize you. I'll make sure of that. Then I'll introduce him to anyone else who's cleared to visit. First, I need to write and debug the software code, and after that . . . Never mind. I'll figure it all out."

Sophie's eyebrows drew together in misgiving. *Who is this man? He might be a little bit crazy.*

She forgot about the tin man when Carl put his arms around her, and they made love all night and talked until the sun poked at the treetops. She'd tried to go back to her place, but he'd asked her to stay, so she did.

He was hard to refuse when he wanted something, and Carl wanted her. She didn't know how to say no.

Sophie massaged a cramp in her calf that woke her and listened as shower water serenaded and then died with a squeal of pipes. An awkward blush crept from her chest to her cheeks, and she wished she'd gotten dressed before he came back into the room. But she'd waited too long. His towel wrapped body stood at the end of the bed, still damp, curls clinging, and she pulled the sheet up to her neck, dislodging several calicos with the sharp tug.

"Get up, lazy bones," he said, whipping off the towel and surprising her.

"I . . . Well, alright."

She found her bra, shoved a cat off her blouse, and shook loose hair from it before sliding her arms through and buttoning it up.

Did I just get out of bed naked in front of a man I barely know? This isn't real. Is it?

"Do you have a brush?" she asked.

"Hardly. Comb do? You'll come here when you get off work, right?" he said in a tone more command than question.

"I don't know how late I'll be at work. The dinner crowd sometimes hangs around a long time."

He grabbed an arm and pulled her against his chest. "But I know you want to come and cook dinner for us. Last night you said you'd make goulash. Did you lie to me?" His eyes narrowed like he peered into her soul, looking for the answer to his question. He gave her ponytail a playful tug and grinned. "Well?"

"No. I told you; I don't lie. I'll be here. I just don't know what time it'll be. And I'll have to go to the store first for the fixings."

"I'll be right here, waiting."

Dee saw her pull up to the diner from a kitchen window and met Sophie at the door, expectation and curiosity flashing in her eyes.

"Well? Tell me all."

"I have to prep my tables, Dee. I'm late, and you'll have to wait."

"Come on. When you didn't come home, I was a little worried, but then I thought, hmmm . . . lucky girl. Right?"

She took the salt and pepper tray loaded with shakers to the dining room, pushing through the swinging doors to leave Dee's curiosity behind. But her friend followed and started pouring salt into half-filled containers.

Sophie huffed in a fake show of frustration – fake because she enjoyed having something different to tell Dee for a change, and Carl was something different, without a doubt.

"Okay. Here's the scoop. I stayed at his place last night, and I'm going back there after work today." Her mind drifted over the evening in question, and changing shadows reworked her expressions. "He's definitely a cute guy and smart. I've never met anyone like him. He's a powerful force."

"You don't date somebody because they're powerful. You date a guy because you like him. Because there's some kind of chemistry happening. You know . . ."

Dee laughed and wiggled her pelvis back and forth like a lazy stripper. Sophie couldn't help but grin.

"Oh, there's that all right. Sparks most definitely flew. I'm just not the kiss and tell kind of girl. I will say this, though. We had a *lot* of fun."

"That's it? You had fun?"

"Yeah. All I'm giving you."

"Well, *you're* no fun if that's all you're gonna say. I'll set out the napkins and place mats for your tables, you stingy woman."

Sophie chewed at her bottom lip and wondered why she hadn't said anything about the 'tin man' and why Carl had built him. A robot was interesting, and worth telling her best friend about, but it felt like it should be kept private. He'd probably been teasing her about his plans for it, anyway.

So, she kept the secret, and Carl's odd invention sat rusting in her gut like a dirty deed.

Three – Sophie goes to town

She pounded on the hood of his car, the sides and trunk, too, and walked all around it before she opened the door and lowered her old body to the seat. The noise-making was a practice begun after she'd run over one of his kittens as it slept up on the tire.

It had happened so many years ago, Sophie couldn't even remember what color or make the car had been. She *did* remember he'd yelled at her, and the horror and sadness in his eyes when he picked up the limp kitten and buried it.

And she'd cried – not because he'd yelled at her, but because she'd killed an animal. She loved all the critters on their property, tame and wild, and she thought about that cat every time she hammered on a car fender.

Afterward, Carl had chased her to the car whenever she planned to go to town, banged all around it to scare away cats to reinforce the 'new procedure.' Only then would he nod, giving his okay to start the engine.

She'd never seen any run out from under the car, but he insisted they stick to the plan, and she didn't mind. His love of cats was endearing, and she loved them, too, so she banged away. Now, many years later, it was a habit.

The 1962 Volkswagen Beetle lived a pampered life next to his tractor under the metal lean-to. The car was his, and it looked and smelled new inside because it had so few miles on it. He would hardly use it. He drove her vehicle into town so his own stayed new and shiny, and hers had to brave the sun, rain, snow, and bird poop in the dirt driveway. She didn't care. It wasn't worth an argument.

She honked at the peacocks to scoot them out of the way and watched them fly up into their tree, the only one in which they perched. They were the homestead lookouts. In the tall maple, they were the first to see intruders and would alert Fannie who'd drive the trespassers away, mimicking ferocious growls and coon hound howls.

Today, she drove the Beetle into town, and it gave her a titillating sense of joy. Yes, her vehicle had died, and she had no other way to get there, but using his car still made her eyes sparkle, her heart thump like she was a naughty teenager. Heads would turn when she drove down the main street in town, their covetous eyes glued to the spotless antique Beetle.

She only needed a few things at the feed co-op and grocery store, and she needed to pay bills. When you don't use banks, you have to trot cash around to pay electric, phone and insurance bills. Fortunately, that was all she owed each month. She still heated with wood and figured the huge pile of neatly stacked logs next to the old moonshine house would most likely outlast her.

In the time it took to park safely at Henry's – away from other vehicles – she could have driven home and poured a drink for herself, but it wouldn't have been the same. Every once in a while, she needed to see friends. And she still had some, but they long ago understood they weren't invited out to visit her and Carl.

She snapped the leash on Fannie and opened the door. The dog leapt over her and sat on the gravel, waiting, looking at her with a laugh in her yellow-brown eyes.

"Yeah. You're younger than me. I get that. Just wait until I pry myself out of this stupid car. He could have bought something a little bigger, couldn't he?" She swung a leg out and turned sideways. "No, sir-ee. Everything has to be smaller than him."

Fannie whined. She knew where they were going and was salivating for a burger and fries.

"Come on, girl. I'm thirsty."

She pulled on the leash, heading straight toward the door, and Sophie let her go to tug at her town-blouse, one saved for her trips to Henry's Bar because of the perfect neckline. She'd always had an ample bosom and wore a bra on bar days so she could show off her bustline a bit. So what if she was old? Her friends were too, and they still appreciated a good peek at some nice cleavage. And she had plenty.

The bar hadn't changed since she'd spent time there, years ago, even before Carl. It was dark, smelled of old beer and popcorn, and gray stuffing stuck out of the rips in the fake red leather covering the stools. Heads turned to check the silhouette centered in the yellow light of the opened door, and she grinned and waited for recognition.

"Sophie! Told them you'd be in today. I know when bills are due." Pete patted the seat next to him.

He'd been a good-looking man in his day, and some would say he still was at eighty-something. He had a full head of white hair and a slender, straight body. For many men – and women – that would be more than enough. He'd made moves on her a long while back, even though she was married, but she knew a cheater when she saw one and told him to go home to his wife. Sophie knew her, too.

She walked around Pete to take a stool at his other side, refusing his wide-open arms. Hugs weren't for her. She wasn't going to shove her breasts into any man's chest; it was a point of principle.

"Glass of merlot?" Lainie didn't wait for an answer to slide it in front of her. "Everything good out there in the boondocks?"

Sophie sipped the liquid, and it slid down her throat while she pondered the question. What could she say? Sure? Well, it was. It was fine.

"Animals are squawking at me, grass is growing, and I got food for my belly. What more could I ask?"

"Surprised to see you in town driving his baby again," Pete said.

"I've been driving it since mine gave it up."

"I know, but . . ."

"Pete," Lainie said, butting into the conversation. "Sometimes you're just dumb. Shut up."

"What's going on with the banners up all over town?" Sophie sipped and wiped the red over her lip.

"Big celebration. Town is all gussied up over it." Pete poked her side and she recoiled a bit and leaned away. "Want to go?"

"Keep your hands to yourself, old man, and answer the question," Sophie said with a smile, teasing so he wouldn't take offense even though she meant it. "What's it for?"

"Fifty years since Nam. Every ten years we celebrate the end of the stupidest damned war the U.S. ever fought. Having a parade and all. You'd think we'd just try to forget it ever happened."

"They're honoring the soldiers, Pete," Lainie said, "especially the POWs. You can't have a fit about that regardless of how you feel about the war."

Sophie nodded, thinking about all the strangers who'd be in the area for the celebration and remembered the man on the motorcycle. She scanned the tables now that her eyes had adjusted to the dim light and looked for the sandy haired man. She waved Lainie over.

"A Harley came down my driveway a while back."

"All by itself?" Pete nudged Sophie again. He wasn't a quick learner, or he didn't care.

"Smartass. A thirty-ish man riding it. Long legged and lanky. Seen anybody new in town? Kinda blonde? Beautiful bike."

"What did he want?" Lainie asked, surprise raising the level of her voice. She'd seen all the postings just driving by their property. "Can't he read?"

"That's what I asked, and he said he figured all those 'No Trespassing' signs were for other people, not him. Kinda cocky, huh?"

The creases on her forehead deepened as she thought of the stranger – and the possibility of his presence at her place while she was gone. He could go anywhere, do anything. She hadn't given a thought to visitors before leaving home; people knew not to come out there. Shoot, she should've left Fannie to scare him off if he came back.

"Eat up, Fannie. We gotta go."

"What's the rush. You just got here." Pete put a hand on her shoulder to keep her there, and pulled it back at the dark look in her eyes. "Sorry."

"I know, Pete." And she did. There weren't many of the old crowd left, and he was lonely. Getting old was hell. But she still didn't want his hands on her.

"You oughta come in for the street dance this Saturday," he said. "Jolly Boys are playing. We're all gonna shake a leg."

"The only thing shaking on you, Pete, is your palsy," Lainie said and patted his hand.

"I've got moves you wouldn't believe, young lady."

"You're right. I wouldn't."

Sophie listened to the banter with the edge of her mind. The rest was on the stranger and her land. She climbed off the stool, swigged the last of her drink, and tugged on Fannie's leash.

"Come on, girl. I don't like going out after dark, Pete. Sorry. Maybe we'll come in for the parade, though."

Her foot sat heavy on the throttle all the way home, her eyes scanning the brush at the sides of the dirt road for deer and other critters that would make short work of the small car. She normally didn't mind going slow. It was a habit they'd acquired early on because of the hordes of wildlife in the back country, from ugly-cute possum to stately whitetail deer and everything in between. They always meandered traveling the road, enjoying the animals. Today, she cursed the need for slow.

He was there. She knew it and could smell the strange exhaust clinging to the tunnel of branches and leaves as the car crawled down the two-track path to her house – strange because the scent didn't belong to her, but another. It was foreign to the air she knew and breathed in every day.

He sat on the porch in the chair next to hers, one leg crossed over the knee of the other in an oddly languid pose for an interloper, let alone a man. The hanging leg moved subtly as if in rhythm to a tune hummed in his head, and he didn't alter his repose until she parked the Beetle and opened the trunk.

He could see shopping bags inside and loped down the steps to help. Sophie crossed her arms and stuck a foot in front of her, knee pumping in agitation. Fannie tried to growl, but it wasn't in her, so she wandered over to the peacock tree and looked around for the big birds instead.

"What the hell are you doing?" Sophie asked.

"Helping unload your cute baby car." He grabbed the burlap sack of chicken feed and threw it over his shoulder. Grabbed another and trotted to the shed, looking back at her. "Show me where, girl."

"Stop it! Put that stuff down right now. And I haven't been a girl in a damned long time."

"Don't think it goes right here where I'm standing. It'll get wet if it rains," he said, eyes narrowing in a grin.

"John Wayne! Stop! Hound dog, why you letting him do whatever he wants?"

"Inside this door, I'll bet."

He nudged the old-fashioned lever with an elbow and pushed it open with a booted foot. Hens and guineas ran out squawking and flapping erratic wings, feathers drifting around him in a cloud. He moved through the flock like he did it every day and found a clear spot to stack the bags.

When he turned to leave the coop, she had her back to him and was hobbling up the steps with grocery sacks in her arms. The risers were taller than steps should be, and she wasn't, so it was an effort, especially with her arms full. His long stride ate up the ground, and he was lifting a bag from her arms in seconds.

Daggers flew from her eyes. "You didn't need to do that. In fact, you don't need to be doing anything. This is my stuff, so just get out of my way, and leave me alone."

He opened the door, and she went through while he stopped and looked around the interior of the old-fashioned farmhouse. Wide-planked floors were painted a deep green in both the entry and the kitchen. Light flooded pale, yellow walls and a wide window framed a view of multiple gardens and statues, ones he'd seen from the porch, but hadn't noticed. The place suited her, as if she'd come from the house and property instead of a mother's birth canal. He handed her the bag after she put hers on the island, and he left to bring in the rest.

Sophie wiped a nervous bead of sweat from her upper lip and shifted the vee of her neckline so cleavage didn't show. Mr. Wayne didn't need the view. She didn't know what he wanted, why he was out here. Hell, she didn't know him from the devil, and he could be. She heard the trunk slam shut, and in a moment the door swung open.

"Where do you want the bags of cat food?"

"Here. In the pantry."

He wiped his feet on the entry rug and walked by her to put the bags where she pointed. She was befuddled, couldn't figure this out, and should have just told him to leave, but didn't.

She put her few groceries away and asked him if he wanted coffee.

"I sure do."

"Go on outside, then."

With him out of the room, she settled down and quit sweating. She put grounds in the coffeemaker and filled it with water from a store-bought gallon jug. The well was deep and cold, but it spewed rusty, orange water that tasted different than most. She was used to it, even liked it, but it made the coffee bitter.

She pulled out a couple of mugs, filled them as soon as she could drag the pot out from under the stream, and carried them outside, questioning herself. Why had she offered him coffee? Why not send him away right off?

Refusing to look at him in some sort of childish retribution, she put his cup on the small table between them and stared out at the distant statue standing guard in the flower lined path beyond the yard. Weeds littered it now. Her own creaking limbs made it impossible to keep them all pristine like she used to, but they were still wild and beautiful to look at, and she could remember what they looked like when both she and the garden beds were young.

"How long you lived here?"

"Why?"

"I just wondered. It's an amazing place. A sanctuary of sorts. A wild nature preserve."

She finally looked at him.

"You running from something? Maybe the law?"

A shadow crossed his face, but he gave a soft chuckle, leaned back and crossed his legs. "I'll tell you a dark secret. I jaywalk all the time, but they haven't caught me yet. Your turn."

"Fifty years. We bought this house and the acreage fifty years ago and paid it off in five."

"You must have been a youngster."

"I was." She smiled thinking back. "I was a baby and married an older man, but not right away. We bought this first. They all said he robbed the cradle."

He wondered where the robber was but didn't want to ask. Thought he must be ancient by now. He skirted the issue hoping she'd volunteer the answer.

"Has to be wonderful out here with nature all around, no neighbors to bug you. A man could pee off the porch if he wanted to. Hell, a man and woman could run around naked as chubby cherubs, for that matter, and nobody'd be the wiser."

He glanced at her, thinking she might be offended by the idea of her running around without clothes, but she wasn't. She was smiling.

"Yes, you could. Wild and naked." Her gaze probed further than the yard, beyond the forest enclosing them to someplace in another time, and sorrow melted her smile. "But I don't appreciate you calling me obese."

"Excuse me? When did I do that?"

"Chubby cherub."

"Oh. Merely an adage."

The sun had made its way across the sky and was trying to drop behind the tall trees, but it was still light enough to call it daytime. She tossed the remnants of her coffee over the edge of the porch and looked into the dregs at the bottom like it might provide a prophecy.

"You like dandelion wine?" she asked.

"I guess I wouldn't know. You make it?"

"No. Not me." She grabbed his cup, went inside, and brought back two small glasses of pale, yellow liquid. She didn't even like the stuff, but, for some reason, it felt right drinking Carl's homemade wine with this stranger.

"You have kids and grandkids?" he asked, sipping and trying not to make a face. It was strong stuff.

"No. Kids weren't a good idea."

"Why not?"

"There were reasons. Maybe because we liked to run around like those fat cherubs you're so fond of. Maybe that's the reason for the gate, too. Put it up so there'd be no surprise guests. Like you."

John tried for a neutral expression, but it was hard. In a way, though, he could see her doing the nude thing, stripping off her clothes and enjoying the feel of sunshine and warm breeze on her skin.

"You grow up in the sixties?" he asked. "Wear flowers in your hair and say 'peace' and 'far out?'"

"I was already grown, but barely, and I guess I'm an old hippie now. Carl's more hippie than me, even though he doesn't think so, and boy does he hate the government. Hates politicians and anybody telling him what to do. But that's alright because he's special. Everybody knows how rare he is. And he's a hard man to refuse."

"He must be something else." John looked a long time at Sophie's face, her eyes. "I'd like to meet him some time."

Four – The Rat Race

Sophie bribed Dee to stay at the diner and outwait the people eating at her last two tables. Checking her watch every few minutes wouldn't make them leave any sooner, but she couldn't help herself.

"Go on. I'll save your tips for you," Dee said. "Maybe. Looks like you have another hot date."

"I'm making dinner. I promised, and I have to go to the store first."

"Wow. Carl works fast. You excited?"

"Sure," Sophie said, grinning with enthusiasm. "And he knows when he sees a good thing."

"How about you? Do you see a good thing, too?"

"Absolutely." She said so, but she wasn't sure. And the not knowing bothered her.

She raced to the store and then to his house to make more of the promised goulash he liked. He liked her pot roast, too, and many other succeeding meals. In fact, the original steak dinner was the only food he'd ever cooked, but that was fine because Sophie enjoyed making meals for him. It felt right cooking for someone who enjoyed eating as much as he did, and she liked doing little things for him. It helped make him happy, put the grin she loved to see on his face.

"I have to run or I'll be late," she said in the morning, blowing him a kiss, her hand on the doorknob. All her clothes still hung in her apartment closet even though she hadn't slept there since the night of his steak dinner. When Sophie thought back to that night, she saw what might have been a watershed event in her life, a defining moment she couldn't change.

And she wouldn't want to alter anything. Carl made every day special because he was original, unlike anyone else she'd ever known. She'd heard people say every person is unique but figured that wasn't true. *She* was simply Sophie, easy to overlook and not exceptional at all. That had been made abundantly clear. Just ask her mother and father.

Ask Uncle Thomas.

Carl yelled at her retreating back as she sprinted through the door.

"Wait! What's for dinner? I like to know these things ahead of time so I can think about it all day long."

"Don't know. What do you want?"

He scratched his chin and lit up like a boy. "Spaghetti. That work for you?"

"Sure. Spaghetti's fine. See you tonight."

She left on the run, showered and dressed at the apartment, smeared on some red lipstick, and was only a few minutes late for work. Unfortunately, she was late leaving work, too, so she didn't stop at the store for spaghetti stuff and hoped the ingredients could be found in his cupboard.

They were staples, right?

A tired sigh slipped out as she slid into her car. How long could she continue the frantic pace she'd set for herself? She ran a constant race, a marathon – his place, her place, work, store, his place, kitchen, bed and start again.

She was exhausted and glad not to see his vehicle in the driveway when she got there. He'd probably stopped at the bar for a couple of beers. She hoped so, wanting a few moments to herself while she sorted through his food pantry, regrouped, and took a few breaths unfettered by demands, even pleasant ones.

She popped a beer for herself and opened the cupboard doors looking for marinara sauce, canned tomatoes, noodles, anything to makeshift some spaghetti. Deciding it was hopeless, she switched to chicken and pulled out the pressure cooker to help speed up the cooking of a whole frozen fowl.

She had potatoes peeled and boiling in water, cream gravy in a saucepan, peas ready to turn on, and a brown bottle chilling in the freezer. She congratulated herself for a job well done as he opened the door.

"Good timing," Sophie said with a grin. "I was just about to sit for a few minutes while the chicken and potatoes finish cooking. Happy to see you, Carl. Want a very cold beer?"

His face changed into one she didn't recognize, a stranger's, and he banged a fist on the stove, leaving a dent and rattling the metal pans. He glared at her with instant mistrust.

"What do you mean chicken is cooking? We were supposed to have spaghetti. You said so. Why'd you lie to me? Damn it, Sophie. I wish you wouldn't do that."

Sophie's shoulders thumped against the wall when she backed away from his loud words. Her breath caught in her chest, and she grasped her apron as if it might protect her from whatever projectile his anger expelled.

He glowered at the pressure cooker as if he could turn chicken into spaghetti by the sheer magnitude and power of his frustration.

"It's alright, Carl," Sophie whispered. "It was too late to go to the store, and you didn't have the ingredients to cook spaghetti in your cupboard. That's all, and I was too tired to go back out and buy it. We'll eat chicken today and tomorrow I'll . . ."

She stopped talking, confused by his narrowed eyes, and watched as he grabbed the pressure cooker and stalked out the door with it. He threw the metal container into the mole riddled yard and stomped back in, grabbed a shotgun from the corner and loaded it.

She'd never noticed the long gun before and didn't know if it had always been there or been put there today. The idea didn't set well. Arms crossed over her chest, Sophie gave a nervous half laugh, sure it was all a joke. He wouldn't shoot her because she didn't cook what he expected. Surely not. She waited, her heart pounding too-rapid beats, watching as he strode by and out the door.

Several blasts of the gun fractured the night, and lead pellets zinged the metal of what she assumed had been the cooker. They must have dislodged the pressure vent, as it shrieked with released steam.

She expected police sirens to scream down the street toward the house, scared neighbors' fists to bang on the door, the phone to jangle as other neighbors questioned what was happening. Who had gotten shot?

But there was nothing. No knocking, no sirens. Was everyone used to guns going off in this neighborhood? Is that what they did for fun in his town at night? Her back stayed stuck to the wall as she thought about what had just occurred. She considered Carl's odd behavior, and her pulse settled. Fear abated in unlikely waves of hopeful peace.

She swallowed, wrinkled her nose, and wondered if the chicken was fully cooked. He'd want to eat later.

What's wrong with you, Sophie? Carl shoots the pot and you're worried about how cooked the chicken might be?

In the strange silence, she pondered what had happened to her serene evening. What had caused him to shoot the pressure cooker? What could he possibly accomplish by doing that? No way could shotgun pellets penetrate the metal of that cooker. They're made like armored tanks.

What was he thinking?

What was he doing? *There are too many questions, and you don't have any answers, Sophie.*

She left off bracing herself against the wall to turn off the flame under the potatoes before the water boiled away and scorched his pan. She scanned the kitchen for something else she should be doing and decided there wasn't anything she *could* do.

Pulling out a chair, she did what she'd wanted before he came home. She sat with her opened beer, sipped and looked around at the neat kitchen. She'd left nothing out of place she noted with hopeful satisfaction.

But she gnawed a ragged fingernail, too, and kept an ear tuned to the outside as she waited.

He came in scratching his head with one hand and carrying the shotgun in the other. She considered leaving, wondering why she hadn't already, but stayed put as he stood the gun in the corner like it was supposed to be there, a part of the furniture.

Striding to the door, he said "Be right back," and left.

He had the cooker in both hands and a guilty grin on his face. Did the look indicate an apology or some explanation was on its way? No. He didn't say anything about shooting the pressure cooker or the chicken or his anger, nothing at all.

"You want to talk about this?" she asked, getting up to turn the potatoes back on.

"Nothing to talk about."

"Why on earth would you shoot our dinner, Carl?"

He opened the beer she'd offered earlier, sat, and appeared to ponder her question as if the question, itself, was complex or crazy.

"It wasn't spaghetti. It was supposed to be spaghetti."

Sophie nodded and sat next to him at the table and put a gentle hand on his arm to get him to look at her face.

"So, you shot it because you were . . . disappointed?"

"It wasn't what it should have been. That's all. I didn't hurt anything."

She stared at him, looking for clues that could explain his bizarre behavior. They weren't there, at least not at the moment, and the way he handled his frustration troubled her. But she understood how it felt when things weren't the way they were supposed to be, things you'd like to change but couldn't. Uncle Thomas came to mind, but she wasn't going to tell anyone about him.

"You gonna set the table?" he asked.

She did.

And the chicken was fully cooked.

Five – John Wayne Settles Back

"If it isn't what he wants or expects, or if it doesn't work exactly right, he shoots it to smithereens because it's nothing but a target to him, a disposable thing – even if it's mine and not his to destroy. Do you know what I mean?"

"It's pretty hard to understand why anyone would do something like that," John said.

"Shoot stuff?"

She looked surprised, maybe because she'd gotten used to it over the years. It still turned her stomach sour when she thought about the frustration packed in his eyes, but the shootings no longer seemed unusual. Just dumb and full of exploding anger. Only a bit fearsome.

Sophie drained her glass of the dandelion wine and checked out John Wayne's. He still had some, but she was ready for more.

"Tip it up, John."

He did and she pushed herself upright using the arms of the chair, making an effort not to grunt like an old man as she rose.

"I can get us the refills, you know."

"I'm not letting a stranger wander around my house while I sit here and let him rob me blind. Do I look like a fool to you?" She grabbed the glasses with two fingers stuck inside them, and they clanked together as she toddled off. "Yeah, I know. I probably do resemble a fool in a whole lot of ways. Act like it, too," she muttered to herself.

He had wandered around the back of the house by the time she came out, and he heard her shouting his name, panic raising the volume.

"John! Where the hell are you? What you doing? Where'd you go off to?"

He poked his head around the corner of the house and grinned at her.

"Think I'm stealing your whole house with you in it?"

"Course not. But you have no right to go wandering around. Did I tell you, you could do that?"

"No, ma'am. You did not. But since I already did it, and since I saw a firepit in the backyard, I thought it would be real nice to see a fire flickering in it." He gave her a cowboy grin she couldn't resist. "What do you say?"

Sophie lifted her eyes to the sky and traveled inward, remembering. It had been a while since she'd enjoyed a fire. She jerked her head toward it as a gesture of compliance and dragged her feet down the steps. John relieved her of the drink burden and led the way to the backyard like it lived behind his own house.

Trees surrounded the ragged lawn, encircling them as if the house sat in the middle of a Michigan jungle, which he thought likely given what he'd seen as he motored down the long driveway. The woodland began in earnest at the edge of a wide expanse of green grass sprinkled with a wide variety of gardens and statues and boulders.

Attached to long ropes and staked a good distance from each other, several goats munched grass, and he now understood the lawn's scruffy nature. It hadn't been cut by an iffy mower but was landscaped by billies, nannies, and kids. His happy chuckle forced a raised eyebrow from her.

"The goats," he said.

"They gotta eat, too."

A faded, overstuffed couch and several metal chairs flanked the rocks and defined the fire. Between the couch and the fire pit perched a low wooden table that had weathered years of sun, rain and wind, but its battered, splintery surface matched the surroundings.

He put the drinks on the table and turned to Sophie.

"So . . . why is Carl hard to refuse?"

"What are you talking about?"

"You told me he's a hard man to refuse. Why couldn't you say no to him? Seems to me you're a pretty tough woman and know how to speak up for yourself. You've put me in my place plenty."

He put his booted feet on the coffee table and his back against the surprisingly dry couch. He was where he wanted to be and happy. If anyone had told him they decorated their outdoors with inside furniture, he'd have laughed and called them crazy. But the whole thing was perfect. More than picture-perfect; he was home.

"What the hell are you doing here, John Wayne? What do you want from this old lady?"

She sipped from her glass and plunked it on the table before pulling several branches from a decaying mound of kindling and dragging them closer. One by one, she snapped them into pieces and stacked them like a teepee in the middle of the stone circle.

John watched, fascinated by her precision in creating the foundation of her fire. When she sparked the lighter and held the flame to the teepee, it smoldered for only a second before igniting and spewing orange flame from the center.

Sophie sat back on her heels and stared, willing the flame to take hold and waiting for an answer to her question.

"I told you. I want to buy your property. It felt like mine the moment I saw it, and now I'm liking being around you a little bit, too. There it is. You have the long and short of my story, Sophie."

"You don't know me."

"Neither did your man at first, but he liked you right off, didn't he?"

"He did. I wanted to go back to my apartment and friends, but he convinced me I needed to be with him, so I did."

"You always do what he says?"

"You're pretty nosy, you know." She pushed herself up from the ground, her knees making noise like the crackling and snapping of the kindling in the fire.

"I need logs. You bring them here, and I'll put them in. Don't you do it."

"Yes, ma'am." He stood and saluted before heading to the stacked logs. "You heat the house with wood?"

"Always have. Saved a lot of money over the years."

He made several trips and dropped the logs next to the firepit for her to arrange, which she did with the same practiced precision as the kindling teepee.

"You've done this more than a few times, haven't you?"

She nodded, concentrating on the task of building a perfect fire. "Cooked out here a lot, too."

In between watching her work, he let his eyes roam the gardens and statues scattered behind them. One figure in particular caught his attention.

Several boulders stood one on top of another, situated as magically as the monuments in Stonehenge. He knew they didn't just happen that way rolling in from the ice age, and he visualized Sophie and her husband spending the time and energy to create the giant. Like England's ancient treasure, the enigmatic, strategic pile of rocks guarded an enclosed plot of land that held a variety of concrete and wooden headstones.

"You have a cemetery right on the property?" he asked, in awe at its proximity and at the number of headstones marking graves.

She dropped the log she'd been about to place and sparks scattered and soared with the avalanche of carefully placed wood.

"Damn it, John, don't disturb me with stupid questions when I'm building a fire. It has to be done right."

"Sorry. But it looks pretty darned good to me as it is. Let's sit and enjoy it."

He reached to help her stand, and she glanced toward the cemetery, picked up her glass of wine and took a drink before taking a seat on the couch. "For pets. Not people. Fifty years of our fur-bearing children are buried there. Our dogs and cats, anyway, not all the farm animals. Mostly cats. We've had a lot of them. You have a pet?"

"Dog followed me around some in Iraq."

Sophie's head twisted around like it might disconnect from her shoulders. She didn't know why she was surprised he'd been a soldier, but she was. He didn't seem like the shooting kind, is all.

"You were there? In the war?"

"Wasn't anything. Tell me how you got so many cats. Looks like a lot of pet graves."

"It was him. Twenty-something all at the same time one year. He was always bringing them home for me to take care of – feed and worm, do the damned flea baths. Cats aren't cheap, you know, and in the winter the darned things take up every flat surface in the house. You can't move or sit for cats and hairballs."

"Have to have a big, soft heart to love cats so much."

"You'd think so. I did, too. But I might not have been right about that. One thing might not have anything to do with the other."

"Doesn't seem likely, Sophie."

"What I mean is, a man can admire a cat and still not like people. That's what I meant. And some do. You don't need a big heart to like cats."

She patted the couch, calling a long-haired tiger who'd ambled by to climb on her lap.

"How many cats in your flock right now, Sophie?"

"Don't know, and they don't come in flocks. They're not pigeons, John."

"What do you call it, then?"

"Clowder. A bunch of cats is called a clowder, city boy. And a bunch of ducks is a paddling. Elephants are a parade, and a whole strew of crows is a murder. Want more or does that much information already crowd your little brain?"

John's hand flew into the air with the crows.

"Wait. The word for crows can't be murder. Besides, it's a verb."

"Listen to you, John. You just gave me an English lesson."

"Sorry. Bad habit of mine. But really, a murder?"

Sophie spent some time staring at the cat on her lap, finished the wine in her glass and grimaced.

"Never liked this stuff of Carl's. Bitter junk, isn't it? And yes, crows gather in a murder. Strange, huh?"

"It's sure an odd term to ponder in this garden of Eden. And I'll bring the wine next time," he said.

"Next time?"

John grinned at her, raised his glass to his lips and didn't respond. His tranquility was complete, and he melted into the scruffy couch cushions as if they were clouds.

Six – The Slow Dance

Their relationship was idyllic when it wasn't horrific, and she learned to feed her lies with wishes.

They took road trips to the Upper Peninsula and swam in the lake near Carl's home, took his dog for long walks and ate out at every restaurant in the county. Sophie learned to pay attention to what he said he wanted for dinner and how to behave when they went out for drinks after work, but she held her breath wondering if the shotgun would reappear some day without notice.

Carl was a charmer most of the time, and he loved her, only her. Sophie was sure of that, and his love buoyed her, kept her afloat during the tough moments.

She also learned when to talk, when to keep still, and when to walk away if he got agitated. Conversation and logic didn't do any good, then. Not hers, anyway. Words wouldn't walk him down whatever mountain of frustration he sat on. Conversation only created a volcanic eruption.

At their favorite bar, he liked talking with people about things he knew, and he knew a lot.

"Man," his buddy said. "Where do you get this stuff? It's like your brain is a sponge, but it sucks up information instead of spilled beer."

"I listen and read. And I think. Most people don't do any of those complex things." Carl grinned as he cast out the blanket judgement.

"You talking about me?" Freddie asked.

"No. Not you. All the ignorant idiots. They're all over the place. Look around you. The whole world is crawling with stupid people and they're reproducing like rabbits, Arabs and Jews," he whispered. "And niggers."

"Carl," she said and put a hand on his arm to make him stop saying such prejudiced garbage. She thought he spouted ridiculous bigotry sometimes just to get a reaction from people – watch their eyes and learn if they were who they pretended to be, down deep. Some faces showed obvious horror, and some would laugh and slap his back in approval. Most people looked away like they wished to be somewhere else, uncomfortable because they didn't know how to respond to his narrow-minded ideas, and didn't want to cause a scene. She believed he didn't mean it. She hoped he didn't.

But Carl meant what he said and knew he could reveal his aberrant thoughts to his old friend, Freddie. They'd been close since kindergarten.

Freddie knew him well. Sophie didn't, yet.

Today he'd tempered his voice so not everyone heard. He was smart enough not to insult everybody in his favorite bar. People here liked and admired him even if they frequently didn't understand what he was talking about, and being liked was important to him.

When Carl started talking about computers, she left to join a couple of girls she knew at a nearby table.

"About time you came unglued from your man," Dee said. "He's cute and all, but . . ."

"He is, isn't he?"

"So how is it being a married woman?" Dee asked.

"I'm not."

"You might as well tie the knot; you're at his place all the time. You live there."

Sophie frowned without realizing it. "It's too soon. I'm not ready, and I don't know if I ever want to get married. Look around at all the divorces."

Lisa, a dark-haired young woman who worked at the diner with Sophie and Dee, snorted and chugged half her beer.

"I'd worry more about the cheating than the leaving. All men are cheaters," she said.

"Not all of them." Sophie glanced at the bar. "Carl isn't, and my dad is true blue – mean, but a good man."

"Can you be both at the same time?" Dee asked.

"You know what I mean."

"No, guess I don't." Dee had seen mean firsthand and knew it couldn't exist right next to good. Not in the same body or in the same brain. And not in the same fisted hand.

Sophie knew from personal experience it wasn't only men who cheated, but she didn't want to talk about it. Dirty laundry stayed in the hamper, like the man she'd called uncle since the second grade. The man her mother spent all her spare time with – for years. The man Sophie believed sired her brother who looked just like *Uncle* Thomas.

Her mother had taught her how to feed a lie with wide eyes and smiles. People buy words coming from smiling lips – without question. Sophie practiced it on Dee when a friend asked her to dance and she said yes.

"You sure Carl is going to be alright with you dancing with another man?" Dee asked, hanging on to Sophie's arm as she stood.

"Course. Why should he care?"

She let Dave pull her through the crowd to the dance floor and stayed for the next slow one, too. Sophie knew he liked her, and her shoulders settled in comfort as they shuffled through the sawdust spread over the hardwood planks. The music filled her, and the room grew distant, fading from her conscious mind. A soft smile dimpled her cheeks.

"How you doing, Sophie?" Dave asked.

"I'm perfect."

"You sure are. Been meaning to tell you for a long time. Guess I didn't get around to it soon enough." He glanced from her face to Carl's and wondered if she would be in trouble for dancing with him.

Sophie's light laughter filtered through the room.

"Could be you got around to it in time," she whispered. "Never know."

"You're like your mother, aren't you?" he said as they pulled from the parking lot. "Flirting and dancing with any man who smiles your way. I should've known you would be. The whole town probably knows it, too." He glanced at her, anger and disappointment mingling in his eyes, and shrugged. "Just like her. You don't use your brain."

"Stop it, Carl. You don't mean that. You're just jealous right now, and you don't need to be. It was a dance and that's all." She tried to sound firm, but it didn't work. The words came out weak and uncertain.

Her shoulder pushed against the door, and her elbows pressed into her sides as she made her body as small as possible. Her chin trembled, and an anxiety caught in her chest and flamed into a righteous anger she deliberately stoked like the backyard fire.

"You can stop the car right now and let me out. I'm not going home with you. Not like this."

"We're going home, Sophie."

She argued, even tried to open the door, thinking he had to stop if she was climbing out of the car, but he grabbed her arm and held her in the seat.

"Shut the damn door, Sophie."

When they got to his house, she went inside intending to gather her things, determined to go back to the apartment she had shared with friends, to a simpler life with simpler people. She told him so as gently as possible, trying to leave the argument in the car behind.

"This isn't working, Carl. You can't tell me what to do all the time, and sometimes, I swear, you don't even like me.

Not at all. I disappoint you every time I speak or move." Her eyes filled when she said the words. It was important he liked her, liked who she was.

He shook his head. "You need me to monitor what you do, Sophie, because you don't think for yourself. Women aren't as capable of rational thought as men." He softened his words with a dip of his head. "You know. The old Venus and Mars thing?"

She let his words go, telling herself he didn't mean them. It was the beer talking.

"I need to leave. I can go back to Dee's apartment, my old place. She'll love having me back."

"Go ahead," he said with a half shrug and a smirk that conveyed information only he knew. "Remember this, though. No one else will want you. Not now, not ever. You're used goods, and everybody knows it."

When she realized he wasn't kidding, she was stunned and then angry all over again. He didn't bring up her being used goods when he was taking off her bra and panties. He hadn't cared how secondhand she was when he wanted her the last time and the time before that and the time before that.

"This is the sixties, Carl. Nobody cares. Haven't you heard of the sexual revolution? Make love, not war? Flower children? Burn your bra?"

Her voice raised with each pronouncement.

"I'm no hippie," he said, spitting out the words. "Just because I recognize bureaucratic government bullshit when all the stupid sheep in the world buy into whatever they're being told, it doesn't make me a damned flower child. What the hell is the matter with you?"

"Nothing's wrong with me. And if I'm second-hand goods, what about you? You're used, too."

He marched to the refrigerator and grabbed a beer.

"Don't you think you've had enough, Carl?"

"I'll stop when I damned well feel like stopping. I have a brain in my head, and unlike you, I use it."

Sophie deflated, her anger gone, and she couldn't rekindle it. She was empty, and tears gathered, but she wouldn't let them fall. She tried to rekindle her outrage by fighting through the hurt and reclaiming her anger. Anger was a head, not heart, kind of thing and much easier to speak through.

But it was useless because she wanted his smile back in place and his eyes looking at her with approval, not dissatisfaction. She sat on the short end of a teeter totter, going up and down between what to do. She believed in Carl's wisdom and agreed with him about pretty much everything – mostly.

He was smart, and she wasn't. Sophie knew that much for certain. And when he looked at her like she was special, she *almost* believed what his eyes said.

Maybe he was right about what others might think – what kind of man would want a cast-off woman? It could be he spoke the truth. What kind of man would look at her now?

Her mind was a battleground, and she wanted the war over.

He didn't mean every single thing he'd said.
She was lucky to be with him.
She didn't want to leave him.

Sophie stemmed the tears and moved toward him, a smile wavering on quivering lips, her hand rubbing her forehead as if to wipe away all the hurtful words. He wrapped an arm around her and patted her bottom, and Sophie knew everything would be alright.

She loved him. He loved her.

Some days were dream-like, a fantasy of what every young woman believes marriage and love should be, and on just such a day, they bought their dream property.

"It's perfect," he said. "We can buy a tractor to plow ourselves out in the winter and haul wood in the summer. We can be by ourselves, away from people."

"It's pretty far from town. What about getting to work on snowy roads?"

"You could quit. Just take care of this place and me. We'll get chickens for eggs and frying and goats for milking."

"I like my job, Carl. I like being around people."

Seven – The Joy of Farming

"So, did you quit work?" John asked.

"No. Not right away. We wanted to pay off the property mortgage as soon as we could. All my checks went to pay the bank loan, and we did it in five years. Carl never trusted banks, so other than the mortgage, we never used them. He never trusted anything at all, actually. Or anybody."

"Maybe he was smart not to have any faith in banks."

"You're telling me he's smart? Everybody in the whole world knows that." She scoffed and snorted. "Of course, he is, and you're not listening."

John grinned her way and nodded toward the guinea hens edging closer to them as evening fell. He heard *Buck wheat, buck wheat*, and thought he might have to learn guinea talk. It was sweet.

"I'm not sure I trust banks either," he said, "but you can't get along without them, can you? Are those birds looking for food?"

Sophie thought about the jars of money and squinted, examined his eyes searching for two faces. She saw only one and was satisfied.

"What are you getting at, John? If you've got a question to ask, just do it and stop beating around the bush."

"I did, but I'll repeat it. Are the guineas looking for food?"

"You're an ass, John Wayne. Anybody ever describe you like that?

"Frequently. I guess you've noticed I'm always alone. Nobody likes being around a smart ass."

He chuckled at his own humor, but it wasn't a happy sound, and Sophie felt a twisting in her gut. It wasn't a sick stomach like when Carl got mad and shot things, but like when a coon got in the chicken coop and killed her favorite hens.

"No family? Never got married?" she asked.

He sipped at his glass, shook his head, and stared at the perfect fire. "Nope. You called it right. I'm too much of an ass."

Her eyes narrowed, accentuating the spiderwebbed creases spreading from the corners as she pondered John Wayne. She tugged at the long mass of silver hair hanging over one shoulder and let her hand hang from the tail of it, forgotten.

She didn't know what to believe about him – particularly his spending time out in the boondocks with an old lady. She wanted to mistrust his motives but couldn't make herself. There was something markedly trustworthy about John. She didn't know what it was and couldn't put a name on it, but it was there.

He grabbed the jug of bad dandelion wine, filled both their glasses and settled back into the mushy couch. The air had cooled as evening dropped over them, and he was glad for the warmth of the crackling fire. Its orange light made a circle around them, beyond which lay thick, purple darkness, a deep ebony broken only by the stars blinking on and the glowing eyes of night creatures.

He spotted two sets and pointed at them.

"Coons," she said and called to Fannie. "Go, girl."

The dog took off baying like a movie hound he'd seen in a story about a Georgia cop chasing an escaped criminal. When she came back, Sophie patted the dog's head and scolded her for not spotting them herself.

"She's a good dog," Sophie told him, "but she's lazy."

"Seems to me she took care of them pretty fast. Bet she keeps out all the intruders. Cept me, of course," he added with a grin.

"I trust her. She knows what to leave alone, like possums. Most people think they're just big rats, but possums are good citizens to have around. They eat ticks and grubs, pests you don't want bothering your animals."

"What about deer? Do you fill your freezer with venison?"

"No hunting on the property. Never. Ever. But I got a freezer full," she said with a sly tilt of her head.

He nudged her foot with a boot tip, getting a kick out of her crafty look.

"What are you hiding, devil woman? Spill the beans."

"Road kill."

His face scrunched, his nose wrinkled, and he made a choking sound that made her laugh.

"It's fresh meat. People call us to go pick it up when they hit a deer with their cars. And it happens around here all the time. I've got more than I can use. I'll make some burgers if you're hungry . . . if you can wrap your mind around eating roadkill."

"I'm game."

"Gotta milk the goats first. You can feed the chickens and guineas. Grab the eggs, too, when you shut them in for the night."

She took off for the far edge of the lawn where the goats were tethered, her rubber-booted feet slapping the ground with faultless certainty and taking her directly to them. They bleated, calling her name, knowing they were going to their shed. Their bellies were full of fresh grass, and they were ready for their straw beds.

John wasn't sure how to do what he'd been told, but he swallowed the last of the wine in his glass and headed toward the rickety chicken coop. The guinea hens who had gathered around them at the fire pit followed, cooing their appeal for dinner and making him smile.

"I could get used to a couple goats and some guineas," he told them. "You're kind of sweet."

He knew where the feed was because he had put it there, himself. He dipped a tin can into the bin and scattered seeds on the ground, watching in delight as they scooped up their dinner. Spotting a few eggs, he pulled his shirt tail from his pants and made a nest of it to carry them.

All went well until he tried to corral the fowl and move them into the coop for the night. They squawked, flapped their wings, and ran from him as if he wanted chicken dinner and they had the drumsticks. He chased and flapped one arm at them, the other holding his shirt tail turned egg nest. Their combined ruckus kicked up dust and filled the night with audible angst – fowl and his own.

"Sophie, help!" he called as she neared, three goats trailing behind. "They don't want to go inside. They're acting like recalcitrant children."

"Recalci . . . what?" She halted, and the goats nudged her butt to get her moving again.

"Wayward, unruly. They won't do what I want them to do. They won't go to bed."

"Well, why didn't you just say that? Didn't you give them feed?"

"Yes. They ate it."

"In the coop?"

"No. I put it on the ground. Like I saw you do."

She chuckled. "Some farmer you'd make. Morning is outside. Night is in. Why would you give it to them out here? Not too smart, John Wayne."

"Oh yeah?" He popped his knee forward and jutted out a hip because he was at a loss for words. "Well, you didn't know what recalcitrant meant."

"I do now." She shook her head and ambled toward the goat enclosure and the milking stool.

And she did know now. Sophie never forgot. Her brain stored information like a file cabinet, each little bit in its proper folder and filed away with like categories. She might not have won any secretarial awards for her filing system, but it worked. Recalcitrant would likely be filed under 'R,' but it would have been for rotten children, Sophie organizing style.

John carried the bucket to the kitchen for her and watched as she strained the milk and poured it into glass bottles. He felt like they'd stepped backward in time, and he was fascinated. For Sophie, it seemed that time had stopped fifty years ago and never moved on. She'd begun milking goats right after they bought the land and the animals.

She cooked the venison patties on the firepit grate, slapped them on buns, and watched as John ate one and asked for another. Sophie liked a good eater and noted he didn't even flinch at the first bite of his roadkill burger.

Bats, coons, possums and owls took over the night, and Sophie kept a hand on Fannie's head to keep her from chasing them away. She'd seen John's enjoyment as his eyes followed the shadows, and she liked his pleasure. As long as her chickens were safe, she didn't care who came around. When she went to bed, she'd send Fannie out on her rounds of the property. She'd clear it of predators.

With a full belly, John rose to leave, thanked her for the evening, and meant every word when he said he'd not enjoyed himself so much in years. It was a place of peace, with abundant life existing in harmony. He hadn't been anywhere in all his travels that displayed such complete accord.

"You have a special place here, Sophie. It's serene. Thank you for sharing it with me."

His words prompted memories of the too many times it hadn't been serene at all, the times when Carl got drunk and shot whatever he was angry with at the moment. But she didn't say so. Instead, as they walked to the front yard and the Harley, she pointed to the peacock tree.

"That big old tree in front of you?" She said it like a question, and he nodded. "I shot a coon out of it once. Didn't know how to load the damn .22 caliber rifle properly, so I stuffed in one bullet at a time. Couldn't see anyway I was crying so hard."

"Why would you shoot a coon if you were gonna be sad over killing it?"

"He managed to get into my chicken coop the night before and killed some of my favorite guineas and injured some layers. You reminded me of that when you talked about this place being so peaceful. Sometimes it isn't. Sometimes life just isn't."

She paused for so long, he wondered if she'd blacked out or something, but she shivered and looked away from the tree and back to him.

"Anyway, I shot over and over again. I wasn't a very good shot. Then. Finally got him to fall to the ground where I finished him. Carl made me skin him and eat him."

"Really! Were your chickens alright?"

"Some were. Some I tossed into the field. They were gonna die."

"That's harsh, Sophie. How could you do that?"

"They're chickens, John."

"I know, but you love your birds."

"Yes, but I couldn't save them, and I couldn't eat them. There's a fine but really deep dividing line between what the head knows and what the heart wants. I am queen of living on that line."

"I get it."

He climbed on his bike and made it growl to life. Its thunder filled the night, but it was a sweet grumble and didn't even stop the crickets' chirps. She stayed in place until the sound turned onto the road and faded out of hearing before ambling back to the fire.

She poked the coals until they flamed around a couple of slender logs. Sophie didn't want to spend all night outside, but she wasn't ready to go to bed. The pleasant evening with John Wayne had prompted memories of other nice nights by the fire when Carl still grinned at her, thanked her for cooking, and made love to her on the outside couch -- cool air on bare skin and stars overhead, a forbidden world made delightful in the middle of their own forest.

Sophie poked at the fire one last time and collapsed onto the couch. It was still warm where John Wayne had been, and she let her hand soak up the heat and reminiscence. She wasn't lonely now, but could be if she let herself.

Her foot bumped the dandelion wine jug, and she reached for her glass, filled it, and lay her head back to watch the sky fill with twinkling light. She wanted to remember the pleasant nights. She wished they had all been, but wishes were paper that burned into ash and floated to the sky, and she knew the flames too well.

Morning had nearly nudged out the night before she stood, hand clutching the ache in her back, and climbed the steps to her concrete porch. She went into her tiny house to sleep on the inside couch, not wanting the big bed upstairs.

She never slept there anymore.

Eight – Putting up Barriers

"You should see the place, Dee. We're all by ourselves in the middle of a forest. I can garden, get an all-over suntan, and cool off in this little swimming pool Carl made for the two of us. I love it so much."

Dee's eyes grew wide, and her smile said she'd like to run around naked, too, but would be afraid her mother or the mailman would catch her. That was her luck. All bad.

"What if somebody shows up? I mean, people do go out visiting, you know. Maybe even a Jehovah's Witness group coming to tell you how to find your forever place in heaven."

Sophie giggled. "Getting caught by a Jehovah would be kind of funny, wouldn't it? I worried about it for a while, but he fixed my little problem. He put a gate across the driveway and rigged up lights that flash and bells that ring if anybody tries to open the gate or drive up the driveway. He really is something else; he has a scary kind of genius."

Sophie's eyes were lit in admiration with only a small cloud left over from the day he came home from work and found her mowing grass in the nude. His eyes had blazed with fury as he yanked off his shirt and threw it over her shoulders.

"But you wanted this, Carl. You said this was our own little nudist colony." She stopped talking to chew on her lip, hoping he'd smile and forget his anger. "And you like me best without clothes on. Remember?"

"When I'm here, damn it! What kind of woman runs around naked all by herself? I should've known about you," he mumbled and stalked off, shoulders bent, to his work shed.

She swiped at the tears leaking from her eyes and rolling down her cheeks. She couldn't stop them, and she was mad at him and madder at herself for falling into the trap it seemed he was always setting for her.

He wanted her to be free in their perfect paradise – for him, but not for herself, it appeared, and he would show his annoyance in a fit of temper if she or the world didn't conform to his requirements. When she tried anything on her own, Sophie paid the price. He didn't physically hurt her, but he didn't need to. She hurt all by herself when it became clear she'd disappointed him. Again.

He banged away in the work shed, taking his anger out on metal pipes he was turning into a gate, and she finished mowing the lawn with his shirt over her shoulders. She'd stuck her arms in the sleeves but would be damned if she'd button it up. She and the cotton shirt flapped in the breeze created by racing the mower across the lawn at high speed, and she shivered from the thrill of the flapping shirt, as well as fear of his fury.

He didn't quit working until he had the metal gate in place, and it was dark when he finally came in the house. She slid a plate of steak and potatoes from the oven and put it in front of him.

"I kept it warm for you."

"Gate is up. Keep it closed at all times."

"I'm sorry. I didn't think about anybody coming out and seeing me. Why would they come all the way out here?"

"That's the problem, Sophie. You don't ever think. Keep the gate closed from now on. And locked, hear me? Get me a beer?"

Sophie popped the metal cap off the glass bottle and handed it to him. He guzzled half before setting it on the table to eat his dinner.

"We needed a gate anyway. Should've put it up right away. We don't want strangers and busybodies coming out. Don't need anybody here. Just us."

She perked up after hearing what could have been construed as an apology for his anger and harsh words, but probably wasn't. She took it as one, anyway, because she knew it was the best he would offer, and she needed some words of repentance. A contented heart depended on it.

"It feels a little bit like we're shutting ourselves off from the world, Carl. Like nobody's welcome in our home," she said as she took the chair next to him.

He patted her shoulder and grinned, the kind of smile she liked to see reflected through the glint in his eyes.

"Now you're getting it right. We are. Because we don't need anyone. Being by ourselves is why we have this big chunk of property. And on the weekend, we're going to start building our underground bunker. Wait until you see what I have in mind, Sophie. Before long, we won't need anybody for anything. But we do need a windmill."

His eyes glazed over and wandered as he considered how he could construct one, and as the glow of creation burned in him, he forgot her.

She didn't know why he wanted a windmill but assumed it was to make electricity. He always talked about being totally self-sufficient, and she understood his desire and wanted it, too. But hers wasn't a need, not like his. And it sounded like fun, something to do. Together.

They spent evenings by the fire and made love in the moonlight. She wanted to quit work at the diner to enjoy the freedom to create more gardens and experiment with canning and freezing vegetables, but they needed her money for the mortgage. Soon, she thought, and her love for their paradise grew.

She painted the living room walls beige, the plank floors green, and scattered red flowered rugs around the rooms and at the entry ways. The house reflected her personality – light and cheerful and liberally sprinkled with splashes of bold red. Their home gave her joy with every stroke of love she painted it with.

She created flower beds throughout the woods so when she and Carl's huge Dane, Charlie, took walks they'd come upon bright flowers as if it had been unexpected, like she hadn't planted them. At least, that was the plan. She knew it wasn't realistic, but she liked to pretend the angels had spread gardens there just for her. Pretending was easy for Sophie, and, in many ways, her imagination was better than reality.

Charlie became her new best friend, and she let her hand rest on his head as they ambled along together. She talked to him, and he would bump her hip and stare up at her face. Charlie knew confusion when he saw it, and he saw it in his friend, Sophie. It disturbed him.

"You trying to push me over, Charlie? What are you doing that for?"

He moved over a few inches, but before they'd taken too many steps, he grazed her leg again. She needed him, he thought. Needed his warmth.

"It's alright, my friend. You can shove against me all you want. But we need to hoof it. Your papa will be home soon and wanting dinner."

When snow fell in December, they rejoiced, cut a spruce tree from their woods and stuck it in a bucket of sand. They bought a single ornament and decorated the rest of the tree with old fashioned strung popcorn and colored lights from Walmart. And every year afterward, they'd buy one ornament together. It became a tradition, a part of their Christmas holiday, and they both treasured it.

Their second year in the woods, after the tree stood brightly lit and perfect in the corner of the living room, Sophie went to the diner to invite Dee out on their next coinciding day off work.

"I want to make Christmas cookies," she said. "And drink some beer. We'll make a day of it."

"Absolutely. I've been dying to see your place, but you've been so secretive about it . . . I've been afraid to drive out, what with the gate and all."

"Yeah. I know, and I'm sorry. Well, come out on Tuesday. I'll have everything ready."

Sophie waited for her at the end of the driveway to handle the gate for her. After locking it back up, she climbed in Dee's passenger's seat, shaking her head at the expression on her friend's face. When they neared the lights and they flashed and clanged, Dee put her hands over her ears in pretend fright. Sophie laughed, mouth wide, eyes sparkling.

"Keep driving," Sophie said. "They'll quit when we get far enough away from them."

"This is crazy! You know that, don't you? Tell me you know it's crazy."

Sophie shrugged. "Maybe. But we won't get robbed, will we?"

"If you're actually home to hear the bells when the robbers come." Dee couldn't believe what she was seeing and hearing and thought Carl might be a little bit nuts.

Several guineas and two peacocks met them as they neared the house, and Sophie had to get out of the car to shoo them away so Dee didn't drive over them. She slapped her hands together and shouted, "Scoot babies! Fly away or the foolish lady will run you over."

Dee cracked up. "Between goats bleating, peacocks screeching, chickens clucking and guineas making whatever sound it is they're making, you don't need bells. You've got all these – things," she said, her head spinning around trying to take it all in. "Holy moly. Grab the wine bottle from the back seat. I'll get the rest of the stuff."

"Wine?"

"Yeah. Thought we'd go high class today."

"Roll your window up, Miss Class, or you'll have cat and chicken stowaways when you leave."

The house smelled like Christmas from the cinnamon and vanilla cookies cooling on every counter to the pine tree in the tiny living room, and Sophie sucked it all in. This felt exactly right. This was how a home should feel, and she was glad she'd invited her friend to help her fill it with friendship.

She poured another glass of wine for them both and began frosting the last batch of cooled cookies cut into Santa and tree shapes. They'd already finished the angels and candy canes, and the cookie jar was filled to the brim.

"Where's your Tupperware container. Is it full, too?" Sophie asked.

"Almost. We'll have to wrap these in foil when they dry."

"Thanks for coming today. Aw . . . There's Elvis. I love his Christmas songs. Fills my heart with hope."

"You're a mush ball, Sophie. You're getting teary eyed, you softy."

"I am. Christmas makes me happy-sad."

"That's a new one. Uh-oh. Speaking of hearing the Santa bells . . . Your man is home. At least, I think it's him."

Sophie got a beer from the fridge and opened it, ready to welcome him to the festive activities. She bubbled with excitement. Today, she'd made their house a warm holiday home.

He scowled at the car in the driveway and plodded up the steps to the door.

"Merry Christmas, Carl," Sophie said, holding the bottle of beer out to him. "Would you rather have wine? We have some left."

He nodded at Dee, took the beer with a shake of his head, and looked at the trays of frosted cookies lined up on the counters.

"Dinner?" he asked with a grin.

"Uh. Not made yet." Sophie grinned back. "But have we got cookies! Lots and lots of cookies."

She pulled the red elephant cookie jar to him, the one that had belonged to her grandmother, and took the top off.

"Feast your eyes on those."

"You've been busy," he said, taking one out and biting the head off an angel.

"We have, Carl," Dee said. "And as soon as these are frosted and my wine is gone, I'll get out of your hair."

"I don't think you're in it. I'll just sit here, eat cookies, drink beer and tell you about my stupid day. Damn but people are dumb."

Carl started in on his co-workers and didn't quit until Dee packed her car with half the cookies and backed out of the yard. Sophie guarded the birds and cats while she maneuvered the driveway and met her at the end of it to open the gate and relock it.

"Thanks for coming, Dee! I had a great day," she shouted at the retreating car.

And she had. She hustled back up the long driveway knowing supper was late and feeling anxious. She tried to shake it off and wore a smile on her face when she went back into the house. Carl did not.

"Who in the hell said you could have a cookie party out here. No one! I mean no one needs to come into my house!"

Sophie stumbled backwards into the entry, away from the distorted expression on his face. Away from the heat of his intensity.

"We were making . . ."

"I can see what you were making. Do you think I'm a fool? While I'm working my ass off with an ignorant bunch of jerks, you're here playing and drinking wine. Where's dinner? Where's my clean house?"

His arms swept the room in violent broad strokes as he complained, and his nostrils flared. When she tried to respond, he cut her off, and the more he talked, the angrier he got and the further away from him Sophie shrank.

She found herself in the small bathroom and hid there, rocking back and forth, arms gripping her knees, until the gun went off. Three times the blast shook her until she crept from the house to see what object had been his target. When she got to the bottom step, she saw the massacre.

Shards of the red elephant and colored frosting were scattered in a circle on the grass, like bad parade confetti waiting for the cleaning crew the day after a celebration.

Sophie turned toward the house.

The party had ended. She clutched her stomach and climbed the steps. The kitchen needed to be cleaned. Dinner fixed. What had she promised to make? She remembered saying something that morning, but not what it was she'd said. Should she ask him?

No. Not right now.

She checked the refrigerator, found a package of ground venison, and talked to the meat like a friend.

"Good, hamburger. You're goulash soon. Thank God."

When he came back in, the kitchen was clean, cookie pans put away, and his favorite dish simmered on the stove. There had never been brightly frosted Christmas cookies. A red elephant cookie jar had never existed, regardless what her grandmother had thought.

She handed him a beer and set the table.

Nine – The Parade

When full sun hit her face, she stretched and groaned even louder than usual as she sat up. Fannie groaned, too, and licked Sophie's nose.

Come on. Wake up. I'm hungry and you're late.

"I know, girl. It was a long night. I blame John Wayne. He doesn't know when to go home."

She shuffled into the kitchen and poured food into the cats' bowls and kibbles into Fannie's, made coffee and stood at the sink looking out at the nymph in the furthest garden as it spewed water into a basin and recycled it to spew all over again. Sophie loved the figurine, loved that it was a constant flow of liquid in an erratically tedious world.

How can it be both? Fannie waited, expecting a nonsensical answer but getting no answer at all. She prodded. *Did you even hear the question?*

"I heard you, and it can be both. Don't get snarky with me, Fannie Amelia. I wonder if he even has a home."

Fannie rolled her eyes and would have told her, but Sophie wasn't looking for an answer, and they both knew it.

She took her coffee to the porch and watched several fat squirrels squaring off in a battle for the peacock tree. Back and forth they scampered and stood on their hind legs, chattered ferociously, and raced back to the thick trunk.

"Foolish creatures," she said. "Share. There's plenty of tree for all of you."

Fannie finished her breakfast, pushed the screen door open and ambled out, heading to the peacock tree to pee. She could have lifted her leg to get the point across but wouldn't act like a male for anything, not even for the comedic, fluffy tailed rodents.

The squirrels scolded, the peacocks floated awkwardly from their low-branch perches to the ground like airplanes with bad wings, and Fannie wandered back to lay by Sophie.

"Nice day, isn't it, Fannie girl? Want to go to a parade later?"

Fannie didn't lift her head from its resting place on her two front paws, but she darted an eye toward Sophie making it clear she wouldn't be left behind.

"After chores, we'll take the Beetle to town. You always enjoy riding in the Bug, don't you? We'll stop for a burger if you want."

She bathed in lemon laced lavender water and dressed with care, donning her favorite blouse, the one she saved for wearing to Henry's Bar. She yanked her bra straps tight so a deep cleavage showed above the vee neckline and clasped on a necklace so the locket hung at the perfect spot on her chest. She looked good.

Her long silver-white hair glistened as she brushed and fastened it back on the sides with two of her grandmother's combs. She'd always hidden them from him and was pretty sure that's why she still had them. She turned a circle in front of the full-length mirror and nodded appreciation.

"You still look good, Sophie, even if you don't have much of a waist anymore. Don't you let anyone tell you any different."

Fannie waited by the car, and Sophie opened the passenger door for her. She slapped around the Bug and watched for cats to race out from underneath. None did. None ever did, but . . . Everything dies hard. Habits, too.

She backed into a slot at the river park where they used to walk Charlie, and the next dog, and the one after that. All of them. And she remembered their names but didn't like to dwell on them. Fannie sat tall in the seat and drooled at the scent of hamburgers and hotdogs on all the grills fired up and readying for picnic lunches.

"Leash up, Fannie."

Sophie held up the flimsy lead and waited for Fannie to move closer so she could clip it on. It was so thin it wouldn't do any good if the dog determined to take off on a run, but rules were rules on parade day.

"You're a good girl, Fannie. I love you."

Sophie smiled at all the semi-familiar faces lining the main street. The town's different generations resembled each other, the mothers and daughters and grandmothers. Same with the men and boys, and she wondered what all their names were. It didn't matter, but she wished for her own sake her mind could dredge up who they were. They looked like kids, every damned one of them. Where were all the adults? People like herself? Gone?

When he grabbed her around the waist, she knew who it was, and knowing someone in the sea of nameless acquaintances prompted a huge grin.

"Damn, Pete. You know I don't do hugs."

"You weren't the hugger. I was. Glad to see you."

"You, too."

"I brought you a chair," he said.

"How'd you know I'd come? Pretty cocky, aren't you?"

"Just hopeful, Sophie girl."

Their conversation started and stopped in brief, half-sentences, the kind of talk common with folks who had known each other a long time, the kind that grew out of an eternity of association. She wouldn't say friendship – but maybe it was. Maybe by now. Whatever it might be soothed them both like a warm bath you didn't want to get out of, like a neck massage you didn't pay for but got from a loved one.

Air filled her lungs, down deep and satisfying. She released it slowly through her nose and wondered if she had been going about life taking in little, shallow breaths like some mincing princess.

"Do you take big breaths?" she asked him.

Pete twisted his head and stared. "Can't. Makes me cough. Why?"

"No reason. I just wondered. You used to smoke, didn't you?" Sophie leaned in to sniff the air coming from his mouth.

He didn't smell like a smoker anymore, but his breath smelled like old person, and she wondered if hers did. She put her hand an inch from her mouth and puffed air into it, snuffled and thought about it. Her own scent wasn't like anything except breakfast and maybe a little bit of the bad tooth she needed to get fixed.

"What are you doing, Sophie? Does my breath stink? Got any mints?"

"No. It's fine. Does mine?"

Pete didn't respond because the fire truck hooted and wailed, signaling the start of the parade and making it difficult to have a conversation. That was fine with her. She was done with talking anyway.

They watched baton twirling little girls and dogs dressed as soldiers, some even wounded. A huge-footed black horse pulled a carriage holding the town's mayor who took up the entire seat with his wide bottom. Flower bedecked floats vied for first prize in the annual contest, and the queen sat in a southern-belle style, ruffled gown surrounded by her disappointed court. But they all smiled and waved while the high school band played *America*, and Sophie's eyes teared up.

Pete put his hand over hers, and she let him.

"Where are all those young men who went to war, Sophie? My friends. Why didn't they come home?"

The wet gravel in his voice made her look at him, and she wished she hadn't. She didn't want his tears. She didn't need anyone's grief. But she couldn't pull her hand away. He needed it, and there were too few left who looked like them. She waited for him to remove his hand, and the parade ended. Fannie stood and picked up her leash.

"Sophie, Lainie said to come by for one on the house."

In the parking lot behind Henry's, Fannie leapt from the Bug carrying her leash like she had a dog of her own on the other end. It hung from her mouth as it would from a hand. She knew where they were heading and led the way, eager for her hamburger.

The bar was empty except for them. Lainie tossed two napkins on the bar and followed up with Sophie's merlot and Pete's beer, a smile of welcome on her face.

"Glad to see you two. Pretty lonesome here today."

"Glad to be seen, Lainie," Pete said, his usual corny response to a polite greeting.

Shadows hovered at the far end of the long room and in the dim corners.

"How was the parade?" Lainie asked.

"Same as 1970, 1980, 1990, 2000 – cept Mayor Hart shows every hotdog he ever ate and more. Doesn't he, Sophie? And I'll bet he's eating one right now, at this very moment. Maybe two. They're going to have to get a bigger horse to haul his lard around."

"Be nice. Some of us enjoy our food, Pete. We can't all still wear our high school clothes like you and Sophie."

"And I *can*, too. How'd you know?" he said, sucking in his flat belly and puffing out his chest. "We were something, back then, weren't we, Sophie? Lainie, you should have seen this girl."

Pete made an exaggerated hourglass shape with his hands and wiggled his eyebrows provocatively. Sophie's laugh echoed across the empty room, and she looked like the young girl he remembered and still saw. Her laugh remained unrestrained and eager, her smile toothy, dimples deep and infectious. She could have married any man in their class. And she never knew it.

"Way back, Joe was nuts about you. Freddie, too. And Tom and Terry. Did you know that?" he asked.

"They all were, you crazy old geezer. Every last one of them. Even you," Sophie said but didn't mean it. She hadn't known at all.

"You're right. It's the absolute truth," he replied as his feet hit the floor. "Sorry. I gotta use the little boy's room. Can't get five minutes away from the damned john anymore." His mumbled words followed him as he left.

The shadows Sophie had seen in the dim corners of the room rippled, and from them emerged a youthful Carl and his friend Freddie. She spun around on her stool and put her back to them, but he drifted into the corner she faced, determined to gain her attention.

"Stop."

"What?" Lainie said. She stepped out from the kitchen pulling several boxes and cardboard cases on a dolly and came to a halt in front of Sophie. "We're gonna be getting busy soon," she said pointing to the beer. "Did you need something, sweetie?"

"Umm . . . Fannie was taking herself for a walk, and I told her to stop. Can you make a burger for her?"

"Sure."

"Me, too," Pete said, coming through the door still buckling his belt and causing a blush on Sophie's cheeks.

"Get dressed in the bathroom for crying out loud. You're obscene."

"I know. Am I giving you any ideas?"

"Hey, Sophie," Lainie asked. "Did you ever find out who your biker man was?"

"Yeah," she said grinning, anticipating their response. "John Wayne. And he was there when I got home."

"You don't need to fib to us, Sophie." Pete wagged a finger and peered at her over his glasses. "You can just say it's none of our business. We can take it."

"I'm serious. He said his name was – is John Wayne. Maybe his mother loved westerns. Who knows?"

"Was he really at your house when you got there?" Lainie asked, concern wrinkling her brow. "That's kind of creepy. Did you call the police?"

"Course not."

"Lied about his name, for sure," Pete said.

"Maybe. He unloaded supplies from the Bug for me, and we had coffee and then wine. Dandelion." She watched their eyes go from surprise to shock to concern and chuckled. "He's fine."

"What does Carl have to say about him?" Pete asked.

"Nothing. He didn't say a thing."

Ten – Wedded Bliss

"Carl!" She shouted to break through the ear-splitting sound of hammer on metal.

He didn't stop his work, nor did she expect him to. She merely wanted to let him know she had entered his workshop and didn't want to startle him. He held the foot-long piece of thick metal up to the light and squinted at it, brow furrows telling her he wasn't happy with whatever it was.

"What do you want, Sophie? Could I get a cup of coffee out here?"

"Sure. I'd be glad to make some, but I have a question, first." She shuffled her feet, wishing she'd planned ahead and knew exactly how to ask for what she wanted. But she hadn't.

He waited and watched her eyes dance around her fluttering thoughts. "Well, woman? You had a question. Did you forget it already?" He grinned and waited again while she fidgeted. "Sophie. Just spit it out"

"Sorry. I got interested in what you were making. Dee asked me to be a bridesmaid at her wedding, and I'd really like to do it."

"So, go ahead. Why bother me about it?"

"I'll need a special dress and shoes, and it's in Leland which is really pretty in the summer, and you'll like it, I know. And the hotel might be kind of expensive, but it's worth it because it's right on the water."

Her words spewed like an overfilled, boiling tea kettle as she tried to get everything out at once. Carl's eyes opened wider with every wave of words.

"Wait just a minute. I'm not the one going to be a bridesmaid. Why do I have to go? I don't even like the damned cookie woman."

"You don't *have* to. I thought you might enjoy Leland. And it's something we could do together. Go away on a kind of a romantic trip. You know?"

He leaned against the work bench and crossed his arms, tipped his head and waited. She didn't know what he expected from her, didn't know what else to say about it.

"Well . . . I'd like to be her bridesmaid. I thought you should know about it ahead of time."

"What about your goats and birds? And the cats. Who's gonna take care of them? And who's gonna pay for the clothes and the room? Dee?"

"Course not. Brides don't do that. I'll pay for them out of my savings. And . . . if you're not going, you can take care of the animals. Right?" She smiled at him and wrapped an arm around his back.

"I could. But why would I? So you can go galivanting around?"

"You'd do it because you love me. That's why."

"When is this stupid shindig?"

"Summer. But it won't interrupt any of our plans at all. I promise. And I'll only be gone a couple of days."

The time leading up to Dee's wedding spiraled her up and down like a kite in a storm. One moment she flew high, couldn't wait to leave, enjoying all the preparations and meetings with Dee and the other women in the bridal party.

In the next, the wind slammed her to the ground, and she dreaded leaving Carl and her animals. Would he take care of them? Feed and milk them? He'd said he would but . . .

And she castigated herself. Carl always did what he said he would do. She knew that about him. He didn't lie, and she trusted that.

As the big day grew near and for many days in advance, she cooked meals and stored them in containers with breakfast, lunch and dinner written on them so he'd know what and when to eat each one. A big pot of goulash, a bowl of spaghetti, and pot roast leftovers filled the refrigerator shelves. She made three plates full of bacon and eggs to reheat in the small counter oven. He'd have to toast bread on his own. She couldn't figure out a way to keep toast fresh ahead of time, or she would have done it, too.

It made her happy doing everything for him. She'd be taking care of him from a distance and figured women did those things for their husbands. Good wives did, anyway. She hummed while she cooked and wrote out instructions for eating and heating.

She poured measured cat food in bags, labeled and dated each one. Dog kibbles, too. The pantry shelves grew full of baggies and instructions. She smiled and took a long look at the packages, shelving the last container to be used in her absence.

The bells rang, and she looked up from washing dishes, waiting to see him drive in. She was packed and excited. The house had been cleaned and everything he could possibly need or want was ready and waiting – except for her. She'd be leaving for Leland in the morning and wanted to know what he really thought about it. He'd never say.

"Want a fire tonight?" she asked as he came through the door. "I can cook the steaks on the grate over it."

She handed him a beer as he tossed his lunch box on the table, leaned in to put her lips on his, and he raised an eyebrow in question.

"What's this?"

"Just wanted to say I'll miss you, Carl. And thanks for being alright with me going."

"You got everything ready, right?"

"I do."

"Then what's the big deal?" He slugged down a couple big swallows of his beer and took a stool at the island.

"I thought you might miss me being around."

"Course. Don't do anything stupid while you're there. You'll be back Monday morning, right?"

"Noonish. You'll have to feed and milk in the morning before work. Sorry."

He shrugged, and Sophie smiled. It would be alright.

She people-watched at the wedding rehearsal and the dinner afterwards. Drinks were free and plentiful, and most took full advantage. Dee was too busy to pay much attention to her guests, but they didn't need her. They entertained themselves and each other.

Late in the evening, a stranger bearing two glasses of wine took the chair next to her.

"Sophie, right?" he said, setting a glass on the table in front of her and holding out a hand.

"That's right, and you are . . .?"

"Dee's cousin, Travis. Where's Carl?"

Sophie's head tilted thinking it was an odd question for a stranger to ask. "You know Carl?"

"Nope." He smoothed his perfect hair and chuckled, squinted his perfect eyes and showed thirty-two perfect teeth. "Why would any man let his beautiful wife out and about so far from home all by herself."

"Because he's home taking care of our animals."

"Well, he's a lucky man," he said.

His words confused her. "Lucky to be home taking care of the animals? Excuse me?"

"Don't pretend ignorance, Miss Sophie. Fishing for another compliment? How's this one . . . you look spectacular and have a great body. But you know that."

She backed up against the chair slats. "I thought you meant . . . you know, about the animals."

He took a drink from his glass and winked. She hated him instantly, and even more so when he let his hand drop to her thigh. Her cheeks flamed with embarrassed anger as she shoved the hand away.

"You're an ass, Travis. Touch me again and I'll break that hand for you. I do know how."

He raised his arms in a gesture of defeat and continued an offensive grin. After he left, she breathed through the tears threatening to ruin her makeup.

Jerk. Who does he think he is? Or she is?

Travis had diminished the evening, and she no longer felt like joining in the fun. She stood at the fringes and listened, drank her wine and watched, instead. When Rob – the groom – slipped furtively into the cloak room with one of the bridesmaids, Sophie had had enough. She walked back to her room, watching to be sure the handsome Travis didn't follow.

Standing at the third-floor window, she watched lights shimmer on Lake Michigan and the far-off orange glow of bonfires on the Manitou Islands. It was beautiful, and she wished Carl was with her. Sharing made everything better, more beautiful. Even made jerks more tolerable.

Her face burned hot with the night's events, and it occurred to her she might be stupid like Carl always said. Was she really ignorant about things? About people?

She slipped on her nightgown and crawled into bed. Perfect Travis and adulterous Rob had ruined the weekend. Maybe people weren't very smart after all. Maybe he had been right all along.

Sophie fell asleep smiling and thinking about Carl, wishing she was home with him and the critters in their tiny slice of Eden.

Eleven – John's Goulash

A strange discontent settled over her when she drove down the driveway toward the peacock tree and didn't see the Harley parked in the yard. She tried to swallow it back and to understand the bereft feeling but couldn't quite get there. Her peculiar sorrow made no sense at all.

Fannie sensed her chagrin and chased the peacocks to get a rise out of her. When racing around didn't work, she spun in a circle and chased her tail. That always got to Sophie. She ran and ran, chasing herself, until she heard the desired laugh and dropped to her belly on the grass, panting.

"You're a fool, Fannie. And I was going to suggest we take a walk. You're probably too tired to go, now. You wore yourself out acting senseless."

Fannie sat erect; her ears perked.

"Okay. I'll change and be right out."

She pushed away what might have been construed as missing John Wayne and decided to do something to lift her spirits. Digging up a couple of the money graves would help; dollar bills did that – especially the ones with big numbers.

She stopped at the shed for a burlap bag and a small spade, and they meandered to the furthest back forty. She knew where she was going, but they walked with purpose so she wouldn't miss the signs.

There were no paths to guide her through this part of their woods, and it appeared she wandered aimlessly. It was slow going searching for the marks because time had changed everything. Didn't it always? Even people; we get weathered, wrinkled, old and die. Pets do, too. Even the trees age from young saplings into giant oaks, and they give it a nice name, like *mature* forest.

"They don't call it old like us. Well I'm mature, too, just like the damned trees," she muttered, sputtering her displeasure.

She and Carl hadn't wanted to advertise that this land was used for anything other than growing trees, mushrooms and moss to anyone who might wander through their forest. *No Trespassing* notices were posted all over the place, but everyone knew those words made no difference to people who thought they had a right to encroach on others' property. In fact, the constraining signs most likely did the opposite and invited poachers to wander. Carl was right about that.

And he had always been paranoid about his land. About money. About strangers. About people who, according to him, had zero personal responsibility, and he made no bones about it to Sophie and anyone else who would listen.

When she spotted the first mark, she turned toward the sun, checked her watch, counted twenty steps and rammed her spade into the soft earth. Around two feet down, she gentled her shoveling until the spade head connected with something besides dirt and stones. It clinked distinctively, a muted thunk sound, and she knelt to brush the dirt away, finally pulling a jar from the ground, a quart jar surrounded by coarse feed bag fabric and packed tightly with money.

She put it in her burlap sack and refilled the hole, stomped all over the fresh dirt and covered it with leaves and branches afterwards so it appeared the area hadn't been disturbed. Twice more, she spotted a mark, checked her watch and the sun, and counted her steps. Two more jars stuffed with money went into her bag.

"Let's go, Fannie. This should do us for a long while."

She heard the rumble of his bike before they were half way back to the house, and she hustled her step, doing her best to get there before he did. What would she do with the bootie bag? Chicken coop? The underground?

He sat sidesaddle, the kickstand down, and watched her and Fannie quick-step out of the woods. She wiped the perspiration from her lip with a sleeve, nodded, said "Hello, John Wayne," and didn't stop striding until she had passed him by and was inside the house.

She hadn't been sauntering at all, he thought. It had been a walking fib. His grin was bemused, and he wondered what precious cargo she had her arms wrapped around, but he wasn't worried when she'd marched straight by. He'd come to expect bizarre behavior from Sophie and figured she'd be back outside soon.

He called to Fannie who readily took the affectionate head caress from him, flipped the flap on his saddlebag and pulled out a box of wine and two stemmed glasses. He chuckled as he climbed the steps to the porch, opened the box and made its content drizzle from a plastic faucet like the supply was endless. Like it was attached to a deep well just for the winos of the world.

He didn't know if she liked red, but she seemed like a red wine kind of woman. He heard the intake of her breath when the screen door opened and she came outside.

"What in blue blazes are you doing?"

"Pouring some wine. What about you?" He handed her a glass and took the other for himself.

"I mean it. Why are you doing this?" Sophie was growing madder by the moment. Her foot twitched up and down, and the sole of her rubber boot slapped the concrete. "Why aren't you off making out with a young woman instead of hunkering down here and plying me with wine?"

"Sit and relax, Sophie," he said, not understanding her irritation.

"Don't tell me what to do, John Wayne."

"Okay. How's this? Would you like to sit and relax a little? If you do, I'll show you my cool underwear all covered with red valentine hearts."

She cackled a laugh she couldn't help. "Hearts? Are you serious? No. Do not show me!" she added as he stood and began to unzip his trousers. "What is it with men and the zippers in their pants today? You're the second one."

"Really? At the parade in front of everyone?"

"How'd you know where I was? Are you keeping tabs on me? Stalking me?"

"Course not. I couldn't get across the main drag and was forced to watch it. Dogs were cute. The mayor wasn't. Neither was the town queen, I'm afraid."

Sophie sat and sipped. She fancied red more than any other kind of wine. How had he known her preference and why did it matter that he had?

"So what. Big deal," she muttered to herself.

"What'd you bring back from the woods?" he asked, curiosity making its way to his mouth.

Sophie jerked back in her chair and glared at him. "None of your darned business. Maybe you need to leave."

He made no move to go. In fact, he settled in further, grinned, and crossed his legs at the knee in the way she'd gotten used to and even kind of liked. She thought it unusual for a man to sit that way. It looked languid or maybe big-headed. She wasn't sure which in John's case.

"I'm just making conversation, not snooping. You don't need to tell me what was in the bag."

She stared out at the garden angel that used to pour water from her bowl over and over.

"Money," she said, hoping for the lilt of sarcasm. "Jars full of lots and lots of money,"

"Nice. Wish I had property growing money trees. Did you plant them or did they come with the land?"

"Planted every single one. Saw 'em in a Japanese seed catalog and sent away for them.

"You read Japanese?"

Her brow raised and she smirked. "Pictures. They had pictures of twenty-dollar bills hanging from the trees, smart guy. Started the seeds inside on the windowsill one January and transplanted the seedlings when it got warm enough."

"Fertilized them, I suppose?"

"I did. With bullshit."

"You can certainly shovel piles of that, Sophie. Ready for a refill?"

"I'm making goulash for dinner. Want to stay?"

"Absolutely. You don't need to ask me twice. Carl's favorite, right?"

Sophie brushed her silky hair back, drawing her fingers through it and remembering.

"Yes, his favorite. I must have told you, huh?"

"You did."

"Come on. Might as well show you the amazing underground, too."

She needed a couple jars of canned tomatoes from storage to make the goulash, but she wasn't going to leave John Wayne alone on the porch right now. Who knew where he'd wander? He was a certified roamer. She knew that much about him.

"Grab your glass," she said.

They walked up a hill behind the house, and he began to think she'd forgotten where she was going when the hill sloped dramatically downward. At the bottom, a door appeared that opened into the hill they'd just walked over. At least that's what it looked like.

She unlocked it and stood back, watching his face as he entered, and it occurred to him she might lock it behind him. It was black as pitch inside and cold. Goose bumps prickled the hairs on his arms and he shivered. From the cold?

He waited, the prickle of fear crawling over him, and started when she spoke close behind his back. Something nudged his legs, and they wanted to buckle.

"Hang on. I'll get the light."

He felt foolish when it flickered on and he realized the nudge was Fannie. Inside, shelves were lined with canned goods and other supplies like paper towels and toilet paper. Bright blankets covered two beds, one hanging over the top of the other attached by bolts to the wall and chains to the ceiling where thick timbers revealed the sturdy construction. Fannie climbed on the lower bunk, turned in several circles, and lay down like she'd been there many times before. It was her bed.

A dozen water jugs lined the floor, a two-burner stove sat wedged into the corner on a home-made wood counter, a small recessed sink next to it. A plank, pine table took up another corner, flanked by two chairs. They could live for a long time in their bunker, could survive chemical catastrophe or other disasters. And he said so.

"That's the point. We were – are prepared for anything."

She pulled two quarts of tomatoes from the shelf and set them on the table. Dropping into one of the chairs, she ignored him and let her eyes wander into the dark corners where light from a single overhead forty watt didn't penetrate.

"We have fun here. Kind of like kids playing house."

"You really constructed this unbelievable bunker by yourselves? You and Carl?"

"With a little help from Freddie on the rafters."

She nodded, remembering the work and sipping from her glass as he joined her at the table.

The air around them was unrealistically still, unlike being outside on a windless day, not even like being in a house where walls kept air motionless. In the underground, it seemed an absence of air existed, but he knew it wasn't true. They breathed. Air had to fill the dark void in order to fill their lungs. But it didn't move around them, and the sound of their voices had a lifeless quality like they spoke from inside a grave.

Twelve – The Underground

In the kitchen, in between cooking sausage and pancakes and staring out at the garden, she listened to the backhoe as it tore through the hill. She could tell what Carl was doing from the determined growl it made as the earthmover dug deep and by its whine as it backed up to dump the dirt.

He'd been at it since dawn, and it was exciting but scary as she watched the hill move from one place to another. He'd rented it for the day and wanted to get the digging done in that amount of time. No sense paying for two if it wasn't necessary. He'd have it brought back out when the shelter was built and ready to be buried, the hill put back where it had been for hundreds, maybe even thousands, of years.

A load of lumber piled high with two by tens, four by fours, and two by fours stood off to the side, wood thick and strong enough to hold a hill on top without crumbling. Sophie came out and sat on the stack of boards to watch the huge shovel dig into the dirt.

Carl knew what he was doing, of course, and teeth bit into solid ground like the prehistoric dinosaur it resembled. It was obvious he was expert at running the machine, and she wondered, as she always did, where he came by this particular knowledge. It was mysterious, even creepy, sometimes. Did he slide from the womb with a cache of collective information from ancestors he didn't even know?

When the noise of the excavator stopped, startling her and leaving a sudden vacuum of silence in its wake, she stood and hollered to him.

"Breakfast is ready, Carl. Come on in and eat while it's still good."

He climbed down and walked beside her toward the house, his eyes sparkling, his grin wide. He grabbed Sophie around the waist, lifted her off the ground, and took off on a run. She could feel the vibration of his excitement through his body, could see it in the glow on his face, and she laughed, leaned into him and wrapped an arm around his neck.

"You're having fun, aren't you?"

"It's alright. If you know how to run these monsters it goes pretty smoothly. I want the hole dug by nightfall when they come to get it."

"Come on. Admit it. You look like a little boy with a new, really big toy. You should look this happy every day. You're handsome with a grin."

He gave her one and asked for his food.

"Feed me, woman."

He finished the hole by dark, and she went with him as he drove the backhoe down the driveway where it would wait to be transported back to the excavating company. Not wanting to leave it there on the side of the road, they stayed with it, him on the seat and her on his lap.

Inside the dark cab, Carl explained the workings of a backhoe, moved levers back and forth, let her move the front-end loader, and kissed her neck until the men came to take his toy away. Sophie wanted to buy one for him, wanted him like this every day.

He asked Freddie to come out the next morning when it became clear he couldn't hold the rafters and secure them in place by himself. He and his friend had the building framed by the next night. Sophie worked alongside both of them and brought them food when they needed it. At the end of the day, she grilled hotdogs over the flames in the backyard firepit and kept them supplied with cold beer.

"Wish I didn't have to work tomorrow." Carl pushed half a hotdog into his mouth and talked around it. He followed it up with gulps of beer.

"You could take the day off," she said, "but it's going to take more than that to finish. What's the rush?"

"None. Unlike some people, I like to finish what I start in a timely manner. No use even starting otherwise."

"You'll get it done. And thanks for your help, Freddie. Another dog?"

"No, I'm done. But speaking of dogs, where's Charlie?"

Carl grinned. "Treeing a coon. Can't you hear him baying?"

They went silent, and in the distance heard the distinctive howl of a dog on scent.

"Whistle for him, Carl. He shouldn't be running so far from home." Sophie added a couple of logs to the fire and moved her chair closer. The night had taken on a chill.

Carl gave a shrill whistle, the kind made between two fingers Sophie couldn't for the life of her figure out how to do, but the sound stopped before it really got started.

"What's the matter, Carl?" She poked at the fire with a stick and watched the sparks climb.

"He's not on a coon. Bet anything it's a man he's chasing."

"Why would a man be out there at night? Can't hunt in the dark, and, anyway, it's posted."

He tilted his head to glare at her, letting her know it wasn't something he wanted to discuss, not with Freddie sitting right there, and boy was she stupid – all thoughts conveyed within a single glance.

"Sorry. Will you whistle for him? He needs to come home."

"I'm gonna take a drive and find the damned dog. Be back shortly."

When they saw his taillights disappear down the driveway, they half-settled into the quiet night. They couldn't hear Charlie's baying any longer, and without Carl's near constant talking, Freddie thought he needed to leave and said so.

"Wait for him to come back. Sit with me, please."

Being alone didn't feel right, not tonight. And she knew Carl wasn't looking for Charlie. He was looking for a trespasser, a poacher, or more than one, and the visual made her sit on the edge of her seat like she was watching a horror movie. When the thought crossed her mind, she wondered if he would create terror in his own woods. He had a pistol in his glove box, and knowing he had it didn't make her more comfortable, but less.

"What's wrong, Sophie?"

"Nothing's wrong. Truly. It's just nice to have company. Thanks again for your hard work today. Carl appreciates it even if he won't say so."

"Sure thing. Carl and I are better than brothers. Always have been."

"I know."

Freddie nodded at her, and his mouth opened, shut, and opened again.

"Look, Sophie. Carl needs not to drink so much. His lips get loose when he drinks. He's out there thinking somebody is looking for his money, isn't he?" The sharp intake of her breath told him the truth even if she wouldn't.

"I . . . I don't know what you mean."

"Sure, you do. I don't think other people know, so far, but . . . he loves to talk, and he loves to drink, too. A bad combination"

"What can I do? You think I can tell him he can't have his beer or a rye and coke? And I certainly can't follow him around to make sure he stays sober, either."

Freddie lifted his broad shoulders, held them there, and then dropped them in defeat. He shook his head and crossed long arms over his chest. He didn't have an answer.

"I've known him all my life," Freddie said, "and he's a good friend, but I've never figured him out – let alone had a clue what to do with him." His dark chuckle hung in the air, fitting backdrop to the picture in her mind. "He would never let anybody interfere with what he wants to do even if they tried all day and all night. He knows more than anybody else. Always has."

She watched the fire, a better alternative to seeing the knowledge in Freddie's eyes, and listened to it snap and spit, sap sizzling. The conversation he'd begun was a terrible idea, and they both understood the unspoken truth. Carl would be furious if he knew about it.

But if anyone ever found out about the hidden jars, it wouldn't be her who'd spilled the beans. She was far too tight lipped. And Carl wasn't.

When his lights appeared through the trees, they glanced at each other, the pact for secrecy acknowledged with a shared look. Neither wanted their earlier words repeated. Neither wanted to deal with Carl's response.

Charlie beat him to the backyard and leaped up onto Sophie, knocking her chair over in his jubilance. She didn't care. Freddie said goodnight, and Carl popped the top of a cold one.

Every night after work, he built forms, and Sophie mixed cement in his wheelbarrow, dumped it and started all over. The labor was back breaking. He removed the wooden frames from set concrete poured the day before and repeated the process. He was a machine, himself, as he moved from one part of the project to the next without stopping to take a break. He focused his energy, drove toward the desired end. He was a man on a mission.

Yard by yard, they poured the floor, lined the concrete walls with sturdy lumber, and built the ceiling with massive timbers covered in thick tar paper and painted with more tar. He worked late into the night by stringing electrical wiring and hanging a trouble light. When the building was complete, he rented the backhoe again, and they rebuilt the hill like they were gods of the earth.

Sophie raked the dirt smooth, scattered grass seed, and covered it with straw to keep the birds from eating the tender grains. While she worked, she considered ways she might decorate the space to make it feel homier, maybe a couple of red rugs, Indian blankets on the walls to counter the chill, a picture or two. She'd enjoy fixing it up. Decorating made her happy.

Except for the door leading to the shelter and facing the woods, it became an unassuming hill again and blended into the backyard as if it had always been there. And the mound had likely existed since the house had been built but was bigger now with a building underneath. No one would ever suspect a good-sized crypt existed under the ground.

Carl liked to tease about the tomb he'd created – maybe for her – and when she was dead, he'd carry her there and set her up in a chair so he could play cards with her and win.

"I don't need to be dead for you to win. You do now." She poked him with a finger and giggled.

"Yes, but I won't have to listen to your babbling at me if you're dead."

She glanced at his face, checking for a grin and finding it there alongside the matching twinkle in his eyes. He turned a circle in the middle of the room and admired his handiwork. The time and effort had paid off.

"This is just what we needed," he said. "Now we put up some shelves and supplies. Add a couple beds and we can sleep down here when it gets hot in the summer. Maybe some furniture and a gas stove, too. What do you think?"

"I love it! You did a great job, and it will last forever, probably a lot longer than us."

"Hell, yes, it will. Now, the idiots can bomb the crap out of the United States if they want, and you and I'll sit in here and laugh at the fools."

"Wait here. Don't go anywhere."

He was still admiring his work when she came back with an arm load of blankets and a basket filled with food and drinks. She spread thick wool layers on the floor and handed him a cold beer, opened a bottle of merlot and poured a generous amount in a stemmed glass.

She clinked their drinks together. "Here's to our new adventure. I hope you're proud of what you've accomplished, Carl. You are truly something, and I am always amazed by you."

She listened to him tell about the problems he'd encountered and solved while building their bunker, and the room grew warmer with alcohol consumed and their warm breath. Sophie fanned her rosy cheeks and unfastened a couple buttons at the collar of her blouse.

"Did you put any ventilation in here?" she asked. "We need a fan or something."

"You just need me," he said, a glint in his eye.

He toppled her to the blanket and unbuttoned the rest of her, and she giggled.

"Christening the crypt?"

"Whoever said you weren't smart?"

"I think it was you."

Thirteen – John in the Crypt

"Did you ever have need of this solid shelter? For a tornado or something like that? Maybe some nuclear fall-out I'm unaware of?"

He presented a scholarly lift of his brows and raised the glass to his lips, marveling at the quality of boxed wine. She emptied her own and held it up to show him the need for a refill before answering.

"Not really. We used it a few times during bad storms but mostly we came out here just for the fun of it. It felt like camping, but we didn't have to pack everything up and cart it to some nature preserve. We had our own. Why didn't you bring the fountain with you, John Wayne?" she asked.

"Fountain?"

"Looked like one to me. Or maybe it was a faucet connected to a magical reservoir kept filled by the great gods of fermentation, although grape gods might be more appropriate."

"Oh, the box of merlot. I'm ready when you are. Need help with the tomatoes?"

"You take one. So, what do you think? Pretty nice place, huh?" she said, calling for Fannie on the way out and locking the door behind them.

"It's amazing, Sophie. Hard to believe it's there under the hill when you're not standing inside it or coming through the door."

"That's the whole idea. Carl likes his secrets, places and things people don't know anything about."

John squinted, wondering again about Carl. He'd not seen evidence of him yet, didn't know if he was still around or not and pondered several possibilities. He wanted to ask her but didn't . . . He wasn't sure why, but he knew prying into her personal life didn't settle well with him. She was a remote woman, and his question would go unanswered unless she chose to share something about it – or whenever the elusive Carl came out of the woods, up the long driveway or down the stairs after a nap.

In the kitchen, Sophie sautéed onions in the cast iron kettle, threw in some ground venison and let it brown.

"Get in here, sit down and stop wandering." She raised her voice for emphasis. "I didn't invite you into the rest of the house, John Wayne, so don't be traipsing around where you weren't asked to go."

"Sorry." With knees high, exaggerated for humor, he hotfooted it back into the kitchen from the dining room where he'd been checking out the family portraits on the walls and the cats sprawled on every available surface. "You have a set of silver spoons you think I might slip into my pockets?"

"I might. You don't know what I might have. And you might fill your empty pockets. I don't know you."

He cocked his head at her, thinking she was right about all of it, and that was one reason why she fascinated him. She said the obvious truth, and he never knew what would come out of her mouth or pop up on her property. He took one of the two stools at the island, one where he could see the front yard and watch her cook.

She moved around the kitchen like she didn't have to think about it. Her hands automatically grabbed chili powder and garlic, dumped in a bunch and shoved the containers back where they belonged without looking. An orange cat leaped to the sink, and she turned on the faucet to let it stream so he could drink from it.

"Speaking of faucets," she said.

"Uh . . . I didn't."

"I did. My glass is empty."

He jumped to his feet and ran to retrieve the magical box, filled their glasses and sat before getting into further trouble.

When the stewed tomatoes bubbled in the iron pot, Sophie threw in half a box of macaroni, turned it down to a simmer, and suggested they move to the porch for some critter watching.

"It's coming into evening," she said, holding the screen door open. "The best time to see all the beasts sneaking into the yard. In a bit, we need to tend to the goats and chickens."

"You including me in this tending thing?"

"You eating goulash, John Wayne?"

"Guess I'll take care of the chickens, feed them in the coop this time," he added with a guilty grin. "See, I can learn."

"Then I'll have to teach you to milk a goat," Sophie said as she lowered herself into the porch chair. A weak groan escaped despite her efforts to restrain it. She hated being old. Maybe even hated old people – except for Pete, of course. Okay, she admitted, she didn't mind being old, just feeling it. That's what bugged her.

"You okay?" he asked, not looking at her, sensing she needed him not to watch, not to see her struggle.

"Course. What a stupid question. Why would you ask a dumb thing like that, John?"

"Because you seemed . . . I heard . . . No reason at all other than I'm an idiot."

"Yes, you are. And a horse's ass to remind me I'm old."

"I didn't, but I guess what you say is true. I am an ass. Want to see my pretty valentine heart underwear?"

"Geez," she sputtered, and clamped a hand over the laugh that wanted to spit red wine. "Didn't your mother teach you to change your underwear every day?"

"Good to see you laughing, Sophie. My grandmother did. How about you?"

"Don't need to change them if you don't wear any. I'm still gonna teach you to milk my goats. You need to know how."

When he quit staring at her, he leaned back, crossed his legs and nodded in satisfaction. The world spun correctly.

Guinea hens raced across the lawn, and two fawns poked their noses out of the woods where the small stream flowed. A long line of Hosta plants separated the stream from the yard, and the whitetail doe led her babies up to the water and kept an eye on the porch where he and Sophie sat.

A male peacock strode to the middle of the lawn like he was Anthony Hopkins assigned to center stage, dragging a nearly six-foot-long train and readying for a monologue. When he neared the peahen, blue and green feathers spread until the tail fan, dotted symmetrically with iridescent eyes, dwarfed his body. He stepped back and forth from foot to foot and the feathers shimmered and quivered.

"He's calling her," Sophie said.

"I don't hear a thing."

"Course not. It's low frequency. We can't hear it, but she can."

He raised his eyebrow in question, doubting her words.

"I tell the truth," she said, and the peacock screeched.

"This is Eden," he whispered.

"It is, John Wayne."

They watched nature wander out of the woods and meander across the lawn until light began to fade, sipped their wine, and told stories. Some of them true.

He learned her sisters had died a few years back, and she had one brother who'd died long ago. She learned his father lived in Florida in one of those golf cart communities with swimming pools and canasta or gin rummy games every afternoon. Dinner was at four o'clock, and somebody other than John was taking care of him. She'd wanted a baby when she was twenty-nine but hadn't had one. He was an only child and didn't like it much, but he had loved his grandmother.

"This would be a great place to raise kids. Lots of room to run around, build forts, play cops and robbers."

A snorting sound of scorn came from her throat.

"Probably would be the game of choice, because kids can't play cowboys and Indians anymore like we did. It's not politically correct, anymore."

"Why didn't you?" he asked.

"Didn't I what? Play cowboys and Indians? I just told you I did. I was always the one getting scalped."

"No. Fill this place up with a passel of kids?"

"You're a nosy son of a gun." Her eyes grew hard.

"Just making conversation, is all."

He ran a handkerchief over the dust on one biker boot, rubbing at the scuffs on the heel, then crossed his left leg and repeated the process on the other boot.

"And you're a fastidious kind of a fella, too. Is that why you didn't have children? They're too messy? Or maybe you do have some. Maybe you left them with their mother and ran off and left them to fend for themselves. Maybe you're a dead-beat dad, a no-good cheater man. Who knows what you are, John Wayne? I certainly don't. I don't know you from Adam." Sophie hurled the words at him like they were darts and could wound. Her nostrils flared.

The night she found out they would never have kids had injured her so much more than words or darts or broken bones. The vasectomy she'd had no say in. The choice he'd made for her, for them both.

John put a hand on her arm and scrubbed his face with the other. He sat back and closed his eyes. How in hell could she get spitting mad in the blink of an eye – and how could he undo the harm he'd done with one stupid question?

"I truly was just curious, Sophie. Sometimes my curiosity and my mouth get in the way of my common sense. I'm sorry."

Sophie glanced at his face, saw him chewing at his lip, and believed what he'd said. She'd been angry at Carl and had taken it out on John.

"Another time. I'll tell you about it another time." She tried to soften the effect of her angry words. "I'm going to milk the goats, and you're on chicken duty. Don't forget the eggs."

"Right behind you."

By the time they finished chores and ate overcooked goulash, it was late, and Sophie worried about him driving the Harley after drinking a few glasses of wine. She pondered it while piling dishes in the sink and came to a decision, one she could live with. And he'd live, too.

"You can sleep in the underground tonight, John. You shouldn't be on the road."

He tilted his head at her. "You're probably right, but I could bunk on the couch for a while or drink some coffee."

"That's where I sleep, and I'm going to do just that in a minute. I won't be staying up to make coffee for you. You'll sleep in the underground. Blankets are already there." One last dish clunked into the sink as she did a quick turn to him. "Don't go wandering around. Hear me?"

He hitched a hip on the edge of the island. "What's wrong with the upstairs, Sophie? If it needs some work, I can put some time in up there. I'm fairly handy." A glare from her made him stop, and he raised his hands in defeat. "Okey dokey. Got the key?"

"I'll let you in. Let's go."

He spun toward her. "You won't lock me in, will you? I can't be confined. Claustrophobia, you know."

Her chuckle made him think twice.

"Now why would I do that, John Wayne?"

"I'm not sure," he murmured, not really to her. Walking to the bunker in the dark made shivers crawl again, and he wondered why she didn't sleep upstairs. He assumed it was a bedroom. What else could it be? Curtains hung at the windows; he could see them from outside, which made him think it was a finished space. He told himself to get a grip. He was letting the night shadows and Sophie's strange behavior get to him.

When she unlocked the door, he waited for the light this time before entering. She smiled, said goodnight and left, another chuckle following her through the dark.

He wedged a gallon water jug between the door and the jam and put a chair in front of it. He didn't want it closed all the way just in case.

In case of what? He had no idea. Just in case.

Fourteen – The Clock

Dee hadn't been invited to Sophie's house since the Christmas cookie baking day – and she didn't understand why because Sophie hadn't told her, and friends didn't pry. If Dee had been a braver woman, she'd just come right out and ask her friend to explain. But she couldn't.

And Sophie had wanted to, but what could she say?

By the way, Dee, Carl shot my red elephant cookie jar. Or Carl joked about the cookies and smiled when he got home, but he wasn't happy and took it out on a porcelain elephant.

And Sophie could never explain. So she kept the tale to herself and said nothing. She only shared the good parts of her life with friends, the way she wished it to be.

"I think I'm going to quit work, Dee," Sophie said. "We don't need my check anymore."

She said it softly and had looked around the diner before speaking. Others didn't need to get wind of her plans. She folded white napkins to look like birds the way she'd taught the other girls and peered up at Dee's face, looking for a reaction. She got the one expected. Dee gasped and Sophie put a finger over her lips to shush her.

"Must be nice," she said. "I wish Rob made enough for us to live without my check."

Sophie's face took on a sly look, and her eyes squinted with mischief. If quitting her job was shocking, this would surely send her over the edge.

"My maternal clock is ticking, Dee. It might be now or never, and we've been together a long time. I want a baby. Soon. What do you think?"

Dee's chin dropped, and her eyes opened wide and turned into a grin spreading from ear to ear.

"I say it's about time. Yes!" she said, her arms flapping and feet dancing. "That is so cool. You're not pregnant already, are you?"

"No. I've taken precautions because . . . well . . . I haven't talked to Carl about it yet. But why wouldn't he like the idea? Doesn't everyone want children at some point?"

"I don't know. He *is* older than you. He's not too old, to make the magic, is he?"

"No. He's definitely not too decrepit for the making part." Sophie laughed and grabbed at the pile of napkins toppling into a messy bird heap on the table. "I don't know how he'll feel about the daddy thing, though. I'll let you know what he says."

"Let's go celebrate motherhood with a drink after work. Henry's, okay?"

Carl's truck was next to Freddie's when she pulled into the parking lot. Good, she thought. She'd buy him an early congratulatory drink. She waited for Dee to pull up and park because walking in alone always made her feel skittish, an odd fact given Henry's was always filled with friends.

"Hey," he hollered when he saw her. "You two women out on the town and available?"

"Sure thing, sailor," Dee said.

"Nope. I'm taken." Sophie knew better than to joke like that. "I saw your truck," she said. "Can I treat you boys to a beer?"

Carl patted the stool next to him, and she hopped on, smiling.

"We had a good day. How about you?" she asked.

"Same old stuff. Too hot. Too long. But a couple of beers sounded like they might fix what ails me."

The bartender set up four as Bryce strode up and put a hand on Carl's shoulder.

"Just the man I needed to see. I have a little project at home, and here you are waiting for me."

Bryce showed his big teeth in the pleading and wheedling kind of smile Carl frequently saw on people needing his help. His vast and recognized knowledge brought it out like a snake charmer coaxing a serpent from a basket. Everyone wanted to make use of his talented brain and skilled builder's hands, and he never, ever said no.

Carl gave him an eye roll and a grin. "What is it, Bryce? What do you need?"

"It's a tiny little job. Electrical, and you know me and electricity. If I even touch a light bulb, it explodes." He laughed and slapped Carl on the back. "You, on the other hand, are the guru of light, an immortal Edison beyond compare, a . . ."

"Okay. I got it, Bryce. When do you need me?" Carl enjoyed the accolades. They completed an unfinished part of him, the single thing he knew nothing about.

"Tonight? Please? I need an electric cable strung from the house to the garage. I mean, it's already there but not connected. Haven't had electric out there at all, and the wife is tired of waiting for a door opener. Told her I'd look for you. And here you are like a gift from the gods!"

"Please, not tonight, Carl," Sophie said. "Can't he help you out tomorrow, Bryce?"

She had plans for the night. Big plans that could result in turning the attic into a nursery, and she didn't want to wait. The pendulum in her clock had gonged, and Sophie wanted to discuss it. Tonight.

"Won't take long," Carl said.

She knew he'd go. He always did. Doing for others was an elixir to him, a tonic for his mental health, his power. She couldn't complain, though. He stayed busy around their place, too, always fixing and making something, but working at home didn't offer him the same kind of tonic. Not like helping out other people.

She tried to smile and be happy Carl could help their friends. He had a valuable gift. She slid from her stool and laid her arm across his shoulder.

"See you at home," she whispered in what she believed a sultry, come hither voice. "You'll find me at the fire pit. Waiting."

Carl tilted his head at her and rubbed his five o'clock chin. "How much did you have to drink?"

"Just one little beer." She waved and told him to hurry home.

Sophie milked the goats, fed the chickens and guinea hens, collected eggs, and talked with Charlie about what it would be like to have a baby in the house.

"You'll like it, Charlie, but you're really big, so you'll have to be extra gentle."

The Dane wrinkled his brow, either questioning Sophie's sanity or disliking the news. She didn't know which, but thought he was almost as smart as his master, and she stroked his regal head.

"I don't know why we waited so long. I really want a boy. No, a girl. I guess I don't know or care which. What do you think?"

Inside the henhouse, Charlie sneezed, and the chickens squawked and flapped their wings trying to get away from him. Dust filled the air, and Sophie fled, yelling for Charlie to hurry. She slammed the coop door and laughed, her heart light, her cheeks rosy under the powder of dust.

She turned her face to the sky, marveling at the color of countless stars, the darkness of the night and the warmth of the air. Her world blossomed with hope.

"So many stars tonight. It's a good sign."

Sophie threw together a ham and potato casserole and put it in the oven, built a teepee of kindling in the firepit, and drew a hot bath – with lavender. In her favorite whimsical nightgown, she poured a glass of wine and took it with her to the fire waiting to be lit.

With logs properly positioned and the flames reaching skyward, she relaxed on the overstuffed sofa, a crystal glass in her hand and a dream in her heart.

A baby.

Her thoughts wandered. She saw *him* toddling around the property, maybe chasing the peacocks and guineas, getting into all kinds of trouble. She saw *her* in tiny, pink rubber boots – looking like her ma – following and helping weed the flower beds but getting into her own kind of trouble later on. Maybe she should only have boys.

She added a few logs to the fire as it burned down and poured another glass of wine. He'd be home soon. She knew she looked good in her gauze nightdress and stretched her legs, trying out different poses intended to entice love making.

She should have waited to talk about having a baby. It wasn't the right time.

It was late.

He'd had a few beers.

And a vasectomy.

The burn of resentment built into a flame and grew.

"When? When did you have a vasectomy and why wouldn't you tell me that important little piece of news? Why wouldn't you discuss it with me first?"

"Years ago. Right after we got together. About a month after you moved in."

He didn't sit next to her on the sofa but moved across the fire from her, as far away as he could flee from her anger. For the first time in the many years she'd been with him, her fury raged hot and red.

"You made a decision that should have included me, Carl. How could you? You had no right!"

"It's my damned body. I can do what I want with it, and I didn't want it to make any babies. The world has too many brats in it already. And I didn't want kids and still don't.

Their pains in the ass, and I don't even like them. Have you seen even one kid you can stand?"

Sophie threw her wine glass at the fire and deflated. Its hissing and the crash of breaking glass were so loud, she covered her ears. She couldn't stand the sound but wanted another one to smash. Wanted to throw one at him for killing her dreams.

She changed out of the nightgown and into clothes, packed a bag and, without another word to Carl, left and got into her car. She didn't know if she'd ever go back.

He hadn't tried to talk her out of leaving, hadn't even looked her way when she came down the stairs and walked out of the house. She couldn't tell what he was thinking, except for one explicitly defined idea. He didn't like children. She knew that about him -- now.

She backed her car out of its parking spot, wanting to ram it into his truck and praying she didn't run over a cat. She had forgotten to bang on the vehicle and toot the horn to scare them away, and she'd never forgive herself if she hurt another one.

Tears streamed down her cheeks – for herself and the cat she had killed long ago. For the death of her and Carl. For the life she'd thought they had – but hadn't. They'd had something else she couldn't put a name on.

She opened the gate, drove through, stopped to close and lock it again and wondered why she bothered. Why did she continue to let herself be ruled by him and his choices? What was wrong with her?

She shouted at the gate as if it was responsible. "Should leave the damned thing open and hope some stranger turns in, drives all the way to the house and scares him senseless. Serve him right."

Tears tightened her voice, and she didn't recognize its nasal sound. She drove around town, hugging the outskirts and looking in windows showing lights inside, people watching television, sitting together on sofas and smiling. She pictured kids tucked into their beds upstairs – two each – and a dog and cat. The mother put on an apron each morning, and, before the dad went off to work with a brief case in his hand, they kissed goodbye at the door like they meant it.

She sniffled. "Don't be stupid, Sophie. Mom's don't wear aprons anymore. Carl is right. You really are dumb."

Fifteen – Milking a Goat

Guinea hens woke him, one from a perch on his chest and appearing either curious or menacing depending on the viewpoint. John couldn't tell which. He put a hand over his nose in case it looked like a giant, tasty tick to the bird. He'd heard they kept down the nuisance insect population. Several other hens looked for their own bugs in the corners of the underground, crying *Buck wheat* and *Chi-chi-chi* at the top of their tiny lungs. He tried out his own guinea talk, and they looked but didn't answer.

"Holy corn fritters but you guys keep early farm hours," he muttered, swung his legs over the edge of the bed and sat with his head in his hands. "Guess it's rise and shine time?"

He pulled on his pants and boots and headed out into the breaking morning. Dew dampened the grass and increased the vivid scent of some flower he couldn't name. He stretched and tipped his face to the opening sky.

Seeing him, the goats bleated and stomped, all lined up at their wire fence. He waved a hand at them, and they scampered away in a game of goat chase. Chickens scrambled out when he opened the door to their coop. He scooped feed into a cut-in-half milk jug and flung it outside so he could gather eggs unmolested by the fowl. When his shirttail was full, he ambled to the house and went in.

The smell of bacon roused Sophie from a sweet dream about still water, a boat and a fishing pole. Confused by the scent of breakfast, she moved with stealth toward the kitchen and spotted him.

"What the hell, John Wayne. Don't you ever ask permission for anything?"

"Not unless I have to. It's simpler to just do things and get punished afterwards. I'm used to chastisement, and I figured you could use a good breakfast after the 'fountain of red' last night."

"I need coffee."

"Brewing and done soon."

"Don't you have a job? Somewhere to be?"

"No and yes. No job at the moment, and I need to be right here. You need me." He deliberately sparkled. "You simply haven't come to terms with it yet."

"So, you're independently wealthy. Nice."

"Now who's being a nosy Nellie?"

"You must admit . . . Never mind. It's a free country. You can do whatever the heck you want."

He grinned. "Thanks."

"Except stay here today. I have things to do, and you need to leave."

John turned the sizzling bacon over, eyeing her in between flipping strips. He cracked six of the washed eggs into a bowl and opened a drawer, then another.

"Those are some bright colored egg yolks," he said as he searched for something to stir with. "And I think Fannie wants food. She's looking at me like I might be it."

Sophie thumped an elbow onto the island and cupped her forehead with the hand. She was at a loss about what to do with him.

"Sorry," she heard. "I should have asked for a fork instead of looking for it. But really, Sophie. Are you hiding gold bullion in these drawers? Does it matter if I look for a piece of silverware?"

"Yes. It does."

He lowered his head and peered up with a sad puppy look on his face, an expression not designed to work well on classically angular features.

"You're right. It does, and I'm sorry. I'll respect your property from this moment forward if you'll tell me where I can find a fork. The spatula was easy. It was staring at me, and I think it spoke my name."

"Jeez. Drawer to the right of the sink. Seriously. You need to leave after breakfast. I have things to do."

"I understand. I'll be gone, and you can miss me when you turn around and I'm not there."

"I need to go into town. Do some shopping. Pay some bills. You know, things normal people who are not independently wealthy and have actual lives need to do."

"It's Sunday, Sophie. Do you want to change your itinerary to going to church?"

"Drat." Fannie nudged her arm, forcing attention.

He chuckled and the color of her face showed she'd been caught lying. Why did she? What was she hiding?

"I'll be going in after breakfast," he said. "Do you need anything from town? Something I can dig up on a Sunday?"

She pitched a towel at him, and he ducked, groaned, and grabbed his back. Fannie fled the room.

"What's wrong with you?"

"Nothing. Hitch in my git-a-long is all. Old war wound."

"Some men say it's a football injury. Others say a long-ago war wound. Men lie. Sit, John Wayne."

"I'm fine, Sophie. I just turned wrong. Give me a minute, and I'll be perfect."

"You've never been perfect in your entire life. Even before the war and football."

"Ha. Did I tell you I fed your chickens and collected their eggs – all by myself?"

"Ha, yourself. And aren't you a big boy? Did you milk the goats?"

"No, but I had a flock of guinea hens in the underground, one on my bed, no less."

"Well, aren't you special? And it's a covey. Why'd you leave the door open?"

Sophie heaved from the chair and grabbed the spatula he was waving around, picked the towel off the floor, and shoved him out of the way.

"Go sit down. Give me back my kitchen."

He sat and she poured coffee. When they faced each other across the small kitchen island table, he rubbed a two-day growth and hummed in indecision.

"Just say it, John."

It's the vasectomy, Sophie. It bothers me. I find it hard to believe any man would do something so contemptible, make a decision as momentous as childbearing without having a single conversation about it with the one he's supposed to love. How did you deal with it?"

"Like I told you, I was furious and left."

"You obviously came home. How long did you stay away?"

"Couple days. I considered leaving for good, but, well . . . I didn't. Several years before, Dee had moved in with her boyfriend and then eventually got married, so she didn't have our apartment anymore. It changed things."

"She must have welcomed you to their place. Right?"

"Sure." Sophie scooted her chair closer to the table, laying her heavy breasts on the tabletop in front of her. "I'm not going to apologize. They are what they are. Not going to wear a bra today. It's Sunday."

John didn't know what to say. What *could* he say? He chuckled and drank some coffee.

"I don't mind, and you don't have to apologize, Sophie. Like you said, it's a free country. Don't wear one if you don't want to."

She tisked. "I just said I wasn't going to do either of those things. You don't listen very well, John Wayne.

"Are you avoiding the conversation?"

"Maybe I am. I didn't like her boyfriend much. He was a cheater and always had been. Would still be today if he wasn't dead."

"Sorry to hear it. Is Dee still alive?"

Sophie's head swung back and forth. She didn't appear distraught, more like reconciled to the inevitable, as if death was similar to the sun coming up in the morning and setting at night. It always did, and you knew it would happen. You only thought about it every once in a while, when it was a special sunrise or sunset, and then you forgot again. You let thoughts about dying go, too, because you didn't dwell on a thing you had no control over and couldn't change if you tried all day and all night long. Or tried and failed your entire life.

True to his word, John got ready to leave after a long, lazy breakfast with several cups of coffee on the porch afterwards. But he wasn't in a hurry to go, and she didn't seem interested in pushing him away anymore.

"Follow me out to the goat pen. I'll show you how to milk the goats."

The male butted him out of the way as he stood near Sophie and tried to watch the process. But the goat was a jealous beast and only allowed a stranger's proximity if he got his horny head scratched. It worked on John. Billy's friendliness suckered him in, and he left off watching Sophie milk to make friends with the goat.

"You don't want to touch his beard," she mumbled.

"Why not. Looks like It itches him. He's rubbing it on my leg."

Sophie snorted, yanking on the female's teat, and the nanny bleated in surprise.

"Sorry, Petunia. He pees on it, John. You won't much like your smell afterwards."

He yanked his hand away and stared at it as if the offensive odor might disintegrate his fingers.

"Why on earth would he pee on his beard?"

"He just does that during rut, usually. And on his face and chest, too. Thinks it makes him attractive to the females and more manly." She settled into her milking again before continuing. "Not so different than human males."

He found a wad of fairly clean straw, rubbed at his hand and gave it up to scratch Billy who continued to butt his head against his legs. The goat was a glutton for affection, but John's fingers moved along his back this time, as far as he could get from the beard.

"I take offense to your extrapolation about men based on goat behavior. I've never peed on myself. Not even to appear manly."

"Ever puff your chest or stretch the truth a bit around a pretty girl?"

"Well, that's a different . . ." John colored, recognizing the accuracy of her words. "Not since I was a much younger man."

"Billy's a filthy goat, but he's my baby. I bottle fed him after my last male died. Made a big baby of him."

"What did the other one die of? Old age? How long do they live, anyway?"

"Fifteen to eighteen years. And, no. He was only eight."

"What happened to him?"

"Killed by a crazy man. And I'll save that story for another day." Sophie finished milking Petunia and moved the bucket out of her way.

"Can I give it a whirl?"

John was interested in the process *and* the crazy man, but he wouldn't push her. Not today.

"Try your hand on Gladiola," Sophie said as she patted Petunia away and called to another female. "She's gentle and tolerant."

They washed the udder, sprayed it with sanitizer, and Sophie backed away. The first squirt landed outside the bucket, and he yelped with a laugh and an apology.

"Knew that would happen," she chuckled. "You want the first few squirts to go outside the bucket, anyway. Any contamination will lie close to the teats end. No, John. Don't pull on it. Gently manipulate. Like this."

She reached across his shoulder to show him the gentle wave of fingers that one at a time undulated the teat and brought forth milk.

"Now, you try it."

After a few awkward moves, his hand worked without connection to his brain, and he forgot Carl's vasectomy, poor Billy's death and Sophie's disappointments. His fingers moved as gently as butterfly wings. He nearly hummed with the pleasure of milking Gladiola and wondered why, and wondered, too, if this was why men starved to death for the privilege of farming. This pleasure. It transcended other kinds of contentment, other joys, was different than simple happiness. He couldn't define it but knew he had to do it again.

Sophie watched his face transform and got an inkling of why she welcomed his company.

His spirit was kindred with hers.

Sixteen – Sophie in the Crypt

Dee and Rob lived in town on a side street where the houses were well over a hundred years old. From their home, it was an easy walk to downtown, and people paraded up and down the tree-lined sidewalks on summer, Sunday evenings. Many pushing baby carriages.

The small town was made for young families, artists, and old people. It was comfortable and safe.

As Sophie drove near her friend's house, second thoughts flickered through her tired brain. It was late. Dee and Rob were probably sleeping. But where else could she go? She looked for lights as she drove by and finally saw one flicker in the kitchen window, so she turned around and went back.

It didn't take long for Rob to answer the door, and he came with a handgun behind his back and eyes wary until he flipped on the porch light and saw her.

"What on earth? What's going on, Sophie?"

"Can I come in?"

She heard Dee's voice asking him who it was from the kitchen, and he told her. She appeared in an instant, saw the swollen red eyes, and pulled Sophie into her arms.

"Can I spend the night?"

"Sure. You can spend the year if you want. Right, Rob?"

"Absolutely," he said with an exaggerated eyebrow wiggle. "I always wanted two wives."

"Go to bed, please, Rob. Sophie and I would like some privacy."

She dragged her to the kitchen, filled the tea kettle, and pointed to a chair.

"Earl Grey?"

"That would be nice."

"Would you rather have alcohol?"

"No. Maybe later."

"It *is* later," Dee said and wrinkled her nose in an effort to lighten her words and the mood.

"I'm so sorry. I needed to leave and didn't know where to go."

"I'm kidding. You can come here any time of the day or night whenever you run away from home."

When the kettle whistled, she filled the china teapot, dropped in several bags and brought it to the table. Two matching cups with saucers waited. Dee used mugs for coffee, but tea must be served in teacups. It was her only pretention, and she insisted on it. They sat and waited for the tea to steep.

She cocked her head at Sophie, saw the puffy eyes, the heartbreak in them, and cursed Carl. She didn't have to ask what had happened. He'd said 'no' to babies.

"Want to talk?"

"When I have the tea in my hands."

Dee poured, and Sophie wrapped her fingers around the cup as if they needed warming, and they did. They felt stiff with cold. Ice covered her body, too, inside and out. She trembled, and Dee asked if she wanted an afghan over her.

"No."

"But you're shivering."

"It was someone walking over my grave, is all."

"Paflooie. Nobody can walk on a grave that doesn't exist. You're still very much alive, woman."

"I don't feel like it, Dee. I was furious, more than I've ever been in my entire life. The anger went away – off somewhere on the drive into town, and now I'm all hollowed out. So maybe I actually am dead and gone, and I just don't know it, yet. Maybe I'm not really here, and Carl buried me on the property with all the dogs and cats."

"You're talking crazy, Sophie. Tell me what happened. I assume you asked him about having a baby, and it didn't go well."

Sophie told her about the nice fire and the nightgown and the waiting with dinner in the oven. And the waiting and waiting. At long last, she came to the vasectomy part and the words dried on her tongue. She couldn't say them, couldn't tell her. His decision was private. It belonged to Carl.

She gulped the tea, pushed the cup away and said it was time for something stronger.

"You were right. He said no. He doesn't want kids. Doesn't even like them."

"I'm sorry," Dee said, wondering how you could be together for so long and not know such an important piece of information about someone you love.

Finding a bottle of brandy in the cupboard, she poured two small snifters, sat back to stare at her friend, and considered her lifeless eyes, ones that typically sparkled with life. Tonight, they were bathed by new wounds and dried tears.

"Not everybody needs to have kids," Sophie said, protecting Carl . . . or maybe herself. "Lots of people nowadays are choosing to be childless. Babies are expensive, you know."

Dee pushed a glass toward her and sipped from her own, eyeing her while she assessed the words.

"Is this you talking or Carl?"

"Both of us, I guess. I was really mad, at first, but now I've thought it over, and I think maybe he's right, and I was being silly."

"If you want babies and he doesn't, Sophie, it's possible you're not married to the right man."

Sophie twirled her glass on the Formica tabletop and stared at the connected circles formed by condensation on the outside. She frowned in thought.

"You know we're not really married, don't you?"

"I guess I did, now that you mention it. Well, that makes it easier. You can leave and go find a man to love who wants kids and a real family. You're young enough."

"But I love Carl. He's a good man, and we're lucky we found each other. He needs me."

"But you ran off, my friend. Are you forgetting why already?" Dee wanted to shake some sense into her and couldn't stop her tongue. "You were furious with him and for a damned good reason."

Sophie sipped and the warmth of the brandy claimed her body. She ran her tongue over her teeth, tasting the after-sweetness of the drink, giving herself time to think.

"I was, but maybe I should go home. I'm not so upset anymore."

"No. Not tonight."

Dee put her in the small guest room, one she'd decorated in the Victorian flowered wallpaper she loved and Rob hated. She smiled thinking of his strong negative reaction when he first saw the flowers and white lace curtains, and she told Sophie about it.

"His opinion didn't matter," Dee said and laughed. "If he'd wanted to do the work, he could've picked the wallpaper. He made his choice."

Sophie was wide-eyed as she listened to her tale – and a little bit envious. Dee might be married, but she maintained her individuality. Her wishes didn't get put on a back burner for his, and her thoughts niggled like hungry mice as she said goodnight.

"Stay for a day, Sophie. Think about it and let Carl think about it, too. He can miss you for a little while. It'll do him good."

She stayed for two.

She worried about what Carl would say when she got home but hid her concern under a smile and told Dee stories about the fun they had together at their little farm. She talked about the goats and guinea hens, the chickens, peacocks and Charlie. She bragged about all the plans Carl had for their property, all the creations he'd already developed and completed.

Only Freddie knew about the new underground, so she didn't tell Dee because Carl might not like it. But she did tell her about the tiny swim pool he'd made out of a water trough and about playing in it with him. And about the balcony.

Carl had built a veranda off the upstairs bedroom where they cooled off on hot nights. They watched the stars in their birthday suits, two stories high in the middle of their wooded preserve.

"Sounds like it might be a nice bit of heaven," Dee said. "It would be hard to leave such a place."

"I can't. I'm packed and ready to go home. I miss it."

Dee didn't say anything, but she took note of the *it* she'd said and the *him* she hadn't.

The closer she got to home, the harder her heart pounded. She wiped her palms on her pants and saw the sweat prints left on the steering wheel. She breathed in through her nose and slowly let it out through pursed lips, trying to still the rapid beating of her heart. And she snorted when it occurred to her she was practicing childbirth breathing. Appropriate, she thought.

Forget it, Sophie. You don't need babies. They'll spit up on your shirt.

She looked at her wristwatch and picked up her speed, wishing she'd gotten home before him. Maybe she still would. Maybe he'd be late, stop for a beer or something.

She opened the gate and drove slowly on the limb-covered tunnel of the two-track drive, avoiding cats, and stopped a distance from the house as she always did. He wandered out of the tool shed as her door opened.

A piece of aluminum swung from his right hand and a hammer from his left. She couldn't read the look on his face and shuddered seeing the things he carried. It took forever for her feet to leave the car and for her body to unfold from it and follow. She thought a bigger car would be better, something easier to get in and out of and then snorted at the timing of car shopping.

Not now, Sophie.

She smiled.

"I'm home."

"I can see. Want to tell me where you've been, what you've been doing? Whoring around, likely."

She blanched and stopped walking toward him.

"You know better than that."

"Do I? Like mother like daughter?"

"Stop it, Carl. I'm sorry I ran off." She moved to him and put a hand on his arm – the one dangling the hammer. "I was really mad and hurt. I think I understand now, and I agree we don't need to have kids."

"Course we don't. We have everything we need right here, and you know it. Glad you came back. You shouldn't have taken off."

She saw the corners of his lips move and the hint of a sparkle in his eyes.

"I was ready. I missed you, and I won't do it again."

"No. You most likely won't."

He dropped the aluminum and grabbed her arm.

Her lips trembled, and she pulled her elbows into her sides to make herself as small as possible as she eyed the hammer.

"Don't squeeze my arm, Carl. What are you doing? That hurts."

He lurched toward the underground, trying to pull her along next to him, but her legs locked, and she couldn't make her feet move.

"Come on," he growled and yanked. "I'm not gonna carry you. Something needs to get through your thick skull if you're too damned stupid to understand how the real world works on your own."

A knee buckled when she tried to take a step, and she dropped to the gravel driveway, crying out as stones embedded in her skin. He jerked her up and dragged her forward as he pulled.

"I said move, Sophie."

Her back stiffened as fear and rage blended and took over. But in a matter of moments, a strange indifference followed.

What could he do? Beat her? Kill her?

So what?

He opened the door, flicked on the light and shoved her inside. She fell to the floor in a disheveled heap and didn't bother trying to rise, not knowing what he'd do if she moved, if she was safer simply laying where he'd thrown her.

She didn't know this man. Didn't know this Carl.

He wandered around the room as if he'd never seen it before and admired the handiwork as if someone else had built it. He picked up a glass from the narrow shelf and inspected it.

She covered her head thinking he might fling it at her.

He unplugged a small radio, stuck it outside the door and continued his examination of the interior. Grabbing all but one blanket, he tossed everything outside on top of the radio and turned to nudge her with the toe of his shoe.

"Glad you felt ready to come home. I'll let you out when I feel ready to have you here."

He stepped through the door, shut and locked it. She listened to the horrifying sound of the latch snap into place. She was locked inside the crypt.

Sweat trickled down her back even though it was chilly in the damp underground, and her shoulders shook with the fear of being confined and having no way out.

The lights went off.

Sophie gasped and leaped to her feet in total darkness, a black so complete you couldn't tell if your eyes were open or shut. The blackness of a hell without flames.

She reached a hand in front of her, feeling for the switch and scraping nails and knuckles. Finally finding it, she toggled it back and forth over and over, ramming it up and down, panic rising until her lungs had taken in so much air she thought they would burst. She spun around and around and banged into things that didn't budge and gouged her leg on a sharp corner of the bunk. A panting scream built but wouldn't release. It couldn't. It was stuck. Confined. Like her.

She slid to the floor and grabbed her head, pulling at the wild hair until it hurt, until her brain hurt, until tears streamed over her face in rivers and pooled in her lap.

He'd had the key in his pocket.
He'd planned this.

Seventeen – Hide and Seek

He stood, lifted the milk pail, and handed it to her with a gruff, "There you go. I milked a goat."

"You sure did, John Wayne. Didn't do so bad, either."

Gladiola nestled her head against his leg, and he scratched behind her ear and looked around. The goat pen needed to be cleaned, the grass cut and flower beds weeded. But not at all a bad place to be.

"I'll be going, then."

At the door, she watched him bring the Harley to life and duck-walk it out of the yard. At the path he gave it a little gas, and at the dirt road he let it go. She listened to the honied thunder until it faded into a soft purr.

"Come on goats. Want some fresh grass?"

She tied ropes to the collars of three, led them to stakes she'd pounded into the ground, and left them to graze and save her from having to call in someone to mow. The lawn mower was dead and the goats served the purpose just as well and didn't stink as much. Well, other than Billy.

Inside the house, Sophie plodded up the stairs, her hand holding the wall for security, back bent and knees objecting. They were narrow and steep, something Carl had been going to correct, but hadn't, along with installing a handrail which didn't exist, either. She went up like a toddler, one hand on the stair in front of her face, her butt in the air.

At the landing, she walked to the window and pulled the curtain aside, peered around the yard and listened for the bells that signaled someone was on the driveway to the house. Convinced she was alone, she opened the door to the attic.

It was short – even shorter than herself, and she had to stoop to enter, but, once in, she could stand upright and did so, knuckles rubbing the ache in her back. She maneuvered around boxes and stray pieces of furniture all the way to the back where she unloaded old blankets stacked on top of a box.

She knelt and opened it. Inside were the money jars – quart Mason jars filled with hundred-dollar bills, and twenties and fifties and tens and ones. She didn't mind the ones. They spent easily at garage sales and secondhand stores where dollar bills and change came in handy.

One by one she carried them out of the attic and laid them on the thick, rag rug by the bed. Smidgeons of dirt clung to them, but not a lot because of the burlap they'd been wrapped in before going into the ground.

She wiped them, cleaning away the leftover dirt, and worked at unscrewing the rusted lids. They resisted the efforts of her knobby, arthritic hands and brought tears to her eyes, but she didn't want to smash the jars unless she had to. It was a waste and would make a mess. Her hands ached by the time she had the last lid off.

When they were all opened, she dumped the money on the bed and stood looking at it. A smile lit her eyes.

"Thank you, Carl. You saved well."

She stacked the bills into piles, putting enough for a good month into each one, and secured them each with a rubber band. Shoving aside a hope chest at the end of the bed, she took a prybar out of it and pulled up a loose floorboard. Inside was a metal box which she pulled from the hole, unlocked, and filled with the carefully counted, rubber-banded bundles.

Once it was back in the hole, she replaced the floorboard, shoved the hope chest back into place, and took a lungful of air. She groaned as she pushed herself from the floor

– partly because of her old, aching bones, and somewhat with the effort expended, but mostly with satisfaction. The cash filled jars she'd stashed in the attic for lack of a better quick solution had been worrying her.

Fannie, who had kept watch just outside the bedroom door, tilted her head at Sophie and looked for something in her eyes that said the world was spinning correctly. Her master's angst had filtered through to her, and she whined her displeasure.

"It's all good, girl," Sophie told her. "It's all okay, now."

She and Fannie walked out onto the balcony Carl had built and they'd both enjoyed. She stood for a while, brushing her hands together to rid them of collected dust and dirt. A chair still sat in either corner, a small table in between where they'd put their coffee mugs in the mornings or drinks on warm summer evenings.

From this height, you could see a great distance if it weren't for the surrounding forest, but it still felt like she was on top of a mountain and surveying her kingdom. It *was* her empire. Hers to love, maintain and protect.

Who would care for it, if not her?

It wasn't often she let herself think about mortality. But every once in a while, like a stealthy predator, it crept up from behind and touched her. Its clawed hand rested on her shoulder, squeezed to the bone with intent, and she knew unease, felt the ache. It bruised her now.

For a moment, she froze in its feral grip, and her heart fluttered too hard and fast as perspiration layered her upper lip. She trembled before shaking off its grasp, and it tried to hang on, but her snarl of determination cast it away.

Sophie straightened her shoulders, laughed out loud at herself and went inside. She had too much to do to be caught up in a stupid anxiety over death.

Her fishing poles lay on a shelf in the shed collecting dust. When she took one down, it occurred to her she hadn't been to the pond in ages. She always caught big sunfish from that little hole in the ground, but she had no way to haul her old ten-foot aluminum boat anymore. Her little truck had died. Seems like everything was giving up.

Ponder another day, old fool.

She pulled the reel from its metal clamp, put the rod back on the shelf, grabbed a hammer and a few small tacks, and went back to the house. At the bottom of the flight of stairs, an inch out from the first riser, she pounded a tack into the side wall, wrapped fishline around the head, and further seated it. She hammered a tack on the other side, too, and wrapped the end of the thin, two-pound line around it, pulled until it was taut, and knotted it securely.

Standing, she stepped back to view her handiwork. Her head tilting from side to side, she moved closer and repeated the inspection.

"Perfect," she said to Fannie.

You couldn't see it unless you knew it was there and were looking for it. It was invisible. A smile grew and she threw out a hearty snort, pleased with her work.

She repeated the process, making two more trip lines, one in the middle and another at the top – in case a thief was too agile to stumble on the first one. She didn't want to kill him, just to know if he snooped. If the stairs had a door she could lock, that would be better, but it didn't. This was the best she could do, and it would have to be good enough.

"What do you think, Fannie. Is he a light-footed dancer or a two left feet kind of guy?"

Fannie asked her to explain who 'he' might be but didn't get a response.

She changed into her gardening shirt, an old white button down of Carl's, donned her rubber boots and gloves, and plodded to the flower bed between the woods and the front yard. It was the bed she saw from the kitchen window and when she relaxed on the front porch. The one with the angel statue that poured water from a bowl – when it was plugged in and when it had water. She wasn't always diligent in taking care of it, and it hadn't worked in a while.

The weeds around it bothered her most because the bed was visible during her cooking and daydreaming moments, important times to have beauty unencumbered by rampant crabgrass.

"John Wayne will be surprised," she told Fannie who walked beside her. "Harrumph. Him and his chubby cherubs."

He who might or might not be a dancer? Fannie pondered.

Sophie looked toward the driveway as if she might see the Harley pop out of the trees and into view at any moment. She knew better. She'd hear the rumble of that big old bumble bee even if he skirted the electric eye of the bells. She giggled and reminded herself to call his bike a bee.

To his face.

She refused to miss him, though. And it had been her idea for him to leave in the first place, right? She threw down the thick pad she'd brought along to protect her bony knees and bent to kneel on it.

"Damn joints, Fannie. Damn weeds, too. Can't even see the lilies."

She yanked grassy stalks and swore for half an hour, moving her knee pad as she progressed through the front of the bed. Sweat darkened her shirt, and she threatened to remove it and work in the yard like she used to, but she glanced toward the path and decided against it.

"A half-naked old woman flopping around would surely surprise him, wouldn't it, Fannie? That'd teach you, John Wayne."

Fannie sat up expecting to see the show and whined when it didn't happen. If she couldn't roll in the dirt, this wasn't any fun at all.

"I know. Be patient. I'm gonna work until we can see the whole statue, girl, and then fill it with clean water and plug it in."

She cleared the front half of the bed and stood to survey the lilies now exposed to sunshine. The angel needed a bath and so did she – later. She found the thick electric cord buried in dirt and weeds next to the outlet Carl had installed on a nearby post for that purpose. She hauled a bucket of water to the flower bed, scrubbed the statue clean, and then plugged her in.

"Hah! You still spill water. I'll get you some fresh stuff in a minute. Thank you for this, Carl."

The peacock screeched, Fannie's ears perked, and Sophie's face lit as she tramped to the shed with her tools, rubber boots squeaking with each step. She listened for the familiar Harley growl but heard only a disappointing silence underneath the bleats and clucks from the animals as she drew near them. She saw accusation in Fannie's eyes and tried to ignore her.

"I have to move the goats before they make mud pies in the yard, and you could help by not looking at me like that. I had things to do today. By myself. Besides, you can't be too careful, Fannie. You don't know about people. Even people you might sort of like."

A map of other money graves was etched in her brain so it wouldn't have to be put on paper. Oh, they'd had paper maps originally, but when Carl was certain she remembered where they all were, they burned them in the backyard fire pit. They had celebrated with corn liquor he'd bought from a friend, hotdogs and marshmallows on sticks, and loving under the stars on the overstuffed couch by the fire. Life was more wonderful then than she'd imagined it would be.

Years later, she had recreated the money jar map. Afraid she'd get old and forget where they were, she drew it from the one in her mind. It had been without his knowledge, but age did funny things to people. She knew that too well and was happy she'd made the copy. She'd tramped through the woods noting the position of each dirt deposit, making sure the ground around each one was covered in leaves, naturally, as the trees and undergrowth normally provided their cover. Her teeth worried at the skin on the inside of her cheek all the way and only quit when she found each spot undisturbed and the map accurate.

"I need to tell John Wayne that parts of life *were* wonderful. Don't let me forget, Fannie. Carl could sparkle with love sometimes."

Musing and weeding done and satisfied with her angel garden once again, she stood and turned toward the house.

"I need a bath. Want to go into town, later? Unless we get company, that is."

She took her time in the lavender scented bath water, listened for the rumble, and dressed in her Henry's bar clothes. She dried her thick, silver hair, dotted some blush on her cheeks and smeared red lipstick on her lips. Turning in the full-length mirror, she let her dimples deepen.

"I still got it Fannie girl. I look good, and so do you. Let's go."

She banged all the way around the Bug and watched to see if any cats actually flew out from underneath. None did. None ever had. Maybe years of making noise on them had trained generations of cats to steer clear of automobiles. She chuckled with the thought and wanted to tell Carl about it. He'd claim he knew it all along.

"Arrogant man. But maybe you did know, Carl."

She stopped to open the gate, drove through, and stopped again to shut and lock it, cursing as she did and always had. It was a pain in the neck.

All the way down the narrow gravel road, Fannie's head spun, looking for plundering trespassers like chipmunks and squirrels. With no one at home to stop them, hordes of critters could invade the property and take over. They wouldn't be stopped by a silly gate, and she'd have her work cut out when they got back. A smirk pulled at her lips showing two long canines. She knew her worth.

Sophie froze in the doorway of Henry's, staring at the man on the stool next to Pete. It couldn't be him. Not after all these years. The dim room after bright sunlight was playing tricks on her.

Fannie nudged her further inside, and, when her eyes adjusted, she squinted to see him better. He was older, of course. Weren't they all – except for the dead ones, and they only stopped getting older when they died.

Pete tapped the man on the shoulder, and he spun her way, a look on his face she couldn't define. Shock? Anger? Hurt?

"Would you look who's here? The sweet young thing we were just now discussing," Pete said, loud enough for Sophie and everybody else in the bar to hear.

He patted the stool next to him but changed his mind and stood, leaving the one between him and the other man empty. He slapped his hand on that seat, leaving Sophie little choice but to take it.

"Recognize this beat up old codger?" he asked as she drew near.

"Course I do. How are you, Joe? What you doing back in town?"

"My brother died. Funeral is tomorrow."

She watched him struggle with the words as they caught in his throat, and she placed a hand on his arm.

"I'm so sorry. That's hard."

He looked the same to Sophie, just a little older. Maybe better, though. His hair was thick, his shoulders broad and back straight. He looked good, but sad.

A drink showed up in front of her, and Lainie asked if Fannie was ordering a burger and some fries. Sophie nodded, the best she could do at the moment, and time emptied its memories all over her.

"Where have you been?" she asked.

"Montana. Worked the fields till I retired."

"Married? Kids?"

He shook his head. "Thought I'd be by this time." He drawled his words now like a western cowboy, and a slow smile lit his eyes. "I let the only one for me get away a long time ago. How about you. Got children? Grand kids?"

Pete interrupted, never one to be left out of a conversation.

"She's got one big baby. Carl's enough of a child to take care of. Isn't he, Sophie?"

She didn't respond and listened to the strains of an oldie coming from the juke box. If she closed her eyes, she could believe it was decades ago.

"Would you dance with me if I played our song?" Joe asked. "We could talk without Pete helping us."

"You don't remember what it was."

"You'd think so, wouldn't you?"

He plugged coins into the juke box, and she knew what would play, *The Most Beautiful Girl.* She remembered, too, and to this day had to turn off Charlie Rich songs when they came on the radio. She couldn't help it.

"Come on, Sophie. Let's dance."

They settled into the easy rhythm they'd known long ago, dancing at the riverbank to music on his truck radio. Sophie's cheek nestled against his shoulder exactly as it had before and she saw the sunshine on the water as if they'd been transported back in time, back to their long walks and talks, and plans.

Years hadn't passed. They were thirty again.

He pulled her closer. He didn't want to let her go this time. Didn't know why he had before – except for Carl. She didn't leave him then, but it had been clear she'd wanted to. Sophie had wanted a life with him.

"How long you staying in town?" she asked.

"I'm not sure. Most of the family's gone, except for a couple of nephews I don't even know. And I got kind of used to Montana country and miss my home. You should see it, Sophie. It's spectacular."

"Tell me about it, Joe."

"Mountains everywhere you look. Sky so big it scares you. Makes you no bigger than a minute. I'm tucked into the Badger Hills in Big Horn County where you can get lost walking out your back door. The fishing and hunting, and air so clean it hurts if. . . sorry. I go on about it a lot."

"I can see you love it. It's tumbling right out of your eyes."

He released the tight hold he had around her waist, and they came back to where they were now . . . Henry's bar.

"You and Carl should take a trip, come stay with me in up in the hills. I've got a spare room, so it won't cost much of anything."

"Maybe I will," she whispered.

They danced again, and he told her about the fishing trips he planned to take and about playing in a bluegrass band made up of a bunch of old men.

"Well, we're all old now," she said.

"That's my life. Wish you'd been there with me."

She didn't tell him about hers. Some people you just don't lie to. She squeezed his hand, and they ambled back to Pete who was carrying on a discussion with Fannie and Lainie.

She wished for a horse instead of a Bug because her eyes weren't working well. They were tear-filled, and a horse would know the way and take her there without any help from her. For years, it had hurt to say his name, so she hadn't in more than forty years. But she said it, now. All the way home.

Sophie strained to see a Harley in the yard and stuffed down the disappointment when straining didn't produce one. She changed into work clothes and tended the animals.

"You should be here to collect the eggs, John Wayne. That's your job," she told him as she filled the egg basket. "And you can milk now, too. Where the hell are you?"

She scattered chicken feed and let herself take in the pleasure they always gave her. She needed them tonight. She needed . . .

"You're a damned fool, Sophie, looking for a man who's hiding who the hell knows where. Hike up your girly britches and stop whining."

She hauled the basket and pail to the kitchen, washed the eggs and put them in a bowl, strained the milk, and put both in the fridge. Repetitive, mechanical movements she'd performed how many times? She couldn't use all the milk and eggs she collected and didn't know what to do with it all.

"Maybe I should just quit," she mumbled.

Fannie's tail thumped the floor as she stared at her empty bowl.

"Still hungry, girl? Coming right up. Keep me on my toes. That's what all my babies do for me. You keep me honest. Keep me sane. Maybe. What I know for sure is my babies keep me true and alive. I won't quit on you."

She stopped at the screen door to listen, heard only the night, and went to check the trip lines on the stairs. They were all intact. She knew they would be. He hadn't been here since morning.

In the upstairs bedroom, she turned in a circle, looking at the pristine room like it was new to her, the rocking chair, the dresser with her jewelry box on top. No jewels were in it. She'd never cared for the shiny, fancy things.

She ran a hand over the handmade bookcase and read the titles of the few books she'd kept over the years. There weren't too many, just the ones she knew she'd read again and again.

She pulled off the bedspread, shook the dust from it and put it back, smoothed it out and tugged at a corner so it was perfect. She plumped the pillows and replaced them, tilted a little against the headboard so the big red flowers in the centers stared right at you.

With a sniff of satisfaction, she turned to leave, calling for Fannie to follow and telling her not to trip on the trip lines on the way down the stairs.

"That's funny, Fannie. Don't trip on the trip lines," she sang, in a singsong refrain she repeated while pouring a glass of merlot. She held the screen door to save it from banging, keeping the harsh noise from interfering with the gentle night.

Fannie pushed against her leg when she sat, and together, they looked and listened. It was too dark to see the angel, but she could hear water splashing as the cherub poured and poured and poured. The crickets sang, the treefrogs chirped, the owls asked their questions. None had answers. Not a damned one.

There was no Harley noise, and Sophie called herself a fool for missing it.

Eighteen – Sophie Gets a Grip

She didn't know how long she stayed in a fetal position on the cold concrete floor of the underground because time doesn't pass normally in pitch blackness. The absence of light becomes everything. Without it nothing else matters.

And there was no sound – beyond hers.

When her sobs quit, she strained to listen without realizing it. Tree branches didn't rustle in the breeze. Birds didn't sing. The peacocks and goats were silent, and even the guineas made no noise. Where were they? The earth's slightest whispers had died, and dark silence defined the space. A world without sound closes in, and you have to breathe your way out of it, push through like passing through the birth canal.

She rubbed at her salt crusted eyes and cheeks, working up the courage to move.

Get a grip, Sophie.

She did, and she took hold of the dire situation with grim resolve. "Candles. I need candles and matches, and I know we have some because I put them here."

She pushed herself up and reached a hand in front of her face so she wouldn't bang into anything. She found the crate of emergency supplies and took it from the overhead shelf. After several moments of feeling around inside, she adapted to letting her fingers *see* what she wanted.

It took forever, but they finally connected with two fat candles and, soon after, the box of wooden matches, and she let out a victorious whoop.

"Hah! Light!"

She struck the match and felt for the wick, burning herself as it flamed. She didn't care. She had light, and her lips fluttered with an expulsion of thankful breath.

Standing in the middle of the room, she gazed around her cell and let her eyes explore. The length of her stay was unknown, but the underground was well equipped for a long while – as long as she had air – as long as he didn't take that away along with the electricity.

He wouldn't. Would he?

She knew he'd installed an air vent. It stuck up above the ground, and she avoided it when she mowed. As long as he left it alone.

Relax, Sophie. Just make yourself comfortable.

She moved the candle to the table, found a book she hadn't read, and settled into a chair to while away the time until Carl came for her. She pulled a knee to her chest, rested her chin on it and opened the book. This wasn't so bad. She could relax and get in some good reading time. She should thank him for the vacation.

A while later, she didn't know how much, her stomach grumbled, and she decided to explore the food supplies. She lit the alcohol burner and hummed a tune while fixing dinner. She called it dinner even though she had no idea what time of day or night it was.

Pretty good you can hum from your grave, Sophie.

She didn't know where that thought came from, but she shoved it away.

Carl loves me. He was just angry because I ran away. I shouldn't have, and I knew it as soon as I got to Dee's house.

She licked dinner from her lips and fingers and decided to take a nap, thinking he would probably come get her while she slept, wake her with kisses, and it would all be over. She pulled the single blanket over her and tried to get warm. It wasn't really cold, just damp, and it seemed to seep into her bones. She tossed around and thought about lighting the kerosene heater but was afraid her crypt was no longer properly vented, so she didn't.

That's silly, Sophie. Carl wouldn't hurt you, and he was right all along. We don't need a baby. We don't want kids to mess up our perfect lives. I was so silly.

She slept and dreamed, woke and laughed at herself lying in the underground. She fixed another meal, read some more and napped again. After a while, getting out soon didn't matter so much. She had been wrong to leave him like she had, and he had every right to be angry. When he came for her, she hoped he'd be over it and chuckled thinking how she'd make it up to him.

She was half asleep when the atmosphere changed. The scent, the density, the noiseless sound. She sat up, bumping her head on the underside of the overhead bed, and saw the glow of twilight from the open door.

"Carl?" she whispered, afraid he wasn't real, afraid he'd turn around and leave again if he was.

"You ready to come out?"

"I am, Carl. This is a nice underground, but I missed you being in it with me. I had everything I needed except for you, and you knew that, didn't you? This was a good test, though. Now we know we can survive down here, and . . ."

Sophie rambled on and on without trying too hard to make sense of her words and Carl watched while she put on her shoes and put out the candle.

"Let's go. I'm hungry," he said. "What are you making for dinner? Yesterday, I ate leftover goulash, but it's gone."

"I can thaw some steaks in the microwave. We'll celebrate with fried potatoes and grilled steaks over the fire pit. How does that sound?"

"Sure. You milking first?"

"Did you milk while I was gone?"

"Of course. I had to. That was a stupid thing to do, Sophie. Don't do it again."

She wrapped an arm around his back while they walked to the chicken coop, and she reveled in the pleasing clamor of their clucking as they dove at the feed kernels. The goats bleated their greetings, and Sophie grinned.

"This is love, Carl. They missed me."

Sophie milked and gathered eggs, felt evening dampness on her skin and exulted in new awareness of fresh air surrounding her, and sounds and differing shades of light. She thought about thanking Carl for giving her this new gift of mindfulness; first, the experience of nothingness, and now its opposite, a fullness that hadn't existed before.

But she didn't tell him. A nagging at the back of her brain wouldn't let her put voice to the thought.

"I need a bath, Carl. Will you start the fire while I get cleaned up?" She moved toward the bathroom but stopped and turned around, curiosity making her bring up a subject that might be better left unsaid.

"How many days was I in the underground?"

"Enough."

"You aren't going to tell me?"

"No. I'll let you wonder. Or figure it out."

He gave her the boyish grin that had drawn her to him in the first place. He knew what he was doing. He tipped his head and glanced sideways at her just to see her cheeks flush. It always worked.

Her heartbeat quickened and she wanted to touch the dark blonde hair curling over his ears and the back of his neck. So, she did. He deserved her adoration because Carl was a special man.

"Want to join me in the bathtub?" she asked.

"I'll build the fire. I'm hungry."

Sophie scrubbed the underground off her body with lavender soap and washed her hair with lavender shampoo. She loved the scent, and it relaxed her, told her – no matter how inaccurately – the world was a wonderful place to be. Lavender lies stayed with her until the smell of reality competed with it and won.   But it lasted a long while, sometimes even until her next bath.

She hummed and slid further into the water, enjoying herself until Carl's voice penetrated.

"You staying in there all day?" he called out.

She let the water drain and toweled off, grabbed the nightgown hanging on the back of the door, and went to the kitchen to gather what she needed for dinner.

They listened to the radio, country and bluegrass, as he told her about work and the dumb things his fellow workers had said or done.   She nodded and clicked her tongue in agreement at appropriate places while adding wood to the fire and flipping the potatoes.

"Want to go fishing tomorrow?" she asked.   "I'll put the battery on the charger tonight if you do."

"It's boring just sitting there with a stick in your hand. If the fish don't want to bite, they don't, and you can't make them."

"But if you relax, Carl, it's fun.   A good way to unwind and enjoy the sun on your face."

The pleasant activities of the evening mended their differences and patched the anger and misunderstandings like stitching denim squares on worn out knees, and they went fishing the next day at a small but deep nearby lake. They'd tried swimming there before, but the shore was lined with weeds, and Sophie shrieked every time one touched her.   The panfish loved it though.

With the sun high overhead and the air warm on their skin, she propelled the small boat around the lake with her trolling motor.   It made little noise, so they were alone in their own heads.

Sophie caught a good-sized smallmouth bass, slid it onto the stringer, and let it hang in the water to stay fresh. Hoping Carl would catch the next one, she frowned when the tip of her rod dipped and came up with a fat bluegill on the hook.

"Did you poison my worms?" he asked.

"Never would. You need to keep your rod still so you can tell whether the bobber is moving because of you or a big ole fish."

Her bait wasn't back in the water long before another bluegill took it and found himself on the stringer with the rest. She tried not to be too happy with her catch.

"Why don't you check your bait, Carl. Maybe a fish took it, and you didn't notice."

He scowled but did what she said and found an empty hook. She passed the can of worms to him, and he threaded a whole worm on the hook in a giant ball of bait.

"You don't need all that, Carl. Pinch it in half first; they last longer and work just as well."

He turned and glared. "Don't tell me how to fish. This lake is cold and could hold a body down so deep no one could ever find it."

Sophie laughed off his words. "You talk big. You'd miss me, and, besides, you can't cook. Remember that before you toss me over."

He grinned and cast out. The glob landed near a log, and Carl let it sit. When the fish hit, it came out of the water, and he jerked back, rocking the small boat in his joyous effort to land the monster. It bent the rod in a 'U' shape and jerked it up and down.

Carl didn't know what to do. He wasn't a fisherman, but he wanted to land this one – he needed it.

"Keep the line taut," Sophie said.

"I am, damn it. Can't you see that? And quit nagging."

"I know. I – nothing."

He fought the giant largemouth all the way to the boat on tiny, two-pound test line, and Sophie scooped it up with the net.

"Wish we had a camera with us. That's a beauty, Carl. You did great."

"It's not rocket science. It's a stupid fish."

"But . . . Never mind. You win the biggest fish contest, so I'll clean."

"You would anyway. That's women's work."

He grinned to remove the sting, but he meant it. He had defined ideas about what men and women should do. Clearly defined ideas.

On Monday, Carl was late getting home from work, and Sophie feared he'd stopped at Henry's and would come home with a snoot full. He wasn't at his best then.

Dinner was done, the table was set, and she sipped a glass of wine on the porch while she waited. Charlie sat next to her, his head on her lap, and she absently stroked it, liking the contact and his warmth.

"They say winter will be early and hard this year, Charlie. I don't think I'm ready for cold weather."

He rolled his eyes to check out hers and commiserated with the mood and her tone. He didn't mind winter as long as he wasn't chained to a doghouse like the last owner did. He was too old for that now.

Charlie heard the truck before it came through the gate and rang the bell. His ears perked, and he left her to welcome his master home. Sophie joined him at the edge of the porch.

Carl threw the door open, a wide grin lighting his face and his eyes crinkling at the corners in the way she loved.

"You look happy, and I'm happy to see you," she said.

"I have something for you. Look what I found at the secondhand shop."

Intrigued, Sophie ran down the steps to peer into the truck bed. He lowered the tail gate and pulled the canvas from a four-foot-long object. Her jaw dropped, and her eyes grew.

"I went to find a used riding mower because the other one got all shot up. It wouldn't . . ." He ducked his head and grinned because he'd shot it full of holes when it didn't start with a pull of the cord. "Well, anyway, look at this. I found it in the pawnshop shed out back with all the lawn stuff and knew you'd love it."

The statue angel held a bowl, and a serene face tilted up like it watched over the sky.

"Water pours from the bowl and runs into a reservoir. It gets pumped back up to the bowl and goes on forever and ever. I mean until it evaporates. Then you'll need to refill it."

"Carl, I love her, and I know exactly where she'll stand. Right where we can see her from the porch when we have coffee in the morning. And from the kitchen window."

He beamed. She smiled. The underground forgotten.

"I'll need to run electricity for it, but we can set it there now if you want."

Sophie took him to the garden bordering the woods in the front yard and showed him where to position her so she could watch over the house, them and all the animals.

"She'll bless us, Carl. Thank you."

"I don't believe in blessings and all that, but I knew you'd like it. Get me a beer?"

Nineteen – Sophie gets a Goat

The grandfather clock struck five times, one for each hour she'd spent on the couch listening to its deep bong. She groaned, rolled over, and went to the floor on her knees so she could push herself upright with her hands on the cushions.

Three calicos leaped from the arms and back of the sofa where they'd spent the night watching her eyes open and close. They raced to the kitchen for breakfast and joined a horde of others assembled around several empty bowls, eyes wide and trusting, feline pupils narrow, upright verticals surrounded by all shades of green, blue and yellow.

The guineas had wakened and greeted the world with their raucous song. The peacocks, too, added to the din. Goats would start in a minute, as would the chickens when they heard her voice.

She scratched her head, yawned, and followed the cats.

"Come on, Fannie. I'll let you out. Want scrambled eggs this morning?"

Sophie fed the felines and finished her chores in record time. She had a funeral to go to and wanted to get her bath, make herself beautiful and find Joe. She needed to see him before he headed home – needed to explain.

The church stood at the edge of town and provided a cemetery for believers at the back. The bubbling sound of a river rose like mist over the rise of a hill, backdrop to the picturesque scene. Sophie stood next to the Bug, listening and wondering if she was making a fool of herself. Why would he care about her reasons?

Doesn't matter, Sophie. You care. That's enough.

The minister's hands were in the air, mid-prayer, when she walked in, which was good because eyes were closed and she could slip in unnoticed. Seats were available since the pews were only half full, and she chose an isolated one at the back so she could exit easily.

At the front, in the family pew, Joe sat alone, and Sophie wished she could join him, put a hand on his arm in consolation. Be someone who cared.

Looking around, she recognized most everyone over sixty and not a single one of the rest. She would pass the time with the old ones after the service but wouldn't bother with the others. What could she say to those youngsters? She didn't speak their language, didn't understand their love affair with cell phones. She owned one but rarely used it. Who would she call?

I wonder if John Wayne has a cell phone?

At the end of the service, he acted as if he knew she was there before he stood and turned. Like they were connected by the airwaves or she had bored painful holes into his back by staring at it. He rose from his seat and made eye contact. Immediately.

Joe led the way when they carried his brother out of the church, and he kept his eyes on her the entire aisleway. Her pulse fluttered.

You're too old to be fluttering around, Sophie.

She followed to the graveyard out back and listened to the reverend's brief words, saw the mourners wipe tears, and wished she had some for the deceased brother, but she didn't. The tears she shed were for Joe as he threw in the first handful of dirt and gave his brother up to God. And they were for Joe and her, together, because, like the dirt he'd tossed in, she had done the same a long time ago with whatever it was they'd had as two people who loved. She'd tossed it away.

After the casket lowered into the grave, and after the people moved a short distance from the gaping hole, voices incrementally raised in jovial greeting. The mood changed, and they slapped backs and joked with one another.

Sophie had noticed this funeral phenomenon before. A bubble of sorrowful, respectful voices surrounded the dearly departed as if mourners feared normal speech might raise the dead or cause the speaker to be the next one to go. Still, they refused to acknowledge extinction was a possibility, and, as they moved away, they felt a need to brighten the atmosphere, pretend today was no different than yesterday – for themselves. Death couldn't happen to them; the dark hole was for other people.

She waited by the Bug and watched as folks drifted to their cars, and eventually the parking lot emptied. Bug and a Silverado sat side by side, and she knew the truck would be his. He shook the reverend's hand and walked toward her.

"Didn't expect to see you, Sophie. I'm glad, though."

"I figured I'd come. When are you heading west?"

"Right now, actually." He saw her disappointment. "I'm all packed, but I can postpone for an hour or so."

"I'd like to talk to you, explain some things – without Pete helping. Can we take a walk? Maybe by the river that's making all the racket?"

Joe held out his arm, and she took it. Sophie couldn't find words until they were nearly standing in the water, and he didn't have any. He'd said it all yesterday and years before. Mostly years before. Too many.

Splashing sounds from the river's current against the rocks helped her sort through the long silent words she needed to say and renounce her betrayal of Carl in saying them. They were words Joe should have heard years ago. He deserved to have answers.

"I'm so sorry," she said after she had finished explaining. "I would have let you know sooner, but . . . Do you hate me?"

She was exhausted but satisfied, and he had heard the truth.

He gave a harsh laugh that landed somewhere between humor and dismay. The lines at the corners of his eyes deepened, and he looked like the cowboy he'd become. She expected him to call her *little lady* and slap a dusty hat on his thigh.

"I knew something like that had to have happened. I didn't hate you, Sophie. I couldn't."

He wrapped an arm around her back, and she leaned against him wondering what life would have been like with this tender man. Different than it had been, for sure.

"You're a good man, Joe."

"Not so good I'll let Carl stop me from getting a goodbye kiss. He earned this . . . and we did, too."

He headed his truck west and waved. She sat in the Bug, watching for as long as she could see the Silverado, which was difficult because of the tears. Maybe she'd go to Montana one day. She'd like to see the mountains, fish in the trout stream, sleep next to the man she loved like no other.

There was love, and then there was love.

Fannie met the car at the end of the driveway and threw herself into the passenger seat while Sophie was shutting the gate.

"How'd you know it was me, girl? You have some good ears, and I'm glad to see you and your funny face."

Fanny raised a brow.

"I'm sorry, but it is comical sometimes. Anything happen here I should know about? Trespassers? Rotten, killer rodents? John Wayne?"

She knew better since she hadn't smelled the distinctive scent of Miss Lily's exhaust along the driveway

146

tunnel. She lifted her shoulders in defeat and struggled out of the tiny car. On the way to change clothes, she stopped to pour a glass of wine.

"I've earned it today, Fannie. It was a hard one."

She poured it into a plastic cup and took it with her to do chores. By the time her work was finished, the animals had lifted her spirits to one notch above her normal good-nature, and she had a seat on the porch to gaze at the newly cleaned angel. What memories she evoked.

She sat for a couple hours and a second glass of merlot, thinking about Joe, about her choices, and the life that hadn't happened. She knew her fantasy was likely much more wonderful than the reality would have been. Right? It couldn't possibly have been that good.

Light had all but faded when she heard the rumble. She wanted to curse him and be mad but couldn't come up with an acceptable reason, and her lips tilted in a strange, indestructible grin. She nudged Fannie.

"The rogue returns, girl."

The Harley pulled right up to the front porch, and John grinned back.

"Hey, Sophie. I missed you. Did you miss me?"

"I've been busy. Have you been gone?"

Leaning back against the seat, he put one boot on a highway peg and glanced around the yard. His position looked comfortable, like he lounged in a recliner while watching television. Fannie sniffed at him and pressed her nose at his stomach.

"Get back, Fannie," Sophie said, but the dog knew something was different and poked again.

"How are the goats? My Gladiola good?"

"Of course. I know how to take care of my own darned goats. What's the matter with you?"

He squirmed when his leather jacket wiggled, and Sophie stared. As he unzipped, two legs popped out of the opening, and then another two, followed by a fuzzy head . . . a baby goat head.

"What on earth have you gone and done, John Wayne?"

"Brought you a present. You said you have to bottle feed a goat in order to make them yours, make them friendly. Well, here's your bottle baby. Didn't get a Billy because I didn't know if you could have two males in the same pen."

He got off the bike and put the kid in her hands. She nestled into Sophie's arms like she'd been born to her. For long moments, she forgot John was there. She checked her hooves, her eyes, and her teeth. She let Fannie sniff her until she got bored, and it wasn't long before the kid was asleep on her lap.

"Well?" he said, eyes like a kid's at Christmas. "Do you like her?"

"Why'd you do this? Why did you get me a goat? I have several, in case you didn't notice."

"I know it isn't the Billy who died at eight years old, but someone should give you a sweet goat, not take it from you. That's all."

Her throat got tight, and she swallowed. She hated it when someone did something nice. It hurt like hell.

"Let's light a fire," he said. "I'll fix it this time, and you can get acquainted with your present. I've got burgers and fries in the saddlebags. And wine."

He looked up to see her smile, glad he'd bought the goat. And the food and wine.

Sophie sprawled on the outdoor couch with Peony, the name she'd come up with on the stroll to the backyard, and watched John fuss with kindling. She tried not to interrupt his work with directions, but it was difficult.

"A teepee, John. It's simple. The Indians knew how to build things."

"It's going to go. You just watch. Got any lighter fluid?" he asked after several failed attempts.

"No. Would never use it. Here, hold Peony."

He laughed. "She's named already?"

"Of course. She was born Peony, silly man. She just didn't know it until she met me."

She handed him the goat, and he took her spot on the couch next to Fannie while she built a fire which flamed in two minutes.

"I'm gonna make a bottle for her. Be back in a few."

"Bring wine glasses, too."

John was stretched out on the couch with Peony on his chest, asleep, a picture she would remember forever. He woke when she knelt beside them and put the bottle to the goat's mouth.

"You're a lousy fire watcher, John Wayne. And goat watcher, too. She could have gotten close to the flames and been hurt."

"Goats are smarter than people, Sophie. We are the only animals who allow ourselves to get burned. Over and over, it seems." He sat up and cradled the kid.

"Did you do that, John? Did you get burned?"

Her words were a soft invitation given birth by an intimate moment, the feeding of a baby, the ache in a friend's voice.

He could talk about his pain, but not now. This night was for Sophie. He touched the back of her hand.

"I never had anyone shove me in a dark underground and keep me prisoner. Or had a crazy man kill my pet goat. How did that happen? Why would anyone do that?"

Sophie ran a hand over Peony's back and listened to her mouth suckle at the nipple. It made an unmistakable sound, like she was all fauna from the beginning of time nursing at mother's breast. She didn't want to blacken the beauty of Peony feeding with thoughts of Carl dragging her goat to its death. She'd worked too hard at forgetting, too hard at forgiving.

"So that's why you brought Peony to me." She sniffed and stared at him, a challenge. "It was an accident. He didn't mean for him to die. The rope tightened around Billy's neck and Carl didn't realize it."

He searched her eyes for authenticity, but Sophie was an expert storyteller. He knew that for certain because she'd told many to him, and her eyes didn't give him the answers he looked for. Storytellers don't.

"Seems unlikely. Wouldn't you see it if the goat couldn't breathe?"

She dropped the bottle and Peony bleated her displeasure.

"Sorry, girl," she said, trying to bring back the lost serenity.

"And I'm sorry, Sophie, if talking about it brings you pain. But maybe it's good for you?"

She stood, tossed the bottle at him and told him to feed his own damned goat.

"Since when is pain good for you? Where's the wine you brought?"

"In the bag." He pointed at the low table.

She freed the fountain from the box, filled two good sized glasses and sat next to him.

"Why in hell do you want to know these things? Does this stuff give you some kind of sick pleasure?"

Her questions met with silence as he scratched the fuzz behind Peony's ear and listened to her bottle run dry. The goat fell asleep in his lap and Sophie handed a glass to him.

"Thank you for the wine and the goat," she said, her annoyance easing and her next words coming fast like she wanted it over with, done. "He was mad. Billy kept getting out of the pen; he was a clever goat, and he was curious too many times. He wanted to explore, and Carl didn't like it. He didn't like to be thwarted, but he didn't mean to kill him." She dropped her head and stared into her lap, whispering her last words. "I don't think he meant it. He loves animals. It's . . . He . . . I don't know."

John sipped his wine and watched her face in the flickering firelight. The creases engraved by harsh memory turned soft, and he wondered what thoughts were responsible for the change.

"Did you go into town today?" he asked.

"Yes. To a funeral."

"Darn. I'm sorry. Someone you've known long?"

"Didn't know him at all."

Sophie poured more wine for them both even though their glasses weren't empty. It was something to do while she pondered Joe and watched John wonder about her sanity.

"Why would you attend the funeral of a total stranger?"

"You're a nosy man, John Wayne."

"I am, Sophie." He gave her a 'humor me' grin. "Why'd you go?"

Peony bleated in her sleep, making a cry somewhere between a kitten and a child, and Sophie rubbed her belly.

"She's dreaming. I'm here, Peony. Mama's here."

"You should have had children, girl. You're a natural mama. You going to tell me about the funeral?"

She snorted to let him know he was a persistent pest.

"He was the brother of a man I would have had children with, would have moved to the mountains with. Wanted to."

She snorted again and gave a jagged laugh to go along with it. It was good to surprise Mister Wayne. He opened his mouth and closed it again, unsure what to say that wouldn't be a leap off the cliff of her revealing words. But they had been unashamed and pure. She'd given him the gift of trust, of disclosure, and he didn't know what to do with it.

"Take a drink of wine before you choke, John. I was young once. I loved. I had sex. All those things you young people think you invented."

"I know. Course you did. You probably invented it."

"Might have done just that, John Wayne. You'll never know, and I'm not saying."

The fire crackled and sparks flew as a log fell from the pile. Sophie got up, poked at it, and added a couple more to the flames. She rammed the hot end of the poker into the ground and rested her hands on the top.

"He was at his only brother's funeral today. After all these years, we had a chance to talk. I explained why I couldn't go with him back then, why I didn't show up when we were supposed to leave town. He never knew why, and it killed me he didn't know."

"Want to tell me about it?"

She nodded and gave him the story.

"I went back to work at the diner for a while, and he was one of my regular lunch customers. Joe. So damned handsome, tall and blue-eyed. He took my breath away with his looks. But what got to me the most was his gentle nature. He loved me – and everything that had anything to do with me. That was really something. I never, ever forgot what it was like being loved like that. Being liked."

Twenty – Love and Reality

When Joe strolled through the door at work one day, Sophie saw a god. She skipped across the room to seat him in her section before the other girls could get to him and wondered how she'd had the nerve. She was the new girl. Tossing a menu in front of him, she stood there grinning, dimples deep.

"Do I know you?" he asked.

"I don't think so. I'm Sophie," she said, thrusting her hand toward him. "And I know I'd remember you."

"Are you flirting with me, Sophie?" He checked her out. Tiny waist and a Marilyn figure.

"I didn't think I was, but maybe. And I can't do that. I'm sort of married."

He raised a thick eyebrow and let it go.

Sophie took a step back and made waitress talk, asking all the right things like 'coffee with your burger?' and 'why are your eyes so blue?' In between customers, she asked herself what kind of fool she was. And she answered.

All kinds, Sophie. You're every damned kind of fool imaginable, and you're acting exactly like the woman Carl says you are.

She had convinced him they could use her money to buy the car they needed, so he gave consent for her to waitress at the diner again. He said they'd try it out for a few weeks and see if it worked for him. She made sure to have dinner on the table even though he frequently didn't make it home on time. Laundry was kept up, animals taken care of, and she met each sunrise happier. Seeing people brightened her world, let her know it was bigger than their hundred and twenty acres.

Her smile made tips, lots of tips, and she had a good time working. Laughter and chatter filled the diner during lunch periods, and Sophie soaked it up. It filled her. She made friends with folks she'd barely known and hadn't seen in years, and it felt good to be part of life again.

The first time Joe stayed to nurse his coffee after the lunch crowd left, she joined him at his table, refilled his cup and brought one for herself.

Conversation flowered and persisted, meandered here and there like a lazy river. He asked about her life as if he was interested in what she did, who she was when she wasn't a waitress. He looked at her when she talked – and he smiled – at her.

"Sounds like paradise where you live."

"It is, Joe. It's a great big Noah's ark."

She listened, too, and got excited over the things that excited him. The forests. The mountains out west where he wanted to build his own cabin and till up a small farm where he could raise his children.

"How many?" she asked.

He scrunched his eyes like he was peering into her brain.

"How many do you want?" he said.

She played the game with him. "Three. Two boys and a girl."

"What about four? Two of each."

"Alright," she teased, "but it's easy for you to say. You don't give them birth."

"I'm sorry. Three then. Do you like to fish? The trout streams out there are magnificent. I'll bring dinner home."

"I love fishing, and I'll bet I catch the biggest and the most."

"Do you want a big garden? You can put up vegetables for the winter."

Her face shut down, and reality came crashing in.

"I have one. A big one. And I have to go."

She whipped off her apron, grabbed her purse from the break room and fled.

In the car heading home, she chewed her fingernail ragged and swore at herself. Images plagued her, and wishes turned to fantasies. She let out a roar of frustration and spun her head to see if anyone she knew was nearby.

She needed to atone, but not for something she'd done. She'd only wanted to, and she did her best to put it out of her head and concentrate on the life she had. It was a good life. Wasn't it?

"Come on goats. I've got things to do," she cajoled, trying to hurry up the chores.

Chickens had been fed and eggs collected. Milking was nearly done, and she wanted time to spruce up, to show Carl an outside job along with taking care of the home was as easy as a country apple pie.

In the kitchen, she seasoned steaks and sliced potatoes to fry at the outside fire, one of Carl's favorite meals. The flames were hot, and she relaxed on the couch with a glass of wine. The potatoes sizzled, and her mind wandered to the diner.

She jumped when gears shifted on the lane and set off the guineas and peacocks. Warning bells rang, Charlie howled a welcome, and Sophie's heart pounded. He was home.

Carl grabbed a beer from the kitchen and found her in the back tending the fire. He gave an appreciative glance at the food and dropped onto the couch.

"What's going on? We celebrating something? Did I forget your birthday?"

Sophie chuckled and winked at him.

"Can't a girl do nice things for her man?"

"Sure can. We can eat and do nice things all night long. Right here under the stars."

Joe came into the diner for lunch every day and stayed until the crowd cleared out in order to have coffee with Sophie. And every day he told himself to go somewhere else. There were other diners where he could find lunch. But he didn't.

And there were days when Sophie's eyes darted to the door every time it opened. Waiting for him. She tried to seat him in another server's section, but failed. She couldn't make herself do it, and he wouldn't go when she tried. Eventually, they went for rides into the countryside and took walks.

He held her hand as they trekked through a small thicket toward a stream he'd fished before. Light sifted through the overhead leaves and mottled the ground, turning it into a grassy jigsaw puzzle.

"I should pack a picnic lunch," she said.

He chuckled. "We just left lunch. But some water would be good."

At the stream's bank, they sat, shoulders touching, and talked and looked at each other.

She noticed the fine lines at the corners of his eyes and thought they were distinguished. Like the sideburns he wore, his carved jawline would be perfect with a black cowboy hat – somewhere in Montana.

He watched her dimples flicker in time with her smile and wanted to make sure she'd never do anything else. Just smile. He plucked her hand from the grass she was shredding and looked at it.

"You work too hard, Sophie."

"Keeps me sane, and I don't mind work."

"Me neither." His pulse quickened. "I really need to kiss you. I know it's wrong, but . . ."

She knew it was coming. She'd thought about it, visualized it, dreamed of it, wanted it, but his words took her breath away, and she thought she might die for lack of air.

When his lips met hers in a kiss she *would* die for, and happily, she knew unmistakably. Joe was everything. She couldn't help herself.

Her watch said five o'clock, and she pressed the gas pedal hard, praying she'd get there first. Charlie met her like he always did, and she had hope. She cursed the long driveway and wildlife that forced her to creep along at a snail's pace. When the car came out of the tunnel of trees into light, she saw his truck.

"Damn."

She raced in to change, hoping Carl was in the shed working on some project, and she wouldn't run in to him. Her work clothes hung in the bathroom, so she headed there. She had stepped out of her uniform and was standing in her underwear when the door slammed open, and his form stood silhouetted in the doorway.

"Where have you been?"

She turned her back to him, a reflexive action, while sliding into her clothes, cutoffs and one of his old shirts. His hand touched her shoulder and she flinched.

"What's the matter with you? Why are you hiding your body from me? You think I haven't seen what you've got? I've seen it plenty."

She turned, and the hot red spreading over her neck to her face told a story she didn't want him to know, didn't want anyone to. Moisture beaded her upper lip, and she licked it away.

"Nothing's the matter, Carl. You just surprised me. Sorry I'm late. Let me get to the chores so I can get dinner started."

He lounged against the doorframe instead of moving out of the way and observed her. His words came out soft and a kind of grin slanted his lips.

"You didn't answer my question. Where were you?"

She finished the buttons and tried out a smile.

"I went for a walk. It was a beautiful day, so I spent time by the river. That's all. I lost track of time. I'm sorry."

Sophie raced through her chores, smiling when she could and trying to pretend the day was like any other, but she knew her thoughts were written on her face. Carl had to have read the words. She was rotten, through and through.

She fried fish outside, and her hands trembled as she placed the fillets in the pan, splashing hot grease. She momentarily closed her eyes and breathed through the pain. When the pan was full, she stuffed the burns behind her back and out of sight.

"How about a beer, Soph?"

She went inside to get one for him and poured a large glass of wine for herself thinking she might relax. But she couldn't stop the pounding of her heart and the face that showed every single thought charging through her brain.

The fish were burning when she got back, and he scoffed at her cooking skills.

"Couldn't you move the pan, Carl?"

"That's your job, girl. Why'd you burn my dinner?"

"They'll be fine," she said, moving the pan to a cooler place on the fire and flipping the fish. She gave him a hopeful grin. "You like them crispy, right?"

"What I like is my wife here to take care of the house and my dinners."

"I'm not even your wife, Carl. We never got married, remember?"

"Well, we're going to remedy that."

Joe came for lunch the next day, and Sophie tried to tell him to stay away. Eat somewhere else. She failed saying it, and he couldn't do it.

"I'm in love with you, Sophie," he whispered. "Come with me to Montana. We're perfect together, and you know that's true."

158

His eyes lowered. He didn't want her to see his need. His adoration.

Joe asked her to marry him every week – regularly, like that's what Monday's were meant for, marriage proposals, and that's what he was destined to do. And she was created to say she'd be his wife.

"I know you love me, Sophie. I feel it flowing from your eyes, from your fingertips. Please, say yes."

One day while they were walking by their favorite spot on the river, she threw her arms around him, felt a dark weight lift from her back, and a shadowy dread she didn't understand melted away. Freedom gave her wings, and her soul soared across the sky for the first time in years.

They made plans for Friday after the end of her work day at the diner.

The days dragged.

Carl hassled her about quitting work, and Sophie prayed for Friday to hurry.

"My wife doesn't need to work. I make enough for both of us, so, you can quit. It's a stupid waitress job, for crying out loud."

She held herself rigid and chewed a lip in fear he'd beat her down, defeat her resolve. Her bag was packed and stuffed in the trunk of her car – under a blanket in case he happened to open the trunk lid. Her mind was made up, and she needed to leave, wanted to leave. Being with Joe meant life, air, and she'd finally chosen to live.

Sophie coaxed and reasoned with Carl, trying to keep her job. This week, it made everything easier. She needed to be at the diner, needed to see Joe and be reassured by his presence.

"I said no, Sophie."

She drank half the wine in her glass in a gulp and faced him, ready to tell all, ready to leave him tonight. She threw her shoulders back, filled her mind with strength and shivered at the look on his face.

His smirk said he already knew what was coming and wasn't afraid, that he had the solution to her intended desertion. Her family. Joe's family.

But he couldn't know, could he?

"If you're thinking of leaving me, forget it. We're good together, Sophie. We even have some fun once in a while." He gave a meaningful pause. "And I know where your brother and sisters live. I know where your mother and stepfather live. Does that make you think a little? And I will tell the entire town – including *his* mother and brother and sisters what kind of a slut old Joe wanted to run away with."

She never went back to the diner.

He showed up for lunch every day that week hoping to see her, excited to whisper plans to her, eager to share his dream for them in Montana. Joe never knew why she didn't show, but his packed truck sat in the diner parking lot until sunrise Saturday morning when he headed west and never looked back.

Twenty-one – Good, Bad and Humanity

Peony lay asleep between them, and they took turns stroking her. Periodically, the fluffy kid murmured a tiny bleat in her sleep and her back legs kicked as if she defended herself from a predator.

"She'll be spoiled rotten," Sophie said.

"Isn't that what you want? A brat kid? A goat you bottle feed and turn into a real kid?" John chuckled at his joke and checked to see if he'd ticked her off.

"Probably true. Sorry about the gloomy story. I'm a real-life soap opera star, aren't I? But you asked."

"I did, and I'm not sorry. I'm glad you told me. It explains some things I didn't understand. I don't know why you put up with it. You're a strong woman, Sophie. You don't let anybody push you around. Why did you allow it after all that? Or did you?"

Fannie howled and tore off into the dark chasing an interloper, startling Peony who nudged her nose into Sophie's hand, snuffled, and fell back to sleep.

"Coyote," she said. "Fannie can't stand a coyote."

"How do you know? Could be a whitetail or coon. Maybe a possum."

"No. That's her coyote howl."

John gave her a skeptical grin, and Sophie glared at the dark corners of the back yard wondering why she would bother to explain anything to the Harley riding upstart sprawled on her outside couch – either coyote or Carl related.

"Really?"

"You don't know anything, John Wayne. Were you born under a rock or in Detroit where they killed off all the wildlife to make room for people?"

"Both, I think. That's why I love your place. It's unspoiled and primitive – like you."

"Good God, John. What balderdash. Shut that stuff up." She paused in thought. "People aren't all good or all bad, you know. Including Carl. We had some fun."

"What kind of fun did you have? Tell me." John leaned sideways on the arm of the couch so he could watch her face as she talked. Eyes were his bullshit barometer – usually. But Sophie was a hard read.

"He had a little motorcycle he liked to run around the countryside on. Not a fancy Harley like yours, a little Honda Cub. He looked like a big kid on it, long legs hunched up, knees sticking out. And one day, shortly after I quit the diner for the second time, he came home with another bike in the back of his truck."

She lost years from her face as she remembered the day, and John cursed his youth. At that moment, he would give up forty years to see Sophie as she was then.

"Was his broken?" he asked.

"No. His ran fine. I was in the chicken coop when I heard him coming up the driveway. Between bells, guineas, peacocks and goats, nobody sneaks up this driveway, not even Carl." She gave him a sideways glance. "Except maybe you. I went outside to say hello and knew from the slant of his happy eyes it was going to be a good night."

"Happy eyes?"

John chuckled over her choice of words.

"Sure. When he was in a good mood, they slanted or squinted, kind of, and lines went out in a triangle from the corners. He wasn't big on lip smiling. Just his eyes. Anyway, he called me over and went around to the back end of the truck and waited."

"So, I'm guessing he had something back there for you, right?"

"Yes! My very own bike. Even smaller than his and kind of black and grimy, but he was a good mechanic and told me as soon as I learned to ride it, he'd clean it up and paint it red." She looked at John to check for understanding. "He knew I liked red."

"Did you learn to ride?"

"I did learn. I was scared, too, but he was a good teacher. He ran along beside me in the yard and up and down the driveway. He mowed a big patch in the pasture next to the yard so I could practice turns and figure eights. It was great fun."

"And did you forget about Joe?"

"Never for a day, and don't you be asking about him again. Carl and I took long bike trips. Bought a little tent to stow on the back of his Honda and attached a crate on mine to hold camping things and took off for the north, always on the back roads. We rode side by side with the wind blowing in our faces and bugs sticking in our teeth."

"That sounds wonderful, Sophie, like freedom. Do you miss it now?"

She shook her head. "I miss Carl being happy. He wants to be, tries to be, but every day he turns around and looks behind him, waiting for bad stuff to creep up and clobber him. It makes him crazy and mean. It's like he shouldn't ever be happy or wasn't allowed to for some ungodly reason. I think some religions make people sad or scared."

"You blame churches, then?"

"Some of them. Maybe." Sophie's eyes followed the return of Fannie, and she pointed to a chair. The dog climbed up, lay with her head on her front paws and stared at John.

"That's a big leap, don't you think?"

"Maybe I didn't say that right," she said, finishing her thought. "Maybe it's just the way his mother thought about

God. She wasn't a very nice woman, and he had nothing good to say about her or his life with her when he was a boy and then trying to be a man. Whether she meant to or not, she taught him smiling was wrong, even sinful. So was fun and dancing and drinking and anything except working or sitting around being miserable and praying."

Sophie reached for the half empty wine box and lifted it in question. He nodded, and she poured a little more in their glasses. She sipped and watched him stroke Peony, a look of contentment smoothing the few shallow lines spreading out from his eyes.

"You spend a lot of time dissecting Carl and me, John Wayne. What about you?" she said. "What makes you happy and sad? What gets your goat." She tilted her head and grinned. "But wait, you don't have any, do you?"

"Well, let's see if I can answer that. You make me happy, and so do Peony and Gladiola," he grinned at that. "Your beautiful gardens, too. Any kind of conflict makes me sad. War, in particular."

"Which one?"

"All war, but I only saw one. Iraq."

"You lived through it, though. That's something not everyone did."

"Surviving doesn't mean living." He balanced the wineglass on his knee and stared at the flames through it. Red liquid danced like a firestorm, like war, like Iraq, and he had to drag his eyes away from the memory. "I'm betting you know that, Sophie. You've become the queen of contented endurance."

Stillness hung around them, and unshared thoughts hovered, infiltrating their pores. Like an unknowable God breaching personal barriers, their individual dreams teased them with promises and tantalized them with threats. The gods of their youths had disappeared.

Sophie had come to terms with her spirituality as easily as she mastered most everything else. She believed in the God she envisioned because it made sense to do so – and because she wanted to. It was a simple process. Choose belief and it was done. She didn't need to ponder or question it anymore.

John saw God all around him, in the fields and flowers, the animals and forests, and now in Sophie. He couldn't tell you why He was in her, but he knew it was true.

And he'd already seen hell – in war. He knew no God lived in battle regardless of the number of deaths claimed in the name of a deity. So he'd seen both heaven and hell, divinity and the devil, and thought he knew the difference between them. That was the best he could ask of himself.

Peony squirmed like she wanted down, and Sophie stood and called to her.

"She probably needs to pee," she said. "She's been asleep a long time. Take her for a walk, and I'll fix another bottle for her."

When she returned, man and goat were nowhere to be seen. She called, and his voice answered from the direction of the pet cemetery. Peony raced toward her on wobbly legs, bleating for food, and Sophie picked her up, still looking for John in the dark.

"Where the hell are you, John Wayne?"

He moved out from behind what he thought looked like a totem of some sort. Stepping back from it, he took in a monument made of huge rocks stacked one on top of the other.

"What are you doing over there?" she asked, miffed to see him near the graves. "You're standing on our private burial ground, and you know that. Could be walking on a dog. Maybe a cat."

"Sorry. Peony ran off, and, in chasing her down, I got clobbered by Aunt Jemima."

He looked up at the top rock. The pile stood so high he couldn't reach it, and he gazed up in awe.

"Aunt Jemima?" she asked, her face set in furrowed confusion.

He laughed. "Racist, right? We're not supposed to use names like Uncle Tom and Aunt Jemima – Little Black Sambo, either. But I'm not meaning to be a bigot. I just remember the shape of that syrup bottle, and the silhouette of this stone formation looks like her.

"I get it, John. You're not prejudiced. Just fanciful. Get away from there now."

"Did you and Carl make this? Don't tell me it was here all along. That a tribe of Neanderthals made it back when this acreage belonged to them and the stone age."

"Come on. Get away from there. And I don't think Neanderthals were around during the stone age. Science channel," she said with a grin and tilt of her chin.

She took Peony back to the couch and stuck the bottle in her mouth. When he added a log to the fire, she told him not to put on more.

"Unless you're gonna watch it because I'm going to bed. Where are you sleeping tonight?"

He grinned at her. "The underground? Will that be alright with you?"

"Fine. I'll get the key when I'm done here."

"Tell me about the rock formations. I saw some in the front yard, too."

She let the years float away, let herself be young again, and told him about hauling and stacking their stones.

"Boulders are everywhere on this property. And there was a time Carl could do anything. Everything. He could calculate which stone would sit on top of another one without wobbling. How to settle it securely so it wouldn't fall off and hurt a cat. Couldn't let a cat get killed. That couldn't happen, not ever."

John whistled his admiration.

"They're huge, and it must have taken forever to lift and move them, place them just so. I mean, why would he want to make them in the first place?"

"Because he could and because other people couldn't. Nobody else has giant stone gnomes in their yard, do they?"

She giggled like a schoolgirl with a secret before growing somber. "And because I like stones. He did it for me, and we did it together – with the tractor and chains and me shoving the stones into position as they swung in the air, making sure they went exactly where he told me to put them."

"Wasn't your part in the process kind of dangerous with a thousand pounds or more hanging in the air next to you? What if a chain had broken or it slipped?"

She gave him an enigmatic smile. "It was a risk. He told me that."

"They're something, Sophie. Like spiritual guardians made of granite."

"They speak to me."

"Now you're just joshing," he wrinkled his forehead and narrowed his eyes at her. He wasn't going to push the idea because he thought they just might talk. Who knew?

"Yes. I'm ribbing you. And I'm going to get the underground key and then head to my couch, the inside one. I need sleep. I'll tell you the stone stories another day."

Twenty-two – Don't Shoot the Help

Carl ripped off a large piece of pancake and held it under the table for Charlie who swallowed it whole and bumped his head on the table when he got up. On all fours, he stood hip high on a tall man, and he didn't understand small spaces.

"Get out from under there," he said, giving his giant Dane mix a fake frown. "You're too big for this house. You should be out in the pasture like the horse you are. Should be eating grass instead of eating me out of house and home."

"Come here, old boy," Sophie said, and burrowed her face in his gray muzzle when he lumbered over to her. "We still love you. We're lucky to have you around for so many years."

"Danes don't usually live so long. You gotta get mutts like Charlie. Mongrels always live longer." He rippled the dog's ruff and stood. "You need to come out and help me today," Carl said.

When she tried to pick up their plates, he grabbed her arm and tugged her toward the door, his face burning with excitement.

"Can I clean up the kitchen first?"

"No. Do it later."

"Where are we going?"

"I told you. Outside. It's a surprise."

When he was excited or wanted to hurry, Carl leaned forward at the waist like he would get there faster if his head arrived early. He pointed it in the direction of the back of the property and took off, hauling her along with him.

Twenty minutes later, he stopped his half-run at an old fence row, crossed his arms and leaned back with a satisfied 'See, I told you,' grin in his eyes.

"Well?" he said.

"Well what? I see a bunch of big, beautiful boulders all in a row."

"Aren't they spectacular? I knew they were here, but I'd forgotten. Ran across them again the other night when I was looking for Charlie."

"They're something, Carl. You know I love enormous stones. Bigger the better. I wish they were in the yard where I could see them all the time."

Fun jumped out of his eyes, and his smile showed the tips of his teeth.

"They're going to be."

"Be what?"

"In the yard. We're going to put them there. You, me and the tractor."

Sophie stared at him, then at the stones and back at the crazy man. "We're going to pick these monsters up off the ground and move them?"

"We are. The tractor's already here. Chains, too. I'll tell you what you need to do. And you've got to listen, too, Sophie. These are heavy. You don't want them dropping from the chains and landing on you. Not even on a toe."

Her eyes grew wide, and he didn't know if she was afraid or happy. She didn't either, but she wanted the rocks. Charlie moseyed over and nudged her arm. She patted him absently, imagining the monster stones in her flower beds.

They walked the stone fence row, and Carl pointed out the ones he'd picked to move first. She couldn't even respond as he prattled on and on, naming each kind of rock and explaining the particulars of every single one, how long it had been there in geological terms, and what he planned to do with it. But when they came across a large pinkish stone, she jumped up and down and pointed.

"That one. I want that one in a front flower bed."

"You can have it, and I'll put it on top of three others so you can see it from the kitchen window."

He brought the Oliver 550 tractor close to the biggest stone, one meant to be a base for others, wrapped a heavy chain around the bottom near the ground, hooked three more to the first chain, and clasped them together with another, making a kind of tripod. He handed the last one to her.

"Grip this tight. Hold it high, and don't let it slack, not the least little bit," he said and climbed on the tractor. "You got it tight?"

"I do. But don't make me stand like this for too long. It's heavy."

"Don't be a sissy girl." He gave her a wink and lifted the front-end loader to just higher than the stone. "Now wrap the chain over the loader bucket and hook it to itself."

"I don't know if it's long enough, Carl. It isn't reaching around completely."

She tugged and pulled, and chains clanked against each other and the tractor. Her arms turned to lead from the weight of the tripod contraption and from holding them above her head. He climbed down and took it from her, stood back and looked over the tangled mass of chains.

"Okay. This is what we'll do. I'll scoop this one into the bucket because it's going to sit on the ground, not on another stone, so I won't have to raise it, just dump it and roll it into place. The next ones, we'll chain, but I'll make some adjustments in how we secure them. Ready?"

He looked at her, and Sophie nodded, but her eyes held more fear than excitement. Carl's entire face radiated exhilaration.

He removed the chains, backed the tractor away, lowered the bucket and moved forward again, digging into the dirt under the massive boulder. It tried to teeter away from him, as if it feared the noisy machine, but he revved the Oliver and kept forward pressure until it toppled backwards into place, dirt and all.

Carl had won.

Sophie watched the battle from a distance, looking back and forth between the stone and Carl's face, worried he would get angry and the day would turn ugly. She didn't understand how or why, but frustration changed him, and she couldn't help him cope. She didn't know how.

With a sigh of relief, she watched the boulder tumble into the bucket and rock their small tractor with its weight. It settled, and Sophie ran to Carl, climbed up and threw an arm around his neck.

"You scared me." She whispered into his cheek. "Don't get hurt, please."

"Course not. I know what I'm doing. Let's go." She started to climb down, but he pulled her to his lap with an arm around her middle. "Stay here and take a ride with me."

They walked around the front yard looking for the perfect place for their first stone totem and decided on the edge of the yard bordering the woods, up near the stream.

"I'll put flowers around it. I wanted a garden here anyway."

"It can guard the place and watch for intruders slinking down the driveway," he said.

Sophie's dimples deepened. "With all your bells, lights and the gate, Carl, how could anybody sneak down this driveway?"

"You can't ever be sure. People want what somebody else has. You know that. People are basically no good. Thieves."

He strode back to the tractor, started it up, and motored to the spot they'd selected. Sophie waited there and pointed when he drew near. He lowered the bucket, tilted it, and their first colossal boulder tumbled out and rested like it had always been there in the shade of the nearby trees.

The next three were smaller but still monstrously large and heavy, and they needed to be chained and carefully lowered into place. He perfected the chaining process, but Sophie still had to hold the chain assembly high and without slack while he moved the tractor into place so she could attach it to the bucket and he could lift it. The boulders slipped in their nests as weight settled, and, each time, she waited for a chain to slide and allow the rock to slam back to the ground. Or into her.

As soon as it lifted into the air, Sophie hopped backwards, eager to be away from the hundreds of pounds that could escape the restraints and smash her feet or arms or legs. Carl laughed at her fearful face and quick-step scamper. He patted his leg, inviting her to climb up as the second stone swung from the bucket and came to a slow, grudging halt.

"You're a big chicken, aren't you, Sophie?"

"I'll drive the tractor and you go play with the boulders and chains."

He chuckled. "You can't. You don't know how, and I do. I'm not going to let you get hurt. Who'd make my supper?"

It took all day to make one four-stone boulder statue, mostly because it was an intricate and possibly deadly process, but Carl had something to do with the length of time, too. He was a perfectionist, and simply putting one stone on top of another wasn't enough. They had to sit acceptably and satisfy his artistic eye, and they must rest securely, as well. No critters should ever be threatened by a toppling pile of stones. People? Maybe.

Charlie quit following them back and forth, contented to lay his tired body on the concrete porch. Three cats curled into his belly, and, rather than disturb them, he followed Carl and Sophie's progress with just his eyes. He was satisfied to watch, happy to rest his old legs.

They finished as the sun threatened to take away its light and after the pink rock rested at the top of the stack. Carl sent her into the house for a whiskey and coke. She brought his drink, a glass of wine and a blanket, spreading it far enough from their work of art so they could rest and admire it.

"It's a shrine," she said.

"To what?"

She shrugged and sipped her Merlot. "Does it have to be *to* something. Or somebody?"

"Shrines usually do." He raised his brows and gave her a look that made her bite her lip and stutter to find a response. "I won't have a shrine to some god I don't believe in," he added. "Not on my property."

Sophie straightened. "*Our* property, Carl. We both worked for this acreage."

"You're right. Let's lay back and admire our work. It was a hard day, but you did alright."

She flushed in the stolen praise, and he finished his drink and sent her for another. She brought a small cooler this time, so she wouldn't have to go back for more too soon, along with snacks and a couple of pillows. The sun left them in darkness, but the moon soon glanced off Sophie's shrine as it observed them undressing each other.

On Sunday they built two more monuments, one at the head of the pet cemetery in back of the house and one near the chicken coop flower bed. Late in the day, sweat dampened their clothes, and they were tired, ready to be done with the project. Sophie's legs shook and her feet didn't work as well when she scampered back out of the way. They were spent, and she feared an accident.

"We could finish another day, Carl. We don't have to do it all this weekend."

"We can make this last one. Come on. Get over here and hold the chain up. Move it, Soph."

The work was grueling in the heat, and as the last stone raised from the ground, a chain slipped, and the rock fell back to the earth inches from Sophie's toes.

"What did you do?" He shouted, anger contorting his face as he climbed down from the tractor to fix the bed of chains.

"Nothing. I didn't do anything different."

"You must have. You let them go slack. I told you not to do that. It could have crushed your foot."

He tried to adjust the chains, but one lay under the boulder and wouldn't budge when he pulled on it. He glared as he handed her the assembly and went back to the tractor.

"I'm going to tilt the stone with the back of the bucket. When you see it move, grab the chain it's laying on. Keep it up high, and don't let the stone lay back on it – or on your foot."

"Seriously? You want me to put my hand under that rock?"

"Not under it. Just close enough to grab the chain."

The stone moved as he said it would, but Sophie's hand shook with fear and exhaustion. She didn't say anything about either, and she didn't resist when he handed her the assembly and told her to do it right this time. It wouldn't help to deny she'd done it wrong in the first place.

The last monument caused problems. The last stone, the one that should perch on top, beautiful for all to view, refused to stay in place. Every time he let it rest where he wanted, it tried to slide off, even with Sophie pulling at the chains holding it.

"It won't sit, Carl. Lift the bucket and let me rotate it. Or come look at it and tell me what else I can do."

He got down to inspect the rock and said it had a perfect seat on the flat top of the third stone. There was no reason for it to fall.

"It's your imagination," he said. "Pull the chain back toward the chicken coop as I lower it."

"This time, you're gonna kill me, Carl."

"Maybe I will, but not with a rock, woman."

The tractor made a grinding noise when he tried to lower the bucket, and it quit its downward trajectory. He pushed the lever forward and backwards over and over, hearing the same grinding noise but seeing no movement of the bucket. He swore at the tractor, at the stone, and at Sophie whose numb arms were stuck high over her head, hands still pulling back on the chains.

After fifteen minutes of trying to lower the bucket, he climbed off the tractor without a word and disappeared into the house. He came back with his twenty gauge, and Sophie let go of the chains and ran toward the porch. She stood with her back against the house and watched him shoot the tractor – five times – until the gun was empty.

Lead pellets zinged as they slammed against the metal and ricocheted off into buildings and trees. Chickens and guineas screeched and scrambled into their coop, goats bleated and raced to their shed, and the Peacocks flew up into their nighttime roost tree, shrieking their panic.

He pumped it again and swore because it was empty.

In the kitchen, cool air against her damp skin created shivers as she poured a healthy glass of red wine and slugged half of it. She chewed her thumb nail, pulled off a ragged piece and spit it to the floor. A sleek, black cat called Satan leaped to the counter and bumped his head against Sophie's hand. Wine sloshed over the rim and drizzled over her forearm, looking like a bright streak of blood that pooled and dripped from her elbow.

"I know," she whispered to Satan. "I love you, too."

She rested her hands on either side of the sink in front of the window and tried to admire the yard and gardens – and the shrine they'd created the day before, the one that had watched them make love in the moonlight. The same one who'd seen his tenderness. She reached for her glass and sipped, slowly this time, wondering where that man was, the one who had loved her so well.

Surely, he wasn't the same man shooting the tractor because it frustrated him? Surely not the same one who had screamed at her, swore at her.

While onions sautéed, she thought about the stories she'd tell Dee when they went to lunch next week. She knew how to make their working together sound romantic and make the shrines be his glorious tribute to her. And they were. He'd done all this for her because he loved her and she loved stones.

Shooting the tractor was history. It was over. Done. She'd not include the gun in her tale; she'd forget that part – wish it gone.

When the goulash simmered gently, Sophie put on her rubber work boots and fed the chickens, looked for eggs and milked the goats. She spotted the peacocks still in their tree and Carl under the tractor removing parts.

"Want a beer, Carl?"

"Yes. I'm done here. We need a new tractor."

"Because you shot it?"

He scowled. "No. Because it didn't work like it's supposed to. And that's why I shot it. Things should work like they're supposed to. That's all there is to it. They should just work right. Did you make dinner?"

"I did. Your favorite."

"Good. I'll have a couple of beers first."

Twenty-three – Taking a Ride

The Harley's throaty rumble woke her from a dream about stone gnomes wandering around the yard in the darkness and peeking into her windows. She bolted upright in time to see the gnomes evaporate into the mist and the motorcycle disappear into the trees as it headed down the driveway.

"Well, thanks for the good morning words, John. Good riddance to you, too."

She dislodged several cats asleep on her legs and moved her feet to the floor. Fannie stood and shoved her nose into Sophie's cheek, her typical salute to the day.

"I'm coming, Peony. Damned man woke up every animal for a square mile. Listen to them screeching and shrieking like banshees, whatever the hell they are. What's a banshee, Fannie? Do you know?"

She shoved herself from the couch and shuffled to the coffee pot. It was hot and full, and surprise brought a smile to her face. She poured a cup, fixed a goat bottle, and headed to the door.

"Come on, Peony. Get outside all of you," she muttered, holding the screen door open while Fannie led the kid and a variety of cats, tails skyward, out to the porch.

The sun poked at the tops of the trees, and dew had sprayed the grass white. It looked as if it had snowed in the night and left thin traces. Birds threw their favorite songs out for the world to admire and scolded when the cats stalked them as breakfast. It was a summer morning paradise, and, for a moment, just a single one, she wished to share it with John Wayne.

She held Peony's bottle with one hand and managed her coffee cup with the other, spreading her legs wide to make a nest of her nightgown for the baby goat.

"So, he sneaked in and made coffee for me," she said to Fannie. "Doesn't make him a saint. And you didn't even bark at him. What kind of watch dog are you? He could've robbed me blind."

After two cups of admiring the break of day, she fed Fannie and the cats, threw Carl's white shirt over the top of her nightgown, and pulled on her tall, rubber boots.

"These boots stink, Fannie. They make my feet smell."

Fannie rolled her eyes, thinking it wasn't the fault of the boots.

"Don't be a smart-ass, Fannie. Nobody likes a smart-ass mutt. Maybe I ought to wear socks. Next time. Come on Peony. Let's go see the big goats."

Fourteen eggs nested in the basket, and as many chickens happily pecked at the ground outside the coop. In the goat pen, Sophie milked Gladiola, watched Peony pretend to use horns she didn't have on the big Billy, and wondered what to do with her day. Take a bath, for sure, what with her stinky feet, but what next?

She stood and was calling for Peony to follow her when she heard the Harley's sweet growl grow louder as it left the road and thundered down the lane. She waited at the door of the pen, holding the milk bucket and Peony's collar so John wouldn't run her over.

He came to a stop when he saw them, knocked the kick stand down, leaned the bike, and sat back.

"Well, good morning to you, Sophie, Peony, Fannie, Gladiola and Petunia. Oh, and Billy. Can't forget you, my smelly friend. I'd greet the peacocks, chickens and guineas, but I don't know their names." He squinted at her. "Do they have names, Sophie? They should. Everybody should have a name, even the animals."

She couldn't decipher the look on his face as he stared at her and thought it was somewhere between laughter, surprise and disbelief. She squared her shoulders and lifted her chin, making an effort to dislodge a growing sense of annoyance.

You don't laugh at me, John Wayne. I'll whitewash you with goat milk.

"Good morning, yourself. I need to get this stuff inside before it spoils."

"I'll take it." He climbed off his bike and held out his hand. "Then let's go for a ride. Go get dressed."

She tilted her head at him and strode off toward the house. He followed, still grabbing for the milk bucket.

"Stop!" he said, and she spun around.

"Who the hell do you think you're talking to, John? You don't order me around."

"What's wrong, Sophie? Are you mad at me?"

She swallowed and scratched a broken fingernail at her cheek.

"I . . . Uh . . . Course not. That's just stupid talk. I have things to do. A life to live. I don't sit around waiting for you to come riding down the road, John Wayne."

He took her elbow and guided them up the steps and into the kitchen. He poured the milk for her while she held the cheesecloth in the strainer and put the container in the fridge.

"Want another coffee? There's some left," he asked while pouring one for himself.

"No. I need to take a bath."

"Wait. Don't do that right now."

She narrowed her eyes and glared.

"You giving orders again? About when I can take a bath, for crying out loud? You need to leave." She went to the screen door to let Peony and a bunch of cats in and held the door for him to go out through.

He deflated. She saw him shrink from six foot something to a little boy and flattened along with him.

"I didn't mean that, John. But I do need a bath. My feet stink. Well, my boots do, but Fannie thinks it's my feet."

"The dog said so?"

"Sure. She rolled her eyes when we were talking about it. You know."

"I do. Yes."

"So, why do you think I shouldn't take a bath?"

"Because I brought a picnic, wine and all, and I thought we'd take a ride on Miss Lily, since you know all about riding bikes." He saw more confusion and tried to clear it up. "That's her name. You probably forgot. She's Miss Lily, prettiest lady this side of the Pecos, cept you."

"You saying I'm old and forgetful? I remember just fine, but what does the damned bike have to do with my feet and a bath?" Sophie's forehead furrowed in an effort to make a connection.

"Oh." He grinned. "Forgot that part. We're going to a lake so wear a bathing suit under your clothes. You can take a bath in the lake. I brought you a helmet."

The vibration coming through the foot pedals and leather seat ran up her legs, along her spine, and centered in her brain. Euphoria settled in, and Sophie counted the years as they fell away. She turned sixty, and fifty, and skipped straight to thirty.

The Harley sang when John kicked it into fourth gear, and Sophie peered at the part of his face she could see, wondering if he was feeling what she did.

"Good girl, Lily," he said, crooning to his bike.

He dropped back a gear as they came to a curve and they leaned into it together. John grinned at the synchronized movement.

Sophie had become someone else, someone immortal. Creaking joints and worry were things other people suffered – old people.

From a vague, imaginary distance, she heard another gear and knew when John kicked it up another notch. She heard the growling purr, and John looked back at Sophie and smiled.

"Miss Lily's a temperamental girl," he yelled.

"Aren't we all?" She relaxed her shoulders and let her eyes take in the countryside.

She'd forgotten how close blades of green grass grew on the side of the road. Seated on a bike, she could reach out and touch them. Her vision sharpened, and she saw small critters in the woods, ones she never saw when riding in a car. And the wind . . . It washed her face and flung her hair, tangling the strands with abandon. She was liberated.

She loosened her hands on the handles, let them curl with careless ease around the chrome grips, and chuckled as she leaned back in what John had called the bitch seat. The leather, warmed from the sun, leaked through her back and into her soul. She hadn't known the Harley could take her into another world, transport her to another time.

Over his shoulder, she saw water glisten in the sunlight, and he turned Lily's wheels onto the path circling the lake. They had the place to themselves, and Sophie thanked him for the treat.

John shut it off, and silence penetrated in the absence of the Harley's throaty grumbles. Sophie didn't want to move. She wanted to hold onto the freedom and air and sensation. And being thirty.

He swung a long leg over and to the ground and held a hand out to Sophie.

"I'm not so old I can't get myself off a motorcycle."

"Slide on off then, woman." He slipped the buckle on the side bag and hauled out a bucket of chicken, a bottle of wine and a blanket.

"Spread it out, please, Sophie. Isn't this place a great find? Trees all around us. Water. We're in paradise in the middle of nowhere."

She spread the blanket and tilted her head with a wicked grin. "You thinking about skinny dipping?"

"I could do that. You asking?"

"Hah! You foolish man. You don't know who you're messing with." She plopped on her butt and looked around. "Where's the corkscrew? I need some wine before I go swimming in my birthday suit."

John's face turned to stone and his tongue clucked coming unglued from the roof of his mouth.

"Got me good, Sophie." He pulled a folded tool from his pocket, pried a small corkscrew from the side of it, and handed it to her.

"Got glasses?"

"In the bag. Fancy plastic."

She uncorked, poured and held one out to him.

"Here's to you. Thanks, John, for the wonderful ride. I got young again."

"Any time. Where's your bike, Sophie? Could be worth a lot of money now."

She chuckled without mirth. "Full of holes and rusting away, more than likely."

John's eyebrow rose. "Shotgun pellets?"

"A long time ago."

Sophie sat with her legs straight out in front of her like a little girl and held the plastic glass in both hands on her lap. She'd removed her shoes, and polished toes pointed to the sky. Two ruby red lips curved in pleasure. Her hair, loosened from its tie during the ride, hung around her shoulders in tangled silver strands.

John couldn't stop staring. He wanted her to remain immobile so he could paint her because he certainly couldn't describe what she looked like with words. And there were no metaphors for her, no like images to say what she resembled. No song praising the woman inside. She was Sophie.

Simply Sophie.

"If you could see yourself as I see you, my friend, you would think it wasn't so long ago."

"You talk like a fool." She swallowed the last of the wine in her glass and said, "Let's do this. By the way, I'm afraid of weeds. Weeds and water."

"You're kidding. You? Afraid of a little old weed? What can lake vegetation do to you?"

"I don't know." She removed her shirt and pants and stood. "Tangle up in my legs and drown me. Come on. I'm not going in without you."

"I'll save you, Sophie."

He was a strong swimmer and towed her along with him to the middle of the lake where their feet couldn't touch weeds. There, they floated on their backs and found shapes in the clouds. They treaded water, and she concentrated on keeping her head above it, with a hand on his shoulder to help. He told her a story to take her mind off drowning.

"There's a little stretch of road nearby that I like to ride," he said. "It has two sets of light curves all within half a mile. Heading north, the curves are tight and require some lean. They're posted fifteen, twenty, and thirty miles an hour. I got through the third curve and was entering the fourth at thirty-five, five miles over the limit. At the top, I rolled on."

"What's that, John? And by the way, you're an idiot going over the limit on a bike. You know that?"

"Rolled on means I increased the speed because the throttle is on the handlebars and you roll on and off. Anyway, as we began to leave the curve, Lily righted and started to make noises I hadn't heard before, so I clutched to fourth and she made more noises that startled me."

"Was something wrong?"

He scratched his head, dripping water into his eyes.

"I couldn't tell if I heard the sounds in my ears or from my insides out. They were low, loud, and guttural, and I didn't know if she was in agony or ecstasy. What I did know was they were noises no lady should make, especially in public. Then again, Lily's no lady. She just poses as one – fools some folks, too."

"Shame on you, John, saying that about Miss Lily." Sophie tried to look at him for emphasis and sucked in some lake water. She coughed and sputtered for a while as John continued his story, ignoring her near drowning.

"At about seventy, I realized she was in ecstasy, not agony, and she wanted more. At eighty, I realized she was an experienced and wanton woman with a hunger for asphalt, and I was not her equal. I used the excuse that our turn onto Willow Road was near, and I had to roll off. She was not happy. It was the first time in my life I have ever felt inadequate with a woman."

Sophie waved her arm and sent a spray of water over him, regardless of the threat of drowning. "Jesus, you're a lousy storyteller, John."

"I thought it was pretty good. You got over being afraid of weeds and water, didn't you?"

Their skin had puckered by the time he kicked back to shore with his rider in tow.

"Thanks for the lift. Guess I'm a remora, now, and you know what that makes you," she said and wrapped herself in the offered towel.

"A mean old shark? Not very flattering."

"No, it isn't, and I'm not eating your parasites and picking your teeth, either." She laughed, but her searching look gave him pause.

"Something bothering you?" he asked as he poured them both a little more merlot. "You're looking at me as if I really could be a Great White."

"Just wondering about you as I always do. Why you're here hanging out with an old woman instead of a pretty, young one? Asking me questions. Wanting to know all about my life. The stone monuments. The bikes. Children. Why? What are you doing?"

John contemplated her questions and answered honestly. He didn't want Sophie worrying, and she was. This wasn't the first time she'd asked.

"I have no place to be right now, except here. Is something wrong with that? And speaking of stones. I can't believe you put yourself in harm's way. Why would you do that?"

She tilted her glass and swirled the red wine, watched it creep close to the rim and slide back into the bottom of the glass before it spilled over.

"Keeping it in the glass is just physics, Carl would say. He always knew what he was doing. I trusted him. I trusted what he said was what he knew as the truth. He had a thing about lies, and he never did. Never does. I knew that right from the start."

"He seems a little . . . um, off kilter. Shooting things and all. You weren't afraid he might hurt you?"

She chewed her cheek while she thought and rubbed her forehead.

"That's not it. I wasn't exactly afraid and I wasn't unafraid, either. He didn't say he would kill me and he didn't say he wouldn't."

"Well, that's not a thing most people talk about over breakfast, now, is it?. Like – Hey, do you think you'd ever like to kill me?"

"Course not. I know that. He said he *could* a lot, just not *would*."

"He could what?" Shock, pure and unconcealed astonishment exposed itself in his eyes because he knew before she said it.

"Kill me, silly."

"Jesus, Sophie. That's nuts."

"Seems like it could be, but John, you don't understand. Some things are more important than others. Trust is one of them. He was depressed and negative and bigoted and hated the world and everybody in it, but he was always doing nice things for me – some of the time, anyway. And for other people. They thought he was wonderful."

"Didn't you ever talk to your friends about him shooting things? Or maybe . . . maybe about some of the other stuff he did? Didn't they talk to you?"

She leaned back on one elbow, propped her head on her fist and studied John. His age hid behind the lines on his face along with, she supposed, his battle with war memories. She appreciated his reticence, most of the time, but the thing about fair play pushed her.

"Do you go around talking about all the death you saw in Iraq, John?"

His mouth opened and closed, and his face shut down. An apology slid to her lips, and she bit it back.

No. I won't. He doesn't need to talk about his dreadful days, just understand my own silence.

"Hell, he doesn't even need to do that. Not if he can't," she mumbled.

"He who? Who are you talking to?"

"Nobody. I didn't talk about the bad things *because* they were bad. In a way, it would have been unfaithful to him, and I was stupid and didn't want anyone to know. There. Now *you* know."

His lips quirked and he patted her shoulder. She jerked it from under his hand, irked at the show of kindness or his grin. One or the other.

"Yes, now I know. Want the last of the wine?"

She shoved the plastic glass to him and he poured, stole a sip from it and handed it back to her.

"And I do get it, Sophie. Bad things should be buried – but pretty much after they've died, been autopsied, and the disease understood."

Twenty-four – All Things Wonderful

Carl sprinted into the room and let the screen door bang behind him. He had a big box in his arms and a half grin on his face. At the sink, Sophie glanced his way and returned his smile, feeling it swell in her chest.

"What's in the box?"

"A surprise. Found it at the secondhand store and knew you'd like it. Take a look." He set it on the table and stepped back, waiting for her exclamations of joy and appreciation.

She dried her hands and lifted the lid. The sparkle in her wide eyes didn't disappoint him.

"Twenty-two-quart capacity," he said. "Takes seven quart jars or twenty pints. You'll get a lot more done with this beauty."

"I really wanted one, but it's a lot of money, Carl. Can we afford it?"

He pulled her to him, hands on her back and sliding over her bottom.

"Course. I wouldn't have bought it otherwise. And you'll make up the money on canned tomatoes and spaghetti sauce. Think of all the food you can preserve with this. Even venison."

Sophie gave him a fake pout. "So, you're just trying to get more work out of me?"

"Don't be like that. You wanted it. You said so. Did you lie to me?"

"I'm teasing, Carl. I love it. And thank you."

"I know. Get cleaned up. I want to have a couple of beers at Henry's and get a burger."

"What about the pot roast you planned on for dinner? It's in the oven."

He shrugged. "It'll keep till tomorrow."

"You sure? Weren't you counting on it?"

"But now I want a burger at Henry's. Are you coming?"

Carl went to sit at the bar with Freddie, and Sophie found Dee waiting for friends at a table in the corner.

"Sit, Sophie. It's really good to see you. Where in hell have you been?"

"Home. Doing homey things." Her dimples showed, and she shared them with the bartender when he brought a drink to their table.

"All day, all night, all the time? For crying out loud. You've got to get out once in a while."

"I'm having fun, Dee. Don't be a poop."

When the bartender walked off, Dee scrutinized Sophie's eyes, looking for lies or hidden truths while she ran a finger in the liquid overflow from her beer mug.

"Are you? Is everything alright now?"

"Course."

"I mean – since you stayed at our place for a couple of nights. And the baby thing. He was alright with you being gone? No consequences?"

"Course," Sophie repeated. "Carl's great. You should see the pressure canner he bought for me today. It's huge. He's always bringing presents home to me and making things I want."

Sophie told about the bike he'd brought her, taught her to ride and painted candy apple red. She laughed with abandon as she talked, and Dee bought some of it. She told about the stone gnomes and the weekend of working together, and Dee thought it sounded fun and like her friend was giving her the facts. She told her they made love in front of one by the moonlight, and Dee sensed truth in the story.

"So, it sounds like you two have worked it all out and you're happy as clams or peas in green pods or something like that."

"Yes. We are. Carl is brilliant. I couldn't ask for anything more."

"Well, you could," Dee said. "You could ask for Tom Jones. I wouldn't mind his shoes under my bed."

Sophie smacked her arm and glanced around to see who might have heard.

"You're crazy. Don't talk like that."

Dee sat back and eyed her friend, trying to figure out what was different about Sophie. She couldn't put a name on it, but something had changed. What was it?

"Where's Rob?" Sophie asked.

"He had to work late. I got bored at home."

"Doesn't he care you're at the bar without him?"

Dee shoved back against the chair, and her eyes opened wide, surprised her longtime friend would ask something so old fashioned, so nineteenth century. That was it – the difference she'd noticed. Her clock had moved backwards to another time.

"Why would he care, Sophie?"

"I . . . I don't know, I guess."

"It's not like I plan on dancing naked on the tables." She grinned and leaned to bump Sophie's shoulder with her own. "I never *plan* it. It spontaneously happens when I get the notion to shake my bottom."

"Right. Now you're just joshing me."

"And that's when Rob would get mad at me . . . because he'd miss the greatest show on earth – no elephants, though, and he'd be sad he missed my dance."

"You'd make it up to him later, I'll bet."

"Sure would, and here come the other two trouble-makers," Dee said as two women joined their table.

Somebody ordered shots, and someone else reciprocated. The women's voices rose, laughter intensified with each drink, and Sophie cringed along with the loud guffaws. She didn't want to worry and tried not to watch Carl to see if he noticed, but every once in a while, she saw him look their way and a frown crease his brow. Not knowing how to extricate herself from the group without appearing rude, she smiled and tried to enjoy the conversation.

Not so long ago, she wouldn't have been bothered by the noise; she would have had fun without caring about being rowdy. She would have giggled like a fool if that was what she wanted to do. She tried to do it now, but it came out a croak, and she straightened her spine in frustration, angry at herself and her silly fears.

I can still laugh, damn it.

She threw her head back, opened her mouth, closed her eyes, and let it rip. She was still laughing when Carl tapped her head to get her attention.

"Time to go, Sophie."

She expected him to be angry, to yell at her, but he didn't. Still, the expectation hovered like a cloud about to be split with lightening.

"I'll be late tomorrow," he said after starting the engine. "Gotta fix the air conditioning unit in Glen's trailer. And this weekend, Mac needs my help with his car brakes. He doesn't have a damned clue what he's doing. People are idiots."

"You're a good friend, Carl. Anybody else need you?"

"Yeah. Freddie has some wiring he needs done, but he's not ready, yet." At a stop sign, he turned to her. "You were doing a lot of laughing with your friends. Do I know them – besides the stupid cookie lady?"

She ignored the name calling, hoping he'd leave it alone, too.

"No, I didn't know two of them. And they were pretty loud, weren't they? Sorry about that."

"Women," he scoffed. "What do you expect? They don't have any sense at all. Probably not a whole brain between all of them put together at that table."

"That isn't true, Carl. You don't really mean that, do you?"

"What do you think? Course. Even a dog has more common sense than a woman."

She wanted to argue with him, tell him how wrong he was, but thought better of it. He'd had a few drinks, and so had she. Any attempt to persuade him with logic would have to wait for sober minds. She'd learned that much.

And she didn't want him angry and driving. They needed this vehicle, and she didn't want to die. She went quiet and encouraged him talk about the work he'd be doing for his friends. He liked to talk about that -- in detail.

The headlights glanced off Charlie sleeping on the porch surrounded by a bevy of cats. He didn't rise with the noise of the truck and squawking of the peacocks. He didn't stand to greet them as they climbed the steps, so Carl knelt to wake the Dane.

"Come on, Charlie. Let's go to bed. Let's go, Charlie. Get up," he repeated in several attempts to pretend the animal wasn't dead.

Sophie put a hand on Carl's back trying to bring him to reality with her touch.

"Charlie's gone. He's passed on, honey. You know he was old."

The glare he gave her was both fire and ice, and he put his face into the Dane's ruff, felt for a heartbeat and pushed at his chest. When he sat, tears fell from his chin in rivers, and he swiped his face and eyes in annoyance. He needed to see. He needed to help Charlie.

He swatted Sophie's hand away when she tried to console him. He didn't want consolation. He wanted his dog. He ran his hands under Charlie's body, lifted and stood, but when he tried to figure out what to do, he turned in a circle waiting for the miracle that would make his dog live again.

"Where are you going, Carl?"

"Inside. We're gonna watch a little television."

"You and Charlie?"

He nodded and she opened the door for him.

They sat in Carl's big recliner chair, Charlie in his arms like a giant baby, and watched television until morning. Sophie watched with them until falling asleep on the couch.

When the clock chimed the hour six times, she opened her eyes. His hands had stopped stroking Charlie's fur, and the tears had stopped running in rivers. Carl's eyes were puffed and red, but peacefulness had washed his face.

"Want help?" she asked.

He nodded.

Sophie helped pull Carl and the dog from his chair; both had stiffened during the long night.

"Where you taking him, Carl?"

"Gonna let him lay in the grass while I make his casket. He'll like watching the sun rise and listening to the morning."

"I'll bring you some coffee."

She opened the door for them and turned back to her kitchen. When they'd gone down the steps, her first tears for Charlie gathered, and she blinked them back. But a few found their way from her eyes, and she cursed.

She carried a tall coffee to him and set it on the worktable where he was pounding nails into boards that would soon hold Charlie's body. It didn't take him long. He'd made many over the years for his cats – but never one this large.

Later, she brought more coffee, saw him sanding the outside of the huge pine coffin and tried to help him with the mahogany stain. He waved her away, and she went, unable to do anything else, unable to find solace in her own work. When he strode to the back yard with a shovel, she followed with one of her own, yet he waved her away again.

"Why not let me help, Carl? I want to help you."

He thrust the shovel into the ground and jumped on it, slamming the point deep into the dirt.

"Leave me alone."

The guineas had screeched all morning, and Sophie recognized the edginess in their *Chi-chi-chi* call, the sound they make when they're alerting mates to distress. She wanted to screech, too. She wanted to howl until the sky cracked open and poured its tears over the earth. But now wasn't the time. It would be her turn when Carl could no longer hear the release of her anguish.

She opened the door to the chicken coop, filled a bucket with grain and tossed it outside, apologizing to her fowl for the lateness of the day. Eggs lay snugged in hidden nooks, and Sophie collected them in the wire basket hanging on a nail inside the door. She nested it in the corner of the coop while she milked the goats and spent some time petting and talking with the females before brushing Billy with a damp rag and a stiff brush. With the milk pail in one hand and eggs in the other, she headed for the house.

Carl's head and shoulders showed above the hole he stood in, and she knew it would soon be time to bury Charlie. She fixed a strong whiskey and coke in a mason jar, poured red wine for herself, and carried both to the back yard. It was only two o'clock, but she didn't care.

Without asking his permission, she helped lower the casket and return the dirt to its original place. She handed him his drink, and he didn't say a word, but his eyes did, and he put an arm on her shoulders while they said silent goodbyes.

Twenty-five – When a Lie is a Wish

"Good things get buried, too, John Wayne, not just the bad. You saw the pet cemetery in our back yard. Every animal in there was good."

"I agree. Animals are naturally good. I don't think they understand anything at all about the kind of venom people know and use every day. And they don't know anything about bullets."

They sat on the blanket by the small lake soaking up the afternoon sun and talking about Charlie and the other dogs who had followed him. While many cats lived with them simultaneously, a dog was king or queen of the castle all alone. They didn't have to share the love or the kingdom with another canine.

Sophie tapped at the plastic glass that held the last of her merlot with a hard fingernail and let her eyes rest on the smooth glass of the lake. A gull swooped in, and ripples circled out from its disturbance before settling back into a mirror of the sky.

"Charlie was a good dog, and Carl loved him. He loves cats and dogs – lots more than people. He doesn't like them at all."

"Thank you for telling me about him, Sophie. But it makes Carl even more difficult to understand. Do you know what I mean?"

She chuckled without humor, and he realized what a stupid question he'd asked. Of course, she knew the dichotomy of Carl. She lives – or lived – his contradictions.

Sophie fought with the straps of her bathing suit, shoved most of her unruly breasts back into the cups, and pushed herself vertical, butt first.

"I want to go in for another swim before we head back, but you have to come to. I need your fingers in mine."

He grinned, grabbed the extended hand, and let her pull him upright.

"Come on Chicken Little. Let's go."

He dragged her back out to the middle away from scary, predatory weeds, and they floated on their backs and talked about the clouds again.

"You ever come out here with your husband?"

"Sometimes we went to a swimming hole a lot like this one, at night. It was his favorite time to swim. Brought Charlie with us a lot, and the next one." She spent a moment remembering which one that was. "Most of our dogs were hounds, and Danny was a long-legged beauty. Boy could he howl."

John gave a loud, hound dog wail, and Sophie sunk under the water and came up sputtering.

"Damn it, John. You scared me to death, and I almost drowned myself."

He chuckled. "Sorry. Couldn't help it." He swam in a circle around her, chicken clucking all the while. "I can't believe you'd be afraid of anything, Sophie. You're a tough bird, the things you've been through. How can a howl and a little ole weed scare you?"

"I've always been afraid." Her whisper came from some place far away, deep in her soul, and timid like she confessed to a priest in whom she had little faith. "I was afraid to stay and afraid to leave. Didn't think I had it in me to take care of myself, and afraid no one else would want to. And then it was too late."

Her sorrow turned to anger inside John, and no matter what she believed, he knew Carl had lied to her, over and over, to keep her with him. He wasn't the trustworthy man Sophie thought him to be.

"You realize what he said wasn't true, right? I'm betting many men would've liked the opportunity to take care of you. But you could have done that on your own, Sophie. Very well, in fact, and all by yourself."

He tugged at the long, silver hair floating on the water's surface, haloing her face, and she tilted her head to look at him.

"He told me no one would. And I was afraid somebody would know the truth about Carl and me and think it was my fault. Like somehow, I'd made him mean and miserable. Or I was afraid they'd hear the truth and not believe it; think I was telling lies about him. I didn't give them the chance."

"So, when you told Dee all the wonderful things you and Carl did together and how happy you were, you were lying?"

"I don't lie, Carl," she snapped. Her hand flew to cover her mouth, her eyes grew to worldwide orbs in surprise, and she wobbled trying to stay afloat. "I meant John. Sorry."

His head had popped out of the water to look at her. "Was that Freudian?"

"No. Yes. I guess. Carl hates lies, and I don't lie to him, really. But he thinks if I simply change my mind from one thing to the other, like what I'm going to make for dinner, I'm lying. It's really strange." She spread her arms wide as if hugging the universe and brought them together to hug herself. "I know what lying is. I was taught how to do it at an early age, but I didn't think I used that particular skill as an adult. When I told Dee stories, it was more like wishing. I didn't think of it as dishonest until a few years back. Let's go in now. Take my hand, please."

John towed her back to the grassy bank without comment. He threw a towel to her and dried himself off, put the blanket and picnic trash in Lily's saddle bags and waited for

Sophie to dress. His mind burned with questions about a man he'd yet to meet, a man she talked about like he'd be coming around the corner any moment. And he wondered.

And he angered.

Talk about lies hovered and snapped at pieces of her happiness until the Harley picked up speed and wind blew the memory away. She briefly thought about chores waiting, about Peony needing to be fed and goats milked, but soon settled back and dropped her hands from the handles, let them swing limply by her sides.

Lily moved over the gravel as if her tires were made of clouds, and Sophie closed her eyes to savor the sensation but quickly opened them again so she wouldn't miss a blade of grass, a chipmunk, a thread of sunlight shafting through the trees.

Back in the house, she stripped off her damp clothes and pulled Carl's white shirt over her bathing suit. Grabbing Peony's bottle and stuffing feet into her stinky boots, she slogged to the animal enclosures, Fannie following close so she didn't get left behind again.

"You can feed Peony," she called to John. "Don't you need to get dry?"

"Nope. I'm good. The wind did the job." He caught up to her and took the bottle from her hand. "I'm happy to feed Peony, but afterwards I have to leave, Sophie."

She stopped walking, rubbed her nose like it itched, and moved on.

"Well, that's good because I have places to go, too, after taking care of the animals. People expecting me."

The hard slap of her boots stirred up dust, and the chickens following after her squawked and stirred up more. Sophie threw open the door of the coop to get chicken feed, and he headed for the goat pen. He knelt in front of Peony to hold the bottle while trying to keep Billy from butting him for attention. He didn't need Billy goat smell all over his clothes.

"Will you get Billy out of here, Sophie," he asked, hearing her booted shuffle enter the goat pen. "He's determined to stink up my shirt."

"You need to smell sweet for some special reason? Going to visit a girl?"

He shined a big grin at her. "Did that already. You're my only girl."

"Bullshitter. Get on out of here. Go see your girl."

"Where you going, Sophie? Visiting friends?"

"None of your damned business, John Wayne."

She pulled Gladiola over to the milking stool and sat, sprayed her udders and wiped them dry. In the heavy silence, Peony's bottle emptied, and she pulled hard on the nipple, yanking the whole thing from John's grasp. She ran off, bottle swinging from her lips and him close behind trying to retrieve the stolen bootie. He slid in the loose bedding straw and landed on his back with a thud.

"Jeez. You're a worthless son of a gun, John. A kid goat can whip you. What on earth did they do with you in Iraq? Make you peel potatoes with a butter knife so you didn't hurt yourself? Or somebody else?"

He stayed prone in the dirty bedding, felt the back of his head where a bump was forming, and rolled his eyes her way.

"You mad at me again, Sophie?"

"What have I got to be mad about?"

"I don't know. But you sure seem mad to me. I do something wrong?"

She coughed, swiped at her face and blamed the dust.

"We need a good rain. My allergies are acting up."

He cleared his throat. "Mine, too."

Goat milk squirted into the metal bucket, and he could tell by the change in sound when she was nearly finished with Gladiola. He hadn't moved and lay still, wondering how to leave without upsetting Sophie's – allergies.

She patted Gladiola away and called Petunia over.

"Go on, John. I'm almost done and then I'm going to town. Gonna have a glass with some friends."

"You sure about that?"

"Told you I don't lie."

"Right. You told me."

She stripped off the shirt and bathing suit, splashed her hands and face with cool water, and dried and dressed for Henry's Bar. When her hair and teeth were brushed, she smeared red on her lips and dotted her cheeks with a little. After rubbing the dots together, her skin blushed with health and the effects of the light sunburn she'd gotten floating on the water. She misted cologne in her cleavage and smiled at her reflection. Before leaving the bathroom, she bent over, gave her head a massage, and flipped back the silver-white mass of hair. She was ready.

"Come on, Fannie. Let's get a burger."

Sophie circled the Bug, banged on its fenders, trunk and hood, and let Fannie in the passenger's side. When she was in the driver's seat, she blared the horn in a final effort to scatter sleeping cats. None raced away to safety, but . . .

"Sweetheart," Pete shouted at her silhouette in the open doorway and slapped the empty stool next to him. Two other men she knew only slightly sat at his other side.

"Don't you have a home to go to, Pete?"

"Not when I figure it's time for you to visit Henry's and me."

He grinned, showing all thirty-two white teeth, and Sophie wondered if they were as false as Pete. She vowed someday to find out, even if it meant having to kiss him and stick her tongue in his mouth. It would be worth it just to know, but she made a face at the thought.

"Hey, Joshua, Sam," she said to the other two men.

Lainie came with a hefty merlot and a smile.

"Missed you, Sophie. Where've you been?" She leaned her forearms on the bar, waiting. "I know you've been up to something or you wouldn't have stayed away so long. Fess up, girl."

"I've been busy."

She ran a hand under her hair and rubbed at the back of her head, wondering how much she wanted to share about John Wayne. She hadn't asked for him to appear. He'd done that all on his own. But now, recalling her earlier fit of pique, she questioned herself and took the plunge into the freezing cold water of disclosure.

"I've had company."

Pete's mouth opened, and he sucked in a gasp. "You have? And it's allowed?"

"Yes. Remember when I told you about a stranger on a Harley? Said he came right down our driveway like he owned it?" Pete nodded, and the other men shrugged ignorance. "He's been around a bit. A lot, actually. We took his bike to the lake today and went swimming."

"Carl, too?"

"Carl wasn't there."

"Bet he didn't like you doing that without him," Joshua said, leaning in to look at her.

"He didn't care. We've been swimming there before. And I'd forgotten how much I enjoy riding on a bike. He brought me a kid goat."

"Carl?" Pete asked.

"No, John Wayne. The guy with the Harley."

Joshua guffawed. "You're kidding! He claims his name is John Wayne?"

She nodded. "Beautiful bike. Calls her Miss Lily. And he helps me milk the goats when he's there. Feeds the fowl sometimes. He's a good friend."

"I haven't seen anybody like the guy you describe, and I know everybody in three counties. Where does this man live? I'm telling you, not around here," Joshua said.

"I don't know. He never said."

"Old man? Young?" Pete asked.

"Youngish. Maybe thirty. He's a tall guy and pretty good looking."

"Come on," Pete said. "I think you're making him up, just trying to rile me cuz of me loving you all these years."

Sophie pulled at her blouse to show the sunburn line on her breasts, and the men's expressions went slack as they leaned forward.

"Told you we went swimming today. I don't think you believed me. Now do you?"

The eyes staring at her squinted, changed from adoration to concern, and darted to other eyes for some kind of confirmation. They waited for someone besides themselves to pose the question they were all silently asking. Pete took the brave leap.

"Are you sure there is a John Wayne who rides a big Harley and brings you goats and helps you with chores? You sure you're not making him up?"

Sophie threw back her shoulders and gave each man a glare intended to burn. "I'm not lying. I don't do that."

"I didn't say you lied. There's all kinds of . . . uh, mistruths," Pete said. "Some could be just wishing. You know, about something you want. Some aren't lies at all."

Sophie turned from Pete and sipped her merlot. She knew about the word. Knew it way too well.

"Stupid word, *mis-truths*."

Twenty-six – Big Lies, Baby Lies

Sophie didn't mind Uncle Thomas, even thought him nice and handsome. In her five-year old mind, he was someone who bought her toys and ice cream because he liked her.

She heard the ice cream truck blare *Pop Goes the Weasel* as it rounded the corner, and her eyes lit. Uncle Thomas dug into his pocket for change, and she could taste the cold Creamsicle sliding down her throat. She bounced from foot to foot, heart thumping in anticipation.

"When you get back with your ice cream, Sweetie, stay outside until it's gone so you don't drip it all over Uncle Thomas' nice carpet."

Her mother's voice followed as she ran out the screen door and flinched as it slammed behind her. She knew the porch cautions by heart because they never changed. She practically lived out there when they were at Uncle Thomas' house during warm weather. But it didn't matter. Her mother always called her nice names when she was around him, and she didn't scold if Sophie got sticky stuff or grass stains on her clothes. For that reason alone, she liked him.

She took her time on the wooden porch swing, licking just enough so the ice cream didn't drip, and turned to peer into the window to the living room. They were sitting together on his couch, arms around each other. His hand moved on her mother's thigh, and hers pulled at the back of his head. Sophie stood and moved away from the window. She didn't know what they were doing, but it didn't feel good – or right – and she skipped down the porch steps and walked around to the back yard where she couldn't see them.

Nothing to do. No swing hung from a tree waiting for her to climb on, no sand box for making castles like at home. Uncle Thomas had no need for kid things, so she picked dandelions with the hand not holding ice cream and gathered them into a bouquet to give to her mother. When she looked up from her work, they were in the yard, watching her.

"Finish your ice cream, Sophie. Uncle Thomas and I have a surprise for you."

Sophie jumped up and held the weed bouquet out to her mother. "A puppy? Are we getting a puppy?"

Her mother's frown responded to the question, but she always asked. It was her biggest desire, a constant wish, to have a dog all her own. She'd call him King, and he'd protect her, keep her safe.

"No. Even better. We're going to a rodeo. You'll see lots of horses and clowns, but you have to be good. Hear me?"

"I'm good, Mama. Aren't I good?"

"Well, the rodeo will be our little secret, Sophie, and being good means you keep our secret. You don't tell anyone – not your brother or sisters or your daddy. This is just between us. Promise?"

Sophie licked in a frantic effort to keep the Creamsicle from melting all over her hand. She'd forgotten it in the excitement over the puppy possibility, and now she had to conquer the drips as well as worry over another secret. She had many to keep. Too many. So many they haunted her dreams and turned them into nightmares.

"What if I can't keep the rodeo secret? What if it slips out? What if robbers come and tie me up until I tell?" Her tiny voice whispered a wish to be standing in a different yard, a wish to be on her father's lap touching two-day bristles on his chin, even if he snarled at her like he always did. A wish that Uncle Thomas could turn into her father.

"Don't be so silly, Sophie. You're making up stories like always. Just don't say anything at all, and you'll be fine. Throw away the rest of that ice cream, now, and go wash your hands."

It took a long time to get to the rodeo because it was in another town. They went to a lot of faraway places, and she usually slept in the back seat of his big car until they got there. Sometimes, she pretended to sleep so she could listen to them talk, but she learned a lot she shouldn't know, and wished she hadn't heard it afterwards. But she kept listening.

More secrets for the robbers . . . like Uncle Thomas wanted to marry her mama which would make him Daddy Thomas.

Wouldn't it? Would I have two daddies? And then could I tell my secrets?

She wanted to ask but closed her mouth in time, shut her eyes, too, and lay listening to the hypnotic sound of tires hitting tarred cracks on the pavement, the whistle of the wind through the front window vent, and the hum of their murmuring voices. Her eyes opened a crack when her mother turned to look at her and then slid closer to Uncle Thomas, and opened wider still when she told him she had a big problem. He laid his arm across the top of the seat back and patted her shoulder.

"What's your little problem, Phoebe? Tell me. Let me fix it for you."

"It's not so little, Thomas. Told you it's a big one." She paused, considering her words, ordering her thoughts. "I'm pregnant." The words were whispered but clear, and she checked again to make sure her daughter was still asleep.

"You've been pregnant before, several times, as I recall. You should be used to it by now." He grinned and glanced her way.

Sophie heard the expulsion of her mother's breath and held her own.

Pregnant? Did that mean she'd have a baby?

"It's yours. Not so funny now, is it?"

Sophie felt the car swerve off the road and bump back on, heard Uncle Thomas curse.

"Don't wake Sophie. We need time to talk."

His voice was a whisper. "Come on, Phoebe. How can you possibly know the baby's mine? You can't be sure."

It is a baby! I thought so.

"How do you think I know, Thomas? My husband and I sleep in separate rooms. We have for a long time."

He slapped his hand on the wheel.

"Then why in hell don't you get a divorce? Tell me that? Why!"

"Shhh. What good would that do, Thomas? You have a wife, an invalid wife in a wheelchair. Easy to forget when she lives in the nursing home, right?"

Thomas sucked in his words and glanced away. She knew he'd been wounded, and regret washed over her. It was a difficult life they lived.

"I'm sorry. I didn't mean that. I know you see her as much as possible. Her health isn't your fault."

"I . . . Damn! I hate this."

Her mother shushed him and turned to look at Sophie, sure she'd be awake after her outburst. Sophie groaned and stretched, pretending to awaken. Wishing the rodeo gone, wishing herself at home with her daddy, wishing she'd been born without ears.

"Are we there? I have to pee." She didn't, but she wanted out of the car. Something was terribly wrong. Tears formed, but she didn't understand all of it and didn't want to.

He watched Phoebe's belly grow, and Sophie watched him. Fall came with yellow-red leaves and smoke in the air, and she started school. She liked learning new things but struggled keeping secrets from so many more people. Robbers lurked everywhere, on the swings and merry-go-round, in the classroom and on the floor taking naps with her. That's mostly where they tied her up and she cried.

Mrs. Johnson, the teacher, spoke with her mother about the naptime tears, but when Sophie explained about the robbers to her mother, the expected frown sealed her lips. Secrets were best kept from everyone. That was the only way to be safe.

She wanted to be good, so she made a decision to speak only about wishes because those felt good. She learned not to tell about things that made her feel bad.

Thomas met them at the car and helped her out of the driver's seat.

"Bring him in," he said, "I can't wait to meet my son."

Inside, Phoebe handed the bundle to him, and he lowered himself to the couch, lay the child next to his legs and unwrapped the blue blanket. He looked him over, brushed the wispy brown hair with a trembling hand, his eyes intense with want.

"You can't keep him from me, Phoebe. He's mine, and I want to raise him."

"I'm not keeping him from you," she teased and gave him her best smile trying to bring one to his lips. "We're here aren't we?"

He lifted his son and cradled him like he'd cared for babies all his life.

"What's his name?"

"Silly man. Tommy, of course."

"Jesus. Are you serious? Won't somebody ask about that?"

"Why should they? It's a name like any other. And he *is* your son. He even looks like you."

"This is ridiculous, damned crazy" he whispered, still gazing at his son, his imagination building a home for them all, even the children he'd never met. "Where's Sophie? I miss the kid."

"School. Did you forget about kindergarten? I need to pick her up at noon."

"Can you come back after?"

"Maybe. For a little while. He watches me now. He knows Tommy isn't his."

"Has Sophie said anything? Asked any questions?"

Phoebe's shoulders lifted, and her hands opened showing a question hovering in the air.

"What does she say about me?"

"Nothing. Not a word. But at night she prays no robbers will come tie her up and steal her secrets."

"Damn. I hate that for her."

"I know, but what can we do?"

"You can get a divorce. That's what. It's pretty damned simple, Phoebe."

"I will. Soon."

The ice cream truck didn't come in the fall, and there were no dandelions to pick, so she sat on the porch steps and made up stories about the people she saw going by. Some she liked. Most didn't stop to talk with her but walked on by, going about their own business.

Going about your own business was good.

One old woman paused on the way by, turned and wanted to talk. Sophie lowered her head and didn't respond, hoping she'd move on down the sidewalk.

"Aren't you a pretty little thing. Come here, girl. What's your name?"

"Sophie," she mumbled as she strolled toward her as she'd been told, but slowly and dragging her feet.

"You one of Thomas' nieces?"

She nodded, remembering her mother called him Uncle Thomas. So it wasn't really a lie.

"You don't talk much, do you?"

"No."

The woman cocked her head and peered into Sophie's eyes like she was looking for something sinister hidden in them. Sophie closed them but they wouldn't stay shut and bounced open again. She saw the woman's puckered skin and straw hair inches from her face and stepped back, afraid.

"Uh-hum," the woman murmured, as if she had found what she was looking for. "Are you a good little girl for your mother?"

Sophie laced her fingers tightly together and prayed the lady didn't have a rope. She didn't tell – ever. Of course, she was good. She bobbed her head up and down in a silent yes, and the woman left.

Her eyes stayed glued to the woman's back as it got smaller and smaller before it turned the corner. She wanted to be certain she was safe before heading to the back yard. The front yard had too many people and too many questions. She kicked leaves and pretended she was home until her mother called her.

On her father's lap, she plucked at his watch and tried to tell the time. She wasn't good at it, but she was learning. She showed him how to tie her shoes, ran the bunny around the loop and forgot what to do next. Tears pooled in her eyes until her father told her she didn't need to know how. She was still his little girl.

"What did you do today, baby?" he asked.

"Kicked leaves."

"That's it? You kicked leaves all day?"

"Yes. My friends and me. We rolled in piles of leaves, too, and laughed and laughed, and Sissy's mother gave us cookies and milk. I had the best day."

"I'm happy for you, Sophie girl."

"I have to go, Daddy."

Mostly, her father wasn't very nice after Tommy was born. He'd stare at the baby, walk away with heavy feet and slam the door when he left for the neighborhood bar.

When she turned seven, she knew Uncle Thomas really liked her mother and Tommy the best. But Sophie came with the package, and she figured getting ice cream in the summertime was at least something.

Ice cream was on the wish side of things, but she still kept it a secret. She wasn't sure why. Maybe because it didn't taste completely good.

Twenty-seven – John Wayne the Cowboy

"How can you tell when the beets are ready to be pulled?" he asked. "They're a bunch of ground moles hiding in the dirt."

John beamed over his ridiculous beet metaphor and watched Sophie to see if she appreciated his literary humor. With a hand holding the small of her back, she stood upright and groaned. She'd been picking green beans and had the bushel basket at her feet nearly full.

"You're a regular Jack Benny," she snarled, but her lips slanted in a badly disguised smirk. "Wonder where his buddy Hope is."

"All we really have is hope, Sophie. And we have a garden full of it." He waved his hands expansively, his face a deliberate phony ray of sunshine. "Where's yours?"

"Right here, John Wayne. If you recall, this is *my* garden, and I was talking about Bob Hope. You probably don't know him, but he was a compatriot of Jack Benny who you don't know either. You're a dumb shit."

"Why would you want to hurt my feelings when I'm working in your garden with you?"

She yanked at a tall weed that broke off, leaving the roots firmly fixed in the soil.

"Damned weeds. This is the worst possible place for a garden, worst in the whole damned world. I've been weeding this patch of ground my whole life and never get anywhere. Seems like it, anyway."

"Your back hurt?"

"Course not. It feels good bending over with my head in the dirt and my butt in the air. It's good for me." She shook her head as if talking to him was like talking to a child who couldn't learn or a scarecrow. "How come you're not done with that row, yet? You're slacking."

"I have to study each beet to see if it wants to come out of the earth. Your beans are just hanging there waiting, and you don't have to ponder if they're ready."

"Jeez, John. I like beets small and young, big and old. Pick the damned thing. Don't study it. Didn't you ever have a garden when you were growing up? Didn't your mother put you to work in hers?"

He bent to pull at the greens, and a plump purple globe came from the earth. He wiped his hands over it, dusting away clumps that fell to the ground around his boots.

"Look at this, Sophie. It's perfect. And I didn't have one," he added in a whispered afterthought.

"Well, your mother missed the boat if she didn't have a garden. She should've – and could've made you weed it for her. Would have been good for you."

"I meant I didn't have a mother. Or a garden either, for that matter."

Sophie picked up the basket and turned to him.

She grinned. "You do realize the garden and the cabbage leaf story is a fairytale. Right? Everybody has a mother. That's how you came to be, silly man."

"Nope. I don't. She left long before I could walk. Probably couldn't take being around the ornery man she'd married any longer. Or maybe it was me. Enough about her. Want me to carry that in for you? Are we going to can those beans?"

"We are, but finish your beets, and I'll take these up and get everything arranged. So your father raised you?"

"Sure. That's what we'll call it." His chest tightened, and he bent to the next beet in the row. He pulled gently, and the brown crown at the top gave way to a deep red sphere. His face softened as he wiped the dirt away, and the constriction in his chest gave way to peace. "Beet healing," he muttered to himself.

Watching his dramatic and swift transformation, Sophie wondered but held off asking. "Come on Fannie. Leave him to his produce pondering."

She left the basket on the porch and hauled the garden hose to a waist high outdoor sink standing like a prepared boy scout at the side of the house. She plugged the drain, filled it with water, and dragged a giant kettle to the back yard. By the time John finished the row of beets, she'd filled the sink, made a small fire in the back yard, hung the cast iron cauldron on a trammel hook over the flames, and filled it with water from the hose.

"Lop the tops, knock the dirt off and pop them in the sink, John. We'll let them soak while we snip beans. Want help with the beets or should I go snip?"

"Help, if that's alright."

One by one, they performed the intricate dance. They lopped off the greens, threw them into a basket on the ground, and let the beets drop into water that soon grew muddy. The snick of the knife through juicy stems, the splash of water as each beet plunked in, and their slowed breath of fulfilment serenaded the tango.

She had questions but withheld them in favor of working serenity. Aware of her curiosity, he'd formed simple answers, but a larger desire for their synchronized movements stilled both voices.

"You need a table here, Sophie, so you don't have to bend in half all day long. Do you have one I can bring outside?"

She pointed, and he found a bench in the shed, a narrow, plastic one, and set it up between them with the basket on top.

"You think I'm an old woman? I can't bend over?"

215

"Yup, I do. Not all day long without a pain or two for company."

"You're the only real pain I got." She snipped the beet green off and threw the top in the basket with the rest forming a good-sized mountain. It didn't take long to empty the bushel basket and fill the tub.

"Step back, John, or your fancy boots will get wet." She pulled the plug and muddy water poured from the drain and over the grass. "Spray them down good until the water runs clear and fill it back up." She handed him the rubber plug and headed to the front porch.

Before sitting down with the beans, she fixed two tall glasses of iced tea and took them outside to the porch. She went back in for a bowl of water for Fannie and two lap bowls for snipped beans.

"Here you go, girl."

She set the dish on the concrete, and an automatic sigh escaped as she sat, but it overflowed with pleasure. The scent of early autumn, the twinge of red in the oak leaves, and enjoyable company in work completed her day. She'd not had that last part before.

And this was a pleasant part of gardening, the part where you can sit and touch what you've grown, look at it and know it wouldn't be here if you hadn't planted it. Even nibble on one or two fresh, crunchy beans. So fresh, they snap like they're supposed to when you bend the ends, and you don't need a knife to do the job.

Carl called her names every spring when she asked him to till up the garden. Said she was stupid for spending so much time on weeds and vegetables she could buy in the store. He was a confusing man. After all, he'd bought the pressure canner, hadn't he? He ate the food, didn't he? How stupid could she be? She should have learned to use the tractor and tilled the ground herself.

Thoughts about Carl vanished when John came up the steps, and she handed him the cold tea.

He chugged half of it before sitting.

"Beets are soaking in fresh water. So, how does one snip beans?"

Sophie laughed. "One? Aren't we the proper English chap. One bends the bean until the end snaps off," she said in her version of British upper crust enunciation. "Try to make it break as near the end as possible so you don't waste bean."

"Gotcha."

He took the bowl she handed him and plopped it in his lap, mimicking her. Their hands found an alternating rhythm as a long-fingered brown one and a stubby calloused one reached into the basket for a handful, and for a time crisp snaps filled the silence.

Eventually, his ears picked out the trickle of water from her garden angel, the chatter of warring hummingbirds in a standoff for the nectar feeder, and the scratching nails of squirrels as they scampered up tree trunks.

He didn't forget his job or let his hands go idle but allowed his mind to follow the sounds of Sophie's Eden. Did it fill her the way it did him? He couldn't remember knowing a world with so many pleasing, distinctive voices, and, when he was elsewhere, he found himself listening for them and vaguely thinking something was missing. It had taken him a while to figure out it was the particular melody of this piece of the world.

The clamor filling his youth had been harsh and constant and clogged brains like toilet paper in sewer pipes. It was discord created by cars and trains, dogs barking and people shouting. The noise had made him edgy, even angry, and he didn't notice until he left it and drove north, away from the city, away from the jackhammers and sirens of progress.

The northward search for silence, to some extent, had led him down Sophie's driveway that first day.

"There's a lot of food left in your garden. Will it just sit there and rot?" His words were soft, in tune with the tranquil moment, but troubled.

"Nope. It's gonna turn into chowchow soon. The Brits call it piccalilli. Same thing, though."

He grabbed another handful of beans and waited for an explanation.

"Wonderful stuff. Green tomatoes, hot and sweet peppers, chopped cabbage, onions. Pretty much anything leftover. Chowchow takes all the castoff, the not ready, and not so pretty things still trying to grow. It's kind of like the schools for kids who don't fit in anywhere else but they're still great kids. Maybe even the best ones." She turned to watch his face. "Those things in the garden still plug along like winter won't come if they're still doing their work. Chowchow is my thanks to the garden for growing."

"I like the idea, but it doesn't sound too appetizing, Sophie."

"Castoffs usually aren't all that pretty on the outside, but look close and you'll see. A little vinegar. A little sugar."

"Kind of like some folks," he said. "Angels unaware and all that."

She snorted. "Stay on track, John. I'll teach you how to make chowchow because you shouldn't waste food. You don't disrespect your garden."

They settled back into silence and let the work take over until her glance awakened him from a temporary resting place. He waited, knowing a question hovered on her tongue, and she'd been holding it in since she'd left him pulling beets in the garden.

"Your father alive?"

He should have known she'd loop back. She was like a shark circling an unsuspecting swimmer, all curious and eager. The thought made him chuckle as he visualized the teeth Sophie the shark would have. Small but fierce, sharp ones, for sure.

"No. Passed on a few weeks before you and I met."

"Sorry. Bet you still miss him a lot."

"I don't notice. Wasn't much good for anything all the time I knew him."

"Fed you, didn't he? Kept a roof over your head? Respect your parent, John Wayne. It's in the bible, you know." She snapped a bean for emphasis.

"Grandma cared for us after my father's wife left, and I respected her. When she died, I took over."

"Took over what?"

"Everything. I played like the adult because he didn't know how or couldn't or just plain didn't want to because I was there to do it instead of him. I fixed the lawn mowers and cut the grass. I got a job and bought the food. Cleaned the house and washed the dishes. Cooked the food, too. All he did was eat it and sit outside in the summer and inside in the winter."

John tossed a bean in the dish on his lap, leaned back and crossed one long leg over the other – at the knee. It gave him a relaxed air, and he knew it, used it. But the constriction in his chest had reappeared, and he made himself breathe through the discomfort.

"What was wrong with your pa that he let others, even his own child, take care of him?" Sophie asked. "I never had kids, but I know one thing for sure. I would have taken care of them, not the other way around. Was he sick?"

John shook his head and lifted his shoulders. "Not body sick. Only in his head. First his mother took care of him, then me. He was my father, and that's all there was to it."

"How old were you when your grandmother died?"

"Twelve. Old enough. Fact is, I didn't mind doing it. Didn't think about *not* doing it."

He tossed a bean at her trying to get some levity back into the conversation or to leave off talking totally. It stuck in her wild hair, and he laughed to see it hanging there like green fruit in a white, shaggy tree. She plucked it out and threw it back at him.

"Don't play with your food, John Wayne. And don't think I don't know you're trying to get me to stop asking questions by using the old tried and true method of bean bombardment." She scowled at him, but affection tainted the effect. "You ask me about stuff in my life all the time. Every single damned day."

Rhythm out of sync, their hands collided in the basket as they searched for another handful of beans.

"Ha! Last one!" he shouted, holding it in the air like a trophy he'd earned.

"You're a little boy, John. Guess you didn't have time to be one in the life you lived as a real boy."

"My life was fine. Don't be thinking I mourn what it was. Others had worse."

"So, you're a strong, lonesome cowboy type, huh? True to your name? 'I can take it, mister. Bring it on.' Is that what you told yourself?"

"I didn't tell myself anything. I did what needed to be done. Forget about it, Sophie." He lifted the full bowl from his lap. "What do we do with these now?"

"Rinse them, fill jars, add salt and hot water, and put them in the pressure canner. Then we skin beets."

"Carl's gift canner?"

"You got it. Pint jars, so we can put in twenty. That's a lot of beans all at the same time. One more good picking, and we'll have enough for the year."

She had included another mouth in her calculation of food supply for the year and wondered if he knew it or guessed. If he'd noticed, and she didn't know why or how he would, he didn't say so, and she wasn't about to bring it up. She preferred living the lie, if that's what it was.

In the kitchen, she shooed numerous cats from the counter and table, left a couple sprawled on the refrigerator top like lazy lions after a feed, and washed the beans. He packed jars hot from the oven, beans standing like tall soldiers, and she spooned in salt and poured boiling water over them. She dipped the lids out of another pan of hot water and positioned them on the jars. He screwed on the rings.

"Not too tight, now. Just snugged. You don't need to manhandle them. But you don't muscle anything, do you, John? How'd you get to be an old soul? Your grandma?"

"I was born old."

He tightened each ring until it told the tips of his fingers to quit and watched jars filled with vivid green decorate the table. It was beautiful. It was bountiful, and he wrapped an arm around Sophie's back and thumped her shoulder a couple of times.

"I know. It does the same for me." She turned soft eyes his way, told him to be careful putting them in the canner, and handed him specially designed tongs. "Don't burn yourself. Let me know when it's full, and I'll lock the top."

He heard her blow her nose in the bathroom, even though she'd flushed the toilet for noise.

Calling out to let her know the canner was ready, he left the kitchen. At the outside sink, he drained the water again, piled clean beets into a metal tub, and hauled it to the backyard. He didn't have a clue what step was next but assumed the hot water over the fire was needed for the beets. For something.

He relaxed on the couch and waited. When she came out, she had a beer in each hand.

"Thanks for all your work." She clinked her bottle against his and tipped it up. "I need a little break, John, before the next chore."

"I could use one, too. You're a hard task master, woman."

"Growing and preserving food is work, but worth it. You'll see. You'll figure it out. I'm sure of it."

Fannie climbed on the couch between them and laid her head on his leg. The peacocks strutted over to see what was going on. Curious creatures. Goats bleated hello from the pen, and the guineas answered.

Cold beer slid down his throat, and John rolled his shoulders and let them drop and settle. His eyes closed and his head rested against the back cushion as critter voices seeped into consciousness, the sounds of a natural world. He thought if he listened carefully enough, he'd hear the grass grow, the leaves turn yellow. He'd smell approaching autumn and taste it on the buds at the back of his tongue. His voice was an earth respecting whisper.

"What's next, Sophie?"

"We throw the beets into boiling water, dip them out and put them in cold. When we can touch them without burning our hands, we slide the skins off. It's fun."

"Sounds like it. Shall we begin?"

"There you go again, talking like the proper English cowboy. And if you thought the beans were beautiful in their jars, wait until you see the beets. Blood red. And gorgeous."

Twenty-eight – Mothers and Others

"Your mother was a loose woman, and the whole town knew it, Sophie. For crying out loud. She had a fifteen-year adulterous affair and even had a kid by the man while she was married to your father. Everybody knew that, too. All of it. And she treated you like shit, so why are you so torn up about her dying?"

Sophie's hands covered her ears in an effort to keep his words outside her brain, to stop them from turning into ugly thoughts and finding a home in her head.

She dragged herself out of bed where she'd been hiding since the funeral, but once upright, she couldn't figure out where to go. What to do. She turned slow circles in the middle of the room, her hands twisting in the dirty nightgown. Her mother was a dark hole within, and every day, she looked for her wherever her eyes landed. She searched. She longed for her presence even knowing it was hopeless.

Phoebe was dead. Permanently, absolutely dead.

The thought pierced her in ways she couldn't describe and couldn't get over. Did all children grieve so intensely over losing their mothers? Did they want to close their eyes, curl into fetal positions and stay there because a basic connection had been severed? Had death cut the phantom umbilical cord?

Rivers of tears flowed, and every now and then, even when she didn't realize her mother was on her mind, gushing sobs heaved from her chest like a geyser had spewed. When that happened, Sophie looked to see if Carl had heard and she tried to stuff her grief down deep – somewhere in her private soul where he couldn't go. She had erected her own gate.

No trespassing, Carl.

She moved to the small balcony off their upstairs bedroom and plopped into a cast iron chair, praying he wouldn't follow. God didn't hear her plea. Carl's distinctive shuffle, the walk she'd come to love and loathe, sounded close behind her chair, and the tiny hairs on the back of her neck stood at attention. She thrust her shoulders back and tried to grow strong, to be brave.

"My mother did the best she could, Carl. And she loved us kids. She loved Uncle Thomas, too. Daddy is a mean man, and he's the one who should have died. Not her." She gasped at her words, surprised she'd think them let alone say them out loud, give them voice and substance.

"Your dad is a cantankerous old bastard. We all know that, but your mother made him that way. Women do that to men because they don't think straight. They can't because they're not capable. Women feel. Men think. I've explained all that until I'm blue."

"That's nasty, Carl, and I didn't mean I want him to die. That's not it at all. And she didn't make him mean, either, or make him be anything at all. He was always ornery, but she still took care of him until he found a girlfriend and finally decided to give her a divorce."

Carl crossed his arms and sneered at her, his head moving back and forth like he couldn't believe her simplicity, her idiocy. She recognized his eye rolls, the scoffing tone. They were part of the posture he assumed when he spoke with her much of the time, now. Not always, but most.

She wiped her puffy, red eyes and tried to wade through the knee-deep anger, but she was glad for the fury because it shoved her grief aside. She could talk when anger raged, but sorrow caught her tongue and tangled it in mute threads of emotion.

Lately, she'd been sleeping by herself on the couch, and this morning she cooked his breakfast early and slid the plate of scrambled eggs and toast in the oven to be safe from the cats. She wrote a quick note, whispered 'come' to Danny, the new hound, and slipped out the door as soon as she heard his feet hit the floor above the kitchen.

Brown crisp leaves scattered and circled her yellow, rubber boots, and she took a moment to sniff autumn before releasing the chickens and guineas and heading to the back eighty.

"I'll be back to milk soon," she told the goats as she walked away. "Be patient. Enjoy the morning, babies."

Wet from fall rains, the creek that had dried during summer now squished under her weight as she crossed its bed, and mud pulled at her boots. It would fill with snow come winter and flow like a real stream in the spring. She knew its cycle, knew her land like it was her child.

On her left, red leaves from tall sugar maples littered the forest floor, a fresh layer covering decades of fragrant compost feeding the earth. They piled against the sides of a weathered shed they used when they made syrup. Her lips curved in a reluctant half smile remembering days and nights there. They'd played the game of love waiting for the sap to boil. They'd liked each other. She thought so at the time.

She pulled a heart-shaped catalpa leaf from a tree that stubbornly hung onto summer, refusing to release all its yellow leaves. Fanning her face with the giant leaf caused her morning tears to chill and surprise her cheek with their presence.

"Damn, Danny. When will I be done with it? Carl is right. Why can't I grieve and get it over with, stop this craziness?"

Under a willow tree, a doe and her adolescent fawn awakened in a matted bed of grass and stood to watch her movements. Through feathered branches that reached to the ground and surrounded the whitetails, sunlight filtered, speckling their red-brown coats. The young one took a brave step toward her, and the doe snorted and nudged it back with her head.

She protected her child, and Sophie choked back the wayward sob. When the doe warned her with a stomp of a hoof on the soft ground, she called to Danny and hastened away from the whitetails. From mother and child.

Danny chased squirrels up oaks and pines and barked until she called. She laughed at his antics, forgetting grief for the moment in her joy of him, and watched as he tracked a different critter, his nose hovering close to the ground and long ears flapping. He took off, skin loose and sliding up and down over powerful muscles, throat baying as only a coon dog can, and when she caught up with him, he had his long, talented nose shoved into a hole in the ground.

"Come away from there, Danny. You don't know what lives in that hole. Remember the porcupine quills?"

Danny withdrew his nose and gave her a sidelong look of disappointment. It wasn't nice of her to remind him. Porcupine quills were undignified at best. And they hurt.

"Come on," she said, ruffling his ears. "Let's take the long way home."

They passed several small mounds of earth where she and Carl had buried jars of cash. *Money graves*, they called them, and *dirt banks*. She chuckled at the names and wondered if Carl had buried any she didn't know about. If he had, she would never know because he wouldn't tell her, and it didn't matter. Not anymore.

Carl had insisted on using the ground for retirement security because he didn't trust the banks or the government – or any institution at all. Or people. She hadn't known anything about banks or politics, early on, and hadn't cared one way or another. She'd been young and in love, trusted him exclusively – his knowledge, his magnificent brain.

As time passed, he moved her to his way of thinking. The only safe place for the money they'd worked hard to earn was the ground. Their own ground.

Walking by the burial sites now, she speculated whether or not that had been a wise thing to do with their savings. It could have multiplied many times over if they'd invested it, maybe. But she'd let him lead in money matters, in pretty much all matters, and now it was likely too late. She was older and wiser today, she hoped, and wondered if Carl had been right.

"I don't know, Danny. I don't know anything except I have goats to milk and chickens to feed. Let's go."

She was happy Carl's truck was gone when they got back, and, after chores, Sophie put the new, burlap wrapped plant into her wheelbarrow and pushed it to the nearly finished garden. She'd created the flowering sanctuary in memory of her mother and had taken her time planning and planting it. Today, her mother's favorite lilac shrub and a white concrete Saint Cecilia, patron saint of music, would complete the project.

Hosta plants rimmed the black earth oval, and, every few feet, cone flowers and forsythia dotted the open space. She dug a deep hole in the center for the lilac, filled it with water and patted the shrub into place. Saint Cecilia found its home in front of it, guardian of the garden and custodian of her mother's memory.

Sophie stepped back to look at the living memorial, hoping to leave her sorrow with the statue and the plants, needing solace. When a stream of tears dripped from her chin, she spun around in frustration and trudged to the house – angry and disappointed and calling herself a hopeless fool. She didn't know what to do. Working in the special garden should have fixed her, should have eased the constant ache.

Carl would not be happy.

She heard his truck lumber down the driveway, knew it was him because no one else came here, and no one else drove as slowly. Carl continued to harbor a controlling fear of running over a cat.

She ran to the bathroom to run cold water over her face, brush on a bit of blush and mascara and fluff her hair. She wanted to look like she'd been having a good day and was pouring them both a drink when the door opened.

"Where's the dog?" he said. "I got him a leg bone from the butcher shop."

Sophie swallowed and ran her hands over her shirt, smoothing its wrinkles, before lifting both glasses and turning to offer him one.

"Glad to see you, too. Danny's probably out looking for squirrels," she said, and sipped her wine. "He's been doing that a lot today. Want to sit on the porch?"

He nodded and headed out, taking the long, meaty bone and his whiskey and coke with him. Danny must have smelled the treat because he waited in an obedient sit, his eyes on Carl and the prize. When he had the bone gripped firmly between long canines, he dragged it down the steps and into the grass where he lay, chewed, and watched. His world was good.

"Freddie wants some work done this weekend," he said after a long swallow of his drink. "He's ready to wire the new room."

Sophie alternately watched Danny with his leg bone and her mother's flower bed, trying her best to keep her eyes on the dog.

"We're supposed to go to your brother's this weekend. The annual autumn camp out, remember?"

"Damn. You call Freddie and tell him. He likes you. A lot, if you recall." He smirked as he spoke and flashed an insincere smile her way.

"No, he doesn't. I mean, he does but just because I'm your wife. The normal way."

He glanced at the new flower bed, back at Sophie, and smirked again.

"Kind of like your mother in a lot of ways, aren't you? What'd you do all day?"

"Worked outside. There's lots to do in the fall. And I took a walk with Danny."

"I see you got the *memorial* garden done. Did you work on that all day?"

"Course not. But it's done, now, and I'm glad." She stuffed near tears back and swallowed the lump rising in her chest.

"So am I. I'm sick of all the crying. It's time to move on with life and the living. Get over it."

Her eyes widened and her back stiffened. She lifted the glass to her lips and sipped red wine, watching his face and trying to tamp down the rising anger. The heat on her chest burned and she knew when the telltale red grew from her neck and spread to her cheeks.

"You haven't lost a parent, Carl. You don't understand what it's like. The grief. All of a sudden, you have a deep hole in your life. You . . ."

". . . and I don't need to lose one to know what it's all about. And you need to get a grip on yourself."

She tucked her head and closed her eyes in thought. Her words were gentle when she spoke.

"You'll understand when your mother dies. Then you'll know."

He snorted. "Ha! I'll laugh. I'll dance on her grave. Spit on it. She never did anything for me except make my life a living hell. And I hope she goes there if there is such a thing. But I don't believe in any of it. Heaven. Hell. Purgatory. None of it."

"You don't mean that."

"I've said so since the day we met. She's a pious, holier-than-thou nutcase and uses religion to make everybody miserable. Jesus! On my knees all day long every Sunday. Praying day and night. Praying when a storm came, when it didn't rain and when it did. Praying over me like I was some kind of monster. Nope. She can rot in hell."

Sophie heard the words but couldn't believe he meant them. Though he was right about one thing; he had said the same with little variation over the years. But how could he hate his own mother? He was just trying to get a rise out of her.

Carl glanced her way, knowing he'd gotten to her and wanting to see the reaction on her face, in her eyes. He enjoyed it and thought if he poked enough she'd get over the damned grieving.

"Did you stop at Henry's after work?" she asked.

"I did. So what?"

Indecision plagued her. He made bold, ridiculous statements when he drank, and she didn't know how much he'd had. She shouldn't have offered him any, but he'd get his own if he wanted it.

"It bothers me when you talk about your mom like you hate her. She's your mother. She gave you life and deserves some respect. If not that, at least she doesn't deserve hate."

He slammed his glass on the table making Sophie jump and Danny drop his bone and stare. The air grew cold, and she wrapped her arms around her middle, sucked in air and waited for what might come next.

"I could watch her die and not feel a thing. She's nothing to me and you know that, Sophie. I've said so over and over. She's nothing.

He stood, grabbed the empty glass and strode to the kitchen. When he came back with a refill, Sophie said she needed to check on dinner and went in, letting the door snick quietly shut behind her.

Twenty-nine – Watch and Hope

John's hands looked bloody sliding over the rough textured coverings of the deep purple beets. He wanted to sink his teeth into the shiny flesh after it was freed of the skin. Did they taste as wildly glorious as they looked?

When he turned to Sophie, he laughed at the red stain around her lips and dripping down her chin. She resembled a well-fed vampire.

"Couldn't wait?" he asked. "I've been wanting to take a bite but thought I shouldn't."

"Why on earth shouldn't you? Snacking's the best part of canning. Can't get food any fresher."

He grabbed a small one, slid the bulb out of its hide and plopped it in his mouth. His tongue sang in joy. Tender on the outside and crisp in the middle, the beet couldn't have been better. It tasted of earth and sun, of greens and sugar.

"Jeez, Sophie. If I'd known how good they are, you wouldn't have many left to pack in the jars."

"Do you like them pickled?" she asked.

"I wouldn't know. Don't think I ever had any."

"We'll pickle some. Smells up the whole house and burns your throat with vinegar and spices. But when you open a jar and slice them for a salad or put them beside a sandwich, there's nothing better."

She covered the table with a rubber cloth so it wouldn't be stained by the beet juice, and they sorted for size, quartering the big ones. She made the pickling brine, and he packed the jars.

"Wipe them good," she said when he went to move them nearer the stove and the hot brine. "And put 'em on a towel. I'd have asked Carl to build me a red counter if I'd wanted red."

His eyes shined looking at the bright jars in two even rows on the counter, like a platoon of Redcoats on parade. He whistled a tune Sophie thought familiar, and the light melody brightened the room.

"Remove the bean jars, please. They're cool enough to handle now, and we'll need the canner. But don't quit whistling. You're pretty darned good."

He placed them at the far end of the counter on folded towels and away from the work area, taking his time so the jars resembled another regiment – except bright green this time. He grinned at his fanciful thoughts, and Sophie spotted the glimmer of fireworks lighting his face, wanted to save the bliss in his eyes. Could she preserve it, put it in a jar and stand it next to the beets?

She scoffed at her own thoughts of fancy and gave her helper a once over.

Canning with John was just putting up food, same as every year. It preserved the fruits of her garden, and this year was no different, except John had helped. And was in the way, too, she said, having a little talk with herself.

I wiped sweat from my brow like I do every year because of the excessive heat in the kitchen. I burned the tips of my fingers on the hot lids like I always do because I don't bother with tongs. And it feels good looking at the colorful jars of fresh food because I know I'll eat all winter. That's all. It's the same as every damned canning season, Sophie.

It was the same, and it wasn't. The darned man had turned the work into a novel experience, a new old pleasure. A fun time.

Okay, I'm growing used to his presence. And I like it. He's easy to have around. That's it, and that's all.

She stacked kindling for the campfire and ignited it. Flames took hold, and she backed up and squatted, butt on her heels and poker in the dirt – steadying herself like people had been doing for centuries when they tended fires.

"I'd help, Sophie, but I'd kill it. You're the fire woman, and I'm just good at tending after you've done your special fire thing."

"You're a lazy bum. That's all."

He poured wine into two stemmed glasses and sat back to enjoy the night. His eyes scanned the flower gardens and stone monuments, and a hint of longing seeped from his eyes. This Eden wasn't his, but it felt like he'd come home. He had tried to nest elsewhere but missed this place when he wasn't here.

"I have to be gone for a while. Don't know how long," he said, throwing it out there like bad confetti and waiting for the pieces to hit the parade ground.

She stared at the flames, not wanting to check his face for a lie or maybe just a smokescreen, but when she glanced, a fib wasn't there. He looked like he always did – a cocky cowboy, but tired. He wore fatigue like a frayed, shabby sweatshirt, and darkness circled his eyes.

When did that happen? Why hadn't she noticed?

"Are you alright? You suddenly look like you're . . . not alright."

He ran a hand through shaggy hair and grinned. "Don't be inviting trouble, Sophie. Or inventing any, either. But I do need to be somewhere else for a time."

"Guess I'll survive," she said with a toss of her hair, but a wounded edge hid in her words. "How long?"

"I never know."

He wouldn't explain further but stayed for a second glass of wine at the firepit before climbing on his Harley. It grumbled like her unspoken words down the overgrown driveway.

Red disappeared from autumn's leaves and winter trees became dark, angular sticks silhouetted against a cold sky. From her bed on the couch she stared out the window and watched a woodpecker search for breakfast in the cracked center of a tall oak. Lightening had tried to shorten its life, but it hung on, mending the angry split with sap and overgrowth, and the birds enjoyed its plenty.

She needed to get up, but weariness stuck her to the sofa. Once up and moving, she'd get over the ennui, she knew, but making the first step called for fortitude. Peacocks were already on the ground and parading to the back door, waiting for the handful of broken toast she always gave them. Damned greedy birds. And the goats' insistent bleating said she should put her feet on the floor. Get a move on.

"Come on Fannie. Wish I could train you to feed the fowl and milk the goats."

She glanced out the door on the way to flip the switch on the coffee pot. Nobody there. No bike.

In the bathroom, she took care of necessaries, donned Carl's white shirt that wasn't so white anymore and dragged a ragged flannel one over the top. The coffee gurgled as she poured kibbles for the dog and cats, and it was ready when she was rubber booted, hatted and scarfed. She poured a cup to take with her into the December cold.

Fannie wolfed down her food, met her at the door and leapt through it, ready to track down raccoons and possums that hadn't realized morning had blossomed and they should be in their dens.

Frost whitewashed the grass and showed her boot prints marking a trail from the porch to the shed. Her breath iced the cold air in front of her face, and she coughed as it stung the back of her throat. She hurried through the coop door, scooped feed in her bucket and tossed it outside.

"Gonna open the little chicken door, babies, so I can close the big one and keep some heat inside. Give you a warm place to nest today."

She turned the heat lamp off hoping the sun would do its job and headed for the goat pen. Billy butted her hip and she smacked him away.

"You're too damned pushy, goat. And you stink. Too cold for a bath, so you're gonna stink for a while."

Chores done, she swallowed the last of the cold coffee in her cup, hauled the milk bucket and basket of eggs outside and was glad to see the sun already warming the earth.

She glanced down the driveway, tilting her head to listen, and a curse slipped from her lips but only in a whisper. She wouldn't say it out loud because she didn't want to curse John and didn't care if he came back or not. Ever. She liked being alone with her animals – her land – her thoughts. Just . . . not knowing where he was caused her worry. That's all it was. And he'd looked way too tired for a young man.

"To hell with that," she muttered. "Worrying doesn't do anything for anybody. Think I'll dig a jar and go into town. Maybe even two. Don't know how long I'll be able to stick a shovel in the ground because it's getting cold early this year. It's gonna snow soon, Fannie."

Inside, she poured another cup of coffee and sat on the kitchen stool where she could look out the window at the front gardens. But they were all dead, colorless. Even the statues were gone, hidden in the shed and sheltered in a bunch of straw for the winter. What she saw outside was a desert, not an oasis, and she called winter a killer, a dark reaper, and named spring a rebirth.

She glanced at a mental picture of how her own springtime might appear, hoping, and gave herself a sharp shake. Swallowing everything but the dregs in the bottom of her cup, she called to Fannie.

With a canvas bag and a spade over her shoulder as if it was a rifle, she marched down the path, a gut full of determination churning the coffee in her stomach. The effort required to enjoy the morning's walk tightened the straight line of her lips.

"I'd think you would've learned to carry something on your back before now, Fannie. Dang. I'm gonna make a saddle for you. With pockets. You can carry supplies, too. I'm too old to do this by myself."

Fannie heard but chose to ignore Sophie's words. Her nose wiggled and flickered, sucking in the damp morning scents hovering in the air and waiting for her.

They walked a familiar trail worn through the woods to the back acreage, but it took her longer each year, and she stopped to rest more frequently. She used the pauses to soak in surroundings she knew like her own face in the mirror — maybe even better.

Her land didn't simply exist. It was a living, breathing entity, as much a part of her as it was of the earth or of God. Sophie devoured her property like a starving person, touched the soil with her hands and eyes, sniffed each change in the season's scent. Tasted all the variations of plant and dirt, moss and pitch.

She was the land.

From the marked spot, she counted out the required number of steps that would take her to a buried jar, stopped to look around for snooping trespassers, and shoved the spade into the ground. She knew the jar would be a good foot or so down and covered with several layers of burlap so she didn't need to be careful until she got close.

She worked up a sweat and gave Carl a piece of her mind with every spade full. Why couldn't he put money in a bank like a normal person? She heard the tunk of metal on wrapped glass as the spade tip connected with the mason jar and loosened the dirt carefully with her fingers to free it from the hole. A smile grew when the jar revealed hundred-dollar bills. He'd made quite a few big bill dirt deposits just for the fun of it.

"Don't need to dig two today, Fannie. This will keep us until spring. Need to fill the hole, though. Don't want to break a leg stepping into it. Who'd find me and cart my broken, old carcass back to the house?"

She shoveled the dirt back in, ran the back of her hand over the sweat on her forehead, leaving dirt in its place, put the jar in the bag and the bag over her shoulder.

"Nobody. That's who. I'd be bones by the time somebody looked for me. I be food for the critters, but I guess that's the way life is. In and out in so many ways." She snickered. "Let's go, girl."

The path led down one side of the property, curved across the back, and ended on the opposite side of the yard, near the cemetery. She stopped, as usual, to talk to the deceased critters, put a hand on each headstone or wooden cross and remember each as they had been – some a few decades ago.

"I see you Kate. You're a beautiful girl. And you're a handsome boy, Charlie. I still love you. And Callie. And Thompson. And George, Danny and Rhonda. Bob. Tootsie. And Tucker." The names continued.

It took a long while to address them all, but she couldn't leave any out, from the tiniest grave to the largest at the far edge of the cemetery. She visualized each one as she talked, and they came alive again. For a few moments, they were healthy and walked the earth by her side. Ears perked, alert.

She dropped the bag and spade at the far end and took a seat on a wooden bench. Carl had made it and regularly used it to contemplate as she did now.

Cold seeped through the heavy flannel shirt as she sat staring at the crude concrete headstones and crosses. Her life could be told by the words Carl had written on each. The burial ground was a silent motion picture, a visual of time on earth, years counted by those she'd loved and lost.

"I don't want to put you here, Fannie. I can't do it anymore. I'm cold now, hound dog. Let's go in. Want a burger?"

She wouldn't let herself look or listen for a Harley. She left the spade in the shed and averted her eyes from the driveway on her way to the house.

The bathroom steamed as hot water filled the tub and she shed her clothes. She wiped a clear space on the mirror and glanced at her reflection. Mud streaked her forehead and filled the wrinkles with black, emphasizing the years she'd spent on earth – shouting the years out loud. She grabbed a towel and rubbed at her face, splashed it with cold water and rubbed again.

What's wrong with you, Sophie? You're old, and you know it. And you show it.

She bathed in lavender water, dried, and donned a Henry's Bar shirt. This time, when she looked in the mirror to dot a little blush on her cheeks and apply lipstick, she gave a nod of satisfaction, plumped her breasts for the sake of cleavage and grinned.

"What was wrong with me? I still got it, Fannie. Let's go to town."

The flat of her hand slapped the fenders, trunk and hood, and she opened the passenger door for Fannie. She let the horn blare for a few seconds and they left, crawling down the driveway so they didn't run over any cats. Would the time spent driving this long trail while searching out cats total a week of her life? A month? She didn't begrudge it, only paused to consider the idea and chuckled. The driveway, with its gate and bells and lights, was a monstrosity, at best a curiosity, and totally Carl.

At the metal gate, she stopped, pulled it to the side and drove away leaving it open.

He'll be furious.

"I don't care, Fannie. I'm not gonna stop to open the damned gate when we get back. Won't do it. I'm doing things different around here from now on. And I'm doing them my way for a change."

She pounded her chest, shifted the VW, ground the gears like a teenager, and laughed.

"You should've bought an automatic, Carl. I told you a long time ago, but you don't listen to me. You never do."

Pete's car was in Henry's parking lot, and he was just climbing out of it when they pulled in beside him. His hair showed comb teeth marks and his shirt was starched, collar crisp. He called a greeting and waited for her to get out.

Sophie's eyebrows rose when she looked him over.

"Pretty damned spiffed up, aren't you, Pete? Oiled up hair and all."

"I knew you'd be here, Sophie. Little birdie said so. Where've you been, and how is it Carl lets you drive his Beetle all over the place now instead of fixing up your car?"

She stuck out her chin. "I just do. Remember women's liberation?" She snapped her fingers for Fannie and headed for the bar.

"I've been waiting a long time for you to toss that brassiere aside Miss Liberation."

Sophie called him a fool and stalked off.

"Wait up, Sophie. You're looking pretty spiffy yourself. You get all cleaned up for me?"

"You're still a fool, Pete. Always have been."

Lainie whistled and grinned when she spotted her in the doorway. She liked Sophie, liked her spunk, her sass, and her long white hair.

"You've been a stranger, girl. Is that cowboy biker taking up all your time?"

She poured a glass of merlot and pulled a beef stick from its plastic container for Fannie who smiled back wide enough to show a couple of long canines.

"Don't know what you're talking about. Haven't seen Mr. Wayne in a couple of months. I've been busy doing stuff in the house and yard, and that's the long and short. Taking a break now."

"Hey, Lainie. Am I invisible?" Pete whined.

"Would that you were, Pete. And mute, too. If I blink twice, will you disappear?"

She poured his draft beer and tweaked his cheek just because she could and because it was fun.

"Is your Harley man gone, Sophie? He ride on out of there like a wandering, lonesome cowboy, or did you give him the old heave-ho?"

Pete nudged her shoulder trying to find a crack in her tranquility, pushing her buttons. Sophie breathed hot air through her nostrils and tilted her head down to scare him into shutting up. Sometimes that worked.

"He isn't *my* Harley man. And sometimes I need a little Sophie time. I don't like having a stranger hanging around all the time. That's why . . . Never mind."

"Seems like you liked it fine a while back," Pete said, and Lainie rested her elbows on the bar and her chin on her fists to listen. "Even if he's only in your head."

"That's crap and shut up, Pete."

"Yes. Please curb the tongue," Lainie said, digging in her pocket and slapping a handful of quarters on the wooden bar. "Go play the juke box."

Pete palmed them and did as he was told. Lainie leaned toward Sophie, tapped her hand and lowered her voice.

"Everything good out in no man's land? You're not having troubles with the stranger, are you?"

"No. No trouble. I don't know why everyone is so concerned about John Wayne. I don't know where he is, and I don't need to know."

She slugged down half her wine and let the glass hit the bar harder than intended. Some sloshed over the rim and onto her hand, looking like blood from a gash – or beet juice.

"Sorry," Lainie said, wiping the spill. "I overstepped the bartender code of propriety."

Sophie smiled and reddened. She'd said too much. Words had come out of her mouth and had revealed things she didn't know she thought.

"Yeah. You're a lousy barmaid."

Coming here was supposed to take her mind off the damned man, stop her from looking for him every ten minutes. She and Carl had locked themselves away for too many years, and Henry's was her escape, her refuge from seclusion when she didn't want to be a hermit, a place she could fold herself in the figurative arms of friends. Even when she didn't like them too much, like Pete.

But today it wasn't working. She ordered burgers for herself and Fannie, another glass of wine for herself, and a beer for Pete. She *did* like him, the ridiculous man. He wasn't mean. Or too smart.

And that was a good thing.

Thirty – Watch and Wonder

She didn't think she could make herself rise from the couch and knew it had to be done since she'd heard the grandfather clock gong half past five. But her body was too heavy, too limp. Even her eyelids wouldn't move because they were weighted by weeping sand from crying in her dreams. They had no desire to greet the day, either.

Eventually, they unlocked themselves to focus on the woodpecker drumming on his favorite broken oak outside the living room window. She'd processed the hammering in her sleep-muddled brain as someone breaking into the house and didn't know if seeing the truth was better or worse. She was never sure about truth. Guess it would depend on who was doing the breaking in and why.

Judgment was a vague and transient thing.

But peacocks were at the backdoor screeching for breakfast, and Carl hated to be wakened by their clamoring. She had to admit the screaming bird demands were irritating, and she called out to them as she rolled from the couch to her knees on the floor.

Running a hand through her thick, tousled hair, she thought about cutting it off. It was in the way, and sometimes it tangled under the dog who frequently slept in the bed between them, or it got caught under Carl's arm and shoulder, and she had to wake him because she'd be pinned to the mattress, unable to move. Trapped.

But he liked her hair. And maybe that was true, she thought with a smile. But she believed he liked restraining her with it, too. Accidentally.

"Just cut it off and have done with it. It doesn't matter at all. Not a scrap." She grumbled along, making her way to the old toast container, grabbed a handful and pitched it out the door. The peahens got to the biggest chunks first because they were unburdened by the enormous, wide-spread tail of the peacock.

"Just like a man." She shook her finger at him. "You're all alike. Starved by your own masculine pride. Close your darned tail so you can run, peacock."

Carl had slipped into the room behind her and was mumbling obscenities at the noisy fowl.

"It's no different than a woman walking around on stilettos. Now that's pretty damned stupid. At least there's a point to his tail. It's for mating. It's part of his dance to attract the girls."

"Maybe stilettos are for mating, too," she said, waiting for a reply. But he never responded when she was right.

Sophie flipped the switch on the coffee machine, glanced out the window at fall taking over the front yard and then at the man she'd lived with for over thirty years. He hadn't shaved in the last couple of days, and there was no mistaking the white in the bristles on his cheeks. Carl's landscape showed autumn passing, and his color indicated an early winter had arrived. Some days the approach of that frigid season took over her body, as well. He was ten years older, so if he was winter, she figured she must be autumn – already.

Did they look alike, too, after living together for so long?

Standing with skillet in hand, it occurred to her she shouldn't have to ask what he wanted to eat every single morning. Shouldn't she know from years of doing it – or from having slurped it up and into her brain through some marital meal osmosis? But it wasn't that she didn't know what he liked, she did. She just didn't know what he wanted that day.

Couldn't he just smile and tell her so she didn't have to ask every damned time?

"What do you want to eat, Carl?"

"Don't care. What I want is to retire so I can eat anytime I feel like it, so nobody else owns me and has the right to tell me when to eat. And when to leave the house. And when to come home. I hate those people. They're morons. Every damned one of them." He yanked the stool away from the island and sunk onto it. "And I wouldn't be eating breakfast at six o'clock in the morning, either."

He rested his elbow on the table and dropped his forehead into a hand. "You about done crying?"

"I don't know, Carl. How about bacon and eggs and a good morning?" She avoided his question. Didn't want to talk about mourning or her mother's death anymore. She wanted a pleasant start to the day and to make him smile.

"I know you don't really hate those people. You don't want to go to work, and I get that."

"No, you don't get anything, nothing at all. You work when you want and quit when you want. Maybe if I screw up enough, they'll fire me and I'll collect unemployment." He stared into his coffee cup, his face unsettled, unhappy, and she wanted to cheer him but didn't know how. "Hell, I'm putting in my retirement notice this week. Wait and see."

Sophie ignored his grumbling, laid strips of bacon on the slotted pan, and put it under the broiler before turning to him.

"You should do that, Carl. Retire, I mean. We have enough to live on," she said to his retreating back.

Eggs sizzled on the cast iron griddle when he came back into the kitchen with an armload of burlap and set it on the butcher block. Beside the brown bundle were two jars packed with green. He slapped a paper with handwritten instructions next to the bundle and shoved it toward her.

"These need to go into the ground before it freezes, but I can't do it. I'm working late all week, and they've been sitting around long enough. Who knows? You might sneak a friend out here while I'm gone. A crooked one who'll steal you blind, and you won't even see it coming."

Sophie chuckled, making light of his comment, determined not to react to it, but he glared at her before letting it go and followed it with a boyish grin. He was good at those. They were what had captured her in the first place, and she was glad to see it on his face now. Truth or not.

They sat after she put food on their plates, and he poked a finger at the carefully drawn map.

"You know where this is, right? Near the old maple syrup shed." He lifted his eyes to check comprehension on her face. "Okay, count your steps from this point and take into account the length of my stride and yours. Think you can do this? Do it right?"

"Of course, Carl. I've been with you every time we've made a dirt deposit. I mean, I have, haven't I? I've watched how you do it."

"Put the map in with the others," he said, ignoring her question. "Don't forget."

Steam rose from the hot water in the sink as she slid in the plates and utensils and watched him slap the metal of his work truck before getting inside. She heard the horn blare and listened as the engine's whine faded down the driveway. Bells rang twice as Carl drove by them, but she could no longer hear the vehicle's hum nor the gate swing open and closed to shut folks out – or her in.

In her mind, the process unfolded like a dark movie, and she felt silence and solitude wrap around her, a not altogether comfortable mantle shrouding her. It took some time after his departure before the tranquility of being alone in her home seeped into her bones. The rooms were too filled with him – his heavy shuffle, the trail of his cigars, his body and his scent. She rushed through dishwashing to get outdoors to her animals.

It was too cold to wear the usual white shirt over her pajamas, so she sniffed at Carl's thick, insulated flannel hanging on the back of the door. Her nose wrinkled at the scent of old perspiration, gasoline and tar, but she put it on anyway, stuck her bare feet into rubber barn boots, and called to Danny.

"A fashion model I'm not, boy. Never was. We'll come back for the jars."

Hands wrapped around her coffee cup, she paused on the porch, Danny pressed against her leg, and her eyes strayed to the driveway. She imagined visitors, friends stopping by to pass time, share a coffee. How would she feel if a stranger drove down the driveway and pull right into the yard?

"Well, who'd want to? And they couldn't even if they did want to, could they Danny Boy, what with the locked gate and all. Besides that, I'd know if it happened because of the bells, dang, crazy man."

She moved down the steps and strolled toward the chicken coop and chores. She milked and kissed the nannies, brushed Billy, getting rid of some of his beard stink, and wiped her hands on Carl's shirt.

"You're alright, Billy boy. I think each boy goat I've had has been named Billy. Does that bother you, you're not the first? Bothers some men. I still love you because you're a pretty good old goat."

She left the pen and listened for bells or an engine on the driveway, not really hoping to hear one, not really caring about it one way or another. It was habit. What would she do with a visitor?

In the house, she strained the goat milk, put it and the eggs in the refrigerator and found gloves for her chilled hands. Grabbing the burlap bundle, she stopped at the shed for her spade, put the jars into a gunny sack for easier carrying, and whistled for the dog.

"Let's do a walk, Danny."

She and the dog of every decade had worn a pathway to the back acreage. The trail hadn't been deliberately created, but her years on the property could be counted like the rings inside a tree. In this case, though, the years were told by the definition of the cleared trail. What had begun with their feet picking a way through the tangled forest had turned into an easy and mindless meander on an obvious path.

Danny darted off to chase a scent, sauntered back to Sophie, and she allowed her mind to ramble over the trail of her years. Here on her land.

Her memory saw buds become leaves, turn red and fall; saw timid fawns peek from behind their mothers, grow tawny-red and strong; heard the return of migratory birds and their disorderly flight south when they departed. The pictures were burned on her brain as if a pyrographer had taken up his instrument to create a wood-carved masterpiece called *The Passing of Time.*

She smelled all the seasons and tasted them like pickle juice that salivates in the mouth, especially spring. She liked spring. For some unknown reason, autumn signaled too much time had passed, and winter called forth black and white images of mortality.

But life comes back, Sophie. Every spring. Remember that, you maudlin old woman.

When they came to the sugar shack, she paused as she always did to remember the many hours they'd spent in the shed waiting for the sap to turn into syrup. The loving, the laughter. She waited for the good memory to warm her, ran a hand over the weathered wall to help recollection along and glanced at the rotted cot still sitting along one wall.

And waited.

But waiting didn't work this time.

She left her bag in the syrup shed and pulled out the map, counted her steps, put a booted foot on her shovel and pushed. The ground was rain-soft and digging was easy, but the effort still caused her to perspire. She wiped her forehead and cooled off on the slow walk back to get the bag.

Once there, she glanced around and through the trees, checking for interlopers, and listened for bells that warned a vehicle was coming. Listening was habit, not hope, not fear.

She removed one jar from the sack, tightened the burlap encasing it and tucked it in the hole. With the dirt replaced and the ground once more covered with leaves, it was impossible to see it had been disturbed. She gave it a smirk and wondered which one of them would be digging it up. Her? Him? Some gleeful but unsuspecting future owner of their property out digging worms to fish with, was more likely.

Back at the shed, she turned in a different direction and counted her strides. When the hole was deep enough, she stood back and stared at the empty space, images of graves invading and her eyes turning glassy with thoughts of her mother's. She sagged against a tree and continued to stare at the hole, unable to figure out why it drew her.

Danny broke the trance when he stood up on his back legs and braced on her shoulders to look into her eyes.

"I know. It's time. Thanks, boy."

She buried the second jar without pondering who would unearth it and found she couldn't care.

They paused at the cemetery to pay homage to those who had come before Danny and the current cats. Again, she touched each headstone and wooden cross, said their names and told them how much they were loved or remembered.

Sophie wasn't plagued by the idea she had to love them all equally. She hadn't loved every single cat, but she'd still fed them, respected them. Gave them a pat now and then and what they needed to survive and be healthy. Life gave out odd connections, according to Sophie. Some cats you cared a lot about, and some you didn't so much, just like some people.

Large stone formations marked the corner boundaries of the plot, and she noted the space was nearly full. Sitting on the bench, she called to Danny, wanting the warmth of his body against her leg.

"Only room for a few more at the far end," she murmured. "We'll either have to move the rock statues or make a new graveyard. Don't want to do that. I want to be done with burying."

The dog whined like he understood her words and lamented with her.

"This property was made for life not death," she said, "but sometimes intentions lose out and stuff takes over. You get that, Danny? Sometimes you can't keep reality from raising its ugly head. It's a path you take, and you don't even know you're on it until it's too late to take a right or a left, and there's only one road left. Straight ahead."

She stood and stretched the tight muscles in her back.

"Let's go pull the last of the beets. That's reality. Carl likes beets, but he won't say so. He'll say they're just okay. And that's for real."

Danny stood, too, looked at Sophie and loped on old legs toward the garden. It didn't occur to her to be surprised at his comprehension. He was a smart old hound.

"Chowchow tomorrow, Danny. Don't want to wait for a hard freeze. Garden angels wouldn't be happy we left their bounty to rot, and we don't want to disappoint them."

She'd put the last of the pickled beets into the pressure cooker when she heard the bell jingle. A roast with all the fixings was keeping warm in the oven, and she hurried to clean the kitchen so Carl wouldn't have to see the mess when he came in. She hefted the basin full of vegetable leavings, stepped out the door with it, and saw his lights come around the last turn.

Thirty-one – A Fall in December

In the low light of a gray afternoon, she dragged a wooden rocking chair to the porch, bouncing the rockers against her painted pine floors and leaving scrapes she would be mad about later. She pulled a thick quilt out of the chest, took it outside, too, and wrapped in it to watch winter claim her front yard.

No straight-backed porch chair would do on this day. She wanted to rock like a baby, pretend she was snug in a cozy living room, staring at a comforting hearth fire. But the house had been stifling when she'd tried to rest there, and the outdoors freed her even through cold and aching bones.

A mug of coffee warmed one hand, and she studied the red, swollen knuckles of the other, tried to make a fist and to stretch it wide open. The fingers couldn't do either very well and complained at the effort.

"Darned things don't work right anymore. Nothing does," she said to Fannie who perched beside her, watching. "What do you want for Christmas, girl? Don't know if I'll be driving our Bug into town unless the roads clear a whole lot more than they are now and if I can get the driveway plowed. Maybe I'll make you some dog treats and put a ribbon on them. That work for you? Maybe I'll make some for me, too."

She snorted at the idea of eating dog treats, making a humbug kind of sound. "Some old folks do that, Fannie. They can't help it. Maybe I'll put some butterscotch chips in them, just in case."

Fannie nudged her nose into her arm in response and got the desired smile and ear scratch. She knew when Sophie needed her nearby, and today was one of those days. Her master's eyes looked but never landed, bored deep into the woods searching for something that wasn't there or maybe had been there once or twice – and left.

Snow fell, but it came down in soft, lazy flakes that landed on the porch roof, not her. It was warm for December, but it had already snowed a couple of times, and a few inches lay on the ground, painting the land sterile. It added to the barren feeling she carried around all day long and slept with each night.

Sterile might be hygienic and good for hospitals, but she'd take a few germs over an antiseptic Sahara anytime.

"Patches," she called to a calico slinking up the steps. "Come sit with me. Keep me warm."

Green eyes winked at her and glanced toward the wood pile. Patches had other ideas that included mice and a race, not a warm lap.

"Witch," Sophie said when the cat hunched her back in attack mode, preparing to catch dinner. "You calicos are all the same. Selfish critters. You won't be getting any Christmas treats from me."

The harsh words sat at right angles to her forgiving tone, and Patches flicked the tip of her tail and hopped off the porch. Sophie knew cats were created independent, self-centered, even egotistical, and she'd frequently wondered if that's why Carl loved them. Even halfway worshipped them. They're kindred spirits, he and his idols, and all of them were wholly consumed with their own personal needs. He wanted to be a cat.

"Maybe Carl was feline in another life, Fannie." She gave a second harsh chuckle.

Fannie left the porch to mingle with the hens who didn't seem to care she hadn't any feathers. She snuffled at the ground, trying to figure out what was so fascinating about dirty seeds, and nudged a chicken with her nose. The chicken flapped her wings in play, and Fannie nudged her again. It was a game of chicken tag.

"Maybe I should come play with you and the chickens, Fannie." The sigh came from her toes and spread.

You wanted to be alone, Sophie. You chose it.

Shut up. Who asked you?

Sophie stood, piled the quilt on the chair seat and shuffled to the steps. Goats and chickens were good company. They'd be happy to see her.

Her eyes darted cross country where the drone of an engine slowed and came to a stop.

Probably the mailman.

In seconds, it continued, but toward her as if plowing through the woods. The gate was still open. She still refused to close it in defiance to . . . something.

A visitor.

Her eyes lit and her foot slid from the step, bumped off the second one and thudded to the ground, followed by her back. She lay still, stunned by the impact, unsure if all her parts remained whole and connected. After touching her head where it had hit the ground, she checked her fingers for blood. They were clean.

"Hard head," she said, "but I don't know about my bones. Stop kissing me, Fannie. I'm fine. I think."

Groaning, she tried to sit but fell back and cursed. She tried again as a rusty green pickup pulled up and a pair of worn work boots exited the door, slowly, and then at a run.

"Sophie!"

In moments, he covered the distance between them and was peering into her face, patting her arms and begging her to be alright.

"Stop! I said stop it, John Wayne. What's the matter with you?" She slapped his hands away and grumbled that he was acting crazy.

"I'm crazy?" he said. "You're lying on the ground in the snow and I'm the crazy one? How long have you been lying here? Are you hurt? Did you fall?"

John's face was ashen and grim, fear choked his throat as he grabbed her hand and gripped it tightly so she couldn't rip it away from him.

"No, I didn't fall. I purposely slid down the steps so I could make angels in the snow. Adds to the thrill if you slide first and bump your back and head on the way."

Her scowl wasn't as fierce as she would have liked. She was too happy to see him, so the glare flickered and fizzled and worked itself into a grin.

"Sassy words for a woman lying prostrate on the ground. Don't make me pick you up like a baby and carry you into the house, Sophie. I will, you know."

She tried to sit and groaned with the effort.

"Just give me a hand. I can get myself up. I've been walking for years. Ever since I was a toddler."

She stood, but he could tell it hurt, and he pulled her arm over his shoulder, put his around her waist, and half carried her inside the house.

"You need cleats for those damned rubber boots you insist on wearing. They're not fit for winter wear. If you refuse to buy some for yourself, I will. What size are your feet?"

"Shut up, John."

"I mean it, Sophie."

She stifled the escaping groan as he lowered her to the couch, and his brow wrinkled.

"Get me some aspirin, if you would. Bathroom shelf."

He did, coming back with a glass of water and a bottle of whiskey he found in the kitchen. When she finished the water, he poured in a finger of the liquor.

"That's Carl's," she said.

He raised his eyes in question. "Will he care?"

"Nope. He likes shine or rye better now, anyway."

John pulled the blanket over her legs, pulled a chair closer and sat watching her sip the drink. She shuddered a couple of times, like she wasn't used to hard liquor, but continued until her eyelids drooped. He didn't know if whiskey and sleep were good for a bump on the noggin or not, but her pride not her head seemed to have taken the worst beating.

"Don't sit there and stare at me like I'm a circus freak. I slid on the steps is all."

"I'm not staring at you. I'm just looking. At you." He chuckled and crossed a leg over the other like he was in for the long spell. "There's a difference, you know. I'm looking for signs of things like – concussion."

"How about signs of me cussing at you for staring at me and looking for a concussion? I can curse as good as old man Finkbeiner." She squinted at him. "Don't you know him?"

John didn't answer hoping she'd rest.

The clock gonged top of the hour, and a blue jay called from the treetop. The damned bird never left her alone. The only birds she didn't want to hear – ever – wouldn't even go south. She shut her eyes and tried to loosen her muscles, let them detach from the tendons and bones to lie by themselves so the bruised flesh could heal without her knowing about it. Stupid flesh.

"Thought you went to Mexico," she said in a whiskey muddled voice.

"Nope."

"Could've." After a time, she added, "I wouldn't have cared."

"I'm sure that's true, Sophie. But I didn't."

Her eyes finished closing, her lips opened to release a light snore, and he rescued the glass from her hand. He didn't know if he should drive her to the hospital or not. Nothing seemed to be broken, but how would he know?

He watched her slip into a restless sleep, and the afternoon light grayed into darkness. The goats and peacocks bleated for attention, and he wanted to shush them but knew that wasn't going to work. He wrote a short note and left it on her chest before putting on Carl's flannel shirt, grabbing the milk bucket, and going out to them.

The shirt's fragrance wrinkled his nose, and he wondered when it was last washed. When had the ethereal Carl last worn it? He'd seen Sophie in it several times, but never the man, himself. In fact, he'd never seen him in the flesh at all, ever, let alone in Sophie's work shirt.

Sometimes he had a hard time believing a husband had ever existed. Maybe he was a figment of Sophie's imagination, a product of her desire for marriage and a happy family. The idea perplexed him but it wasn't his business, so he left it alone.

He tossed chicken feed inside the coop and shut them in for the night to keep the defenseless fowl from becoming midnight snacks for raccoons. In the goat pen, he let Billy rub his face on the ripe smelling shirt and knelt in the straw beside Petunia. They were so much shorter than cows, he couldn't sit on anything to milk them, even a short stool. He smiled when they turned their heads to eye him with affection and relief, eager to be liberated from their burdens.

"Goats have long eyelashes. Hmm. Who'da thunk it?"

Although awkward at first, it didn't take his fingers long to get the hang of it again, and he remembered Sophie's instructions. 'Like a lava lamp, John. You're not yanking on a rubber hose.'

The rhythm of the work and the music of throaty goat whispers soothed him, and for a time he forgot Sophie's fall and his own problems. It happened every time he visited her Eden, and, every time he left, the world materialized and drew him back into its rude vortex.

Sophie sat up and the note fell from her chest. She read it several times and visualized what might have happened if he hadn't come when he did. While it wasn't cold enough to freeze to death during the daytime, by nightfall she could have lost a couple fingers and toes. Or life.

The door opened and closed and his boots slapped the wooden floor. She recognized the sound of him straining milk and knew when he placed the container in the fridge. She thought kibbles dribbled into bowls and guessed he'd fed the cats when the bowls clinked on the wooden floor.

"Fannie, too," she said.

"Course. Good to hear your voice. How do you feel?"

"I'm fine. Quit coddling me. You're not my nurse."

"How do you feel about soup for dinner?"

"You making soup?"

He laughed. "I could, but no. I see some in jars on your shelf. Want some?"

"I guess. John, get in here."

When he stood in the doorway, she leveled her gaze at him. "I don't want a nursemaid. I'm old, not sick. And I'm capable of doing for myself. You understand what I'm saying?"

"I do. You're old. But I knew that before." He held a hand over his mouth to hide the grin, but it didn't work. "And you're capable. Got that. I'm a good listener, too." He turned back to the kitchen.

"You're a smart ass," she mumbled. "That's what you are. Probably always was. Even as a boy. That's why I decided not to have any kids. Brats. You all are."

She swung her legs to the floor, bent her knees a bit more to see if they were going to work, and stood. She wobbled, but the legs held her at a slanted upright position, and she shuffled to the kitchen to watch.

"What are you doing up?"

"I want to cut a tree. Will you help me?"

His eyes slammed open along with his mouth.

"You want to be Paula Bunyan? Right this minute? I thought we were going to eat some soup. And it's getting dark."

"And there's a plow blade in the lean-to. Will your old Bone Keesha take a blade?"

"Bone what? Blade? Old woman, you're confusing the dickens out of me. You must have a concussion because you're talking like a nut."

She fixed him with a glare and snuffled, stemming her frustration, needing his help.

"The blade is to plow the driveway. I think the tractor's dead. Carl shoots it a lot, but it might still work. I don't know, but I saw you in a truck. Is it a four-wheel drive? That would be good. Especially for plowing, and maybe it could get us to the back of the property. Won't have to walk dragging a tree."

He stood erect, his hand in the air like a traffic cop at a school crossing and waited for her to stop talking.

"Sit." He pointed to the stool.

She stuck out her lower lip and stayed planted upright, but only until wooziness overtook her and she had to brace herself with a hand on the table corner.

"Sit down before you fall down, Sophie. I don't want to have to pick you up off the floor again."

She sat. "You didn't pick me up off the floor. I was on the ground. Taking a rest."

He popped the top off a jar of chicken soup and hid his grin. "Okay. The ground."

"And you didn't pick me up. I walked into the house."

Soup plopped into a pan, and John set it on a burner. "Yes. You did. Crackers?"

She pointed to the pantry. "What do you eat on, John? You independently wealthy? Don't need to work for a living?"

He stirred the soup before answering, and two lines formed between his eyebrows. Sophie watched and wished she hadn't asked. It was none of her business what he lived on, and she'd hate it if anyone asked that of her. None of their damned business, either.

"Forget I said anything. I shouldn't have," she said.

"We're friends, right?" he said, eyes wide and interested in her response. When she didn't give an answer, he put two placemats on the island tabletop along with a couple of spoons. He left the crackers in the box and put it there, too.

"I'm beginning to wish I hadn't brought up the friends thing," he said, a grin trying to undermine the discomfort crawling up his spine. "It's easy, Sophie. I write for the Marine Corps. I talk to Marines and try to get their stories . . ."

"Stop talking. I was feeling ashamed of myself for butting in – and then I was feeling proud to be called your friend." She pointed at the shelf where her merlot sat, and he got it. When her fingers wrapped around the small glass, she continued. "I do consider you my friend, and I'm sorry I was a nosy Nellie."

He tipped his glass toward hers. "I like you anyway, Nellie, just as you are."

"Want to talk about it?"

"Maybe some. I was wounded, on disability, and they found out I could write and could talk to other wounded men. It came down to me telling their stories."

"In books?"

"No. For the military archives. Someday I might write a book, but I won't be using their stories unless they want me to. It's their tale to tell."

Sophie thunked an elbow on the table and listened to Fannie's howl as she chased stray critters out of the yard. She sipped her wine, left a red line on her pale lips, and licked it off with the tip of her tongue. Her heart missed a couple of beats and then revved up way too fast. She ignored it like she had been doing for a while.

"We think alike. Will you help me haul a Christmas tree up from the back acreage? Carl and I do that every year. Cut our tree from our own woods."

"Tell me more. It sounds like a good time."

"Later. Can your old Bone Keesha make it through the snow?"

"Absolutely. Got a saw?"

"Sure."

"Then you got the man for the job. Good name for my truck, by the way. Sounds African."

"I think it used to be before I butchered it. And where is this man you mentioned? All I see is a smartass little boy."

He beat on his chest and let out a Tarzan yell. When that didn't impress her, he strolled across the room, swaying from side to side in his John Wayne-the-actor saunter, called her his little lady in a down-home drawl, and winked.

That worked. She belonged to him.

And he was the man.

Thirty-two – Oh Christmas Tree

A few clouds kept the sun from warming their world, but they bundled up, climbed on the tractor, and called to their new hound, Tucker, to follow. Carl shut off the engine at each tree she pointed out, got down and walked around it, shook his head and moved on. It had to be perfect – the right size, with even branching, no gaping holes, and limbs jutting out at the correct angles. It had to fill his critical eye with the perfect vision of Christmas, repeat the flawless image in his mind. Carl was sometimes childlike, and Sophie smiled and shrugged with tolerance.

Christmas and Christmas trees were two of the few things he enjoyed. He liked cutting it, the satisfying scent of pine, and flawlessly decorating it. She picked out the tree, and he evaluated her choices, but she'd not trimmed one since they'd been a couple. He did that.

Together, they bought one new ornament every year, and each ball or figurine had special meaning glued to its glitter. The year's memories were firmly attached. Like the path to the back of the property, their years together could be told through each decoration. The year of the property. The year of the new puppy. The year of seventeen cats. The year of the goats.

"Look at this one. It's the silver goat, Carl. Remember when we bought it?"

She pulled it from its nest in the box and put it in his waiting hand. He hung it centered on a high branch where she could see it sparkling from her place at the end of the sofa. They'd moved Carl's chair to make room for the tree, and, from his seat, he could admire all three visible sides of the symmetrically adorned Christmas tree.

"Course I remember. Bought it the first year we got our goat herd. And we had that pain in the ass Billy who wouldn't stay in the pen."

Sophie's eyes shuttered with the ache of remembering how her first billy goat died. She knelt to hug Tucker, the yellow hound, and shoved her hurt away, tamped it down, and reached for another ornament, a crystal cat nursing several kittens who sprawled at her belly.

"Oh, remember this one, Carl. The kitties."

He grinned. She held it up to the light, and Carl took it from her hand.

"Best one of all," he said.

"It does catch the light nice, doesn't it?"

"I meant best because it's a cat with kittens, and that's what makes it perfect."

She bent to look in a box at her feet.

"How about this one? I seem to remember you loving the dove and its real feathers."

"It's a bird. Cats catch them in mid-flight, though, and it's fun to watch."

"I don't want to hear about that. It's Christmas, and this is a dove of peace. Please don't talk about its death."

He didn't respond, but he didn't bring it up again, either. Carl liked Christmas. The lights. The music. The idea of presents, even if he didn't believe in the reason for the celebration.

And the food. He loved Sophie's cooking during the holidays.

She heard the clink of ice against glass from the kitchen and knew he stirred his rye and coke. She picked up the pace of unpacking the decorations even though she loved taking time to look at each trinket and remember, to spend time sifting for gold in the attached recollections. She opened the box holding her mother's antique decorations as Carl came back into the room.

"I'm not gonna put that stuff on our tree. You're not thinking about doing that, are you?"

"Why not, honey? They're part of my past and they lived on our family Christmas trees when I was a girl."

"Because they're not ours. They're hers, and that would make it her tree."

Sophie didn't want to argue, so she closed the box and pushed it into the corner. Tomorrow. She'd talk to him when he didn't have drinks in him.

Carl's tree wore the big, old fashioned lights, not the newer tiny ones, and red, green and blue orbs flickered in the windowpanes like planets in a dark sky. Later, with the overhead light off, they sat in the darkness and stared at the glittering ornaments, remembering when each had been purchased, recalling who they had been at the time, or maybe who they'd wanted to be. It was a time for peaceful reflection.

Their voices were easy, merciful, and conversation drew on fragments of memory, some shared and some not; some remembered through words that nudged a spark of further recollection, and some forgotten but not refuted. Not tonight. Transporting their words carefully, they shuffled over and curved around stumps and holes, the way talk should always travel. And Carl's face became softer as night moved toward morning.

He liked Christmas a lot, if not his mother's Jesus.

When they went upstairs for the night, she brought her glass of red wine and he his mixed drink to the balcony off the bedroom where they stood side by side and watched stars blink in a cold, dark sky.

"Thanks for cutting the tree, Carl. And for decorating it. It's beautiful."

"It does look good, now. It's a fine tree."

She wanted to ask about her mother's ornaments hiding in the corner, behind the tree, not part of it, but didn't want to end the night troubled.

It doesn't really matter. They're inside me where he doesn't go.

She pushed herself into his side, and he drew her against him with his free hand. They didn't make love often, anymore, and that wasn't what she wanted this night, but it would be okay if they did.

She simply wanted connection, to fit together, to link flesh with hers. Lonesome wasn't for Christmas, and she needed his warmth as she said her prayer with the words stuffed deep in her heart where he wouldn't see them. He never looked there.

Sophie wanted to end the night with hope.

Savory sage and thyme shared the air with sweet cinnamon from apple pies cooling on the counter. The strong scent of pine from the tree and cut boughs layered on the windowsills completed the aroma. And without words or sound, the tiny house sang carols in praise of Christmas.

A turkey roasted in the oven, Sophie's contribution to her father's table where she and her siblings would meet for a family dinner. They would share a potluck meal at their patriarch's home in the afternoon so they could all be back in their own for Christmas dinner. One of the pies would go with her and the turkey, soon.

It had been a sleepy-eyed five o'clock morning, and she blinked the grit from her eyes and yawned. Carl still slept. She eyed the kitchen a last time, making sure food was safe from cat burglary, and left to take care of outdoor chores.

She gave the chickens and guineas extra feed in celebration of the holiday and left the small door to the shed open so they could go in or out as they pleased. The overhead trouble light gave enough heat to make a difference in the temperature, and some of them preferred it inside nesting in clean straw during the winter days.

She had pockets full of carrots and apples for the goats, and as soon as she entered the pen, they smelled the treats and shoved against her until she laughed, called them greedy buggers, and gave up the goodies.

"You're not very patient, sweet girls. And Billy, you might've gored me with those big old horns of yours."

She gave each one a second carrot, waited for them to munch it, and swore she saw their eyes light up when she held out the apples.

"Merry Christmas, goats. Let's get to milking because I have places to be."

She hauled the milk to the kitchen and was straining it when he came downstairs. Grunting a reply to her Merry Christmas, he grinned, told her whatever she was cooking smelled good, and pulled the rye bottle from the shelf.

"Why don't you wait until I get back from my dad's, Carl? We'll have a drink together while I put the rib roast in the oven."

He ran his fingers through longish gray hair curling over the collar of his shirt, scratched at a two-day beard, and shrugged.

"Don't have anything better to do." He grinned at her, poured a healthy amount in his glass, and added coke and ice.

"Why don't you go to Dad's with me, honey? You can have two big meals. You like to eat, and we won't have our prime rib here until late tonight."

"Nope. Don't want to spoil my day. I don't like being around all those people."

Sophie's breath released in an expression of mixed relief and worry. She wished he liked her family well enough to eat a polite meal with them but knew the time she spent there would be more peaceful without her husband along. He managed to stir things up every time, deliberately poking them with political or ethnic views they didn't hold, and she spent her own time dancing on ice and smoothing disheveled feathers. It was easier without him. But still.

She put the turkey and pie in her car, banged on the metal fenders, honked the horn, and waved to him as he stood on the porch, the early Christmas rye in his hand.

"Merry Christmas, Carl. I'll be back in a few hours. Please don't . . ."

"Don't what?"

"Never mind. Eat the food I left in the oven for you. See you soon."

It had snowed while she was at her father's house, and she crept home like a slow turtle to keep from sliding into a ditch where shoulders were nonexistent. The back roads were made of clay, making for a slippery drive in wet conditions and a treacherous one with a few inches of fresh snow on them.

Moisture built on Sophie's lip, and she cranked the defroster higher and moved forward in the seat to see better. Dark came too darned early in the wintertime, and threading her way through the murky tunnel of trees was nerve wracking. Her hands gripped the steering wheel until they ached, and she flexed them one by one and breathed out through pursed lips to ease her nerves.

She talked to herself and to the trees creeping by and wished she'd phoned Carl so he would know when to expect her – maybe come looking if she didn't show up. She snorted, startling herself, and laughed. Carl wasn't likely to dig her out of a snowy ditch; she'd found that out the hard way when she had a flat once and no spare. He'd told her he was busy.

"You're a strange man, Carl, eager to help acquaintances, easy with gifts, but unwilling to help me when I need it. What do you think about that, world? What do you say, night owl?"

Through the woods, Christmas lights flickered and disappeared, but she'd seen them, and the lingering sight helped lighten her mood. A farmhouse, she thought, and pictured a family sipping eggnog and opening presents with exclamations of wonder, love pushing at all the cheek muscles and squinting the eyes.

Her fingers relaxed. "It'll be fine. I'll be home soon. Wish you were by my side, Carl."

With a sigh of relief whooshing from her, she stopped before the gate to open it and was out of the car before she noticed it sat parallel to the driveway, open and waiting for her to come through. She saw the taillights of the tractor going away from her down the tunneled path and smiled.

"You're a good man, Carl. I do love you."

Sophie closed the gate and followed the lights, finding it easy going. No snow except what was falling, just a smooth hard surface leading her home. Candles showed in the windows, and the red, green and blue of the Christmas tree shot like the sun's rays over pristine snow in the yard. She swallowed the gathering mist in her throat and cursed whatever was wrong with her. He did nice things a lot.

She blinked and stopped the car as he climbed off the tractor, a shuffling snowman in Carhart coveralls and matching canvas hat with floppy earflaps. He grinned and fell spread-eagled on his back onto the snow.

"Come on down. Weather's nice," he said as he lay staring at the flakes turning the air fluffy and white.

"I'm not dressed for making angels in the snow, and I have to cart this stuff into the house." She leaned to grab the box in the back seat, took a second look at her husband lying on the ground like a boy, and changed her mind. "Thanks for plowing." She took two steps toward him, spun around, and fell backwards beside him. "Dang. Snow is cold."

"The physical properties of snow vary over time and according to region and atmospheric pressure," he said, turning his head to look at her.

"Uh . . ."

"It's an interesting phenomenon. I've studied the clouds, and . . ."

"Carl, I'd like to hear all about snow, and I'm eager to hear your explanation, but I'm in a skirt, and my legs are freezing to the ground. Will this take long?"

He jumped up, offered her a hand and pulled. Sophie's grin went from ear to ear and wouldn't stop. Looking at him like this made her laugh – in a good way.

"Thanks. Will you carry the big box for me? I'll get the rest."

"Sure. Meet you inside," he said.

Thirty-three – A Christmas Gift

Coming up the basement stairs, her hands clutched the rail Carl had screwed to the wall, and she waited for her heart to settle. Light flickered around the edges of her eyes, and for a moment she thought the electricity might be failing. Out in the boondocks, the company didn't bother trimming branches away from power lines, and heavy snow frequently brought wires to the ground.

"Electric is fine," she said when her vision cleared. "It's you who isn't." She grumbled at herself and pocketed her anxiety for later.

Feeding the wood furnace was a chore she hadn't minded before, but right now it irked her, especially the part about getting up in the night in order to keep the fire going. But it was a lot easier to frequently throw in a few chunks of wood than to start it fresh when the coals burned to cold, gray ash. She might need to have the propane furnace checked out and the tank filled. It had been a lot of years since they'd installed it – just in case they lived long enough and got too infirm to crawl down the steep basement stairs several times each day and climb back up.

"Too late now, Fannie. I'm used to wood heat. And I'm too old to change."

Fannie lay her head on her paws and looked up, long ears dusting the floor. She begged for breakfast with a woeful expression only a hound could muster, and she played it like a scene from Macbeth.

"You're a liar, Fannie. I heard you in the cat's food a while back. And don't fib because it'll be Christmas soon." Sophie gave her a meaningful glare. "Want Santa to put coal in your sock?"

The dog turned on her back, paws in the air, and did her best to look innocent.

In the kitchen, cats filled the island tabletop and lined the counters, waiting. She dumped kibbles in several bowls, called the umpteen cats by name and touched a tail or patted a rump. Into two bowls, she poured heated wet food, special diets for the ancients with no teeth, and shut them in the bathroom with their food for a while so the young ones wouldn't steal their gruel. The old ones needed some time to eat – and they deserved a little peace while they gummed their meals.

"I might not have any teeth someday," she said to Fannie. "Think you can learn to work the microwave to heat up my baby food?"

She stuffed bare feet in her rubber boots and tucked the pajama legs inside to keep them out of the snow. With two insulated flannels over her PJ top and the canvas hat on her head with its fuzzy ear flaps down, she made ready to brave the snow.

"Come on, Fannie. Let's go see the goats."

She froze in a stiff halt on the porch, feet rooted in place, when she saw the door to the chicken coop standing open. Her eyes widened in horror; her nostrils flared and gut clenched. She hadn't heard a commotion coming from the coop, but some evil, damned raccoon had obviously been in there. He had opened the door, like coons know how to do, and went in for a nighttime free-for-all and feathered snack.

But why hadn't she heard it?

She cursed herself and moved down the steps thinking about her chickens being scared to death . . . or worse.

And then she froze again.

Why were the guineas milling around, contentedly pecking at the snow like they hadn't a care in the world? And there! Deep boot prints marked the snow.

What the hell was going on?

She'd turned back to get Carl's gun when John Wayne exited the coop, ratty cowboy hat on his head, Carl's Carhart jacket on his back.

"Hey, Sophie. Good morning? Sleep well? Feeling any leftover aches and pains from your fall?"

She stood still, mind racing before an answer made its way to her brain. Recollections of yesterday floated in, and she reddened.

"Told you. I didn't fall. I took a slide."

"Pardon me, little lady. Feeling any, uh . . . twinges from your slip and slide activity?"

Sophie huffed, and fear faded in a trickle down her back as her pulse calmed. She'd forgotten John was here. What was wrong with her?

"Gotta milk." She headed for the pen, not wanting to think about her memory lapse and not wanting to discuss it with him.

He smirked at her and followed.

Inside, he grabbed a pail, settled himself in front of Gladiola, and told Sophie she could do Petunia. Sophie lifted an eyebrow at being told what to do but sat next to the specified goat.

Peony, who never, ever forgot John had saved her from the dogfood factory, nudged his hand and demanded recognition, which he gave. Warmth spread inside, and he wondered how he'd survived without her all his life.

"Everybody should have a goat. And I think Peony's purring."

"It's a goat, John. Not a cat, dang city boy."

"I'm not so sure some of your felines haven't tainted our baby goat."

"Tainted?" The word spewed from her mouth like her cats had been slighted. She plopped on her short stool, cleaned Petunia and had milk streaming into the bucket before John turned back to Gladiola.

"I just meant they rubbed off on her."

"Gentle touch, John. Squirt the first half cup at the cat bowl, don't forget."

A grin flirted with her lips and she turned away so he couldn't read her thoughts. He fit in her goat pen like it was his mother's womb. Like it had been waiting for him and his odd tranquility. Stillness seeped from John's pores like sweet sweat, and the goats accepted him, even begged for his attention. When Billy butted his arm, he didn't get upset or give him the back of his hand. He lifted his nose to avoid the smell, but he didn't yell.

And he remembered their names.

"Amazed you know them all," she said.

"Course I do. Why would that be a surprise?"

"Many wouldn't. A goat is a goat, they'd say."

"Well, they'd be wrong. They're all different. Look different. Talk different." He wrinkled his nose when Billy tried to push between his body and Gladiola. "And they most definitely smell different. Most positively, absolutely and unquestionably."

Inside, she cooked sausage for biscuits and gravy while he attempted to attach the snowblade to his truck. He didn't know if it could be done but had promised Sophie he'd try.

Every now and then, he'd look around for the man the blade, along with the Carhart coat and winter boots he was wearing, belonged to. He wasn't sure but didn't think Carl was around anymore, and he'd given more than a little thought to the whereabouts of the elusive husband.

And Sophie didn't say, or she wouldn't. Or couldn't. It was odd, and he kept shelving his many questions for another time, a different day.

Most of all, he wanted to understand her – to comprehend how she could live with a man who treated her without a shred of respect, had stripped her of the dignity she deserved.

He slid a finger under his cowboy hat to scratch his head and turned back to tackle the blade. She wanted it attached so he could plow the driveway and maybe the path through the woods to find a Christmas tree, and she'd get what she asked for even if he smashed every finger on both hands to make it happen.

He hammered the pins when he fit the pieces together, and the sound drifted into the kitchen where it entered Sophie's subconscious. Her shoulders stiffened and cold anxiety struck.

Carl!

She lifted her eyes to the window and her snow-covered gardens. The plastic covered angel with the stilled fountain wore a halo of white; the bench seat near the back had a thick cushion of white; and, in her mother's garden, the wooden pelican stood tall and glistening – a solitary black statement in a world of all-encompassing white.

Sophie scrubbed at her eyes, dried her fingers, and shook her fear aside. It was *John* outside. John Wayne banged at the metal, not Carl. But it sure had sounded like her husband, always out there tinkering with something, pounding away with his hammer, making something from nothing or madly turning something else into nothing. Frequently, she couldn't figure out which he was doing even while he was doing it, and she'd given up trying.

Carl liked making things, and it confused her to see him destroy them with as much satisfaction as when he created them, but she'd accepted his eccentricity. When she could.

Acceptance was necessary in a marriage, as well as being a little blind, a little deaf.

Bone Keesha plowed a narrow path to the back woods, and Sophie's fingers grabbed at the dashboard before coming to terms with the ride. John wasn't going to crash the truck into a tree. He drove at a snail's pace, pushed the snow off into the brush periodically, and checked on her with sidelong glances.

"I'm fine, John Wayne. Quit looking at me. You just keep your eyes on your driving. You don't want to kill any critters with this monster."

"They'll hear us coming and run off long before we get there."

"You don't know that. You don't know anything about the woods."

Her tightly strung nerves made her irritable. Yet she was honest enough to admit to herself that, while it may be Bone Keesha stress, it was most likely because she wasn't going out to cut a Christmas tree with Carl. You don't get over years of tradition like you're crossing a dry creek bed.

And truth is, she was accustomed to being a little on edge. Carl had trained her well, and that fact made her smile.

She'd wanted to walk to the woods, might even have insisted when John urged her into the truck, but a deep-down niggle hinted she might not make it back if they walked. And she *had* asked for this.

She bit her tongue when they went over a bump and cursed at him. "Watch for critters," she repeated.

He grinned and rubbed whiskers that could use a razor.

"Pretty damned sure they'll run away from the noise. They're a lot smarter than people who plow headlong into peril even knowing a threat is waiting right in front of them."

The tanks wait . . .

His memory surfaced and pooled inside where only he knew it existed, and he was glad she chattered on.

"Keesha makes a nice walking path," Sophie said.

He stopped the truck and cut the engine. "I think this is as far as we can go."

Grabbing the saw out of the bed, he went around to make sure Sophie didn't do her *slide* again. She had the door open and one boot on the rusty running board when he rounded the back end of the truck.

"Wait, Sophie. Let me help you down."

Her head snapped his way, and she jumped, not waiting for his outstretched hand. She landed like a gymnast with her butt stuck out and her arms extended and high as she balanced, doing her best not to fall.

"Jesus, old woman."

But he couldn't stop the grin, and she stayed in the landing position she'd 'stuck' until he applauded.

They found the perfect tree much sooner than Carl ever had, both of them thinking nearly any pine would be beautiful once decorated. Maybe some imperfections would even make it better, she thought. More natural. Sophie jiggled the snow from it before John slipped under the bottom layer of branches to saw its trunk.

"Timberrrrr!" he called out, stretching the word for the whole county to hear, maybe the next one over, too.

Sophie laughed and backed up.

"Think you're a lumberjack now?"

He stood, thrust out a leg and bounced it with pride, a whole lot of arrogance flooding his face.

"Didn't I just chop down a tree?"

"No. You didn't. You sawed it down."

"Doesn't matter."

He pulled a silver flask from his inside coat pocket, unscrewed the cap and handed it to Sophie.

"Merry Christmas tree shopping, Sophie."

"What is it?"

"Brandy to warm your innards."

She sipped, shuddered, and handed it back with glistening eyes. "Thanks. That's good stuff."

"It's medicine. For frost bite. Or maybe snake bite. It's hard to know what'll get you first in Sophie's boondocks."

With their tree in the bed, he plowed a turn around, and let the truck crawl back, enjoying the sprinkle of glistening sunlight poking through overhead branches. He cranked up the heat and opened the windows so they could listen to the songs of birds who liked winters in Michigan and stuck around for it.

Snow periodically plopped to the ground in clouds as squirrels disturbed the laden limbs, and whitetails stood motionless, waiting for their habitat to return to a hushed normal. They wore no fear, but a buck picked up a leg and slammed his hoof to the ground in warning, impatient for his forest tranquility.

Quietude.

It filled the warm cab of the truck, and Sophie wore it on her face. It had found a home in John's eyes.

Thirty-four – Christmas Miracle

It's Christmas day. I love Christmas.

In the kitchen, she unloaded the box of leftover turkey she'd brought from her father's house and Carl fixed them both a drink. She sipped at merlot, looking forward to their evening together, grateful for the peace of her house, for Carl, and for the holiday. She put the food away and cleared the island to make room for prime rib preparation.

"Want rosemary on it like last year?" she asked.

"Want to open presents? Now?" He tried out the grin that worked so well on her.

"No. I need to put this in the oven and milk the goats first. Can you wait for presents, little boy?"

She laughed, liking his eager eyes and matching grin. She loved him best when the boy slipped past his discontent and the creases at the corners of his eyes deepened. Youth was always inside, but Carl did his best to keep it there, hidden, beaten down. She needed to focus, instead, on the man who made angels in the snow, the one who had plowed the driveway so her trip down it would be easy.

Sophie gave herself a silent reprimand and him a return grin. Nothing should disrupt this wonderful day.

"Want to help?"

"Nope. I want to walk in the snow or something like that if we can't open presents."

She slapped the roast with a layer of kosher salt and rosemary and lifted the massive hunk of meat into the oven, turned it down to low, and washed her hands.

"I'll change and be right back."

She donned jeans, wool socks, and a thick sweater, and drifted into the kitchen to see him pouring another rye.

"Why don't you have that when we get back inside – after the goats and the walk."

"Because I want it now. And we can take drinks with us on our walk." He topped off her wine glass even though she had only taken a few sips.

"Hope you ate today," she said.

"Course I did. Put this on over your sweater," he said, handing her his insulated, plaid flannel.

It smelled like tar and gasoline and Carl, but she took it anyway, knowing her wool sweater would never be the same, and gave him a grateful smile.

She milked while he fed and locked in the fowl and they walked the path to the sugar shack, saw the moon sliding over the horizon and beginning to share the sky with the stars.

"Point out the little star," she said.

"What little star?"

"Bethlehem's. We should wish on it tonight."

"You don't believe that stuff. It's a crazy kid's fairytale, and that's all it is."

His words were muffled as if his lips were too cold to work properly, and she glanced sideways at him.

"You okay?"

"Sure," he said but stumbled over a small branch in the path. Liquid splashed out of the glass and over his glove, and she looked his way again. "I just need to get another drink. Spilled this one."

"Let's go around the back way. It's a little longer but it's a beautiful night for a walk. We'll fix another one as soon as we get back to the house."

She hurried to the goat barn to retrieve the milk can and, in the doorway of the kitchen, saw him tipping the rye bottle over his glass, filling it halfway before adding ice and coke. Her tongue tried to tell him to stop, but her brain said it wouldn't do any good, and she knew which was right. She bit the tongue and hummed a carol as she strained the goat milk and checked the roast.

"Almost ready, Carl. Hope you're hungry."

"I've been waiting all day. Course I'm hungry."

She covered the table with a bright green cloth and arranged the set of good dishes he'd given to her for Christmas several years ago. The candlesticks were gifts from him, too. He picked one up and stared at her.

"Where'd this come from, Sophie?"

"From you, Christmas four years ago." He needed to hear words of praise, and she gave it to him. "They're beautiful, and I love them. They're perfect with the dishes."

He touched the gold-edged plates.

"And these?"

"From you, too, Carl. You give wonderful presents, and I love them all."

She hurried to finish dinner and put the roast on a gilt platter surrounded by baby potatoes and browned carrots and carried it to the table.

"You want to carve?" she asked, offering the long knife to him and hoping he'd decline.

He shuffled over, grabbed the knife, and she jumped back a couple of steps as he hacked at the space between the ribs, nicking bone and shredding meat.

She bit her lip and let him hack. Thick slabs quickly lay next to tiny, thin pieces, and he swore at the stupid meat, the stupid knife. Chunks slid off the platter and fell to the floor where several cats waited, whiskers twitching, and Sophie wondered how they knew he'd make a prime rib pile on the floor for them.

He'd be mad tomorrow when he wanted leftovers and blame her for botching the meal and the carving, but a sober mad was safer than correcting him now.

It was still excellent roast beef. It looked funny but would taste wonderful.

He ate, and she was hopeful; maybe the food would soak up the alcohol. But he was fast, and before she'd gotten halfway through her plate, he was making another drink.

She looked back at other Christmases, other days when Carl didn't have to work, and couldn't remember when rye began to take over the day. When did a drink begin to mean more than breakfast? More than her? But she couldn't remember when it hadn't.

"Come on," he shouted from the living room. "Let's do presents."

She left her food and scooted in. He sat in the middle of the room on the floor, a brightly wrapped gift in one hand and a grin on his face.

"From you?" he asked. "Or Santa Claus?"

He shook it, and she reached out to stop him.

"Don't shake it, Carl. You might break it."

"Did you buy me cheap, breakable junk?"

"Open it and see." She knew he'd love the laptop but didn't want him trying to operate it now. He'd shoot it if he couldn't make it work right. As soon as he had the box open, she handed him another – and another, distracting him like a child with a toy gun and foam bullets he could shoot in the house and not do damage.

Sophie grinned, slid the computer away, hid it under the sofa, hoping he'd forget he'd received one. For tonight.

He shoved packages at her, and she cooed over three porcelain angels, tried on her new plaid flannel shirt, told him she loved the hedge clippers – and she did. But her eyes clouded over and filled when she opened the last gift box and say the tall pelican, the bird her mother revered. Her eyes spoke love when she looked at Carl, the kind of love they could have together, should have.

"Thank you, Carl. You're wonderful."

Believing he finally understood her grief over her mother's death, unstoppable tears and gratitude for his special gift doubled. She'd meant her words.

He reached for it, and, wanting to treasure the icon, she pulled it against her chest.

"I want to look at it for a bit, please, Carl. You've given me the best gift in the world."

"You're kidding. This stupid bird is the best thing I've ever given you? After all the things I've gotten for you? Jesus, I never should have bought it." He kicked at the piles of torn wrapping paper and turned in a circle, rubbed his head and cut her a heated glare.

"What I mean is, it says you care about me. It says you understand." Tears clouded her vision. She'd been wrong, and she stared at the bird wondering why it had meant so much.

"I don't know what I was thinking buying that thing. You'll never quit bawling over her. I thought you might be done. Give it here."

She stiffened. "No. It's my present from you, and I love it. I love all of them. Thank you. I love you."

Mechanical, flat words poured from her lips. She didn't care because she didn't mean them, and they were the best she could do. They were routine. They kept peace.

He grabbed for the bird, and she fell backwards, holding the pelican tight to her chest. He tugged on its head, and Sophie held on, refusing to give in, standing her ground because she couldn't help it. He'd given it to her, and it was hers. Hers and her mother's.

Carl let go, and Sophie tightened her arms around it, fearing he'd snatch it away, but he snorted in disgust and stomped out of the room. She heard his boots on the stairs leading to their bedroom, and she wondered if he was going to bed. Hoped he was.

She held her breath as the sound of his heavy tread shuffled back down the steps.

"Put the damned bird down. Now."

Tears slid over her cheeks, and she shook her head. She didn't know he had the shotgun until she saw the round end of the barrel pointing at her temple.

"It's mine. I know you gave it to me for my garden. I know you did, Carl, and I thank you, but you can't have it back. Don't make me."

"I said put it down."

She shook her head again but didn't speak and didn't look at him, didn't look again at the gun pointed at her head. She wondered if he would kill her for the wooden pelican. Or would he shoot her because of the tears she couldn't stop, or maybe he'd trade her for the rye.

She snorted, a cynical, guttural laugh.

When something doesn't work right – like you want it to, you blast it with a gun.

"I could shoot you." He didn't appear angry – unless you knew him well, and then you could see it in the hardness of his eyes. He nudged her with his foot. "You know that?"

Her eyes opened briefly, and she believed his words when she saw the disgust in his.

"I know you could. I've always known."

"I could blow your head off, bury you in the pet cemetery. Put you in with our last dog. You and Dan, lying there together. I wouldn't think twice about it."

"You could, Carl, but . . .

But what? She didn't know. Tears burned behind her eyes, and a painful lump tortured her throat, making more words impossible.

She heard her mother's voice. 'Give him the bird, Sophie. Give him the damned bird.'

Sophie shoved it toward him, her chin dropped to her chest, and her shoulders sagged. Nausea cramped her stomach, and sour bile filled her mouth.

"I'm gonna be sick," she groaned.

He handed her the half full wine glass, and she gulped like a woman dying of thirst, drank it all, and handed it to him.

He went to the kitchen, filled it and gave it back to her. Still holding the shotgun.

He left the house with the pelican, and Sophie heard the bark of the shotgun as he shot it – over and over. She stood and picked up wrapping paper and bagged it, put his new laptop on the footstool so he'd see it when he came in.

Without a word about the pelican or pointing the gun at her head, he sat in his recliner to look over the computer, and she took the paper out to the burn barrel and lit it.

Red flames speared the dark, piercing the night as Carl's anger had. When they dwindled, she moved like a boneless spirit across the yard to the goat pen. They heard her footsteps and came out from the shelter to talk, bleating sweet night sounds and gurgling when she rubbed their ears and soft muzzles.

"Merry Christmas, goats. If a Christmas miracle happens and I'm still alive, I'll see you tomorrow."

She looked in on the guineas and chickens, closed the small door to keep in the heat, and told them to sleep well.

"Lay well, too. He'll probably be good and hungry in the morning."

Thirty-five – Coming Home

They laughed as John awkwardly installed the tree in the bucket and filled it with sand, and they laughed as they battled over where it should stand in the room. They howled and punched each other as they hauled it to the perfect spot in front of a window, leaving a sand trail and cussing each other over having two left feet. And side by side, they toasted and grinned at each other when it stood semi-perfectly in its perfect place.

John swept the needles scattered in a trail from the front door to the tree, and Sophie hauled down the boxes of decorations from the attic. John made sandwiches, and Sophie filled the sand bucket with water to keep the tree fresh.

They ate together at the kitchen island, and she thought about asking what he would like for dinner, but didn't. He'd want hot goulash for a cold day. She knew it without asking.

How strange and wondrous knowing seemed.

While the tree dried in front of a fan, they did early chores. It had dried to dampness by the time they were back in the house, and Sophie poured two glasses of merlot and took them to the living room. Her face was flushed with excitement and her eyes glowed. Dimples made deep craters in her pink cheeks.

John had strung lights together and plugged them into a socket to check for burned bulbs. Two were out, and he asked her for replacements.

Sophie took a backward step and shook her head in enthusiasm. "You trim trees, too?" she asked.

"As in cut the branches with a pruner for uniformity?"

"No, John. As in stringing the lights and hanging ornaments."

"Course." He wrapped a strand of lights around his neck and arms and posed with hands on hips, looking like a brightly lit hooker. "I'm a tree trimmer extraordinaire. It's my specialty."

"Fool," she said, but her face hurt from grinning for so many hours in a row.

She held the strands while he threaded them through the branches, and they both stood back to assess, sipping at the red wine. They both hung the bulbs, and John was every bit as meticulous as Carl in positioning them to hang *from* and not sit *on* a branch.

"We buy a new one every year," she told him. "Cept this one."

He picked up a crystal cat with kittens, held it aloft and asked about it.

"Not sure when we got that one. We have so many cat ornaments."

"How about the silver goat?"

"The year we got our goat herd."

"With old Billie?"

She nodded.

He knew that tale and shot a questioning look her way, but she didn't appear teary eyed with memory. In fact, she was the essence of serenity, and he was satisfied.

When the ornaments were in place, she went upstairs and came down with a small box. She placed it on the floor like it was made of fragile blown glass, and pulled the cardboard flaps open with care. One by one, she touched each bulb and told him its origin. Some she'd been too young to remember, but she explained the stories her mother had told her about each of them when they put up their family tree every year. And she told him the bulbs hadn't graced a Christmas tree since the year before her mother died.

"Why not?" John asked. "They're uniquely yours, and besides that, they're beautiful."

"Carl doesn't like anything on the tree he didn't buy. Anything that isn't just ours."

John pondered over what Carl would think about Sophie's friend helping decorate *his* tree. About hanging her mother's forbidden decorations. But it wasn't his tree, now, was it? It could be a good thing for them all if he didn't come home for Christmas.

Sophie hung the first one, stood back and walked around the room looking at it, taking her time. The second one went on more quickly, and after the third, Sophie raced through the box, giggling with each one. She crossed her arms, lifting her breasts, and breathed a long sigh of satisfaction.

John watched her contented face and wondered again about the elusive Carl.

But his Christmas wish was for her alone.

"I have to run into town. You need anything?" he said when the tree was finished.

"I don't need anything. Not a darned thing, John Wayne. You get on out of here, then. Go on into town."

"Whoa, there, little filly." He stepped back a foot, out of reach of her anger. "Burr stuck under your saddle?"

Sophie kicked at the nearby empty box and grimaced, knowing she had acted like a smitten thirteen-year-old. And that's not what this was. The cinders just felt like it. She'd been having fun, and she wanted more. She was a child again. And she was selfish like one. And eager like one.

"It's mine," she said like a two-year old being asked to share and fighting the idea.

"What's yours?" He melted as he watched her smash holes through self-imposed fortifications and tear them down brick by painful, psychological brick.

John braved putting a hand on her shoulder, and she patted it, knowing she owed him an apology. And he didn't owe her anything. Her head hung for a moment before rising, chin lifted.

"I don't know. You, maybe. Wrong, I know, but what the hell? I'm feeling greedy. Maybe it's everything and anything I can grasp in the time I have left."

"And that's okay. Take hold and hang on like hell for all it's worth, Sophie." He pulled her into a hug, whispered he'd be back in a couple of hours, and left.

John's absence, the projected and imagined coldness of it, collected in her belly and came out her eyes as ice. And he wasn't even down the driveway, yet, or even out the door. She cussed at what she had become, and at her new, appalling neediness. Sophie wandered from room to room in disquiet, put on some music, made goulash and a cup of coffee.

He said he'd be back, right?

She watched the many colored lights flicker in the windowpane and envisioned a pile of gaily wrapped presents underneath the tree.

"What presents? I don't have anything to wrap! Nothing to put under the tree."

She raced upstairs and lifted the lid on the cedar chest at the end of the bed. Pulling a large, wool, Hudson Bay blanket from the top, she giggled and threw it on the bed. He'd like it, she knew, without question.

It was a cowboy kind of thing.

She continued to dig through old curtains and rugs, bedspreads and duvets, thick towels and sheets, until her fingers touched crisp paper at the bottom and her face lit.

"This is it. It's perfect."

Gently taking the found treasure out of the chest, she laid it on the bed and unfolded it from protective paper. Her father's beloved duster, a long canvas covering like the cowboys wore. It was slit up the back to allow for riding a horse and would keep the wearer dry in rain or snow. She saw him in it now – striding across the lawn because he didn't own a horse. But he loved cowboys and wished he could be one.

How could John Wayne not love a duster? It was a real one. Oiled and everything.

She found a box that would hold the large coat, wrapped it and the blanket, put John Wayne's name on both packages and slid them under the tree. They became the focal point of the room for her, and she couldn't wait for Christmas. Couldn't wait to see his eyes explode with excitement.

The driveway bells rang, and she soon heard Bone Keesha's loud engine inching down the driveway. Her lips stretched wide, and she made a guess how long it would take him to notice presents wearing his name under the tree.

"He'll notice right off, Fannie." She rubbed the dog's long ears and snuffled a laugh. "He's a man, and a man is always looking for something for himself. They're a selfish bunch, and don't you forget it. I'm glad you don't want anything to do with them, and I know you'll thank me for that someday."

His boots stomped several times at the entry, knocking off snow before he pranced into the living room shouting *Ho-ho-ho*, a lumpy sack hanging from his shoulder and a ridiculous red hat on his head. The ball on the top bounced erratically as he wiggled his head from side to side, and he grinned at her like she had to love him. Because everybody did.

"You are ridiculous, John Wayne."

"Yes, I certainly am. But Santa still thought I was responsible enough to entrust me with your Christmas gifts. He had some emergency and asked me to deliver them."

John made sad puppy eyes and turned his lips down. "Hope you're not too disappointed he won't be coming down your chimney."

"Fool. What did you do? Buy stuff?"

"Course not. I just told you. Santa gave these pretty packages to me. Got any more wine or should I open the one I brought?"

"I do . . . but . . ."

The picture in her mind flickered to Carl and other Christmases. To too many holiday drinks. To the pelican she'd had to repair and hide. To shotguns pointed at her head.

"You okay, Sophie?"

"Course." She grunted as she lifted from her chair. "I'll pour one for us. Hungry?"

"Always. What are you cooking?"

"Goulash. It's already done."

"I love you, woman. I love goulash."

"I know. So does Carl."

He stepped nearer the tree and saw two packages with his name written in bright red. Sounds without words rumbled from his throat, and he rubbed the scruff on his chin back and forth and stared.

"What the hell?"

"Don't swear, John. It's Christmas," Sophie said as she pushed the wine glass at him.

"*You* do," he said with a childlike pout. "When did you go to town?"

She gave him the Mona Lisa non-grin and sat. "I didn't. Santa stopped by, probably before that emergency you spoke of, and asked if I would please put those two packages under my tree for you because he couldn't find your house. Didn't know if you even had one, actually." She eyed him and took a sip of wine. "Do you?"

"I thought Santa was all-knowing, kinda like God."

"You've got him confused. Santa, I mean, not God. Well, do you?"

John put the sack on the floor by the tree, pulled out a green foiled package and propped it in front of one wearing his name. Then a red one, and then a blue one, and a purple and yellow one.

He forgot Sophie and her question. He had entangled himself in the gifts, in settling them just right on the red tree skirt, in the joy of seeing her face in his mind's eye, in the contentment of this moment.

"John," she said. "Do you have a home?"

He finished designing the gift display before answering, looking for the right response, one that would work for both of them. Not a lie, but not a full disclosure, either. He sat, leaned his back against the couch and lifted his glass to her.

"I live with friends, Sophie. Not always the same ones. I'm a vagabond and haven't been shown where my home is, yet."

She scoffed. "So, you're homeless, huh?"

"If that means I don't own a home, yes. I am homeless. I prefer to say I am free. I'm not hogtied by a mortgage that would make sure I hogtied myself even further with a job I don't like just to pay the mortgage I didn't want in the first place."

"Knowing what you don't want is good, John. And at least you know what hogties you. That's a lot. Most people don't know until we're too old to do anything about it. And we let people tie us up because we don't know they're doing it, or we're fools and think we want them to. And sometimes we wait too long to figure out the knots, and by then it's too late to loosen them."

He squinted his eyes at her.

"Really? That's philosophical, Sophie. Did my words actually make some sense to you?"

She snorted and added a chuckle at the end so he wouldn't be offended. "Surprisingly, yes. They did. So, you want the underground, then?"

He shot a glance her way. "You mean, as in a grave?"

"You know, *my* underground. You spent a couple of nights there."

"Ah, yes. I left the door open once and got covered in guinea feathers. No poop, though. Are you offering me a bed, Sophie?"

"I am. I won't call it a home so you don't feel hogtied. But it's yours. Without strings. After goulash, we'll go check it out. See what it needs."

An albatross lifted, one he didn't know was riding on his shoulders. He could write unencumbered by distracting noise, he'd be around the animals in Eden, and . . . he could keep an eye on Sophie. Care for her.

Not your job, John.
Then whose? Carl's? I don't think so.

Thirty-six – We Need to Talk

She woke, rolled and let her knees touch the floor, memory flooding, and she wished she could dam it up, turn it back, change it. But memories were stubborn as stick-tights when they grabbed flannel pants and wouldn't let go.

She hated stick-tights.

It was early, but she pushed off the sofa and stood without a sound, bundled herself against winter cold and left the house. The goats needed to see her, needed to know she was alive. And the chickens and guineas needed her presence, too. Or maybe she needed them.

Tucker followed, darting his eyes sideways in question. He thought it was strange she didn't feed the cats. She always feeds them – right off.

Like words without sound, a silent movie, Tucker's thoughts carved across the waves of her brain.

"When I get back," she said in response. "Right now, the goats and hens need to know I'm still around and can still care for them. I said a fearful thing last night, Tuck, and I'm sorry I did. I shouldn't drag my mess into their lives. It's not fair to worry them." She let her soft eyes lay on the dog. "You, too. Don't you worry about me, either."

Sophie took her time with the fowl, alternately clicking her tongue against the roof of her mouth and warbling their language. They didn't want to leave the coop, so she swept the straw to one side and scattered their feed on the wooden floor.

"Stay inside if you like. It's kinda cold out there."

She rifled her hand through the straw in their nesting boxes, plucked out eggs, and admired each for the gratification of the hens.

"You're good girls. You make beautiful eggs. Come on, Tuck. Let's leave the birds alone. Happy Christmas, hens."

Gladiola waited next to Petunia at the wire fence and bleated greetings full of joy. Sophie called to them from the door of their barn, and they barreled inside and into her. Billy first.

"Settle down, babies. One at a time. Were you worried about me last night?" She let them push against her legs and tried to hug them all. "Me, too. I worried. But I'm fine today. Let's get to our chores." She passed out small carrots and they backed up to let her milk.

Talking with the goats helped to clarify what she needed to do, and she mouthed sentences as she milked, finding words that weren't too edgy or combative or critical. Ones she thought might anger him, she tossed out like holey socks. Carl didn't like to be criticized. It reminded him of his mother.

It wouldn't do any good to ask him not to drink. She'd tried that before. And it wouldn't do any good to threaten to leave him. She'd tried that, too.

She recalled the dark, open end of the shotgun barrel, and her breath hitched. He could kill her one day; that possibility was certain, and without remorse. It was the *no remorse* part of it that pained her the most.

That – and the love in between the hate. And around and under and through, all interwoven like a worn, wool tapestry showing all the ways love can tangle with hate, all angular and misshapen, a misunderstood Picasso.

And, yet, the picture grows to be commonplace, unsurprising, even expected and accepted.

No. Not accepted.

Sophie knew talk was necessary and – futile. She'd done it before. But she needed to see her thoughts reflected in his sober eyes, and then she could accept his truth – or not. It would be up to her, as it had always been. She knew that, too.

She could wait for him to raise the shotgun again and again, until he wouldn't need to anymore. Or she could run before he pulled the trigger.

She spoke her lines to the goats again, practicing, but the words broke apart, and she quit. Tears shimmered, and she blinked them away.

He sat at the kitchen island pecking away at his new laptop while she took care of the milk and washed the eggs. He mumbled his approval at the computer's speed and played an old Eagles song while he looked at the variety of apps he might find a use for.

"Does about everything, Sophie. It's a good one."

"Does it cook breakfast?" she said, trying for a light tone. "Want waffles and sausage?"

"Sure. Make us a holiday bloody Mary?"

"No. I want to talk with you without any alcohol on the table."

Carl sat back in the chair and glared.

Cold fear struck but fled as quickly. He was sober. He'd never hurt her without the muddle of alcohol.

"What about coffee?" he asked. "Can I at least get a coffee in my own house?"

She glanced at his eyes to see if his words were sarcastic or real, poured a cup and put it in front of him without coming to a conclusion.

"Do you remember putting a gun to my head last night?"

He scratched ragged, gray whiskers covering his chin and ran the hand through his disheveled hair. Sophie saw when recollection moved like a film over his eyes, frame by frame.

"I guess."

"You guess?"

He nodded and didn't attempt to explain away his actions or apologize for them. He didn't grin them gone. He didn't pull them back like they'd been a joke – a silly, meaningless little game of tag, and it was her turn.

The silence-filled air grew heavy, and Sophie struggled to suck in enough to make words float out of her mouth. She wondered how emptiness could have so much weight, and wondered how she could take this moment to speculate about such a ridiculous notion.

"Do you remember shooting the pelican, your Christmas gift to me? Why would you do that, Carl? Why would you buy a wonderful gift like that for me and then take it away and shoot it?"

He bolted upright, anger hot on his face, and she backed up a step, watching his eyes, reading and learning.

"You wouldn't give it to me. You should have handed it over when I said to."

"But it was mine. To keep. I loved it."

"And I told you to give it to me. You don't understand anything, Sophie." He settled back in his chair, ran a hand through his hair again, and let the anger flow away. "I wouldn't have shot you. You're my wife. Just the pelican. It was in the way. And, anyway, I'm the one who bought it."

He shot her a grin, one that asked to be forgiven without using the words he refused to say, and Sophie gave up trying to understand. She didn't know any more now than before. Maybe less. She didn't know how the pelican had been in the way.

"You can't keep threatening to shoot me, Carl." She heard the sizzle of sausage and moved to the pan to make sure it didn't burn.

"I wouldn't really."

"Not sober, you wouldn't. What about after a lot of drinks? Would you then?"

"Probably not.   You just won't do what I say, sometimes, and it makes me mad. Why won't you? And you don't comprehend anything at all."

"Like what? Tell me so I'll get it, Carl. Please."

"Like the stupid pelican. You didn't *get* why I wanted it back. It was in the way. I told you. Your arms were wrapped around that damned bird like it was the only important thing in the room. It spoiled the day. And your mother was right there in the living room having Christmas with us, even dead and everything. She spoiled the day. And you did, too."

Sophie sifted meaning from his tirade.   Was he jealous? Of a wooden bird and a dead person? Maybe she had made too much of it.   But she'd been joyous he finally understood the grief she'd been struggling with, the sorrow that had buried her alongside her mother. With the pelican statue, it had seemed he was telling her he finally understood. Apparently, she'd been mistaken.

Maybe some of the events of the night were her fault.

"Okay, Carl. I get it, and I'm sorry about last night. You, too?" She paused, hoping for a nod of acknowledgement before giving up. "Will you try not to drink so much?"

"Sure."

She didn't know which question the 'sure' was attached to, but she let it go, turned the sausage again and made waffles.

Carl got tired of playing with his laptop and said he was going to Henry's. He wanted to show it to his buddy Freddie. Sophie, curled up on the end of the sofa reading a new book about angels, wanted to stay snuggled there but, after a glance, thought she should go, too.

"Let me put on some lipstick and comb my hair," she said, marking her page.

"You going?"

She swiveled and tried out a grin. "Got a girl there? Want me to stay home?"

"Right. That's what every man needs, another woman whining at him and telling him what to do."

"I'll just be a minute."

All eyes lifted to the light from the opened door when they entered, and, after her eyes adjusted, she recognized men she knew would be there. Henry's provided a home for lonely people, mostly men who were on their own the day after Christmas, the ones who had visited with family the day before and called it good enough. For a moment, she was glad they had come to say hello and Merry Christmas. They were friends.

Pete sat at the bar, Freddie to his left, both nursing drinks that weren't the first of the day. Carl plopped his laptop on the bar and climbed up next to his best friend.

"Need to show you this," he said. "It's the best computer on the market. Fast and memory is huge. Wait until you see me put it through its paces."

Sophie knew his monologue wouldn't quit until somebody made him stop or he ran out of air. Carl could explain a processor down to its last, most microscopic part. He could take it apart and put it back together, and he could shoot it. That's what happened to his last three.

And he liked the sound of his own voice.

Freddie had been listening to his monologues since grade school and knew all he had to do was nod every once in a while and Carl would be appeased.

Within the first few words, Pete slapped the stool next to him inviting Sophie to sit.

"Good Christmas?" he asked, words everyone expected on the day after.

"Sure," she said. "Santa is a good man."

"What'd he bring you? Looks like Carl scored a nice computer. Lucky boy."

Sophie nodded and didn't respond except to order a glass of wine when Lainie got to her. She wanted to steer the conversation away from Christmas and down some road that didn't dead-end at anger.

"I'm looking for spring," she said. "Spring and flowers in my gardens."

Lainie leaned on the bar, eyes lighting as Sophie talked about her flower beds, how they meandered around the edges of the two-acre lawn and provided sanctuaries, places for bees and birds, for sitting and sipping coffee. Or just sitting and thinking, but not too much of that. It wasn't good for you.

"You're a lucky lady, Sophie. I'd like to live your life. Beautiful home and a hard-working man. You've got it made."

Sophie's glance toward Carl blurred as if he sat on the other side of warped glass, and she rubbed her eyes. A couple of blinks straightened him, and she puffed out a little laugh when his moving mouth came in clear well before the rest of his face.

"Yup. When you're right, you're right. Carl's a wonderful man. I'm a lucky woman."

"How'd you manage to catch him – and keep him happy all these years? He's a smart one, too." Lainie cackled and her rosy face wrinkled in a wide grin.

"Guess that's how it happened, Lainie," Pete said, patting Sophie's arm in a way that was friendlier than she liked.

"What're you talking about, Pete?" Sophie slanted her shoulders away from him.

Pete raised his eyebrows, indicating she knew exactly what he was saying.

"Carl's smart. He knows a good woman when he sees her, and he isn't about to do anything stupid to lose her. He knew it a long time ago and still does. That's the long and short of it."

Sophie didn't respond. What could she say?

Maybe this:

You don't know a damned thing, Pete. You're a fool, Pete. Carl doesn't think I'm a good thing, Pete, and he'd as soon shoot me as look at me. What do you think about that, Pete?

Lainie kept asking for an invitation to visit their home, and Pete kept touching Sophie's arm. She kept scooting away from him, and Lainie kept them entertained with bar stories. In a while, Sophie's half-sorrowed chuckles turned to laughter.

Carl ordered another drink and continued his monologue with Freddie. When the drink and his words ran out, it was time to go.

She smiled as they left and thought about left over prime rib when they got home. She'd warm it up a little and make roast beef sandwiches. Carl loved those.

"I'm glad you suggested this. It was fun," she said as they climbed into the car.

He twisted his head to stare at her, a look of wonder on his face. "Seriously? You thought that was fun?"

"Yes. It's nice to see friends, especially when they're alone during the holidays. It would be even nicer to ask them out sometime. Invite them to share our home for Christmas. No one gets to see the tree and all the decorations. That would be pleasant, wouldn't it?"

"*We* see it. Isn't that enough? I don't want people out there, their noses in my stuff. Not on Christmas. Not on any day."

Sophie deflated like a balloon with a tiny hole. The thought of having guests had momentarily and foolishly buoyed her, and her imagination had taken over without direction.

"You're so angry all the time. Who are you mad at now?"

The passenger door arm rest dug into her side as she subconsciously edged away from him, and the roof inched downward, boxing her in, suffocating her as the car grew smaller in his anger. It radiated from him and lodged in her stomach. He didn't shout, but the tone and the words cut, and she saw the shotgun pointed at her head.

"Pete is a joke. Doesn't have a brain in his head. And you sat right next to him. What's wrong with you?" A squirrel ran across the headlight beam, and he slammed his foot on the brakes to keep from hitting it and cursed. She was glad the seat belt kept her from smashing into the dashboard. "We should have stayed home. Damn, people are so stupid," he added.

"Want me to drive?"

He ignored her, not bothering with a response.

"You don't mean that, Carl. Pete and Freddie are your friends. Lainie, too."

"I don't have friends, and I don't want any. Shut up, Sophie, and leave me alone."

She knew how to shut up. It was easy. Out of sight was safer, too. But in the car that wasn't possible, so she took refuge in shallow, quiet breaths and held motionless. She sat in her dark corner, leaning her head against the cool window and thought about him, about them.

After decades, she was learning; stay out of his way when he drank and shut up. She'd leave him alone, permanently, but he wouldn't let her.

And unbelievably, they still had some fun. Like fishing. Out on the lake in their little rowboat, he seemed content. They laughed and soaked up the sun, even caught some fish. At the little theatre on main street, they enjoyed old films and ate popcorn. With Tucker, they took long walks down the wooden bike path and watched the sun set on the river. She tried to focus on those times.

But not too much. That was always a mistake.

Learning what to do and when to do it shouldn't be hard. But the good times made the others come as a surprise. And no matter how often the bad times leapt at you, you were never prepared even after reminding yourself over and over to be ready, expect it, recognize the signs.

Life was a joker and fooled you into thinking it would go along as it should simply because you wished it, but it didn't. The sad joke was on you for desiring something different.

Sophie pulled at her lip in silence broken only by brief comments from Carl, odd scattered observations about people they knew. He had opinions about them all, judgements about the way they lived their lives, their jobs, their children – even the clothes they wore. And that was strange given his preference for dirty jeans. She almost chuckled out loud but bit her tongue instead.

Out of sight, Sophie. And soundless.

She tiptoed through the rest of the holidays, and wore a placid face when Carl was nearby. When he wasn't, she found herself deep in thought about what she needed to do. Safety wasn't a word she'd considered in much depth before, and she didn't know if she wanted to think about it now. Maybe it was best to let fate take over. Let whatever was going to happen, just happen. She chewed the inside of her cheek raw picturing what that might be.

Fear hovered, claimed her when she didn't know it existed. A sudden noise, though innocent like the drop of a pen or the ring of a phone, caused her to flinch, her heart to pound. The bells announcing his arrival on the driveway, turned her stomach to acid.

On a day he went to see Freddie, she found it in the box holding all his other guns. She picked it up, more gingerly than necessary, placed it on the bed and stared at it like it might have been a scorpion – lethal and wicked. When she thought she could handle it with some confidence, she picked it up, rotated the cylinder and pointed it at a tree outside the window, the blue jay tree.

Staying out of sight wasn't always possible, and her nerves jangled, but the Colt revolver soothed them a little. It was small, had a short barrel, and she knew how to use it – just shove the bullets into the holes, flip the cylinder back into place, and pull the trigger. At least, that's what she believed. And it would fit in a pocket.

"I'll never use it, Tucker," she said, patting his head. "But it might make me feel a little stronger having it nearby. What do you think?"

She looked for bullets in Carl's ammunition box, found some she thought were right, and pocketed them.

"Come on, girl. Let's see if we know how to use this thing. He'll be gone for a couple of hours yet."

She grabbed the Colt, threw on a flannel, and headed outside. She was in the backyard stuffing bullets into the gun when the bells clanged. Her heart stopped, and her knees tried to buckle.

She spun around, stumbled back to the house, sweat making streams down her sides and face. She circled the dining room, frantic to get the gun out of her hands and into a hiding place.

His car door slammed shut.

In the bureau chest drawer, she slipped the colt under her mother's hand-crocheted, lace doilies.

Thirty-seven – Talk isn't Cheap

John pondered over Carl's Christmas laptop as he removed his own from its case and placed it on the tiny table. He opened it, turned it on, and light from the screen glowed blue in the dimness of the underground. He could have lit other lamps but preferred the hurricane lantern in the center of the table. It cast a pale, yellow circle and left the rest of the room in vague, mysterious shadow, focusing his words like a spotlight trained on them. When darkness surrounded him, he became a ground mole searching for the path to truth.

Moving into the underground took no time at all. Carl had designed the bunker as a shelter, but Sophie had provided it with every possible comfort and necessity. He brought his clothes, some groceries, his guitar and laptop and moved in. A few books hid in his tote bag, too, and when he mourned not having his Harley with him, Sophie told him to stop whining like a spoiled little boy and bring it out.

"Down here?"

She twisted around and thunked him on the back of his head.

"Sometimes, you're really dumb, John Wayne. Did you notice the barn and sheds out there? Take your pick. But don't put it in with the chickens. They'll poop on it no matter what you do to keep them from it. They'll find a way under any covering. Clever beasts."

Her eyes brightened in approval of her sly birds, and his went soft with visions of his wild Miss Lily coming home to roost.

"I appreciate that. I'll bring her out in Bone Keesha tomorrow. Thanks."

"Tarps are in the basement. I'll bring one up and you can cover her and put her to bed until spring. Hope it comes soon." She rubbed at her knuckles, warming the red, enlarged knobs.

He kept busy trying to save Sophie some energy, but it took clever and subtle determination. Bone Keesha still wore the blade, so he plowed the driveway at least once a week, cleaning it down to the gravel so Sophie could get into town by herself if she wanted. But the Bug wasn't great in winter.

He tried to beat her to the chicken coop and goat pen each morning to get the chores well underway before she arrived, but Sophie rose early, and he realized that working with her animals gave her something inexpressible. It helped instead of hurting her, and she came away from chores looking rosier, her eyes less pained.

And he understood the sentiment but not the why or how. The inexpressible was in him, too, and the word said it all because there were none to describe it. He determined to share the chores – and the joy.

He hauled wood into the basement for the furnace and fed the fire when he was in the house, and he timed his visits for that purpose. He brought canned goods from the underground so she wouldn't have to and lugged bags of chicken feed and cat food from the co-op. If he could think of a chore before she did, he had it done. Her hackles rose when she recognized what he was up to, but she let it go, and seconds later she tugged her ponytail and grinned.

Silly cowboy thinks he's so clever.

Their small world turned in replication of the earth; sunrises and sunsets viewed and treasured, hungers sated with food and friendship, challenges encountered and met. They thrived in the rhythm of their days.

On his way through the kitchen, she stopped him.

"What do you do out there all day long, John?"

"Write. I owe several biographies, and they take a while to create."

"Can you leave them sit for a bit? Take a walk? Maybe the trail back to the woods?"

"I could use some exercise. You up to it? That's a long hike."

"Pipsqueak. Who do you think you're talking to?" she said.

"Annie Oakley? Ma Kettle?"

"How in the hell do you know those two old women?"

His face transformed, warmed by some long past affection. "Grandma. She loved the old television shows. You remind me of Ma Kettle."

"I'm nobody's ma, and you know it."

"But that old ma was sweet and feisty. Like you."

"Bah! Come on. You're talking like an old woman yourself."

She stuck her feet into the boots he'd bought for her, insulated ones that looked like her rubber garden boots but had ridges on the bottoms so she wouldn't *slide*. With a couple of thick flannels, a stocking cap and mittens in place, she turned to grin at him.

"You ready?"

"Will be once we stop at my place for a hat and some gloves."

Another grin split her face. "Your place? Sounds kinda right, doesn't it."

"Sorry about the slip of the tongue. Seems like it's mine, though. And the bunker is downright cozy. Perfect place to write. Hope I'm not putting you out at all."

"Don't talk nonsense, John."

At the underground, she stepped inside and looked around, curious to see if it was different with him sleeping in it instead of them. Did it smell like John Wayne now, not Carl? Did his pheromones rub out the ones Carl had thrown around and left scattered behind him like he had testosterone he didn't need?

"I'll pay rent with the biography check," he said, ushering her up the underground walkway steps and onto flat ground.

"I said don't talk nonsense, John Wayne."

"But . . ."

She spun and stumbled backwards, would have fallen if he hadn't grabbed her arm to steady her.

"What in hell are you doing, John?"

"Keeping you from falling. That's all."

"The rent bull. I offered that place to you and you're turning it into a business deal? What kind of baloney is that? I thought we were friends."

She stomped off toward the plowed trail, bent forward in determination and mumbling invectives until he shook away the shock and followed.

As they moved into the still woods, Sophie's face went as quiet as her tongue. She grew pleasantly devoid of expression as she embraced the winter world, and her shoulders eased back and settled into place. Her eyes searched out sounds, found them and moved on to the next. She became the doe, the owl, the quick cottontail, and wore her peace like a white suit of armor no amount of poking could penetrate.

And he didn't poke. Knowing this was a good time to shut up, he did. He watched instead. Winter sun wove through the overhead thick awning of bare branches and sprayed the nearly white ground with blotches of pale yellow. Squirrels danced across the snow and plunged into it, digging for the lost acorn they'd buried in the fall. A lone woodpecker drilled into an oak, sure of a meal hiding behind the gray bark, and the glorious red cardinal, its plumage the single bright splash of paint in a winter forest of black and white, sang for its own matchless glory.

And John sucked in the scents; the pine, the wood smoke from Sophie's chimney, and musk where the sun's heat melted snow and created a soup made of soggy leaves and moss.

Shutting up was a good thing. He knew that from his childhood, but today he learned how truly wonderous it could be.

When his bike turned down the long driveway on that long ago first day, it had done so because he'd been drawn to the jumbled mess of brush doing its best to hide the fact that a road, however neglected, did exist. And it led somewhere. Curiosity engaged him. But even more, he craved what lay at the end of the path or beyond it, a place where alone meant by yourself. A place where he could think and clearly hear his own thoughts.

He hadn't known each visit would tie him to Sophie's land, to her zillion cats, to her boisterous peacocks and the chaotic birds and goats. And to her. Concern for her grew with each knot tying him, and it loosened his tongue.

"You must have some family around, maybe a distant cousin or two?"

Sophie frowned at the interruption of peace and ignored the question. Her step had slowed, and she found herself more than fatigued on the last leg of their walk. She was glad to see the backyard, even if in the distance.

"None?" he said, digging through her serenity.

"So what if I don't? What's it matter?"

"Guess it doesn't."

The sun took advantage of a short workday and slipped behind the trees as they came into the backyard.

"Want me to cook dinner?" John asked. "I make a mean pot of spaghetti."

She raised an eyebrow. "Trying to make up for being so nosy?"

"I have a giant, straw encased bottle of chianti."

"Got me. I'll do chores and you cook."

"How about this? We'll both do chores, and you can sip wine while I cook."

"God, you're pushy, John Wayne. Let's get it done."

John had mastered the art of milking goats, and he was quick. Sophie told him to get started while she collected eggs, but he liked to do chores with her, chat while they worked, practice the dance that made for good companionship and even better friends. Sophie shared while she clucked to the chickens, and she let him peek inside her soul when she milked. She didn't even know when it happened, but he did.

That's where he learned to love her.

In the underground, he popped the chianti cork, poured and clicked his glass against hers.

"Here's to solitude and to us, Sophie."

"And to you, too, John" she added. "I'm glad you invaded my privacy."

Her grin held a sparkle as she sipped and followed it with a swipe of the back of her hand across the red line over her upper lip – as usual.

"I've grown accustomed to you and your red mustache," he said, shaking his head. He turned to the tiny stove to make *spaghetti spectacular*, as he called it.

Sophie put her glass down and lowered herself to one of the two small chairs, hands bracing on the table as her weight dropped. An unbidden groan escaped, and she closed her eyes against the sound, to block it out and make it go away.

"You're just tired, old woman. We walked a fair distance today."

"What do you know about it, whippersnapper?"

Sautéing garlic and onion perfumed the small room, and Sophie let her gaze probe spaces that belonged to Carl and her; the bunk beds where they slept during storms and sometimes just for fun; the small coffee table where they played scrabble in the lantern light; the rug where she lay sobbing after he'd locked her in, abandoned her there in the dark because she'd left him for two days.

What if I hadn't come home?

She squeezed her eyes shut, blocking that recollection, but it didn't work. Memories stayed put. Forever. They're the bones of your brain; they're grooves in your gray matter that get tolerable only when newer, better days cover them up like flowers on graves.

"What's wrong, Sophie? Don't like the chianti?"

She blinked and came back.

"It's fine. Just remembering. That's all."

"Want to talk about it?"

"No, Dr. Spock. I don't want to talk."

John's belly laugh surprised her.

"What's so funny?"

"Spock's a pediatrician. Did you mean Dr. Phil?"

She snorted and waved a dismissive hand that landed at her wine glass and brought it to her lips.

"Smells good in here," he said, "but I need to open the door for some cool air. It gets warm fast."

Fannie bounded in as soon as the door opened, and she found a rug to curl on.

"The dogs all liked it down here. After they secured the grounds, that is. Especially Tucker. He was hell on raccoons and coyotes invading the yard. But he'd scratch on the door to come in when he finished patrolling his territory and was ready for bed.

"Wait a minute. Who's Tucker?"

"A mutt hound who strayed in after Danny left us."

"Left? What happened to Danny? Did he run away? Why would he do that?"

She paused at one of those brain grooves she didn't want to examine. "Got old is all, a long while back. They do that."

"Don't we all."

John was led back to his earlier question to Sophie. He needed to know about family, anyone she could call kin. Or *he* could call period. Just in case he needed to. And he needed to know the whereabouts of the thought provoking and shadowy Carl. But not tonight. First things first.

"I need to ask a question, Sophie. That alright?"

She knew the path he wanted to take would be full of ruts and holes and pondered before answering.

"You can ask anything," she said, a sly smile forming.

"That's strangely ominous, woman, and so is the evil, dark-witch grin."

"Big word, boy – ominous." She lifted the glass to her lips and sipped. And then sipped again, getting ready. Fortification, she told herself.

"Who should I contact if something bad, God forbid, happens to you? Who do I call?"

"That all? Pshaw, easy one. Nobody."

She lifted her breasts, one hand under each, and lay them on the table, easing the constant ache of muscles in her shoulders and back.

He stirred the sauté, added ground beef, and wondered how to force the issue.

"You're not young, Sophie. And you run around this property like you're a spring chicken. Something could easily happen."

"Yes. It could. But not so easily."

He scratched his head, shifted his feet and stirred the beef. It sizzled, splattering grease.

"You're messing up the stove," she told him.

He turned it down and himself around.

"Where is Carl?"

She hadn't expected him to ask her that.

"Could I have a second glass of chianti?"

He poured, and she called Fannie over, ran a hand over the dog's back and murmured comforting sounds. John could hear her voice but couldn't decipher the words. He wanted to shake her – and wanted to hug her, both at the same time, and she ignored the question.

"You said I could ask anything, Sophie."

The water bubbled, and he slid in the spaghetti noodles, brought them back to a boil, put on a cover and lowered the heat, all while contemplating how to learn what he wanted to know.

"You did. You said I could ask anything," he repeated. "And now I'm doing it."

What the hell was the matter with him? He'd told himself earlier he had learned to shut up, but apparently not. Her white face, her grip on the stem of her wine glass, the position of her shoulders up by her ears, all said he hadn't learned anything at all.

"I said you could ask. I didn't say I would answer."

"None of my business?"

"Wow. Give the boy a kewpie doll."

In the time it took him to apologize, she leaned back in her chair and let go of . . . something. He didn't know what, but her face changed. She no longer looked angry or in any way distressed, just determined, and he applauded her doggedness even as it frustrated him.

He quit pushing, recognizing the stubborn lift of her chin. He'd have to find another way to make sure she'd be taken care of if she got sick or hurt. Stubborn old woman.

"Did you make your chowchow this year?" he asked. "When you gonna teach me how?"

"I did. This fall we'll make some. Chowchow cleans up the garden and gives it thanks. We'll do it then."

He turned back to the stove feeling easy, and his own shoulders dropped into place. He didn't know any more about her than he had an hour ago, but he knew what she didn't want to talk about, and he figured that was something.

And they'd make chowchow together in the fall. That wasn't so far off.

Thirty-eight – Doing the Jitterbug

A stock boy dropped a carton of canned peas onto the floor making a loud bang behind her, and she stumbled into the delicately piled display of apples which collapsed. Red delicious bounced across the floor, tripping shoppers and racing in front of Herb like the winning apple might earn a trophy, or maybe a million dollars. Herb was the owner of Shop Smart, and, when she saw him, Sophie's hands covered her flaming cheeks. Tears of anger formed.

She watched the fruit find escape routes and glared at the stock boy who'd scared the daylights out of her and created the whole mess.

"You alright, Sophie?" Herb asked.

He tiptoed through the apples and took her arm.

"Don't pile apples where they can attack customers, Herb. You should know better. You been doing groceries a hell of a long time, and I would think you'd be better at it by now."

"You look a little jittery. Want to sit down for a spell, let your heart settle?"

"I'm fine. Damned noise your stock boy made sounded like a gun shot, and I thought I'd hide behind some red apples." She grinned. "Should've picked granny smith. They're hard enough to stop a bullet."

She felt edgy and knew she looked it. She couldn't seem to calm herself anymore. Every time she thought she'd found a little serenity, a jarring noise sent her right back over the cliff.

She promised herself she'd get that Colt out of the drawer, load it, and learn to shoot it. She didn't know what else to do. In the months since it had left Carl's gun box to live with lace doilies, she hadn't touched it, and it was time. Past time. Today, she told herself. She'd learn to shoot it today, and she'd feel stronger afterwards. Safer. Calmer.

"You sure you're okay, Sophie?"

"Sure I am. A bit tense because of the break-ins out in the country by us. That's all. I'm not sleeping like I should."

"Hadn't heard about that. You and Carl got a dog, don't you?"

"Yes. Nobody gets by Tucker. For sure."

She walked away from her half-full cart, left the store, and knew Carl would be mad if she didn't make the sloppy Joes she planned for dinner. She had never understood his need to be so exact about meals, but he'd always been.

Maybe she should say she didn't know when he asked every morning. Maybe tell him she would figure it out later and see how he took it.

But she didn't. She said whatever came to mind, and he went off to work expecting to come home to that. To sloppy Joes or goulash or what-ever-in-hell she'd mouthed in a moment of indecision. Anything else was construed by him as a deliberately constructed lie.

She slumped behind the steering wheel and watched star bursts sprinkle in front of her eyes. Her clammy hands trembled, and she wondered if she was having a stroke. That would serve him right. No meal at all. Hah!

She blinked away the stars, took several long breaths, and drove the three blocks to Henry's Bar.

The place was empty, and she was glad. She didn't need Pete or Freddie sidling up to her. Lainie held up a wine glass, and she nodded.

"You alright, Sophie? You look like a ghost or like you just saw one."

"I'm fine. Heart beats a little fast, is all."

"See a doctor?"

"I will. Soon. Don't worry about it. I need to get a few groceries and head home."

"So, you go to the grocery store by way of Henry's?" Lainie teased. "Smart woman. Have a little drink of supermarket courage."

The glass she put in front of her was filled to the brim, and Sophie sipped some out before lifting it for fear of spilling.

"You'll get fired if you give away Henry's profits, girl."

"Just for friends. I make it up by short-changing everybody else." Lainie's grin spread to Sophie, and her heart settled. "Speaking of friends," she added. "Your old friend Dee stopped by. In town for the weekend. Time and that creep of a husband haven't been good to her. The louse."

Lainie leaned on the bar and wiggled her index finger in the moisture left by her coke glass. Dennis the Menace hair appeared in the wood, and under it grew the face of a demon.

"Looks like trouble brewing," Sophie said, watching the watery picture come alive. Lainie's talent wasn't all bartending.

"It did already. He's a rat. Hit her – more than once, I'm thinking. I don't know why women put up with crap like that. It's crazy. You're a lucky lady, Sophie. So few women get the right man."

"Hmmm. Sorry to hear about Dee."

"Maybe you could call her. You used to be pretty close, didn't you?"

"No. I mean, that was a long time ago, before Carl and me. Not so much since."

Lainie toweled the demon dry and gave up. She knew when to let it go. A good bartender looked, listened and learned.

"I gotta go," Sophie said, gulping down the last of her wine. "I'm fortified. Thanks, Lainie. I'll think about calling Dee."

She hauled the groceries from the car and left them on the island table, still in the bags.

Standing in front of the dining room bureau, her chin dropped to her chest as she tried to still her heart. She rubbed sweaty palms on her shirt and lifted her head to stare into the mirror hanging over the chest of drawers. She didn't recognize the woman gazing back at her. Her eyes looked feverish and red splotches dotted her cheeks. She sniffed the acrid scent of anxiety in her own perspiration and berated herself.

"Get on with it," rasped an anxiety laden voice. And fear flew from the mirror to crawl over Sophie's skin.

She thanked God for the value of fear and, with a speck of resolve, yanked the drawer open, slid her hand beneath the doilies, and touched cool metal. The Colt was still there. It had occurred to her Carl might have come across it. He wouldn't have said anything, just moved it to another hiding place – because he could. And he would smile thinking about her surprise in finding it missing.

She stuffed the small pile of ammunition in her pocket along with the gun, changed into her rubber boots, and opened the door, half expecting to see Carl's vehicle parked in the drive, waiting. A surprise visit home simply to thwart her.

She patted her pocket, listened for bells and gave Tucker a treat.

"You can't go, boy. You stay inside this time."

Ground squished under her feet, and she slid a couple of times in the soft, spring ground. It didn't matter how far she traveled from the house to practice. Noise would carry on the air, anyway. She just wanted to be out of the yard and into the woods where no one could spot her.

By the sugar shack, she stopped and squared her shoulders, pulled the gun and a bullet from her pocket, and flipped the cylinder to the side. She fumbled, cursing her bent fingers, and knelt to search the soggy leaves for the dropped bullet. With her knees growing damp and the bullet clasped once again in her fist, she paused for a couple of nerve settling breaths and let her eyes roam the peaceful landscape.

The second time, the cartridge went in smoothly even though her fingers trembled. Squinting at the safety notch, she tried to figure out which way was off and which way was on. She couldn't tell but figured one sure way was to shoot the gun and remember where the safety was positioned when it fired.

She stood to aim the revolver at the sky. How could she miss that? And pulled the trigger. Nothing happened. Not even a click. She pushed the safety forward, aimed and pulled the trigger again. Her hand jerked, and the recoil and blast knocked her backwards. If it hadn't been for the tree behind her, she would have landed on her back. Her knuckles screamed from gripping the gun.

Sophie gawked at the Colt, terrified of its power, and tried to make friends with it, talked to it. She remembered to check the safety again and cement in her brain what it looked like when it was off, when it would allow her to shoot. She could be dead if she forgot its position.

She inserted six bullets, and six spent cartridges came out of the cylinder after she fired all the rounds and dumped them into her hand. They lay in the bottom of her pocket while she reloaded the revolver with six shiny new ones.

She turned the gun in her hand, over and over, noted its smooth metal, now warmed by her hands and the firing. She admired the checkered grip. It was solid and fit her hand. She didn't have to work at holding the gun because it was light and it fit so well.

It was an okay gun. She understood it.

After making sure the safety was in the on position, she put the gun in her right pocket and looked for a place to get rid of the used brass. That's what Carl called the empty casings.

"Brass," she snickered. "I sound like a gun slinger."

Using a rusty can from the sugar shack, she managed to dig a hole deep enough to bury the seven cartridges. Replaced and stomped on the dirt, threw a few leaves on top and left – humming a tune.

She didn't intend to use it, but she'd been right about its healing properties. She felt stronger. More serene. She didn't even mind making sloppy joes for Carl tonight.

She threw an extra tablespoon of brown sugar and a chopped jalapeno into the sloppy joes because Carl liked them sweet and spicy. When it came to a slow simmer, she turned it down, covered it, and slid into her boots.

"Come on, Tucker. You can come with me this time."

She patted her pocket and headed to the coop.

As she scattered seed, the chickens fluttered and clucked, the guinea hens cried *Buck wheat* over and over, and Sophie imitated their sounds back to them. Their music was reassuring, and comfort crept into her bones hearing the guineas' soft words. They would scream *Chi-chi-chi!* to sound an alarm, let her know if a threat drew near.

She'd have to herd them back into the coop before nightfall so the damned coons didn't get them, but the warm spring evening was too good to miss – even for fowl.

She took time with the goats, let Billy push his head against her while she scratched his back where the fur was relatively clean. As she milked, her breath came from a deep baritone, tranquil place. The thrumming pulse of her heart hypnotized her with its soothing composition, and her hands moved in a lullaby's rhythm on her goat's velvet udders. She smiled thinking the words moving through her brain created a symphony.

Where else on earth could she be composer, musician, and conductor?

Nowhere.

Carl didn't come home until well past quitting time. The animals had been put away and she sat bundled in front of a blazing bonfire in the back yard. The bells startled her from a waking dream and she watched his headlights flicker on and off as light danced through the trees and eventually lit up the yard. He had a beer in his hand when he stepped out, straightening himself with a grip on the door.

"Sophie! Where the hell are you?"

Her throat tightened when she tried to respond, and "Back here," came out like a rusty nail pulled from weathered wood.

"Sophie!" he shouted again.

She stood and moved into the still glowing headlights so he could see her and called to him.

"Shut the car off, Carl, and come sit by the fire. It's a beautiful night."

He surprised her by doing as she asked and weaved back and forth toward the fire like a sailboat tracking through a cross wind. She watched and swallowed back the lump as he neared the bonfire. Falling onto the outside sofa next to her, he tipped up the Budweiser.

"You hungry, Carl, or did you eat somewhere?"

"Course I'm hungry. I'm starved."

Sophie stood, wanting to get food into him as soon as possible, but he grabbed her arm.

"Where you going?"

"To get you a plate of food, sloppy joes. You're hungry, right?"

He glared, pupils boring through her as if he could pin her to the ground with his brain and his eyes.

"Where'd you go today?"

She sucked in air, but answering words stuck in her throat.

"I asked you a question."

"You're hurting my arm. Don't, please. I went to the store. For sloppy joe fixings. We didn't have it here, and you said you wanted them for dinner, so I . . ."

Sophie poured her soul over the ground in front of him, begging with her eyes and her soothing words, but it became clear he wasn't looking at her. He wasn't listening to her, and he didn't want to. He wouldn't.

She straightened her spine and yanked her arm from his hand. "I went to Henry's for a glass of wine. I wanted to settle my nerves after destroying the grocery store."

"What the hell did you do?"

"Just knocked some apples over. A loud noise startled me, and I bumped the apple stand."

Carl rolled his eyes like she wasn't worth the effort it took to understand.

"How damned stupid can you be?" he mumbled.

Ire tightened her chest.

"I don't know why you have to call me stupid, Carl. I'm not. Everybody in the world can't be dumb. Everybody but you, that is."

Walk away, Sophie. Stop it. You can't reason with him tonight. Be absent.

"I'm going in, Carl. Watch some television. I'll fix you a plate and leave it on the table."

"I quit work," he said, stopping her like she'd run into a wall.

She turned back to him, eyes wide. He'd be home all day, every day? The thought churned in her stomach, and she thought she might vomit. Words rasped from her throat.

"You just up and quit, or do you mean you put in for retirement?"

"I quit. I'm done. You'll have your ever-loving husband home with you from now on." He grinned at her, but his eyes didn't match the slight upturn of his lips.

"Congratulations, Carl. I'll get your sloppy joes fixed."

He grunted and got up. Thinking he would follow her, she felt his eyes searing through her clothes, burning her skin, and was surprised when he went to the car, instead. Hiding behind the kitchen door, she watched, saw him grab a six pack from the back seat and return to the fire.

She wrung her hands together, rubbed the red knuckles and her stiff neck. She threw two sloppy joes on a plate, added a bunch of chips and covered it with a towel. In the living room, she wrapped herself in a blanket and curled up as small as possible in the corner of the sofa.

It'll be alright, Sophie. Just be quiet.

When his boots hit the kitchen floor, she knew. She recognized the anger in the slapping leather of his footstep, the built-up frustration, his failure to control the world – and her. She flew off the couch, stepped in her boots and ran out the door.

Maybe he wouldn't follow.

She screeched to a halt, head spinning, wondering where she could go, and headed toward the underground, but remembered she didn't have the key and spun back toward the outbuildings.

Opening the door to the tool shed enough to slide in, she watched through the crack as Carl came out to the porch, shotgun in his hand. He stood motionless, a statue, stiff and concrete-still. Only his head moved, searching for her. Ever so slowly, she crept the door closed, backed away, and tried to be a statue, like Carl. But her heart pounded – hammer on anvil, and she was sure its clamor would lead him to her, that and the gasping fill of her lungs and the tempest in her brain.

When the door flew open, he stepped through, raised the shotgun in a calculated, deliberate motion and pointed it at her head in the position to kill her as he always said he could – would.

Life slowed to a crawl, broke into a million pieces and fell at her feet.

She had come to believe his every word. That's the thing about Carl, she mused as she stared into the dark hole at the end of the barrel. He's trustworthy. He doesn't lie. He does exactly what he says he will – every single time, and she's told her friends about his steadfastness over and over and over. Since their very beginning.

So many positive traits. So brilliant. So giving.

The pelican hovered at the edge of her consciousness as she reached into her pocket and slid the safety to the off position.

And he smiled and waited.

She pulled it from her pocket.

The shotgun's safety snicked.

She pulled the trigger.

Peacocks shrieked. The guineas screamed *Chi-chi-chi!* And the chickens burrowed deeper into their nesting boxes. Billy jumped the wire fence and battered his horns at the shed door. The nannies bleated a mournful dirge.

When they quieted, there was utter silence.

Thirty-nine – Another Slow Dance

John helped her plant several varieties of hot and sweet peppers at the south end of the garden where they would catch the most sun. Next to them, stood tomatoes; late and early growers, cherry and roma, yellow and Heirloom. It seemed like a lot, but she said they'd put up juice and sauce. None would lie on the ground and rot. Cabbage and carrots, beets and kale took up most of the north end because they could take colder weather and stay in the ground well into fall. Yellow, wax, and green beans lodged in the center.

It was a well zoned vegetable village.

And it was a magnificent display, impressive even to his amateur eyes. John straightened from his bent position, rubbed his aching back and scanned the neat rows. Pride in the structured plot of ground filled him, creating a hint of a smile even as he groaned his discomfort. He wondered how Sophie managed gardening at her age. Hell, how did she do everything she did? Maybe you had to be born to the labor to not feel it.

She didn't want to quit working until the sun set and forced them inside or to the bonfire. They stopped for the day only when she rubbed her stomach and yelled his name.

"John Wayne! When did we eat last?"

"Eat? What's that?"

"Food, smarty pants. You put it in your mouth and stomach."

"All I know, anymore, is how to put food in the ground and hope it grows into more."

"Ready to go in?"

"More than ready. Head to the underground cuz I've got a pot of chili in the slow cooker."

"You're better than alright, my friend."

He tipped his battered cowboy hat at her and grinned.

"Why, thank you, ma'am. That's mighty kind of you to say," he said in a pretty fair impersonation of the actor. "Come on, Fannie. Let's go get in the chow line."

He ambled along like the silver screen hero since his back was already stiff and sore, but he exaggerated it anyway for her amusement and sauntered across the yard. It never failed to bring a smile and a saucy remark.

"God, John. You're a fool."

"Yes, ma'am, I am. Thank you for noticing."

He'd turned the underground into a cozy den with soft lantern light in the dark corners and bright quilts on the beds. A colorful, thick braided rug covered the cool concrete floor, and Fannie curled up on it.

Taking it all in, Sophie stretched like a cream-fed cat and gave a sigh of content. She'd seen it many times, and serenity still invaded her body when she entered.

"How do you get any work done in here?" she asked. "It's too damned peaceful."

"I need harmony when I'm writing about horror. It's a necessary delicate balance."

"I guess."

He ladled chili into heavy pottery bowls, put crackers on a plate – no cardboard box littering the table in his home – and lined silverware on cloth napkins. John liked a nice table setting.

"Glass of red?" he asked.

She rolled her eyes, like always, and asked for a six ounce. "In crystal. No plastic cup, please, sir."

He lifted an eyebrow.

"Are you making fun of me again, woman?"

"Sure am. It's such a pleasure. And I need something from you."

"Then you'd better be nice. And I'm feeding you, too, so show some proper respect."

"I have money buried in the ground."

He lifted both eyebrows; one first, and the other one followed close on its hairy heels.

"It's true. Carl doesn't believe in banks, so we bury our money. It's our retirement."

He thought It sounded crazy, but Sophie was just the kind of person to stick money in the ground. He had no way of knowing what kind of person the mysterious Carl was – or is – or his state of mind. Well, that wasn't true. He'd learned a lot about him from Sophie and her stories.

"It'll rot. Disintegrate," he said.

She pursed her lips and shot him a withering glance.

"Really, Mr. Scientist? The bills are rolled together in sealed glass jars. Mason canning jars have never before held such bounty. Cept my tomato sauce."

"And have you dug any up to see if they break during winter – you know, frost heave and all?"

"Yes, and they don't. Anyway, I need you to walk the property with me so I can show you where they are and how to find them."

John's back hit the slats of his chair, and his hands flopped to his lap. A blur of thoughts bounced across his brain, and he made a *Quiet, I'm thinking* face as he tried to figure out if Sophie had lost her mind or not.

She hadn't been herself for a while, but he'd chalked it up to aging. She'd been tired lately, too, and often clutched her chest like breath pulled hard and she wished air wasn't needed to sustain life.

Maybe he shouldn't have allowed her to help with the garden. He had tried to make her rest frequently, but stubborn had been invented for Sophie. She refused to sit most of the time, and he needed her nearby, available to tell him what to do, like how to turn plain old dirt into glorious, plentiful bounty.

She wanted him to learn.

"Wear your rubber boots. It's still damp in the woods." She whistled for the dog.

John did as he was told but couldn't believe what she'd said about their money. People used banks, stocks and bonds, not Mason jars for holding their retirement funds. Then again, he thought, most people didn't build earth shelters, either.

"Let's go, Sophie. Want to see if Bone Keesha can make it through the woods?"

"No. It's still too wet, and she'd rut up the path. Let's walk, you lazy bugger."

Just beyond the sugar shack, she stopped, turned, took a few steps and pointed to her boots. "Here's one."

He scrutinized the ground around her feet and found nothing at odds with every other inch of the wooded land. Leaves, acorns, branches, moss. No dollar signs. No message saying something unusual was planted where she stood. The tree didn't have a flashing neon sign.

He scrunched his face and tried to appear cute, not skeptical. He didn't want Sophie to feel silly.

"So, there's a jar right there?"

"Yes. Did you note what I did to get here? I counted. How many steps did I take, John?"

"Uh, no idea."

"Are you paying attention? This is important."

She retraced her steps to the shack and began again.

"How many?" she asked.

"Twenty."

"Good. From what position? In what direction?"

"Jeez, Sophie. I don't know. How many jars are buried around here?"

"More than you would believe."

"I wouldn't believe any," he muttered, but softly, under his breath. "Uh, are you going to point out a bunch today and expect me to remember every direction and number of steps and from what starting point?" He tilted his head and glared, frustrated with her and with himself. This whole thing was ludicrous. "Do you just assume I'll remember?"

"Course not. There are markers and written details for all of them, but I wanted you to get the gist of how it all works."

He rubbed stubble on his chin and listened to its rasp, curiosity and care warring with one another.

"Why are you doing this, my friend?"

Her hand caressed the bark of an ancient oak like it was an old, frail friend and considered how to answer John's question. Lying about life and death came too easily. She'd practiced too long and too well.

She did it again.

"Well, I might not be able to get out here when I need money. Might want you to dig some up for me."

Sophie's words sounded disingenuous to him, and he thought something was off kilter but couldn't pinpoint what and didn't want to ask.

Or maybe he didn't want to know.

At the house, Sophie disappeared and came back with a manila folder full of smudged, wrinkled pieces of paper, a variety from ragged edged schoolbook pages to flower edged stationary. Each sheet held comprehensive instructions to a dirt bank, the name she'd given the jars. She handed it to him.

Perched on the footstool in her living room with the folder on his lap, he studied her face, her pale skin, her folding posture. His long legs stuck out in front of him, and she stepped over them to find a seat on the couch where she measured him – like a hawk eyeing prey, like a doe trailing her fawn into unfamiliar grounds.

They were chess players assessing the board.

Fannie climbed up and laid her head on Sophie's lap, her eyes staring into her mistress's. The air held worry, and it crept through her fur and lodged inside. A low whine rumbled from her chest, and Sophie rubbed the long ears covering her legs like small blankets.

"It's okay, Fannie. We're all fine."

"Are we, Sophie? Are you fine?"

"Never better. Take a look at those and tell me that you grasp every one, every single dirt bank. If you don't . . . well, let me know. You understand me, John Wayne?"

She rested for the next month or so, took her time rising each morning and sat more in the afternoon. John happily took over the chores when she would let him.

And sometimes she did.

With warm summer, they cooked at the backyard fire and sipped wine on the outdoor sofa where they could listen to the critters sing their nighttime serenades.

"Tree frog," she said. "I love the tiny critters."

"I do, too. And the horned owl. Love the *Hoo, hoo, hooooo*."

"They ask a lot of questions," Sophie said. "Just like a lot of people I know. Damned owls can't let well enough alone."

"Feeling ornery?"

"Nope. Making small talk." She tilted her head to listen to a coyote howl and watched Fannie's ears perk and then settle. "Must be in the next section or she'd be gone. I gotta go into town tomorrow."

"Where to? Grocery store? Co-op? I'll take you."

"None of your business, John."

"Sorry. I didn't want you driving by yourself if . . . Never mind." He grinned and rubbed his head. "I'm making my foot-in-mouth condition worse. I keep on spitting out chewed up shoe leather and don't learn."

"I'm old, not dead. I can still drive." She saw him deflate and knew she'd hurt him.

And that hurt her.

"I didn't mean anything by that, John. I won't be gone long."

She banged on the Volkswagen's hood, trunk and fenders, honked the horn, and started the little 4-cylinder. Remembering the day Carl brought it home curved her lips in a smile. She'd told him he ought to ride an electric razor because it had more power. He'd punched her arm and told her to get in. They'd gone for a bug ride and had somehow managed to make love in that baby car.

She swiped at her wet eyes and blinked several times so she could see to drive, glad John wasn't nearby to see her sniveling like a girl.

In front of the attorney's office, one they'd always used, she rubbed her hands together and prayed for a poker face.

You've lied about Carl your entire life, Sophie. It's the single thing you're good at.

She grabbed the property title and went inside.

"You have the paperwork ready, Don?" she asked, swishing in and pretending to be in a hurry. She didn't want to give him much perusal time.

"Sure do, but are you sure this is what you want?" He paused because he wanted her to be sure, and he wanted it to be legal. "And Carl has signed off?"

"Yes. Signed it over to me when he decided to roam the world. Afraid something would happen and he wouldn't get back. Or he might not want to."

"Who is this John Wayne you want the trust written for? I don't know this person."

She glared. "Do you need to know all the people who get trusts made out to them? Since when?"

He shriveled smaller than his hundred twenty pounds of sagging skin, and his balding head reddened.

"Course not. Let's get these signed and notarized."

As the weather changed and leaves turned, the pains in her chest grew worse, and it was difficult to keep John from noticing. She hated him knowing, and she hated the worry in his eyes when he saw it. She frequently pretended to be too tired to get up because of the pain and spent days on the couch.

He brought soups and glasses of wine and watched television with her or read until she kicked him out, sick of seeing anxiety in the fingers holding his book, in the stiff tilt of his head as he stole glances at her, and in the rapid channel changes as he pressed buttons on the remote.

"Go on to your cave and get your work done. I'm a little tired today, so leave me alone."

"Why won't you go to the doctor, Sophie? Why not get checked out?"

"I'm old. That's all it is. Can he fix that? Make me young again?"

"You're not old. Stand up. Let's dance."

"Get out, Cowboy."

"No. I'm not going anywhere."

An old stereo collected dust in the corner by the television, and he rooted around in the stack of LP's piled next to it until he found what he was looking for – Beatles. He brought two glasses of red from the kitchen and played 'The Long and Winding Road,' an oldie even he loved because of his grandmother. He clicked his glass on hers and dared her to refuse his request.

"Drink and then get up. We're gonna dance."

"I don't want to dance, you silly fool. But I'll drink the wine. Thanks."

"Get up, Sophie. Please."

"No."

Disregarding her refusal, he removed the glass from her hand, pulled her to her feet, and wrapped an arm around her back. He held her as if she was spun gold. And she was. Sophie was a rough-cut precious gem, as crude as an unpolished diamond straight from the ground, and as hard. He'd never want her to be anything otherwise.

They glided around the room, and her eyes melted. Her body swayed with his, and only the tips of his fingers against her back directed her dips and turns. She was a dancer.

She was Isadora Duncan, Ginger Rogers, Audrey Hepburn in the soul of a white-haired old woman.

Her eyes were the oceans. Her smile became the sun.

When the song ended, she sank to the couch and asked for another glass of red.

"We'll dance again, John Wayne. But right now, I want to make chowchow."

"Now? It'll be dark in an hour or so."

"You turn into a pumpkin or something?"

"Why tonight, Sophie?" He chewed his lip waiting for an answer he was afraid he already knew. And she gave one.

"Because I want to. Right now. It's my house and my damned garden. Help me up."

On the way outside, she listed off the vegetables he needed to pick.

"Cabbage. A big one. And lots of green tomatoes. They won't ripen anymore because it's too late in the season. Hot peppers and eight or ten carrots. Some garlic, too."

She followed him to the garden and watched him collect the ingredients and fling them in a bushel basket. She turned on the spigot to fill the outside sink and slowly gathered twigs for kindling.

"We'll do a small batch tonight while you're still learning. Go into the house and get the butcher block and a vegetable knife. And turn on the backyard light."

"Yes sir, General ma'am. Anything you say."

In the middle of building a fire, she put a hand on her chest and looked for John as she waded through the dull pain. Flames had taken hold by the time he returned, and she stood without noticeable discomfort or any reflection of what had been.

"Got gloves?" she asked. "Safety mask and glasses?"

"What the hell, Sophie. I'm cooking, here, not making a poison. And you didn't tell me to get them."

"Now, listen up," she said and took a full, deep breath. *"When you're chopping hot peppers, do it in a stiff breeze, Cuz chopping inside makes it hard to breathe. Your lungs'll seize up, and you'll start to heave. Use your head when you're makin that chowchow."*

She'd said it fast and all at once, and John cocked his head. "What was that?"

"A verse from a poem about Magic Bob."

"Who the hell is Magic Bob?" John was trying not to grow testy with the events of the strange night – and with worry. He wanted to get on with the chowchow and be done. Get Sophie resting on the couch.

"He's the man who taught me to garden. The one who taught me about chowchow and life. That to live a right life, you have to start by being right with the earth."

"I don't get it, Sophie."

"Chowchow uses up things a lot of people let rot in the ground. Food they think bad or dead. It isn't. Don't be fooled by what might look dead or not dead. And good and bad can resemble each other a lot, John Wayne."

He thought she was slipping into dementia, going a little bit crazy, but told himself he'd frequently thought so – right from the first day when she held the shotgun on him.

So he listened and did what she told him to do. He got gloves and a mask. No safety glasses; he drew that line. He chopped and chopped and chopped some more. He threw everything in a big bucket, mixed it up like she said and covered it with a ton of salt that he thought would surely give somebody high blood pressure.

He said so to Sophie.

"It's gonna brine the vegetables, draw out the water. You add enough jalapenos?"

"I think so."

"You want it to be bicy, but not enough to make you cry like a baby."

"Bicy?" His eyebrows raised and tears leaked at the corners of his eyes from chopping the hot peppers. "I don't know bicy."

"That's what Magic Bob's mother calls it when the chowchow is hot enough and turns your eyes red – like yours are right now." She giggled. "It was his mother who taught him, and him who taught me."

She stared off into the night like a stranger might lurk in the dark, a shadow hovering between land and the sky. Something or someone he couldn't see.

"There he is." She pointed, sure of the vision.

"Sophie?"

His voice nudged her back to this place and time.

"It's my chowchow friend, laughing and drinking a beer. A Miller, as I recall. I was a kid, but he treated me like a friend, and every damned time I make chowchow, I see his beautiful, bearded face. His black eyes."

He let it go, left Sophie in whatever world she chose to inhabit. Hefting the bucket to the table, he sat next to her with a well-earned glass of wine in his hand. "What's next, my good but goofy friend?"

"Cover it with a plate and a cloth and put it in the barn away from the critters. You don't want it in the house."

"Tool shed okay?"

"Sure."

She didn't go into the tool shed anymore. Memories lived there, squatters she made no attempt to evict.

Sophie sprawled on the overstuffed sofa, her long flawlessly white hair hanging over her shoulders and breasts like a photographer might snap her picture at any moment. Red flames flickered in the glossy white mass, and her red wine glass held aloft made a portrait John wished he could paint. It was totally Sophie and beyond conventional beauty. It was better. As if reading his thoughts, she let her eyes stray from the fire to him.

"I need to tell you something, and if you have a problem with anything I say, keep it to yourself, John Wayne."

"Sounds serious."

"Not so much serious as done. Finished."

"Okay, woman. Have at it."

"I'm dying."

He found his favorite pose, one leg over the other at the knee. It helped him relax, and at the moment, he needed comfort. His mouth opened; she glared, and he closed it.

"You are named as beneficiary to this property. The dirt banks aren't disclosed in the documents, and no one knows about them except you. Everything I own is in a trust and will be yours at my death. See Don, the old attorney on Main Street. He has the original papers. I'll give you copies."

She shot him a look that was half grin and half serious, like a teacher about to scold a favorite, roguish student.

"Now you can talk."

He removed his hat and rubbed at his disheveled head, wondering what the hell he could say. Where should he begin? It was wrong. You don't give away a hundred twenty acres to someone you've known a short time, a good friend, sure, but not family. He tried to be gentle.

"Sophie, you're not dying. And you can't give this to me."

"I am, I can, and I did. Anything else?"

It was obvious her strength increased as moments passed. Her shoulders drew back and her spine lengthened. He uncrossed his legs and leaned his elbows on his knees so he could look directly into her eyes.

"I know you think you can, but your husband must be part owner of this land and house. And everything in it."

"He signed it all over to me and the title has been clear of liens for decades."

John studied her expression. He didn't know what to believe. Her gaze was steady, her hands still. Her lips didn't tremble. If she was lying, she had perfected the art.

"I'll show you the papers," she repeated.

"Alright, you have papers. But answer one thing for me. Where is Carl, Sophie?"

She lowered the wine glass and let it rest on her leg, fingers of both hands entwined around the stem like it was difficult to hold steady. Her eyes focused on the flames and then on the pet cemetery.

"He's gone."

"Please don't think I'm ungrateful, but I have difficulty weaving together some of your statements. Like . . . when you speak of him, it's as if he could stroll downstairs any minute. I've even found myself glancing behind me, staring at shadows. Looking for him.   But he's not here, and sometimes I'm not sure he ever was. I don't want to say you outright lie, but pieces of your story just don't fit.

Sophie's head spun to him, her face bleak and white.

"Of course, I lie. Outright and otherwise. My whole life has been one giant lie, John Wayne."

She was frustrated, and her hand jerked in the air like the truth was hanging right in front of his eyes and he wouldn't see it. She let it drop and went still.

"But mostly, I haven't lied to you."

"You've been telling me tales about you and Carl since the day we met. Want to tell me the real one about him?"

Sophie drained her glass and threw it into the fire. Shattering on impact, the pieces scattered, glittered blood red. She eyed the shards, remembering the last time she'd done that and told her story.

"Carl wanted to shoot me. He shot everything that disappointed him.   And most things did at some time or another because his standards were so high. I mean really high, John. Generally, though, it was me. I was always the biggest disappointment. I tried not to be, but he was a genius, you know. And I'm not. Deep down, I think he always knew he'd shoot me. And one night, with his shotgun aimed at my head like it had been many times over, I knew it was time."

Forty – Making Choices

Carl continued to smile, and she wasn't sure he still meant to. She wondered if he was dead, and maybe it was too late to make his lips form a frown. She froze, her subconscious mind processing the raucous voices of her fowl and goats. They were frightened.

He didn't move. Nor did she.

'*What now, Sophie?*'

"Carl?"

She glanced at the Colt, still gripped in her hand and loosened her fingers from around it. The gun fell to the floor and she followed, kneeling beside her husband.

"Carl?"

When the peacocks quit screeching and silence came from the chicken coop and goat pen, she pressed her ear to his chest. No sound greeted her, maybe because a thirty-eight-caliber bullet had gone into his body somewhere near his heart, if not into it. She put her cheek up close to his face and her hand over his mouth so any breath of air would be forced to come from his nose. Nothing.

She ran to the house for her compact to place where her cheek had been. Still nothing. No hint of breath fogged the mirror.

'*What now, Sophie?*'

Again, the voice.

Her butt met the floor beside his body, and she drew in her knees, clasped them to her chest with one arm like she would spend some time there. She let her fingers feather through the shaggy hair falling over his forehead. She liked his hair a little long, curling over his collar, but not too much. He had a couple days of beard growth she didn't mind, either. It was scratchy when he used to kiss her, a long time ago, but it was masculine, too, and she liked manly. It rasped the tender skin of her palm as she caressed his cheek.

There had been much about Carl she liked. A lot, actually. And only one of the things she didn't drove her to shoot him. Primarily, that he wanted to kill her. Anything else she could live with, but not that.

"You can't live with being killed," she said, surprising herself with the sound of her voice, and snorted a scornful laugh at the outlandish statement.

"You shouldn't have wanted me dead, Carl."

But Sophie thought he hadn't wanted that. Not really.

He'd wanted to shoot her, like the pelican and the tractor and the pressure canner, because she frustrated him like they had. She irritated him, disappointed him. Like all the 'dead' disappointments lying in the yard and full of holes, he thought he couldn't control her. But he was wrong.

He governed her – mostly – but she couldn't relinquish the last speck of self-worth, that last inch in the mile of ego he'd stolen. He'd seen that remaining speck reveal itself in her eyes at the end and knew his authority over her would never be total.

And what he couldn't rule got shot.

But Sophie told herself he didn't want her dead. He loved her. And she hadn't thought beyond having the Colt in her pocket for strength, for reinforcement, not for killing. Using the revolver in that way wasn't the plan.

Stop the lies, Sophie. Her own voice invaded.

Tucker's whine came through the open door, but he only pushed his nose through and whined again, distressed by the smell of blood. Or the scent of Sophie's grief.

"Stay out, boy. Don't come in here."

Instant loneliness found a home inside her breast. Regret, too. She wasn't sorry she'd pulled the trigger – that had been necessary. But she regretted the man he should have been and never was. She regretted the lifetime of lies she'd spun keeping their secrets, and she didn't even know why it had been necessary to spin them.

Who the hell would've cared?

She patted her leg in invitation when Tucker whined again. He sniffed Carl, put his tail between his legs and scooted over to Sophie. With his head on her lap, he alternately stared at Carl's body and up at Sophie's face.

"Remember me telling you about the chickens, Tucker?"

He rolled his eyes her way and waited.

"That old raccoon got to them. I got to him, too, but he'd already killed several and mauled a few others. I threw them over the fence into the field because they were no good for cooking and I couldn't help them. They were gonna die. I always mourned I couldn't wring their necks and hurry their death along. I couldn't do it back then. But I'm older now. I'm tougher."

She got up, called to Tucker, and went to the house for a couple of tarps and upstairs for a thick Hudson Bay wool blanket Carl always liked. She returned to the shed, spread the tarps on the floor and the blanket on top of them. Kneeling behind him, she pushed and rolled until he was centered on the blanket which she folded over him and pinned like he was an Egyptian mummy. She followed that with one of the waterproof tarps.

She dragged her favorite shovel and an axe, in case of tree roots, to the far end of the pet cemetery. After a few tosses of dirt, she went back for a bigger tool and tried again. She jiggled the point of Carl's big shovel into the topsoil, jumped on both steps, and gave a sigh of satisfaction at the clump of dirt she'd removed.

It took all night before the hole was big enough and deep enough. At the edge of dawn, she tied the flat tarp to her lawn tractor and dragged Carl to where he needed to be. She parked him parallel to the grave and left him there.

In the house, she poured a full glass of merlot in a crystal water glass and took it and a cold beer back to the cemetery.

"Maybe I should have made you a rye and coke. Would you like that better, Carl?"

She sipped and tossed Tucker a treat from her pocket, opened the beer and balanced it on the wrapped bundle that was Carl.

"Guess it doesn't matter, does it? But I'd go make one if you wanted me to. You know that."

She perched on one of the huge boulders they'd moved to the cemetery and talked to her husband. Tears stayed put inside, but she chewed her lip like they might appear at any moment, and her bottom lip trembled.

"I'm not at all happy about this, Carl. I want you to know that. I'm not smiling."

She saw the glow rising at the eastern horizon and thought putting this off wasn't a good idea, but she was about to bury most of her life in a deep, black hole. It seemed half of her reason for existing was going into the ground, maybe even more, and her chest filled with the tears she wouldn't shed. She swallowed, tasted the salt, and sipped her merlot.

"Let's go, Carl. I love you."

She moved the beer can, untied the tarp from the tractor and folded it over the other. Behind the bundle, she squatted and pushed and rolled until Carl lay in his grave. She got in, too, realigned him as well as she could and resettled his beer. She told him she'd done her best, patted and put her lips where his face most likely was, and climbed out.

The first few shovels of dirt hurt, but the rest were simply gardening. That's what she told herself. Those were the words she put in her brain.

She tamped it down by walking back and forth across the hill she'd made, packing the loose dirt as much as possible. As she scattered leaves over the mound, the wind blew in a sudden brief squall, erasing signs of overturned soil, filling her senses with fresh air and thought, hiding evidence of her refusal to die.

She was exhausted, had pushed her body to the limit, but the chickens and goats needed tending. They didn't care she had buried her husband a few minutes ago – milk bloated their bellies, and hens and guineas wanted breakfast. Peacocks marched behind her footsteps. She called to them as she trudged to the kitchen to make coffee, filled a cup from the still streaming maker, and took it and toast with her, scattering pieces to the waiting peacocks.

The scent of coffee had refueled her before even taking a drink, and she grinned with the strange pleasure of normalcy, rejuvenated by the ordinary act of sipping the hot liquid as morning always required.

When she opened the coop door, hens and guineas filed outside with careful precision, an orderly troop waiting for instructions. Where were the flapping wings, the squawking, demanding calls for breakfast? She brought out a heaping scoop of feed and stood in the middle of her fowl, scattering seed, carrying on a casual conversation, clucking with her tongue against the roof of her mouth in language they all understood.

"I'm sorry if you were frightened last night. I really am. We'll be fine from here on out. You'll see. I take care of my babies."

Before long, they morphed into their usual, selfish bird-selves, pecking each other away from food, wings flapping in unreasonable efforts to fly, and Sophie clucked with them, heart swelling.

"Stay outside while I find eggs, if you left any after last night."

They hadn't, and she'd expected as much.

"I wouldn't have either," she told them.

In the goat pen, Billy butted her legs hard enough to hurt, and knocked her backward into a wall. It was his way of discussing events with her, and she spent time rubbing his coat and brushing out the filthy beard. She gave him a few apple pieces and turned her attention to the girls who were anxious to be relieved of their burdens.

As she milked, a sense of unusual and unexpected serenity fell in a mist around her, a warm cloud with shots of silver light shining through. She didn't know if this feeling of peaceful euphoria should be happening – but it was, and she wasn't inclined to shove it away. It was her goats. Her guineas and hens.

Outside, she let her chest fill with fresh air and her eyes take in the yard, caress the gardens, see the contours of her home as if she'd just driven down the wooded lane for the first time, ever.

It was quiet in the house. She wandered from room to room, taking her time, touching furniture, seeing each space with widowed eyes. There was a wall where she could hang her mother's framed photo. Here, a small table she could clear off and leave empty. Clutter had always muddled her mind. She made mental notes with neither joy nor sorrow because tasks were merely things to be done.

She had a home to look after.

She had a lot of 'coulds' to consider.

Tour complete, she took the stairs to their bedroom and didn't look at anything. It was a room she didn't need. One she didn't want.

With a comforter and pillow from upstairs, she snuggled on the couch to watch television, a cup of hot chocolate in her hand, periodically glancing at the empty lazy boy across from her. She flicked through the channels on the remote and her fingers rejected the movement. She flexed them.

"I don't use the remote, Tucker. Carl does. He pushes the buttons, and we watch whatever show is on when his finger stops. That's how it is."

Tucker pawed at the sofa, wanting to climb up, and she patted her blanket and made space for him.

When the air grew chill, she trudged down to the cellar to fill the furnace. Her mind agreed this work was exactly right. Putting wood in the furnace when it grew cool in the house was always her job, not Carl's, and he was happy to let her do that little chore. She wondered what else will seem odd.

What will seem ordinary? Breakfast?

Tomorrow, she could pour cold milk on cereal and wouldn't have to cook anything. And dinner? She might not decide what she wants to eat until six o'clock. She might not eat at all. Satisfaction sat like stones on her shoulders as she scrutinized the living room, looking for him. He wasn't there in his big chair.

She sat up, dragged the comforter along with her and plopped into his recliner, pulled up the footstool and lay back. Two cats leapt to join her and kneaded the blanket, nails pricking through to her skin. She smiled around the pain, not caring, and jumped when the phone rang. Cats flew in different directions. She froze as if Carl had called from the grave and stared in the direction of the shrill ringing until it stopped and a voice spoke, leaving a message.

"Haven't talked to you in years, Sophie, but Lainie said you were in Henry's, and she said I should give you a call. So, I'm doing that. Oh, I forgot to say this is Dee. Call me back. Same number."

"Why today?" she mumbled. "Why today of all days? You scared me."

Tucker shoved his nose into her hand.

By morning, nature prevailed and snow covered the land with purity. It was early in the season and likely wouldn't stay, but Sophie was happy for the change. She would see a different scene when pulling into the driveway, if she ever went anywhere again. She would see a new, pristine white one, when sitting at the backyard fire.

If she ever sat there again.

Sophie didn't berate herself for Carl's death. It had been necessary if she wanted to live. Offering herself up to him like a lamb to slaughter was out of the question, not in her nature.

She had come to terms with his death.

What she didn't know was how to deal with the now and forevermore without him. She didn't know how to explain his disappearance to people who knew him and asked where Carl was keeping himself these days – like people always did. She hadn't thought that far ahead and didn't want to.

She didn't need to go in to the grocery store for food. Eggs and milk were plentiful, thanks to her farm critters, and the well-stocked pantry and full freezer meant she could eat for a long while, maybe for her entire lifetime. And she could have the pet and critter feed delivered, a manageable risk.

But someday, someone would miss them, come looking for them, if they both simply disappeared, and she knew that for a truth.

She had a choice to make – to tell the truth or not? What she'd had to do didn't seem wrong, but explaining her reasons might create potential problems. She stewed and pondered until a solution exposed itself like a sixties' streaker.

"Alright, Tuck. This is what we'll do, and we'll see how it goes."

Tucker tilted his head at her for an explanation.

"To prevent rumors and people talking, I'll go into town as usual, and say he's doing *this or that* if folks ask after him. Except for Freddie. I'll tell him Carl came home with a new car and just up and left, said he didn't want to die without seeing some of the world, the Grand Canyon, the mountains in California, places out west. Say I couldn't leave because of our critters, and he didn't want me to go, anyway. Said I'd ruin his 'good time,' and he'd call or come back when he 'damn well felt like it.' Freddie will believe that. He knows how Carl is and how he can be."

She checked out Tucker's rolling eyes and said, "You're right. Freddie needs to be told to keep it under his hat because it might not be safe for everyone to know a woman lives alone out here."

She stepped into her rubber boots and put on Carl's heaviest flannel, poured a cup of coffee and left the house. On the snow-covered porch, she and Tucker paused to admire the pristine landscape before marking it with their prints and heading to the chicken coop.

"The animals will clear my mind, Tuck. They always do."

Tucker woke the peacocks, and they glided from their nighttime tree. He returned to Sophie periodically, checking to be sure all was as it should be. As she carried the eggs and milk back to the house, she told him it was all figured out.

"He said he quit his job. But I can't be sure he wasn't just spouting off, so I'll call there to make sure and ask them to mail his last check if he did or tell them he took off out west if he didn't. Be the good wife. I really was, you know. Good, I mean."

Tucker stared, knew it was not possible to refute her claims, and nudged her arm.

"That's it, then. I like it because it feels like he'll be home at any moment. But I know better, and I'm safer than if he was real. You know what I mean – not dead. It's a great idea. Thanks for the talk, Tuck."

Forty-one – Making Chowchow

John had words for what he'd heard, but they were wedged somewhere between disbelief and trust. If Sophie hadn't thrown her wine glass into the fire, he might think her story was make-believe, and she'd give a hearty *gotcha* laugh in a moment. But she had smashed her good crystal. And the bone-chilling, calm delivery of the killing of Carl rang like truth.

Could she have shot her husband, buried him in the pet cemetery and carried on with her life like he was still alive? It would explain her confusing use of past and present tense when she talked about him – as if he stood right there and then didn't. John stared at the glass shards and tried to choose the right words.

"Why didn't you call someone, Sophie? You shot him in self-defense."

She scoffed. "You haven't been listening, John Wayne. You've sat right here at this fire, on this dirty old sofa, and you've pretended to hear me. I'm a liar. I lied to protect my mother when I was a child, and I lied to save face as an adult, and I continued . . . right up to now. I told everyone how great Carl was, how wonderful we were together. I described the life I wanted to live, the one I wished for, and everyone believed me because I've been trained to tell lies with an honest face, since long before Carl."

Sophie deflated. Hope a forgotten word.

"Who'd believe the resourceful Carl would put a gun to my head? Not once, but a bunch of times," she said and put her chin on her fist, remembering. "I think he liked doing it. It gave him a feeling of control when he didn't think he had any."

John touched her arm with a gentle hand. "But the shotgun was there, you said, lying right next to him. They'd see it and know you had to shoot."

"But they'd say I put it there."

"You were defending yourself, Sophie."

"I know that, damn it!" She shook her head. "But they would raise their eyebrows and ask why I would walk around with a gun in my pocket if I didn't mean to use it." She glared at him. Anger rising again and emanating in waves from her.

"They'd judge me. You know they would. And I would have had to unravel decades of my lies, spill my life all over the ground for them to mess with and pick at. They'd walk on the paths I chose and not recognize where I'd been."

An ache formed in the middle of his forehead and he rubbed it, trying to chase away guns and Iraq. Shooting and noise. And death. He thought it couldn't catch him here, in Sophie's garden paradise. But it had, and he wanted to run, fast and far.

"I don't know, but it seems a mite crazy and . . ."

"I thought you were different, John. How many damned times can I be so wrong about men?"

She heaved herself from the sofa and walked away. He watched her leave, back rigid with pride and offense, long white hair catching the moon's light.

He stayed at the fire, added logs to it, and pondered her shocking story. She'd been filling him with tales of horror since the beginning: Carl shooting computers, dragging Billy to his death with a rope around his neck, locking Sophie in the underground.

Why would he believe all the others and struggle with this one? It's the most logical of them all. It made sense. He rubbed his head again, the pain pooling behind his eyes with visions of tanks blowing people apart.

Sophie had told the truth.

When the fire burned down, he knocked at her door. She didn't answer, so he opened it, called her name and went inside. He heard the television, voices low, and saw her sitting in the recliner bathed in the screen's glow, cats covering her lap and one on her shoulder, remote control in her hand, staring at the screen. Sprawled on the couch, Fannie opened her eyes to check him out and went back to sleep.

John shifted from foot to foot and held his cowboy hat in his hand like any good cowboy should. He had hurt her. Perhaps for the first time in her life, she told the total truth. She gave that gift to him, and he'd thrown it back at her.

"I'm sorry for my words, Sophie. You did everything you could for Carl, and I'm absolutely positive of that, everything anyone could do."

"Except let him shoot me."

He couldn't help the small chuckle that slipped out.

"Right. Except for that. I don't blame you. I wouldn't have allowed him that either. No one in their right mind would."

She turned away from the television to scan his face, ready to look for lies, determined there would be no more. Not from her. Not from him.

And she didn't care about anybody else.

"Now, there's the real issue. Do you believe I'm in my right mind, Mr. Wayne?"

"There's not a person on this earth who is put together better than you. Your feet are on the ground, my friend, and sometimes deep in it. The earth is your kingdom, and you treasure it and care for it like you're its queen. A remarkable, completely sane but idiosyncratic queen."

Sophie rolled her eyes.

"Idiosyncratic? I don't know that word, and you're laying it on a little too thick. Just tell me you believe me, and if you don't understand why I did what I did, keep it to yourself. I don't need you."

"I do believe you. And you do too need me, old woman. You need me like wine and water. Why don't you go to bed? It's been a hard day, and I'm heading to the underground."

"When I'm ready, I will. Don't be telling me what to do."

He raised a hand as if to ward off violence.

"Forgive me, my Queen."

When he turned to leave, she threw the remote at his back. It came apart when it hit his shoulder, and batteries rolled across the floor.

"Leave it," she said when he bent to pick it up. "I don't even know how to use the damned thing. I'm going to sleep. I'll see you in the chicken coop in the morning."

She didn't. He scattered feed while he thought, trying to process the dilemma she'd created. How could he take a trust from her knowing what he did? He collected eggs and wondered how long people who knew Carl would believe he still traipsed around the country enjoying life.

He had Petunia milked and had called to Gladiola when Sophie's bedraggled form darkened the open door to the pen. She threw a piece of apple to Billy and told him he stunk.

"Me or Billy?"

"Didn't get close enough to you to sniff. Do you? I can smell old Billy pee from ten feet away."

"Sleep?" he asked.

"Like the dead."

She smirked, watching for him to cringe or laugh or tell her not to be disrespectfully cheeky, but he cleaned udders, squirted the first half cup in the cat bowl, and didn't respond to her comment.

She put a hand on the door jamb to steady herself and pushed the palm of the other into her chest. When he slipped a sneak peek at her, he saw pain written in the lines of her face. It had been happening more and more frequently, and he suggested seeing a doctor.

She said she had. "And he told me I'm old. Imagine that? I paid that quack, and he said there's a lot of candles on my birthday cake. I gave him money for that bit of news!"

She grumbled and sank onto an overturned bucket, her booted feet and nightgown covered knees spread wide. Her fists planted on the tops of her legs, ready to scrap. She gave the impression of another century, a wilder but more understandable time.

"What about your heart?"

"It's not so good."

"And your shallow breath?"

"It's not very deep. What can I say?"

"Can you let me take care of things around here, Sophie? Take it easy for a while? Get some rest?"

She widened her eyes at him, making the lines on her forehead deepen. "You're gonna get it all soon enough, John Wayne. Don't be trying to take over and put me in the ground before I'm dead."

Billy pushed his stinky beard into her arm, and she pulled the obnoxious goat to her and kissed the top of his head.

"Now, you're gonna smell, too, Sophie. You're gonna stink like Billy."

"I've smelled worse skunks in my life, most of them without stripes and wearing men's perfume."

She lay on the sofa, her skin a blotchy gray, breath shallow and eyes dim. He tucked a pillow under her feet and brought her some chicken noodle soup.

Sophie's downhill slide could be counted in measures from one to ten. But he wouldn't. He hated those preposterous evaluative scales that didn't measure anything except for the logician's pea-sized brain.

Every day, he begged to let him take her to the doctor again, a different one, one who wouldn't talk about cake and candles. She refused.

"Could you sit up for a bit, please."

"Yes. I will, and I want you to bring a folder to me. It's in the center drawer of the bureau – where I keep the Colt." She paused and a grin formed. "Under the white lace doilies."

"You think you're so funny, my fairy queen."

"You gonna argue with me?"

"I might. You can't ever tell."

He found the manila folder, put it on her lap, and she opened it and pulled out several documents.

"Okay, this paper has information about the coroner who agreed to put a stethoscope on my chest and pronounce me dead. He's also the man who proclaimed it good and proper to bury your own body on your own property. Well, I mean, I can't bury me, but you can. Right here."

"Jesus, Sophie. Do we need to talk about this?"

She touched his arm and waited for him to settle, to quit arguing with the facts. She was old. And she was dying.

"Yes, we do, and it's all been decided. My funeral is arranged. No mourners – except maybe you, if you feel like lamenting a little. You know, dredge up a tear or two."

He rubbed the scruff on his face and tried to move his words around the lump in his throat despite her humor.

"I'm mourning right now, Sophie. You've been a wonderful friend to me, the best I've ever had, and I don't want to lose you. Not ever."

"You'll be alright. Just rev up your Harley, fly down the road, and think of me, John Wayne. And when you come home, really come home. Love my babies and my ground and my garden. It's yours, now. And if you get married someday, make sure you know her well." She squinted her eyes at him. "I mean that. And don't ever speak of Carl. You promise?"

He couldn't stop the trickle of rain from gathering at the corners of his eyes and making a stream down his cheeks.

"Don't be a baby, John. I'm gonna go knowing you're here taking care of things. Making a garden. Feeding the chickens and guineas and peacocks, milking our goats. You know Peony is milking like a professional now. She's a fine little nanny."

"Yes, she is. I know how to pick 'em."

"And with all the dirt banks, you'll be able to write. Really write without worrying about money." Sophie lay back on the pillow, peace in her eyes and a light in her smile. "Doesn't take much to live here if you're frugal. You know, heat with wood, grow your food."

"I can do that, Sophie. I'll do it happily thinking of you. Are you in pain?"

"No. That's gone. I don't feel much of anything anymore."

"Cept love for your John Wayne," he said.

"That, yes. I'm happy you trespassed, you arrogant man. Glad you kept coming back like you believed I wanted you to."

He patted her hand and gave it a squeeze.

"I knew you were glad. Saw it in your eyes."

Sophie's body grew weak, but her faculties had never been sharper, her wit funnier, her tongue more caustic. He spent most of his time by her side, watching television or reading, and she came to accept he'd be doing the chores by himself from now on.

He saw the peacocks at the back door one morning, marching back and forth and looking like they wanted in the house. Typically, they waited for signs she'd gotten off the couch before leaving their night nesting tree. Maybe they smelled coffee or heard her talking to Fannie or the cats. Whatever the reason, they knew when to beg for toast.

He tossed off their performance as wacky bird behavior and headed toward the chicken coop, enjoying the morning's pure air. It was warm, but a light snow fell and turned the grass and branches virginal. He tilted his hat forward to keep snow out of his eyes and turned to glance at the peacocks behind him.

Their actions niggled at the back of his brain, and he spun around and strode to the house, waving his arms so he could get to the back door without a pride of peacocks following him inside. He rapped on the wood door a couple of times but didn't wait for a response. He wasn't expecting one.

She lay on the couch dressed in a Henry's Bar blouse and black slacks, a pair of dainty shoes on her feet. Blush painted her cheeks with a pink glow, and mascara darkened her lashes. Her lips were cherry red and shiny. Sophie always wore lipstick – everywhere, in the garden, the woods, and even fishing. Every day. She'd brushed her hair and left it loose, lying over her breasts in a thick cloud of white. She was proud of her hair – and her breasts. She'd donned her good bra so a little cleavage pushed above the neckline of her top as usual.

John smiled and knelt on the floor by her side. He held her hand, struggling not to miss her already, wanting to ask how he could take care of Eden without her and keep it healthy and pristine, knowing he had to be what she expected. *Wanting* more than anything to be what she expected.

She'd asked a lot of him, and her estimation elevated him, made him more than he was. He wanted to beg her not to leave, but asking her to hang on was asking too much, and he couldn't.

Her mouth opened and closed like words were there but trapped inside, or she wasn't sure what she wanted to say, and he leaned close to hear.

"I waited for you," she said.

"Thank you. You look beautiful, Sophie. Spectacular even." His words were feathers on the air, but heavy with grief.

"Do you have any questions?" The trace of an angel's smile tilted her lips.

He shook his head. He couldn't speak. He would have made a fool of himself, and he didn't want to disappoint her.

"Thank you, Cowboy. I've loved you."

"And I you, Sophie."

"I know."

Sophie left in a whisper of smoke, and he thought he saw her soul grin and wave goodbye. She died like she had choreographed it. The clothes. The makeup. The last words.

He pounded a fist on his leg in anger. He didn't want her gone! He wanted life the way it was and had been from his first ride down her overgrown driveway.

Fannie lay her head on Sophie's stomach and whined, not understanding, and neither did John. He ran a gentle hand over her eyes, closing them in sleep, and sat on the floor next to her, not wanting to leave her alone.

Staring at her face, mysteriously young in death, he chuckled because she couldn't yell at him for gawking at her. Couldn't call him damned cowboy or silly whippersnapper. Couldn't punch his arm when he said something stupid. Couldn't teach him the million things she knew about life . . . and he didn't.

"I have to get to the babies, Sophie. I won't be long, but they'll be missing us by now."

After chores, he and Miss Lily crept down the driveway, and as soon as he got to the road, he opened it up, feeling Sophie behind him, hands at his waist, urging him for more speed. He rejoiced with her, and her words were in his ears.

Faster, John. Don't be such a chicken boy. What a great day.

She filled his heart. "You're a nutcase, old woman," he yelled back to her and she asked where they were going.

"Doing what you told me to do, Sophie. Going to get the coroner and find a coffin. You didn't say anything about that, but I want you to have one, the best. One worthy of you, girl. And then we'll take Bone Keesha into the woods. You alright with that?"

John carried on the conversation as if she rode behind him, filling in what he knew she would say. He flinched when she whacked him in the back for being a dunce and smiled when he felt her approval. Except for struggling to see through threatening tears, it wasn't a horrible drive. She was right there. With him.

And he thought of Carl – how she talked about him like he was right beside her or would be at any moment – and understanding flashed like heat lightening.

He bought a cherry wood casket with brass trim, and Edwin, the coroner, delivered it and helped him carry it into the house. The man came to an unexpected stop when he saw her lying on the sofa in her fancy clothes and looking like she was taking a well-deserved nap before going into town.

"Did you do that?" He pointed, wide eyed, knowing that caring for the deceased was not an easy task.

"No. She was like that when I got here this morning. She knew, somehow, and didn't want anyone else picking out her clothes or dressing her."

"Where's Carl?" Edwin asked looking around.

"Sophie said he went out west a while back to do some exploring. Said he told her he'd come back when he 'goddamned felt like it.' Or not."

"Hmmpf. He always hated being interfered with when his mind was set on something. Gonna be a sad homecoming."

Satisfied the cause of Sophie's death was simply old age and a bad heart, not a homicide committed by the man who'd come to fetch him, Edwin took his leave within minutes and left John to the hardest hours of his life.

He carried Sophie to her satin lined bed and wheeled it out to his truck on the trolley the coroner had loaned him. He went back inside for the bottle of merlot and two stemmed crystal glasses, stopped at the tool shed for a shovel and a tarp, and prayed Bone Keesha would make it to the place in the woods she'd chosen – a small rise not too far beyond the sugar shack. He called to Fannie who leapt into the front seat like she'd done it a hundred times before.

The tires slid sideways a couple of times but stayed on the path, John checking in the rearview mirror to be sure she was still safely in the bed of the truck. The tailgate had rusted away long ago.

"Here we are, Sophie. Wish you could help because it's going to take a while."

'Smell the roses, Cowboy. No reason to rush.'

"Easy for you to say." He looked around and saw roses and red berries glistening through the snow and lighting a tree like Christmas. "Thanks."

Shovel in hand, he called to Fannie and trudged uphill to the site. He plunged the shovel into the ground, held onto it as if it was life support, and looked at Sophie's woods. Her birds sang, and her squirrels chattered. Nothing had changed, and he didn't understand how that could be because everything had. The world tipped sideways without the weight of Sophie's life to balance it.

Calling himself a wimpy-ass cowboy before she did, he rubbed at his scruffy chin and let the surroundings filter in. Through the oaks, he could see the back yard and the boulders around the pet cemetery.

"You tricky old woman," he said, grinning. "You're gonna keep an eye on everything from right here, aren't you?"

'Of course, John. You're gonna need my help from time to time.'

"Yes, I will."

He swallowed, his throat thick and painful.

'I'll be right here.'

"Sophie. Damn it," he growled.

He spun, wrapped his arms around the trunk of the huge oak he'd been leaning against and pressed his forehead into the rough bark, needing the pain to lessen the ache in his heart. The side of his fist pounded against it, and his face contorted from the effort to stay strong.

'Do your job, John. Get a grip.'

He didn't know how long it took him to find his grip. It could have been minutes or hours, but find it he did and rammed the shovel into the ground. Yet he knew *exactly* how long it took to dig the hole, four hours and twenty-three minutes, and he could hear Sophie laughing as he rubbed the aching muscles in his back.

He backed Bone Keesha up to where the hill began its upward slope, laid a tarp on the ground, and slid Sophie off the truck and onto it. He tugged her up the rest of the hill, poured them each a glass of Merlot and leaned against her casket. He patted Fannie's head and raised his glass in salute to her forest, her woodland creatures and her.

They had a casual conversation while he drank his wine, and he described the critters who honored her by coming to her funeral. The mourners.

"You are one amazing woman, Sophie. No one died more nobly than you. You truly are a queen."

He slid her satin lined bed into the nest he'd made for it. Her flesh would lie forever in the ground she loved, her property. *Their* Eden.

And she had been right about filling in a grave. After the first few grief laden shovels of dirt, it was gardening. All he wanted now was to be finished because he had chores to do. Goats and fowl were waiting.

He smoothed the mound, nested her glass of merlot where a headstone might sit, told her he loved her and he'd be back when she needed a refill.

And he did . . . whenever he needed her company.

Epilogue – Pepper Tears

Spring arrived and he still lived in the underground. He hadn't been able to make himself move into Sophie's house, even after the attorney came out with papers giving him title to everything, the hundred twenty acres, house and all. Maybe he'd think about it after the garden was planted.

He enlarged the plot and bought bales of straw to put between the aisles and around the plants, increasing the number of tomatoes and peppers. Chowchow was on his mind – lots of it, even if he never ate a single jar. He kept to her planting design.

Because, well, what did he know about a garden?

Several kids were born, and he spent nights with them while the girls were birthing, worrying they'd need his help. He had a conversation with Sophie about it, and she laughed at him, but he did it anyway. Petunia, Peony and Begonia became new mothers, and Billy got downright cocky. John let him, remembering Sophie's Billy who had died.

"You're lucky I'm such a nice guy, Billy Boy, and love you through your stink. I'm taking the hose after you today and I'm going to use some of Sophie's shampoo. You'll smell just like your sweet mama."

He couldn't use all the milk and eggs he collected, so he took some into the co-op in town. After a while, they came to expect him and were glad for his donations to the food pantry, especially a slender brunette with eyes the color of midnight and the size of half dollars.

Fannie followed him everywhere, now, but for a long while she'd slept in the house on the sofa, not with him in the underground. And periodically, John found her curled in the recliner on Sophie's afghan. For some strange reason, seeing Fannie mourn her master brought an instant gathering of tears. He gave up trying to stuff them down, shook his head, and went about his business letting them dry up on their own, making salty tracks on his cheeks.

Counting cats revealed twenty-something. He wasn't sure. He might have counted a few twice but figured some might have come to live with them over the winter, looking for and finding ready food, water and a nesting place. Or Sophie's planned parenthood work had failed, and he needed to talk with a veterinarian. Never-the-less, the felines approved of his care and climbed on his lap with minimal nail holes in his jeans and skin. He wouldn't allow them on his duster coat, though. Not yet.

He found contentment in his solitary life and serenity in the demands of the daily chores. His writing flowered, and, one day, he discovered he looked forward to morning, even with Sophie living on the distant hilltop.

He didn't have visitors because he didn't want any. In fact, he left the no trespassing signs where they were, and the metal gate and ringing bells deterred the curious. He liked it that way. Someday – maybe, he'd let people in.

But he wasn't lonely.

Iraq and the war melted into sporadic nightmares and grew fewer with time. Even the horrific soldiers' memoirs he reinvented stayed in the laptop used to write them. Nothing hateful was allowed to grow in Eden alongside the garden, the critters and himself.

His plants flourished, and he'd canned and froze vegetables like a madman throughout the growing season. He smiled with wet eyes as he bit into a partially cooked beet because he knew he wore red on his face like she had. He'd boiled them to loosen their skins at the backyard fire pit, and sat on the front porch to snip beans, amazed to think he hadn't known how to do all this before. Now, even his fingers knew what to do on their own.

When a light frost fell, it was time to make chowchow. He gathered the green tomatoes, cabbage, onions and hot peppers; the gloves, the mask and the biggest knife in the world, and he started a fire in the backyard pit. A fire she'd be proud of.

He chopped the cabbage and tomatoes and threw it all in a bucket. He put on the gloves and mask to chop the hot peppers, but it didn't help. Tears came anyway – rivers of them streaming down his face, creating waterfalls off his chin like it was a Colorado mountain.

"It's the damned peppers," he growled, seeing her face hover before his glistening eyes.

She knew better.

Sophie and Magic Bob hovered together, pale images in the dark night. John saw him lift the can of Miller Beer and clink it against her wine glass. They grinned as if they knew a secret they weren't sharing.

'*You taking care of Eden, John?*'

"Making chowchow, aren't I?"

He heard her giggle and felt the rumble of a man's laugh.

"Damn it, Sophie. Go away."

'*You don't mean that Cowboy.*'

He mixed the chowchow, squeezing it through his gloved fingers, dumped a bunch of salt on top, covered it up and carried it to the tool shed.

He was tired out – a good kind of tired – and plopped himself on the outside sofa and poked at the fire with a long stick, waiting to see if he'd kill it or make the flames grow. Orange and red shot upward.

"No, I didn't mean it, Sophie. You know that."

A barn owl hooted. A coyote howled, and Fannie took off, baying in defense of her territory. She came back on the run, gave John a satisfied, smug look, and sat staring up at his face. He smiled and scratched her long, hound dog ears.

"Climb on up, Fannie. Let's watch the night critters. You never know what's out there."

Magic Bob, My Friend
A Poem
By Mark Jessup

Well, it's a harvest moon on a clear fall night,
A big orange ball shinin strong and bright.
Lovers is spoonin, and that's alright.
      Me, I'm just squeezing chowchow.

Cuz the growin's all over, and the cannins all done.
We even blanched and froze us up some.
Nothin left in the garden 'cept the ugly ones.
      That's why I'm squeezing chowchow.

There's nothing left in the garden, you know.
Least nothin left that's ever gonna grow.
Ya can't waste what's there, gotta use it and so
      We'll use it, to make some chowchow.

Ya take a big old cabbage and a lot of old green,
Tomatoes, that is, some hot peppers that's mean,
Eight or ten carrots and garlic if you're keen.
      That's how we're makin the chowchow.

So, ya cut it, and ya chop it and mix it all up.
Then ya throw it in a bucket and salt it on top.
Lay the salt heavy so to draw the water out.
      That's how we're brinin the chowchow.

Here's a tip,
When you're chopping hot peppers, do it in a stiff breeze,
Cuz chopping inside makes it hard to breathe.
Your lungs'll seize up, and you'll start to heave.
      Use your head when you're makin that chowchow.

Well, it's got to soak, and it's got to brine,
But I don't bring them buckets in the house anytime.
The fumes comin off would kill me and mine.
      Be careful when you're makin that chowchow.

When you're ready for the squeezing, better have good gear,
Some long rubber gloves goin clean to your ears,
A stout pair a glasses and a mask cuz I fear
      You could die from squeezin the chowchow.

When ya squished and ya squeezed and the chow's all dry,
Take a little bitty bite, and if it don't make ya cry – much,
Add a few more jalapenos; get that fever really high,
      And NOW, we're makin some chowchow.

So, ya pick up all the buckets, and ya take em in the house,
And ya set em in the kitchen, and ya wait for your spouse.
Ya offer help with cannin, but you really just want out.
      Lord, I hate this part of makin chowchow.

And, ya can't just cook it and then put it in a jar.
Gotta add a little spice and a lot of vinegar.
When ya get it all to cookin, you can smell it near and far.
      Open windows when you're cookin the chowchow.

Now, I'm hackin and a gaggin in the kitchen from the fumes,
And my eyes are tearing up from the awful toxic plume.
The vinegar and peppers done peeled paint in every room.
      Why the hell do I keep makin this chowchow?

Well, the chow's all canned, and the house survived.
Me and the wife, we both came out alive.
Walls have been repainted, and they look just fine.
      Don't know why I keep makin this chowchow.

The chow is better if you let it age,
So we let 'er set some till we both felt brave.
When I opened up a jar, it was tense and grave.
      Every year, I'm more afraid of this chowchow.

Well, I took a big bite cuz I was feeling strong.
It tasted pretty good, but it didn't take long
For that heat to kick in, and man it was warm.
      I reckon that's some awful bicey chowchow.

I took another little bite, and my eyes turned red,
And I lost more hair off my balding head.
I was hoping in the morning I'd just wake up dead.
      I'm a quittin this makin the chowchow.

Of course,
I took one more bite, and this one made me cry.
Then through my welling tears, I saw the bearded guy.
He was rearin back a laughin with his hands clapped high.
      Got me wondering bout the making of chowchow.

Cause when I'm squeezing chow I ain't ever alone.
There's a friend right by me with his fall plaid on.
Got a Miller in his hand and a twinkle in his frown.
You know, it's when we're makin chow that it seems he's still
around still around.
      Guess that's why we'll keep makin the chowchow.
            Atta while, Bob.

In Honor

Magic Bob was our friend, and this poem was written by Mark Jessup to honor their singular friendship. It's pretty much true. He did teach Mark how to make a distinctive chowchow out of what remained in the garden – the waste-not want-not kind of thing – the use well the earth and its bounty kind of thing.

Bob lived down the road from Mark's little farm and was the go-to man when help, equipment, or advice was needed. Bob satisfied all those needs with a half grin, a shake of his head, and a comment about folks not knowing much of anything anymore. And he always knew when he was wanted, periodically showing up to help before Mark even made the phone call. There was something unusual about Magic Bob.

He died too soon, and we all miss him and his downhome, enchanted wisdom, but Mark still visits with him when he cleans out the garden and makes chowchow. He can't help it because hovering nearby is that beloved grinning face, mouthing lightly contemptuous but affectionate comments and drinking a Miller.

TO MY READERS

I hope you enjoyed reading *Sophie's Lies.* This work of fiction addresses issues that began when men and women first cohabitated, first pledged to one another. Sophie and Carl are the faces in the mirror of many relationships, have been from the beginning of time to now, and without much change in either the problem or solution.

What made this interesting for me was the tiny spark of understanding that tried to grow into a flame, for both of them. I wish I understood more, but I have no training – my only qualification being a desire to listen and love.

Thank you for spending time with me.

Go to www.julisisung.com for news. If you leave your email, I will let you know when the next book is available.